A BROKEN FAMILY

Kitty Neale was raised in South London and this working class area became the inspiration for her novels. In the 1980s she moved to Surrey with her husband and two children, but in 1998 there was a catalyst in her life when her son died, aged just 27. After joining other bereaved parents in a support group, Kitty was inspired to take up writing and her books have been *Sunday Times* bestsellers. Kitty now lives in Spain with her husband.

To find out more about Kitty go to www.kittyneale.co.uk

By the same author:

KITTY NEALE

A Broken Family

AVON

This novel is entirely a work of fiction.
The names, characters and incidents portrayed in it are
the work of the author's imagination. Any resemblance to
actual persons, living or dead, events or localities is
entirely coincidental.

AVON

A division of HarperCollinsPublishers

www.harpercollins.co.uk

First published in Great Britain by Avon edition 2012

Copyright © Kitty Neale

Kitty Neale asserts the moral right to
be identified as the author of this work

A catalogue record for this book is
available from the British Library

ISBN-13: 978-1-84756-244-9

Set in Minion by Palimpsest Book Production Limited,
Falkirk, Stirlingshire

Printed and bound in Great Britain by
Clays Ltd, St Ives plc

MIX
Paper from
responsible sources
FSC™ C007454

FSC™ is a non-profit international organisation established to promote
the responsible management of the world's forests. Products carrying the
FSC label are independently certified to assure consumers that they come
from forests that are managed to meet the social, economic and
ecological needs of present and future generations,
and other controlled sources.

Find out more about HarperCollins and the environment at
www.harpercollins.co.uk/green

In loving memory of George Frank Warren 1925-2012.
A family man, a kind caring man – and a true gentleman
who is sorely missed by all those who love him.

Acknowledgements

My thanks as always to my family and friends for their continued support. I would also like to thank some of the kind and helpful people I meet along the way, for instance Advantage, an online company who supply printer cartridges and who went out of their way to come to my rescue when I had problems with my printer.

Chapter One

Lark Rise was cloaked in fog on a cold Sunday in late February, and when someone rang the doorbell, Celia Frost huffed with impatience. Though Celia always ensured that she looked immaculate, she nevertheless patted her light brown, permed hair and then whipped off her apron. A quick glance showed her living room looked immaculate too, her plush, blue sofa and matching fireside chairs standing alongside a mahogany sideboard polished so highly that the surface reflected her cut glass rose-bowl.

When she opened the door, Celia wasn't pleased to see Amy Miller and from her superior height of five foot six she looked down at Amy haughtily. 'Yes, what do you want?'

'Hello, Mrs Frost,' Amy said. 'I've just popped up to see how Tommy is.'

'How many times have I to tell you that my son's name is Thomas and I'd thank you not to shorten it.'

'Sorry.'

'*Thomas* had an unsettled night and he's still in bed.'

'Can I see him, if only for a minute?' Amy appealed.

'Certainly not! This is a respectable house and I do not

1

allow young women into my son's bedroom. Also, as I doubt Thomas will be fit to see *anyone* for several days yet there's no point in calling again. Now if you'll excuse me, I'm busy preparing our Sunday lunch,' and with that clipped comment, Celia firmly closed the door.

'Who was that?' George Frost asked as he folded his Sunday newspaper.

'Amy,' she told her husband, who was six foot tall, his good looks in Celia's opinion only marred by dark, unruly, bushy hair and eyebrows. She was forever telling him to get his hair cut, and when short it looked a lot tidier.

'Why didn't you invite Amy in?' George asked.

'I should think that's obvious,' Celia answered. 'Thomas is in bed and in no fit state for visitors.'

'Amy's a pretty little thing and seeing her might have cheered the lad up a bit.'

'She's as common as muck and totally unsuitable for Thomas.'

'Don't talk rubbish, woman,' George snapped. 'Amy's a nice girl and her parents are no different to us.'

'Of course they are,' Celia protested. 'You have your own business whereas Amy's father works in a factory. As for her mother, well, she's just a cleaner.'

'My own business, don't make me laugh,' George said derisively. 'All I've got is a small unit and one van.'

'If you'd accepted my help, you could have expanded, but nevertheless you still work for yourself. We also have a nicer house than the pokey one the Millers live in at the bottom of the hill. Ours is an end of terrace too.'

'That doesn't make us any better than them.'

'Of course it does. We are members of the Conservative Club and enjoy a social standing far superior to that of the Millers. Now if you don't mind, I've got lunch to prepare,' Celia snapped, in no mood to argue. She'd been up half the night with Thomas and was tired. Not only that, she didn't care what George said, she wanted better than the likes of Amy Miller for her son.

From childhood Thomas had been sickly with a weak chest, prone to bronchitis and attacks of asthma. It was just as well Thomas worked for his father, a self-employed glazier, as with the amount of time Thomas had to have off she doubted he'd find any other employment.

Sighing, Celia placed the joint of lamb in the oven, her thoughts still on her son. Thomas had always been intelligent, yet hampered by frequent absences from school her dreams of him going on to further education and finding a white collar job had turned to ashes.

'I'm off to the pub for a couple of pints,' George said when Celia returned to the living room.

'You can hardly see a hand in front of your face out there,' she warned.

'I could find my way to the Park Tavern blindfolded.'

Celia wasn't amused and complained, 'It's like a ritual with you. Every Sunday at noon you go off to the pub while I'm left to cook our Sunday roast.'

'If you feel like that, there's nothing to stop you coming with me.'

'Don't be ridiculous,' she said indignantly. 'I can't leave Thomas and you know I wouldn't be seen dead in a public house.'

'It wouldn't hurt you to loosen your corsets a bit now and then, Celia, and your apron strings while you're at it. Thomas isn't a child, he's a grown man and you should stop mollycoddling him.'

Celia's lips tightened with annoyance. 'Thomas might

be twenty-one years old, but when ill he needs constant care, nursing. I'd hardly call that mollycoddling.'

'You're the same when he's up and about, fussing over him all the time,' George snapped and before Celia had a chance of rebuttal, he stomped out.

Celia heard the front door slam and was left fuming. She had married George when she was eighteen and her elder son, Jeremy, was born before she was nineteen. Thomas came along four years later, both boys before the outbreak of the Second World War.

George had been conscripted into the army, and by the time he came home at the end of the war, he was a stranger to his sons. Jeremy had been sixteen then; almost the man of the house and he'd resented being usurped. He and his father had locked horns, and within two years Jeremy had left home.

Celia had no idea where Jeremy got his adventurous streak from, but he'd gone off with a friend saying they were going to travel, to see a bit of the world and it was rare that she heard from him. His last letter had arrived from Greece a year ago, and though she'd replied with all their news, he hadn't responded.

Now it seemed that George was ready to lock horns with their younger son, but Celia wasn't going to stand for that. She still had Thomas, and there was no way she'd allow George to drive him away too.

Phyllis Miller thought her seventeen-year-old daughter, Amy, looked upset when she arrived home. Amy had gone to find out how Tommy, her boyfriend was, but she was soon back.

There was no hall in their home, with the front door leading straight into the living room, and a blast of cold

4

air came in with Amy which made the flames in the hearth flicker. It wasn't a large room, crammed with an old horse-hair sofa and two mismatched fireside chairs. A wooden table was pushed against one wall where they sat to eat their meals. On the other side of the room there was an old sideboard, and then a gap, curtained off, where a stair-case led up to two bedrooms.

'How is he, love?' Phyllis asked.

'Mrs Frost said he had a bad night. I asked to see him, but as he's in bed she got on her high horse and wouldn't allow it.'

'Frost by name, and frosty knickers would be a good way to describe her,' Stan Miller commented.

Phyllis was amused, but tried to keep a straight face as she looked at her husband. Amy had inherited his blonde, curly hair and blue eyes, but Stan was five foot eight, a lot taller than both of them. 'That's no way to talk about Tommy's mother,' she told him.

'I got told off again for calling him Tommy,' said Amy. 'Mrs Frost insists on Thomas, but when I first met him he said he was Tommy and I've got used to it.'

'If you ask me, girl, you should think hard about finding yourself another chap,' Stan said. 'If you don't, you could end up with that stuck-up cow for a mother-in-law and that's something I wouldn't wish on my worst enemy.'

'Dad, I've only been seeing him for a few months. It's too soon to think about marriage.'

'Good, I'm glad to hear it. Tommy's a nice boy, I won't deny that, but he's a bit of a weakling, always sick and I don't see how he'll ever be able to support a wife, let alone a family.'

'I think your dad's right,' Phyllis said. She too thought that Tommy was a nice boy, but his mother, well, she couldn't stand her. There were five houses at the top of the hill, cut off from the rest by an alley that led to the adjacent Rook Rise. These five houses were different, bay-fronted with three bedrooms, and as Celia lived in one of them, she felt herself superior.

'Tommy works for his father,' Amy said, 'and gets paid when he's off sick, but as I said, it's too soon to think about marriage.'

'George Frost is a good bloke,' Stan said, standing up. 'I'm off for a pint and I might see him in the pub.'

'Dinner will be ready at two,' Phyllis told him.

'Yeah, I know, love, and I won't be late,' Stan said, limping as he went to get his overcoat.

Stan had been wounded during the war, taking a bullet in his thigh, but after so many husbands and sons had been killed, Phyllis was forever thankful that he made it home. He'd been a milkman before the war, but now, unable to walk far, he sat at a bench as an assembler in a local engineering factory.

Phyllis knew that Stan felt diminished by his low earnings, yet he hid his feelings behind joviality. He threw her a smile now as he wrapped a scarf around his neck, called goodbye, and let in another blast of cold air as he hurried out.

'Do you want a hand with the dinner, Mum?' Amy asked as she ran to pull the draught curtain across the front door again.

'Thanks, pet. You can peel the potatoes while I prepare the carrots and sprouts.'

They walked through to the scullery where Amy stood at the sink, while Phyllis found a space, hoping as she began to top the sprouts that there would be enough meat to go round. It was only a cheap bit of brisket, and she had to cook it very slowly or it would be tough, yet it was bound to shrink. As long as there was enough for Amy, Stan, and Winnie, the old lady who lived next door, Phyllis would be happy. As she had done many times before she would go without meat herself if necessary and worried about Winnie's weight loss since she'd been widowed, Phyllis was determined to feed her up.

Next door, on the other side, her neighbour Mabel Povis was known as the local gossip, but despite this, they were good friends. Mabel was always popping in and out with the latest bit of news, but with it being Sunday and her husband at home, there'd be no sign of her today. Mabel's husband, Jack Povis wasn't a drinker. He had a good job as a railway guard, but was a rather stern and taciturn man who rarely smiled. He wasn't Phyllis's cup of tea, but then she berated herself for these uncharitable thoughts. After all, with what he and Mabel had been through, it was no wonder that Jack had lost his sense of humour.

Stan had his scarf pulled up over his mouth and nose to prevent breathing in the smoky fog, but yanked it down as he limped into the pub. It wasn't a lot better inside, the air thick with cigarette and pipe smoke, his eyes stinging as he joined George Frost at the bar. 'Watcha, George. Amy tells me that Tommy's still rough.'

'Yes, he is, but hopefully he's on the mend.'

'That's good. What are you drinking?' Stan asked.

'I'll have another pint of bitter,' he replied, gulping down the small amount left in his glass.

'Hello, Stan,' the barmaid, Rose Bridges, said brightly. 'How's Phyllis? I haven't seen her for ages.'

Rose was Phyllis's cousin and they were around the same age, but Stan knew that his wife didn't approve of her. It was the way Rose carried on, along with the way she dressed, in tight, low-cut tops. Her make-up was always thick, and her lipstick a slash of scarlet. 'Phyllis is fine, but as busy as always.'

'Give her my best,' Rose said. 'Now then, what can I get you?'

Stan gave the order and as Rose pulled on the pump he glanced around the pub. Despite the fog and the difficulty in getting there it was busy, with a good few of his neighbours sitting at tables, some playing cribbage and a team of four were at the dart board. The Park Tavern had been his local for as long as he could remember, and as a pint was put down in front of him, he said, 'Thanks, Rose.'

'And one for you, darling,' Rose said to George as she put another pint on the bar, her manner flirtatious.

Rose's dark roots were showing in her stringy, peroxide blonde hair, yet she wasn't bad looking. She had lost her husband during the war and was always on the hunt to replace him, so much so that she had lost her reputation along the way. 'George, I think you're in there,' Stan said jokingly as Rose took his money and then moved on to serve another customer. 'I reckon my wife's cousin has got her eye on you.'

'Of course she hasn't,' George said sharply.

Stan wasn't sure if it was temper or embarrassment that made George's neck redden and he said quickly, 'No offence, mate. I was only kidding.'

'None taken,' George replied, relaxing his tense stance.

For the rest of the time they were in the pub, they chatted about this and that as they were joined by a couple of other men, the conversation mainly about football, but Stan couldn't help noticing how often George's eyes strayed to Rose.

Bloody hell, Stan thought, surely they weren't having an affair?

The landlord rang the brass bar bell, shouting last orders, and as Stan finished his pint, he decided to make it his last. He hoped he was mistaken about George's interest in Rose, and there was no way he was going to voice his suspicions to anyone. Gossip was rife enough locally, and Stan wasn't going to add to it. If anyone else got wind of what might be happening, especially their nosey neighbour, Mabel Povis, it would spread like wildfire.

Stan couldn't imagine how Celia Frost would react if she got to hear any of it, but one thing was certain, all hell was sure to break loose. He called his goodbyes and with the fog still thick he groped his way home, the wonderful, rich aroma of roast beef assailing his nostrils when he limped indoors.

Phyllis greeted him with a smile, her olive skin flushed from the heat of cooking and her straight, brown hair tucked back behind her ears. She was only five feet tall, with hazel eyes that twinkled as he gave her a hug.

'What was that for?' she asked.

''Cos I love you.'

'You daft sod. You're tipsy,' she said, pushing him away.

'You wound me, my darling,' he said, affecting a posh tone. 'I'm just drunk with love.'

'Dad, you are funny,' Amy said, giggling.

'If he doesn't take his coat off and sit at the table, I'll give him funny,' Phyllis threatened. 'Dinner is ready, and waiting to be eaten.'

'Your wish is my command, my Queen,' Stan said, flourishing a bow.

Phyllis laughed, Amy giggled again, and Stan took off his coat to sit at the table where he picked up his knife and fork, holding them up as he said, 'Right, woman, feed me.'

Phyllis shook her head, feigning disgust, but Stan could see that she was hiding a smile. Theirs was a good marriage, and though hard-up, they were happy. He wanted the same for his daughter, but now his face straightened as he thought about the Frosts again. If George *was* having an affair with Rose and Celia found out, the fact that they were related might affect Amy and he didn't want her taking any flak.

Tommy might be a nice lad, thought Stan, but the sooner his daughter found herself another boyfriend, the better.

Chapter Two

The Sunday roast had been eaten and as her mother stood up to clear the table, Amy saw how tired she looked. 'Leave it, Mum. I'll do it. You go and sit by the fire and I'll make you a cup of tea.'

'There's the washing up and I've got to collect Winnie's plate.'

'I'll do that too.'

'Thanks, love,' Phyllis said gratefully as she took a seat by the fire, kicking off her slippers to rest her feet on the fender. 'Winnie will want a cup of tea too and tell her I'll pop round later to help her to bed.'

Amy stacked the plates before taking them through to the scullery. While waiting for the kettle to boil, Amy dwelled on how hard her mum worked. She was up at five every morning from Monday to Friday to do early morning office cleaning, and then did another stint between seven and nine in the evening at a local factory. To help all she could, Amy gave her mother most of the wages she earned from working in a shoe shop, but there never seemed to be enough money to go round. Though she loved her dad, Amy couldn't help feeling a surge of resentment. If he stopped going to the pub nearly every night he could stump up more housekeeping, but she had never once heard her mother complain.

After giving her parents their drinks, Amy went out the kitchen door and stepped into their small, concrete yard, the back wall so high you had to be over six feet tall to see over it. The fog was still thick and she could barely see the gate, but managed to feel her way along the narrow walkway. The walls on the opposite side were tall too, and the narrow confines felt claustrophobic, but Amy was soon in Mrs Morrison's identical yard. The old lady was in her eighties, very frail now and as she went in, Amy called, 'Hello, Mrs Morrison, it's only me.'

'Hello, ducks,' the old lady said.

'I've just popped round for your plate,' Amy said, seeing it on a small table by the fireside chair, frowning when she saw the amount still on it. 'Oh, you haven't finished your dinner yet. I'll come back later.'

'I've had my fill. Your mother's a wonderful woman and I don't know what I'd do without her, but she always gives me far too much to eat.'

To Amy the food looked barely touched, but she didn't argue. 'I'll make you a drink, and Mum said she'll pop round later.'

'Thanks, Amy,' Mrs Morrison said tiredly.

Amy brewed tea again then gave a cup to Winnie before picking up the dinner plate. 'I'm off now. Bye, Mrs Morrison.'

'You're a good girl. Bye, pet,' the old lady said.

Amy was soon home again, and tackled the washing up, putting everything away before she went into the living room. She smiled at the scene that greeted her. As usual, after dinner on a Sunday afternoon, her parents had fallen asleep by the fire. Amy crept out to visit her best friend, Caroline Cole whose name was always shortened to Carol. She lived two houses down, but to get to her front door you had to pass their neighbour, Mabel Povis. You couldn't do anything without Mrs Povis knowing about it, and Amy was unsurprised to see the woman peeping out of her window. Despite this she was her mum's friend so Amy gave her a small wave.

When Carol opened the door she put a finger to her lips to indicate that her parents too were asleep, before she and Amy went upstairs to her bedroom. It was freezing as they dived onto the single bed, pulling the blankets around them. There were magazine cut-outs of singers and film stars on the walls covering some of the pink flowered wallpaper. They were mostly of an American singer called Pat Boone, but Carol had gone off him lately.

Carol asked, 'Have you seen Tommy?'

'No, he's still ill and in bed,' Amy replied.

'I don't know what you see in him. He's so thin, weedy looking, and when was the last time he was able to take you out?'

'It was a week ago, and Tommy may be thin, but he's tall and good looking,' Amy said defensively.

'You need a bloke who can show you a good time, not one who's more often than not too ill to leave the house.'

'He's sure to get better soon,' Amy said.

'Even if he does, don't let it get too serious,' Carol advised. 'You should play the field a bit first.'

Carol always spoke as if she was worldly and experienced, but though a flirt, she would never let a boy take liberties. To most people Carol appeared older and self-assured, but Amy knew there was another side to her. Underneath the hard veneer she was soft and caring, but with two older brothers to contend with while growing up, it rarely showed.

Amy smiled and said, 'Thanks for the advice, but you know I've been out with other boys and most of them were like octopuses with their groping hands. Tommy's different, he isn't like that.'

'Yeah, all right, I get the picture, but just because Tommy's sick, I don't see why you have to stay at home every night. Why don't you come out with me for a change? We could go down to the youth club to play some records and jive to Bill Haley singing *Rock around the Clock*.'

'You've been on about that song for months now.'

'I know,' Carol conceded, 'but it's so catchy. Davy and Paul reckon that big changes are coming, that singers like Alma Cogan and Ronnie Hilton will be out. Our parents can listen to them or Winifred Atwell on the piano, while we dance to rock and roll.'

Amy was an only child and wished that like Carol, she had two big brothers. Dave was twenty-one, Paul twenty-three, both tall with dark hair, and they were protective of their sister. When the boys had lived at home the house always seemed to be bursting at the seams and with only two bedrooms, Carol's had just been a partitioned-off section of the boys'. Amy had had a crush on both of them, but they only saw her as a kid. When they'd left home to share a flat, Carol had the whole room to herself, but they were always popping home. 'Have you seen your brothers today?' Amy asked.

'Yeah, they came round for dinner, but left soon after, leaving me as usual to help Mum with the washing up. It drives me mad the way they expect to be waited on, and my dad's the same.'

'When you're a girl, it seems to be expected,' Amy said.

Carol pouted and complained, 'I don't see why. When I get married I'm not going to be a slave to my husband.'

'What's this?' Amy asked, smiling. 'Has someone proposed to you?'

14

'Don't be daft. You know I haven't got a boyfriend at the moment.'

'You soon will have,' Amy said assuredly as she looked at her friend. Carol was pretty, with long, auburn hair, hazel eyes and full lips that tended to pout if she didn't get her own way. She was also fairly tall, with a willowy figure that Amy envied.

'I must admit, I've got my eye on a bloke.'

'Have you?' Amy asked. 'Do I know him?'

'You've *seen* him,' Carol said enigmatically.

Amy frowned. 'Where?'

'He's working on refitting that shop opposite where we work.'

'I haven't noticed him,' Amy said, 'but it explains why you've been hovering at the window instead of serving customers.'

'Yeah, well, he is a bit dishy.'

'What does he look like?'

'He's cute. Not too tall, beefy, with a round face.'

'He sounds like your usual type,' Amy said, unable to share Carol's taste in boys. It was funny really, Amy thought, considering that she was only four foot eleven she liked tall blokes, whereas Carol preferred them short and stocky.

'Once the refit is finished he'll be off. I need to catch his eye before then,' Carol mused.

'I doubt he could have missed you,' Amy commented, aware how striking her friend was. 'Unless of course you've been standing at the window so much that he thinks you're part of the display.'

Carol chuckled; Amy giggled, and soon the two of them were in fits of laughter. 'Shush,' Carol finally gasped. 'If we wake my parents up I'll be in trouble.'

Amy managed to stop laughing. She liked Carol's mum,

Daphne Cole. Carol had inherited her mother's good looks and colouring; however she could be hard on her daughter if she was in one of her moods. 'Yes, you might get it in the neck from your mum, but you can't do anything wrong in your dad's eyes.'

'Yours is the same, but your mum dotes on you too. I wish I was an only child.'

'I'd prefer it if I wasn't,' Amy said. 'It can be a bit stifling and you get far more freedom than me.'

'Yeah, there is that I suppose,' Carol conceded, 'though I still have to be home by ten thirty. Talking of freedom, are you coming out tonight?'

With Tommy ill in bed it didn't seem right to go out dancing and if he got to hear about it he might be upset. Amy desperately sought an excuse. Carol didn't know that Mrs Frost had turned her away earlier, so she clutched at that. 'Sorry, I can't come out with you. I'm going to see Tommy.'

'Boring . . .' Carol drawled.

Amy hated fibbing to her friend, but she was really keen on Tommy, keener than anyone knew. She wasn't too worried about Mrs Frost; after all, she'd be marrying Tommy, not his mother. Of course there had been no mention of marriage, but Amy had seen the way Tommy looked at her. He hadn't said that he loved her yet, but she was sure he returned her feelings.

At least she hoped so.

Celia Frost was disappointed to see that Thomas had hardly touched his dinner. She felt his forehead, frowning. 'You've hardly eaten a thing and if your fever hasn't gone down by tomorrow, I think I'll ask Dr Trent to call in again.'

'There's no need to make a fuss. I feel a little better today.'

'You don't look it,' Celia told him.

'Has Amy called in to see me?'

'Yes, but you were asleep and I don't think she'll be back. Young girls are so flighty these days and while you're ill in bed, no doubt Amy's out and about enjoying herself,' Celia said, pleased to see a frown cross her son's features. She had planted a seed of doubt about Amy and she'd leave him to dwell on it. 'Now rest, darling, and I'll be up to see you again later.'

Celia carried the tray downstairs, and after washing the plate she went back into the sitting room where she took a seat by the fire, her eyes resting on her husband in the opposite chair. He was asleep, snoring softly and her lips twisted in distaste. She'd had high hopes for George when they married, expecting him to be as ambitious as she was, but instead, with his problem, he'd never attempted to expand the business. There was plenty of work for glaziers, and by now George should have been in the position to employ men to work for him. However, he'd been too proud to accept her offer to help, instead remaining a one-man band.

Of course Thomas worked with him, but that hardly counted. At least George made fairly good money and was generous with the housekeeping, Celia had to admit. Yet they could have had so much more, still could, if George would only listen to her suggestions instead of dismissing them.

With a sigh of discontent, Celia picked up her tapestry frame to continue working on a cushion; the scene a quaint thatched cottage and garden filled with hollyhocks, delphiniums and roses in profusion. She would love a pretty garden, a place in the country away from the smoke and pollution which would be so much better for Thomas.

There was a snort, a grunt and then George's eyes opened. He yawned then said, 'I could do with a cup of Rosie Lee.'

'You sound so common. It's a cup of *tea*, George,' Celia chastised.

The tiredness left his eyes to be replaced by annoyance. 'When are you going to get off your high horse, woman? You may sound as though you were born with a plum in your mouth, but I know you came from a slum.'

Celia felt the heat rise to her cheeks. She had been born in the East End of London, and when her father died, her mother had been left to bring up eight children on her own. Celia could remember the two small rooms they had been crammed into, the rats, and the bugs climbing the walls. Tuberculosis had been rife, and Celia saw three of her brothers and one sister die of the disease. She'd been terrified that she was going to catch it too, and with that fear came a fierce determination to escape the poverty and filth. Angrily she cried, 'I may have been born in a slum, but at least I had the ambition to better myself, which is more than I can say for you!'

'That's it, bring me down again, but you seem to forget that you only worked in a dress shop when I met you.'

'It wasn't just any old shop! I had to improve my diction, posture and dress sense before I could gain a position in Knightsbridge. We catered for the wealthy and fashionable.'

'Yeah, and you still try to emulate them,' George said bitterly.

'No doubt you'd prefer me to sound like a fishwife, but let me tell you I'm proud of my achievements.'

'If that's the case, how come nobody around here knows anything about it? Instead you've fabricated the story that you were born in Chelsea, of middle-class parents.'

'I won't have anyone looking down on me.'

'No, you prefer to lord it up over them by pretending to be something that you're not.'

'You didn't complain when we met,' Celia told him, annoyed to find tears welling in her eyes. 'In fact you said you loved my voice, my poise, and everything else about me. Lately though, all you do is criticise me and I have no idea why.'

George shook his head, sighed, then said, 'Yeah, you're right and I'm sorry. It's just that I wish you'd lighten up; learn to live a little, to have a bit of fun.'

'We went to the dance at the Conservative Club, and there's another one in a couple of weeks.'

'You can't call that fun. It's all so formal, dress suits and cocktail dresses. We're only in our forties, but we're becoming a couple of old fuddy-duddies, and when was the last time we made love?'

Celia stared at her husband, aghast. George didn't seem to appreciate that lately she'd been worn out with looking after Thomas, sometimes so worried about him that she slept in a chair beside his bed. She didn't bother to point this out; George would only say she was mollycoddling Thomas again, so she rose to her feet, only saying, 'I'll make you a cup of tea.'

'Yeah, do that, and then how about a bit of slap and tickle?'

'George,' she cried, appalled, 'what on earth has come over you? It's four o'clock on a Sunday afternoon.'

'As prissy as ever,' he said bitterly. 'I knew you'd react like that, Celia. In fact the only fun I have with you nowadays is in winding you up. Forget the tea. I'm going out.'

With those words George abruptly rose to his feet, and as he walked out of the room Celia chased after him. 'George, where are you going?'

'For a walk,' he snapped while pulling on his overcoat. Moments later he stormed out, slamming the door behind him.

Celia just stood there for moment, brows furrowed. George had changed lately, had become sharp in his criticism of her, but she felt that something else was going on, something underlying his odd behaviour. Was it to do with his business? Was George having financial problems and keeping it from her? No, that couldn't be it, she decided, he was as busy as ever.

Whatever the underlying problem was, Celia was sure that it wasn't anything to do with their marriage. After all, she was a good wife and mother. It was George who had changed, not her.

Chapter Three

On Monday morning the fog had cleared and Carol's mother, Daphne Cole, stood at the bottom of the stairs to shout impatiently, 'Carol, get up! If you don't get a move on you'll be late for work.'

'Yeah, I'm coming,' she called back sleepily. Carol hated Monday morning, and her boring job in the shoe shop did nothing to inspire her to get out of bed. She didn't mind most of the customers, but dreaded those that had smelly feet, especially if they wanted her to take their foot measurements. However, as she became fully awake Carol thought about the shop fitter who had caught her eye. Now *he* was worth getting up for.

It didn't take Carol long to get ready, but she wished she didn't have to put on the black, pencil skirt and white blouse that all the staff had to wear. She needed something striking to be noticed, and as Carol sat at her dressing table she decided that instead of dragging her long, auburn hair into a ponytail, she'd try something more sophisticated. It took a little time, but at last Carol managed to style her hair into a neat French pleat. She then applied make-up, and smiled at her own reflection. Yes, she looked good. Surely the shop fitter would notice her today.

'Why are you all done up like a dog's dinner?' her mother asked as soon as Carol appeared downstairs.

'I've only done my hair in a different style.'

'It's more than that. You've got far too much make-up on. With all that green eye-shadow and black mascara, you look like a flippin' clown.'

'I think it looks nice,' Carol said, ignoring her mother's criticism as she poured herself a cup of tea. Sometimes she felt that her mum was jealous of her, and she had never been given the attention or shows of affection that were showered on her brothers.

'Come on, girl, it's time you left for work,' her mum now chided.

Carol glanced at the clock, grabbed a slice of toast, threw on her coat and hurried out, calling, 'Bye, see you later.'

Amy was just leaving her house too, and Mabel Povis was on her doorstep, cleaning her letterbox. Carol saw the woman looking at her with disapproval, but ignored her as she linked arms with Amy.

'You look nice,' Amy said as they walked up the Rise.

'Thanks,' Carol said, pleased to hear that after her mother's carping. She saw that Amy was hardly wearing any make-up, just a touch of mascara and pink lipstick. She still looked nice though, pretty in a wholesome sort of way, with her blonde bubble-cut hair, pink cheeks and clear, blue eyes.

'I suppose you're all done up for that shop fitter's benefit,' Amy said, grinning.

'Who else?' Carol quipped. 'I just hope it works.'

As they passed Tommy's house, Amy glanced up at one of the bedroom windows, musing, 'I wonder how he is today?'

'How was he last night?' Carol asked.

For a moment Amy looked surprised at the question, but then she stammered, 'His . . . his chest was still bad.'

'Well then, he's hardly likely to be much better this morning,' Carol said, wondering why Amy looked flushed. If Tommy was so ill, they couldn't have got up to much, but maybe a few kisses had been exchanged. Fancy blushing about that, Carol thought. Now, if they had gone all the way it would be different, but like her, Carol knew that Amy was still a virgin. Moments later they turned onto Lavender Hill, saving on bus fare as usual by walking to Clapham Junction.

When they reached the crossroads Amy was about to turn the corner, as after passing Arding & Hobbs department store they would soon come to the shoe shop, but Carol grabbed her arm, pulling her to the other side of the road, saying, 'Let's walk along to the shop that's being refitted and cross over again in front of it.'

Amy smiled knowingly. 'I suppose you're hoping that fitter will see you.'

'Yes, and I can get a closer look at him.'

Carol wasn't disappointed. He was there, this time standing outside while rolling a cigarette. She planted a smile on her face and began chatting inanely to Amy about the weather as they drew near.

At last he turned his head, eyes roaming over them and then, best of all, with a cheeky grin, he said, 'Now there's a sight to cheer a bloke up in the morning.'

Carol quipped back, 'Glad to oblige.'

'Come on, Miss Winters is opening up,' Amy hissed and after looking both ways, she hurried across the road.

Fuming, Carol did the same, but as she looked back over her shoulder, the shop fitter called, 'I go to the Nelson Café at around twelve thirty for my lunch. Maybe I'll see you there.'

'Yeah, maybe,' Carol called back, her heart racing. She didn't know his name yet, and he looked older than she'd first thought, but he was even better looking close up and nothing was going to keep her from the café at lunchtime.

Mabel Povis put her washing in the bath to soak and then went next door to see Phyllis. She used the back entrance, none of them keeping their gates or back doors locked until they went to bed, and going through the kitchen into her friend's living room Mabel said without preamble, 'I think Amy should stay away from Caroline Cole.'

'Why?' Phyllis asked from her chair by the fire.

'Because Carol looks, and acts, like a tart. You should have seen her this morning, all done up with her face plastered with make-up. Her mother is little better, vain and full of herself.'

'Daphne is all right, and Amy has been friends with Carol since they were kids. She's a nice girl,' Phyllis argued.

'I must admit that Daphne has a lot to put up with,' Mabel said. 'You know how thin our walls are, and Frank seems to be a bit insatiable on the *you know what* side. He's at Daphne every night, and from what I've heard he won't take no for an answer.'

Phyllis chuckled. 'Are you sure you're not jealous?'

'A bit of slap and tickle every night! No thanks,' Mabel protested.

'If I had the energy I wouldn't mind,' Phyllis said, running a hand tiredly over her face.

Mabel was used to Phyllis being a bit worn out, after all, she was up at the crack of dawn, but this morning she looked exhausted, her complexion grey. Not only that, it was unusual to see Phyllis just sitting, especially on a Monday morning when nearly every woman in the street tackled their laundry. A little worried Mabel asked, 'What's up, love? You look a bit rough.'

'I'm just tired.'

'If you ask me, it's more than that,' Mabel said. 'You look ill.'

'I feel a bit washed-out today, that's all. I think I need a tonic.'

'Talking of washing, have you made a start on yours?'

'Not yet,' Phyllis admitted.

'Well you stay there and I'll make you a cup of tea. Then as my stuff is already in soak, I'll make a start on yours.'

'No, I'll do it,' Phyllis protested.

'Don't be daft, it's no trouble and if I was under the weather you'd do the same for me.'

'Yeah, all right, thanks, but there's Winnie's stuff to put in soak too.'

'No problem,' Mabel said, frowning with concern. The fact that Phyllis had agreed to let her help was worrying and she wondered if taking care of Winnie, along with doing two cleaning jobs, had become a bit too much for her friend . . .

Mabel made the tea, determined to speak her mind as she handed a cup to Phyllis. 'Now listen, it's obvious that you're worn out. Winnie isn't your responsibility and you shouldn't have to look after her.'

'Her son emigrated to Australia and with her daughter living in Devon, she's too far away. Winnie hasn't got anyone else.'

'I've offered to help out, but you know that Winnie doesn't like me and she refused,' Mabel said. 'It ain't fair on you and you should get in touch with her daughter. Tell her that her mother needs to go into a nursing home or something.'

'Winnie wouldn't stand for that,' Phyllis said, shaking her head. 'She's lived in that house since she got married nearly sixty years ago and nothing will make her leave it.'

'If you didn't put yourself out, her daughter would flaming well have to,' Mabel snapped.

'They don't get on and she won't do anything,' Phyllis said, her voice weak with tiredness.

'Right then, have a word with the doctor. See if he can get her some sort of home help, 'cos I'm telling you now, Phyllis, if you don't, I will,' Mabel said, concerned for her friend.

'Yeah, yeah, all right, I'll try to sort something out. Now for goodness sake change the subject,' Phyllis appealed.

'While you're talking to the doc about Winnie, you should get him to take a look at you.'

'Mabel, I've told you, I'm fine, and thanks for the tea. As for my washing, I feel up to doing it myself now. You can bugger off and let me get on with it.'

Mabel didn't take offence. She and Phyllis had been friends for years and in reply she said, 'Right, sod you then. I'm going.'

The two women smiled at each other, both knowing that another cup of tea would be shared later that day. Mabel left by the back door again and closed it behind her, unaware that as soon as Phyllis stood up, she had swayed for a moment before crashing, unconscious, onto the floor.

*   *   *

Carol was clock watching. Luckily her lunch break was always at twelve thirty, and Amy's at one fifteen, each of them allotted forty-five minutes – which was generous of their manageress, Lena Winters, as some shop assistants only got half an hour.

Miss Winters was in her forties, and though she had crooked teeth, she was quite an attractive woman. Carol often wondered why she had never married, but she had told them little about herself, only that she lived alone above a shop on Northcote Road. As their manageress, Miss Winters kept herself a little aloof and as questions about her private life weren't welcomed, they knew little about her.

The shop wasn't busy; it rarely was on a Monday, and she and Amy had been given the task of checking stocks. Carol was up a ladder in the back room, calling out any sizes that had sold out, but paused to say, 'Well, what did you think of him?'

'Carol, that's the umpteenth time you've asked me. As I've said before, I think he looks a bit old for you.'

'I reckon he's in his late twenties and I don't see anything wrong with that, after all, I'll be eighteen next month. Oh, I can't wait for my lunch break.'

'You've only got ten minutes to go.'

'Does my hair still look all right?' Carol asked worriedly.

'Its fine, now what did you say about size five?'

'We're out of the D width.'

'Amy, we have customers. Can you come out front, please,' Miss Winters called.

As her friend scuttled off, Carol descended the ladder. She would go to the toilet, touch up her make-up and then it would be time to go. Her tummy was fluttering with nerves as she applied a dab of powder and fresh lipstick.

She had only been out with boys of her own age and this time she was feeling out of her depth.

With one last look in the mirror Carol went out to the shop and spoke to Miss Winters. 'Will it be all right if I go to lunch now?'

'Yes, off you go,' the woman agreed.

Amy was on one knee, helping an old lady to try on some shoes, but she looked up and grinned as Carol passed. With a tight smile on her face, Carol left the shop and soon she was hurrying to the Nelson Café which was a short distance up St John's Hill. She hoped he was already there as she opened the door and glanced quickly around, relieved to see him sitting alone at a table. He waved a hand at her and as Carol approached, he pulled out a chair.

'Take a pew,' he said, smiling.

'Thanks,' Carol replied.

'I wasn't sure you'd come. Do you usually have your lunch in here?' he asked.

'No, I don't, but it looks all right,' she said, her eyes flicking round the café.

'What's your name?'

'Carol. What's yours?'

'Roy,' he replied and handed Carol the menu as the waitress approached. 'What are you having to eat?'

Carol took a quick look to find the cheapest thing and ordered an egg and chips, while Roy asked for shepherd's pie. She usually took a sandwich for lunch to save money, but she'd been up late that morning and a cooked meal would make a nice change.

'Would you like something to drink?' the waitress asked.

'A Pepsi, please,' Carol said, while Roy ordered a cup of coffee.

'Do you live around here?' he asked as the waitress walked away.

'Yes, at the bottom of Lark Rise, off Lavender Hill. Do you know it?'

'No, I can't say I do.'

'Where do you live then?' Carol asked, thinking that Roy really was handsome as she took in his hazel eyes.

He looked away for a moment, but then said, 'In Tooting.'

Carol didn't know much about that area and found herself floundering for something to say, only coming up with, 'Do you live with your parents?'

His eyes widened. 'You must be joking. I flew the nest years ago.'

Carol tensed, and asked, 'Are you married?'

'Nah, I'm still foot loose and fancy free. I've got my own place though, only a small flat, but it suits me fine.'

'Really,' Carol said, impressed. All her previous boyfriends, like her, still lived with their parents. She still didn't know how old Roy was and felt he might even be in his early thirties, yet she really fancied him. He had a round face, with dark blonde, crew-cut hair. His neck was short over wide shoulders, and she could just imagine his muscular torso; Carol hated long, thin men and saw them as puny. She was snapped out of her reverie when Roy spoke.

'Now that you've had a good look, I hope you like what you see,' he said, smiling.

Aware then that she had been staring at him, Carol flushed, but she still managed to quip, 'I was looking *through* you, not *at* you.'

'If you say so, but I've been clocking you too and I like what I see. You're a nice-looking bird, but how old are you?'

'I'm not sure I like being called a bird, but thanks for the compliment and I'm twenty-three,' Carol lied, thinking that if he knew she wasn't yet eighteen there'd be no chance of a date.

Their drinks arrived, followed soon after by their food, and as they ate Carol found that their eyes kept meeting across the table. Would Roy want to take her out? She hoped so, and then at last, between mouthfuls, he asked, 'Are you seeing anyone?'

'Not at the moment,' she replied, wondering if this was the moment.

'In that case, can I take you out to dinner on Friday?'

Carol was startled. That was different. Most boys just suggested the pictures, or dancing, but then again Roy wasn't a boy. He was a man. She didn't want to appear gauche or unsophisticated, so she hid her surprise and said, 'Yes, that would be lovely.'

'I've got a car so do you want me to pick you up, or would you rather meet somewhere?' Roy asked.

'As you don't know Lark Rise, we could meet outside Arding & Hobbs.'

'Okay. Shall we say eight o'clock?'

'That's fine.'

'It's a date then,' Roy said, grinning.

Carol was already wondering what to wear as they continued to eat, and as soon as they had finished Roy beckoned the waitress over to ask for the bill. 'Sorry,' he said when she went to fetch it, 'I only get a half hour break and I'd best get back. You stay and finish your Pepsi.'

'Let me give you my share of the bill.'

'No, have it on me,' Roy said, and after going to the counter to settle up, he turned to give Carol a wink and then left.

Carol sat back, sipping her drink with a small smile playing round her lips. It was her half day off on Wednesday and she'd look around the shops, sure that she'd be able to get round her dad to give her a few bob towards a new dress. She'd find something really sophisticated that would impress Roy.

For Carol, Friday couldn't come quickly enough.

Chapter Four

When Phyllis had come round after fainting, she'd felt disoriented and bleary eyed. What had happened? Her head had been throbbing and she wondered if she'd hit it on something. After struggling to sit up another wave of dizziness had swept over her. She'd remained still until it passed, and then had managed to heave herself onto a chair. It was the first time in her life that Phyllis had fainted, so the feeling of nausea was unexpected. She'd fought the urge to be sick, swallowing bile as she shivered in shock. It had been a surprise to find that only minutes had passed, but why had she fainted? She wasn't ill. She was just tired, that was all, and at last, giving in, Phyllis had gone upstairs to lie down.

It was now three hours later and Phyllis woke up feeling a lot better. It must have been exhaustion; that, or the fact that she wasn't eating properly. Yet they had survived on a lot less to eat during the war. Despite that thought, Phyllis knew that she had lost weight, her arms thin and her ribs showing when she undressed. She hid it well, wearing an extra jumper with a thick cardigan most of the time, and so far nobody had noticed. Anyway, she'd never been fat, so that couldn't be the reason for her lack of energy.

Phyllis changed her rumpled clothes and applied a little

lipstick to give her face a bit of colour, but as she hadn't done her washing, no doubt when Mabel turned up again in about half an hour she'd know that something was up.

For now though, Phyllis was worried about Winnie. She hadn't been to check on her since early that morning and now she hurried next door, pleased to see that the old lady was all right. Winnie's living room was as gloomy as her own, Phyllis thought, with ancient wallpaper and dull, dark furniture. She should polish it, Phyllis thought guiltily, make things look a bit more cheerful for Winnie, but with two cleaning jobs and her own housework to do, she just didn't have the energy. Managing a smile she said, 'Sorry, love, I'm a bit behind today and you must be dying for a drink.'

'I've been dozing on and off all morning, but yes, I must admit I'm thirsty,' Winnie admitted.

'I'll make you a cuppa,' Phyllis offered and soon Winnie was sipping it with pleasure.

However her expression suddenly became sombre and she said, 'Phyllis, I know my Harry passed away, but sometimes I think I can hear him speaking to me. You'll probably think I'm mad, but somehow I think I'll be joining him soon.'

'Oh, don't say that, Winnie.'

'Now don't get upset. I've had a good innings and I'm ready to go.'

'All you're probably hearing is our voices through the thin walls. On the other hand you may be coming down with something, so I'll get the doctor in to take a look at you.'

'There's no need,' Winnie protested. 'I'm fine, as well as I can be, and I don't know why people are so afraid to talk about death. We've all got to go sometime, and I just think that my number's coming up, that's all.'

'You've got years in you,' Phyllis protested, 'and I'm not going to listen to any more of this. Now I'll pour you another cup of tea and then I'll be back later with your dinner. If you need me before that, thump on the wall as usual.'

'I'll do that, and thanks. I don't know what I'd do without you.'

Phyllis managed a small smile, yet she was unable to help noticing how frail Winnie looked. She still managed to use the commode unassisted, but going upstairs to bed proved impossible and now Winnie slept in a single one that had been pushed up against their adjoining wall in the living room.

With a heavy heart, Phyllis returned home where moments later Mabel turned up, saying as she came in, 'I could do with a cuppa so put the kettle on, mate.'

'It wouldn't suit me,' Phyllis said, 'but as I always seem to be making pots of tea maybe I should open a café.'

'Very funny, but why didn't you put your washing out to dry? There's no sign of rain.'

'I didn't do it.'

'I knew you weren't up to it, but you insisted you were all right,' Mabel admonished.

'Yeah, well, as you saw I was worn out and when you left I sort of passed out for a minute or two.'

'You did what!'

'It was nothing,' Phyllis said quickly. 'Once I'd had a bit of a kip I was fine, but you could have knocked me down with a feather when I realised I'd slept for over three hours.'

'You must have needed it, and it looks like it's done you a lot of good. You look heaps better.'

Phyllis refrained from saying that though she was only forty, she felt twenty years older than that as she filled the kettle.

'Leave that, I'll do it,' Mabel said. 'You sit yourself down.'

'You just said I look heaps better.'

'Yeah, you do, but I ain't fooled by that lipstick. You're still a bit pale.'

Phyllis didn't argue and as she prepared the drinks, Mabel continued to chat. 'Daphne Cole got her washing done. I looked out of my bedroom window over to her yard and saw her sheets and towels were gleaming white when she hung them out, but of course she's better off than us with that boiler thing she's got. I still think she should sort her daughter out though. If she doesn't, mark my words, Carol will come to no good.'

Phyllis ignored the comment, only saying, 'At least we don't have to spend time grating our soap now. I think this new washing powder that's come out is marvellous.'

'Yeah, it is, but I must tell you what I heard this morning.'

Phyllis was used to this. Mabel thrived on gossip, but Phyllis knew why and understood. It was something that kept Mabel's mind occupied; a tool she used to shut out the grief that still tortured her. She and Jack had lost their only child, a little boy, to measles when he was only three years old. They hadn't had any more children, and though no reason could be found, it was as though something in Mabel had died too.

Phyllis had always wanted another child too, but though trying, Amy had remained the only one. At least she had her daughter, while poor Mabel had been left childless. Few remained on Lark Rise who remembered what Mabel had been through, or if they did, any sympathy they had once felt had long been forgotten.

With a sigh, Phyllis just wished Mabel would find something else to do with her time, something that could be meaningful, but after all these years she'd run out of suggestions. 'All right, Mabel, as you're keen to tell me, what have you heard?'

'That cousin of yours, Rose, has got her eye on someone.'

Phyllis's lips tightened. Rose was always the subject of local gossip and she said, 'Don't tell me it's a married man again.'

'To be honest it was only a snippet and no names were mentioned. Of course she's had her eye on the landlord's agent for ages, so it might be him. If it is, I don't know what she sees in the ugly sod. I told him that my roof is leaking ages ago, but he still hasn't got the landlord to sort it out.'

'Keep on at him,' Phyllis advised.

'Yeah, I will. My back bedroom is in a right state and every time it rains I have to put a bucket under the leak. It's just as well I don't use it,' Mabel said, her expression saddening.

As it had been the one that Mabel's little boy had slept in, Phyllis understood, but it also gave her an idea. 'If you can get the agent to have a word with the landlord about fixing the roof, you could let that room. It would give you a few extra bob a week.'

'It's an idea,' Mabel mused, 'but to be honest, I don't think my Jack would stand for it. You know how he likes his privacy, and anyway, with him being a railway guard, we ain't too bad off.'

Phyllis's suggestion hadn't been to do with money, though she had passed it off as such. A lodger might have given Mabel something to focus on, someone else to look after instead of spending all her spare time watching all the comings and goings on Lark Rise to feed her insatiable need for gossip.

They continued to chat and when the pot had been

emptied, Mabel rose to her feet. 'I'd best get my washing in. Do you want me to give you a hand with yours in the morning?'

'Thanks for the offer, but I can manage.'

'Right then, I'm off. See you tomorrow.'

'Bye, love,' Phyllis called as she left. She knew that few of their neighbours could stand Mabel, that they found her harsh and opinionated; but Phyllis would always stand by her friend, no matter what.

Amy and Carol were on their way home, Carol going on and on about her date on Friday. 'Did I tell you that Roy's got a car?'

'Yes, several times. Tommy can drive, but his dad won't let him use the firm's van out of working hours.'

Carol gave a little skip. 'I've never been asked out to dinner before and I want to find something special to wear. What about my hair? Do you think I should wear it up, or down?'

'I like that French pleat, it makes you look older, sophisticated, but it looks nice when you curl it onto your shoulders too.'

Carol didn't think that was much help, and her mind drifted to what she was going to wear again. It still seemed ages to Friday, but if she went to the Nelson Café for lunch tomorrow, she could see Roy again before that. The idea was appealing at first, but then she decided against it. After all, she didn't want it to look like she was chasing after him.

As they turned into Lark Rise, Carol saw that Amy was looking at Tommy's house, and said, 'Why don't you go and see if he's any better?'

'If I didn't have to face the dragon, I would. Mrs Frost

made it clear on Sunday morning that Tommy wouldn't be up to seeing anyone for a good few days.'

Carol frowned. 'Hang on, you told me you were with him last night.'

Amy's face went bright red and she stuttered, 'Yes . . . yes . . . I was.'

'If you're going to be a liar, you should make sure you're a good one. You're rubbish at it, Amy.'

'I . . . I'm sorry.'

'If you didn't want to go out dancing with me, you only had to say no. You didn't have to invent an excuse.'

'I . . . I didn't want to upset you.'

'It wouldn't have. I met up with some of the other girls at the club, though I *would* like to know the real reason why you didn't want to come out with me.'

Amy hung her head, saying nothing, and Carol urged, 'Come on, spit it out.'

'I was worried about Tommy. If he found out I'd been out having a good time, it might have upset him.'

'Tough. He doesn't own you.'

'I know that. It's just that I really like him,' Amy said as they carried on down the hill.

Carol just couldn't understand what Amy saw in Tommy Frost. For her, Roy was all man, not a thin weakling, but she didn't voice her thoughts, instead saying, 'Look, Mabel Povis is on her doorstep again. I don't know why she doesn't put her bed on it. She's more outside her house than in it.'

'Mrs Povis is a bit nosey, but she's all right really. My mum thinks a lot of her.'

'Mine doesn't,' Carol said as she watched Mabel trotting up to them.

'Amy, I'm glad I caught you,' the woman said. 'Your mum's so worn out that she passed out this morning.'

'What?' Amy cried. 'She fainted?'

'Yes, but thankfully she's all right now. You, my girl, should do more to help her around the house.'

'Yes, yes, I will,' Amy said, pale as she hurried indoors.

Unlike Amy, Carol wasn't scared of confrontation and she glared at Mabel. 'You had no right to have a go at Amy. She works full time, and on top of that she already does a lot to help her mother.'

'She can do more,' Mabel snapped and turning, she marched back into her own house.

Carol was left fuming, and her parents heard all about it as soon as she walked into the living room.

Frank Cole was listening to his daughter as she ranted and raved about Mabel Povis. He wasn't in the mood for this. After a hard day at work maintaining the noisy machines in the printing factory, all he wanted was a bit of peace and quiet. Daphne, his wife, was of course listening avidly while Frank wondered what it was with women and gossip.

'She was obviously waiting for Amy and had the cheek to tell her to do more to help her mother,' Carol said angrily.

'Well, Phyllis does have it hard,' Daphne mused, 'and I'm a bit worried to hear that she fainted.'

'You should have seen Amy's face. She went as white as a sheet,' Carol continued.

'I'll pop along to see Phyllis in the morning,' said Daphne, 'though I doubt I'll get in the door before Mabel turns up. It's like the woman has some sort of radar system.'

Frank sighed and tried to divert his wife. 'Daphne, what are we having for dinner?'

'What we always have on a Monday,' she replied. 'Meat left over from the Sunday roast with bubble and squeak.'

Frank licked his lips in anticipation of a nice tasty dinner.

To his relief, Daphne headed for the kitchen with Carol close behind her. He could still hear them talking about Mabel, but at least he'd get his dinner soon.

His sons hadn't turned up, but looking at the clock Frank knew that there was still time yet. It annoyed him that Dave and Paul often came round at meal times expecting to be fed, and not only that, Daphne still did their washing. His boys had done all right for themselves in the building game, with Paul a carpenter, and Dave a plasterer. They earned good money, rented a two-bedroom flat above a shop on Lavender Hill, and as far as Frank was concerned, it was about time they looked after themselves.

Frank would never admit it, but though he loved his sons, his daughter was the most precious to him. He also knew that Daphne favoured the boys, who both looked more like him, whereas Carol was so like her mother, both beauties and both his.

He'd never worried about the boys when they went out at night, but it wasn't the same with Carol. He insisted she was home by ten thirty and though she railed against it, she was rarely late. She'd had a fair few boyfriends, but if any of them had dared to take liberties with her, he'd have wrung their bloody necks. Carol wasn't seeing anyone at the moment, and that suited him just fine.

'Dinner's ready,' Carol said, laying two plates on the table.

Daphne followed behind with her own plate, and at last it seemed the subject of Mabel had been exhausted. He sat down, relieved that the boys hadn't turned up, his plate piled high.

'I'm popping round to see my mother after dinner,' Daphne said.

Frank couldn't stand his mother-in-law and knew the feeling was mutual. She lived a few streets away, hated living alone since her old man kicked the bucket, and Daphne often went round to keep her company. He didn't mind, and more often than not he went to the pub where he enjoyed a game of darts. 'I'm going out too. I've got a match on tonight.'

Frank tucked in, mostly a contented man; little knowing that there would come a time when his satisfaction with life was going to turn to ashes.

Chapter Five

Amy had dashed indoors to find her mother in the kitchen preparing dinner. She'd looked all right, albeit a bit pale, but after hearing what Amy had to say, she was now red-faced with temper.

'Mabel had no right to tell you that I fainted!' she snapped yet again. 'Look at you, all upset and for no reason.'

'Mum, I'm more upset that you won't go and sit down. I can finish making our dinner.'

'I don't need to rest. I was just tired, but now I'm fine. Go and get your work clothes off and this will be ready by the time you come downstairs again.'

No matter how hard Amy tried, her mother wouldn't give in and defeated, she went to change her clothes. It didn't take long and five minutes later Amy was back in the kitchen where her mother said, 'If your dad doesn't get a move on, dinner will be ruined. I've only got an hour to spare before I have to leave for work.'

'Mum, no, surely you're not up to going out cleaning again?'

'Of course I am.'

Before Amy could protest further, she heard her father coming in and then his voice calling, 'Where are you, woman?'

'Where do you think?' Phyllis called in reply.

'Probably in the kitchen where you belong,' he said, grinning as he appeared in the doorway.

'It's a wonder you haven't chained me to the sink.'

'Now then, don't go putting ideas into my head.'

Amy usually loved to hear her parents' banter, but there wasn't a smile on her face this time as she said to her father, 'Mum fainted this morning.'

He frowned worriedly and asked, 'Phyllis, what made you pass out?'

'I was a bit over-tired, that's all.'

'Dad, I don't think she should go to work tonight,' Amy said, relieved that her dad was home to back her up.

'Amy's right, Phyllis. You'd best stay home,' he agreed.

'Now look, I told Amy and now I'm telling you. I'm fine and don't intend to lose an evening's pay over nothing. Now get out from under my feet while I dish this dinner up.'

'I'll do it, Mum. You go and sit down.'

'I'm perfectly capable of doing it myself, and you, Stan, go and have a quick wash. Your hands are filthy.'

'Yes Boss,' he said, disappearing.

Defeated, Amy tried another offer. 'I'll give Winnie her dinner if you like.'

'Yes, all right, and tell her I'll pop in after I've finished work to help her into bed.'

'I could do that, Mum.'

'No, love. Winnie can be a bit funny and I doubt she'll undress in front of you. There's her commode to sort out too so you'd best leave it to me.'

'But . . .'

'That's enough, Amy. I said I'll deal with it and I will.

Now get this round to Winnie before it goes cold,' she insisted, handing Amy a plate, covered with another.

With no other option, Amy did as she was told, but she was still worried about her mum and couldn't believe that tiredness alone had caused her to faint.

Celia had seen Amy with her friend as they passed her window on their way home from work. She had held her breath, and was relieved that Amy hadn't knocked on her door. Of course she'd told the girl that Thomas wasn't well enough to see anyone, and thankfully it had worked.

With her son's dinner on a tray, Celia took it up to him. Thomas's fever had gone down overnight and he looked a lot better, but she'd insisted that he remain in bed. 'Here you are, darling,' she said. 'Now do try to eat it all.'

'I thought Amy might call in on her way home from work.'

'I saw her passing with her friend, the two of them chatting and giggling, but she didn't stop to ask how you are.'

Thomas looked forlorn, but Celia hardened her heart. If Thomas became serious about a girl, she wanted her to come from a good family, not unlike the Willards who lived next door. They were members of the Conservative Club too and had a daughter, Melissa, but having seen her all his life, so far Thomas hadn't noticed that she had now grown up. Of course Melissa wasn't a beauty, with a rather large nose and long, thin face surrounded by mousy brown hair, but she was poised and intelligent. Celia wanted to encourage Thomas to notice Melissa, and if he was well again by Saturday night, she intended to invite the Willards to dinner.

'That's your father,' Celia said as she heard George arriving home. She had grown used to his irregular hours.

George could arrive late if an urgent job came up, but not so this evening. She left Thomas to eat his dinner and went downstairs.

George had taken off his coat and was hanging it on the hall rack. Celia knew his routine. He would now go upstairs to have a wash and change his clothes before sitting down to dinner. 'How's Thomas?' he asked.

'A little better,' she replied, her back stiffening at his terse tone and lack of greeting. There had been a time when George would kiss her on his return home, but those days were long gone. They were now like cold acquaintances, Celia thought as she walked through to the kitchen.

By the time George came downstairs again, Celia had their dinner on the table, and pulling out a chair he sat down, looking at his food as he said, 'I'll be going out again in an hour or so.'

'What, again? You're out more evenings these days than you are in.'

'It's work, Celia, I'm not going to turn it down.'

'No, I suppose not,' she conceded, 'and no doubt your profits are up?'

'Yes, they are.'

'In that case, I'd like to buy a new dinner set. Last time we had a meal with the Willards, Libby was showing off her recently acquired Crown Derby. It's our turn to entertain them on Saturday and I'd like to have something equally nice.'

'There's nothing wrong with the stuff we have now.'

'George, it's cheap rubbish in comparison to Libby's china.'

'Celia, I'm sick of hearing about Libby Willard and the things she's got. You wanted a television as soon as they

45

got one, then it was new crystal glasses, and now you want another dinner set. I don't know why you think you have to keep up with the woman. It's getting bloody ridiculous.'

'And I'm sick of hearing your bad language!' Celia snapped, her temper rising.

With that George reared to his feet and leaning across the table he hissed, 'Well you won't have to hear it any more, Celia. I'm going out!'

'Good! I'll be glad to see the back of you,' she shouted in reply.

'And *I'm* glad to hear you say that,' George said enigmatically before marching off, the front door slamming behind him while Celia was left to ponder on his words.

George wished he had kept his mouth shut and as he walked down the hill to the bottom of the Rise he was kicking himself. He wasn't ready to make his move yet and hoped he hadn't given the game away.

It was only six thirty, too early, so with half an hour to kill he headed for the pub. A few blokes were propping up the bar, but George wasn't in the mood for chatting so after ordering a pint, he sat down at a table. He took his time, just sipping the beer, after all, he didn't want to arrive tipsy and ruin the evening.

At seven fifteen the door opened and Stan Miller limped in. George wasn't surprised, the man was a regular, and spotting him Stan called, 'Watcha, George. Can I get you another pint?'

'No thanks, mate. I'm only having this one then I'm off.'

'Yeah, you don't want to upset the wife. Mine's gone off to work so I'm all right.'

George had heard that Phyllis Miller did evening cleaning at a local factory and cynically he wondered if Celia knew how lucky she was. Since their marriage he had been the provider and she'd never had to work, yet despite that Celia had become more and more demanding. It was one thing after another, new this, new that, while he had to work his guts out to provide them.

Stan had gone to the bar, and was soon chatting to another bloke, while George continued to think about Celia. It really riled him that she looked down on people, especially the Millers. Stan had been reduced to poorly paid factory work since he'd been wounded during the war, and Phyllis had to work to supplement their income, yet Celia had never taken that into consideration.

A grim smile of satisfaction crossed George's face. If things worked out the way he hoped, Celia had a shock coming. He finished his pint and rose to leave. It was time for his next port of call, and he couldn't wait to get there.

Stan lifted his arm to wave to George as the man left the pub, feeling sorry for him. Fancy having to go home to a wife like Celia Frost, he thought, old frosty knickers. Stan frowned as a thought crossed his mind. It was Rose's night off. Was George going home to his wife, or was he headed in the other direction? No, surely the bloke wouldn't be daft enough to get mixed up with Rose. If he was going to have an affair, it wouldn't be so close to home – at least Stan hoped that was the case, especially as Amy was still seeing Tommy.

Stan had never been tempted by another woman, not that a nice pair of legs didn't catch his eye. His thoughts turned to Phyllis and despite her saying she was fine, he couldn't help worrying a bit about what had made her pass out. It wasn't like Phyllis. She was usually as tough as a horse and the cleaning jobs had never over-tired her before. Of course she was now looking after Winnie Morrison too; mornings, lunchtimes and after work she'd sort the old girl out, getting her to bed before coming home. Winnie wasn't a relative, she was just a neighbour, and it wasn't as if Phyllis was getting paid to look after her.

That thought led to another, and though it hadn't crossed his mind before, he wondered if Winnie stumped up anything towards the meals that Phyllis provided.

He'd have to find out, have a word with Phyllis, because there was no way he was going to fork out for Winnie Morrison too. As it was, he handed over Phyllis's house-keeping money every week, and with her two cleaning jobs, she always seemed to manage. The rest of his wages he kept as spending money, enough to ensure that he could buy a few pints of beer most evenings.

Frank Cole came in and went to join the darts team, while Stan ordered another pint, his mind still on Phyllis. He was still worried about her fainting and he began to fret. He'd have to put his foot down about Winnie, tell Phyllis that the old girl would have to find someone else to look after her. After all, he didn't want Phyllis becoming so worn out that she had to give up one, or even both of her cleaning jobs. That would mean stumping up more housekeeping money and Stan really didn't want to do that.

Mabel had seen George Frost earlier, illuminated by a street light before he passed her window. She'd been puzzled. He wasn't in his van so he wasn't working, and it had seemed a bit early for him to be going out. Maybe he'd had words with his stuck-up wife and was going to the pub to drown his sorrows. She'd tell Phyllis about it in the morning, but to make it interesting she'd have to weave it out a bit.

She had seen Phyllis leave for work, followed soon after by Stan, limping down the Rise en route to the pub. He did this most evenings while Phyllis was at work and Mabel hadn't really thought about it before, but this time she'd felt a surge of anger. He must have seen how worn out Phyllis looked. Instead of putting money over the bar, he could increase Phyllis's housekeeping money so she could cut down on the hours she worked.

Mabel turned away, her eyes settling on Jack, her husband. He was a good provider, didn't drink, never had, and he worked as a guard on the railway. It was shift work, but this week Jack was on normal hours. He'd been a quiet man when she married him, and he still was, but since they had lost their son all those years ago, he'd also become morose. The only thing that interested him was history books – he always had his nose stuck in one.

Mabel looked outside again, but there was nobody about. It was dark, cold, and there weren't any children playing outside now. She had seen some earlier, playing marbles in the gutter, their fingers blue with the cold which Mabel thought disgraceful. If her son had lived she'd have made sure he was well wrapped up before letting him play outside.

With nothing to see now, Mabel moved away to sit down opposite Jack. The silence of the room was only broken by the ticking of the clock, and for want of some sort of conversation she asked, 'What are you reading now?'

There was an audible sigh before Jack looked up, but he finally answered, 'It's a history of Battersea.'

'What on earth do you want to read that for?'

'It's interesting.'

'Why's that?' Mabel asked shortly, hoping to draw Jack out.

'Because Battersea wasn't written about until the end of the seventeenth century, and it was a lot different then.'

'In what way?'

Jack flicked back a couple of pages and said, 'For instance, in those days, Battersea Park was just marshland. It goes on to describe gentle slopes leading up to Lavender Hill that gave way to untamed heath, sweeping away to the wilds of Surrey.'

'It's all built up around here now and I just can't picture it,' Mabel said, surprised to find that she was interested. 'It must have been like living in the country.'

'Yes, it was,' Jack said, 'and in eighteen forty-six, Battersea Park was known as Battersea Fields. It was fertile land where crops were grown, such as carrots, melons and lavender. Not only that,' he continued, his voice animated, 'where Battersea Power Station stands now, there was a bawdy pub called the Red House Tavern, patronised by Charles Dickens. Now what do you think of that?'

'I still can't picture it, and bawdy? What's that supposed to mean?' she asked.

'Rough and rowdy I should think,' Stan said as he lowered his eyes to the book again.

Mabel knew the signs. She wasn't going to get anything else out of him, and her thoughts turned to Phyllis again. She was fond of her friend, but secretly envied her too – envied that she had a happy marriage, and though he was a drinker Stan was always laughing and joking. Maybe Jack would cheer up a bit if he had a few pints of beer instead of his nose stuck in books.

In truth though, the thing that Mabel envied most was that Phyllis had a daughter. In fact nearly everyone in the street had kids. Daphne Cole had three, two sons and her flighty daughter, Carol.

Mabel felt a surge of deep sorrow. She tried to hide it, buried her unhappiness in gossip, but in reality her life felt empty, meaningless, and she had felt like this since the day her son had died.

Chapter Six

Thomas was almost fully recovered by Thursday, and despite what his mother said, at a quarter to seven that evening nothing was going to keep him in. Thankfully he found he had an ally in his father.

'Thomas, it's far too cold to go out,' his mother complained. 'You've only just got over that nasty bout of bronchitis.'

'I feel fine, Mum.'

'It's damp outside and you need to keep warm.'

'Leave him alone, Celia. He wants to call on Amy and he looks fine to me. A bit of fresh air won't do him any harm.'

'Since when have we had fresh air around here? We'd only get that if we moved out of London. We could find a nice place in the country.'

'Not this again? My work is here, Celia, and I doubt I'd get many, if any, call outs in the country.'

'Your son's health is more important than your volume of work.'

'So you'd be happy if I could only give you a fraction of the money you get now?'

'Money isn't everything.'

'It is with you, Celia.'

Thomas could see this was going to develop into yet another argument between his parents, and quickly said, 'I'm off. I'll see you later.'

'Thomas!'

He ignored his mother's shout, and hurried out, heading down the Rise to see Amy. He couldn't understand why she hadn't at least called in to see how he was. During his time in bed he had at first been bewildered, but then he began to think that she must have found someone else.

Thomas's stomach tightened at the thought. He liked Amy, really liked her and had hoped she had felt the same way about him. If she had another boyfriend, when was she going to tell him? Thomas couldn't stand the wait, he wanted to know and as he reached her house to knock on the door, he found his guts churning with nerves.

Amy opened it, her eyes widening when she saw him, but she also smiled with delight. 'Tommy! Oh, I'm so pleased to see you. Are you all right now?'

'Yes, I'm fine. Can you come out for a walk?'

'Of course. I'll just get my coat.'

Thomas waited, puzzled. Amy had certainly looked pleased to see him. Was that a good sign? In less than a minute Amy was hurrying outside and after pulling the door closed behind her, she tucked a hand into his arm.

They began to walk and Thomas found that he didn't know what to say. If he complained that she hadn't been to see him it would make him appear a bit petulant. He bit on his lower lip, and then said instead, 'What have you been up to while I've been stuck in bed?'

'I've just been to work as usual and then spent the evenings at home.'

'That can't have been much fun,' he said, but his mood

lightened. 'There was I thinking you would have been out having a good time.'

'Well I wasn't,' Amy said, smiling up at him. 'I couldn't have a good time without you.'

His heart skipped a beat. Amy was so cute and pretty. He didn't care that she was less than five feet tall – he loved that about her too. Since childhood Tommy had felt like a weakling and he'd been bullied at school, yet when he was with Amy he felt so tall and manly. 'You have no idea how much I've missed you,' he said.

'I've missed you too, Tommy.'

They had turned the corner, and with nobody in sight, Thomas drew to a halt. He enfolded Amy into his arms, bent his head and she lifted hers, standing on tiptoe as they kissed.

She hadn't found anyone else; Amy was still his, and Thomas was happy. She was definitely the girl for him, and though it was too soon to do it yet, in a few more months, if only she'd agree, he hoped to put an engagement ring on her finger.

'After telling us that Tommy was at the door, Amy soon shot off,' Phyllis said to her husband. 'Not that I mind. It was her half day off today and she spent it helping me to do the housework.'

'She's a good girl,' Stan said.

'Tommy must be all right now, but I still don't think that he's right for her.'

'I know, but if you remember, your mum was dead against me too.'

'What do you expect? She found you taking liberties with me on the doorstep.'

'Liberties!' Stan exclaimed. 'I only had my hand up your jumper and I didn't get far before you pushed it away.'

'True, but it looked bad.'

'Yeah, I suppose so, but there was no need for her to act like I was some sort of sex maniac. She bashed me over the head with a vase – it's a wonder she didn't leave me brain damaged.'

Phyllis chuckled. 'If you ask me, she did.'

'Cheeky,' Stan said. 'Still, I suppose it's possible. After all, I went on to marry you.'

'Now who's being cheeky?'

Stan pulled her into his arms and said, 'I'm only joking. It's the best thing I ever did. In fact, gorgeous, how about an early night?'

'Get off, you daft sod. I've got to leave for work in a minute.'

'Yeah, I know, but I'm still not happy about you looking after Winnie.'

'Stan, we've talked about this and I told you that I can cope.'

'You're as stubborn as your mother.'

'Maybe, but I still miss her,' Phyllis mused. 'I still can't believe that my dad married again just a few months after she died.'

'I know it was a shock, love, but don't you think it's about time you buried the hatchet?'

'Never! I can't stand that money-grabbing woman that he married, and as I protested when Dad gave her all Mum's jewellery, she hates me too. I'll never go to visit them, and I told Dad that he wouldn't be welcome here unless he comes alone.'

'It's not like you to be so hard, love.'

'I can't help how I feel. That woman will bleed him dry, I just know it, but he just wouldn't listen to me,' Phyllis said, glancing at the clock. 'I must go, but talking about my family has reminded me of something. Mabel told me that there's gossip about Rose again, that she's got her eye on someone and he might be a married man. You see her behind the bar in the pub. Have you noticed anything?'

'No, I can't say I have,' Stan lied. He'd noticed all right, seen Rose flirting with George Frost and suspected that something was going on. Of course he couldn't be sure, and he wasn't about to add fuel to the fire by adding to the gossip.

With a flurry of activity Phyllis flung her coat on, and this was followed by Stan getting a swift kiss on the cheek. 'Let's hope Mabel's got it wrong then,' she said. 'See you in a couple of hours or so.'

After a few minutes Stan checked his pockets. It wasn't payday until tomorrow, but he had just enough money left for a couple of pints. He sorted out the fire, put the guard around it and then he was on his way out, taking his usual route to the pub.

At the bottom of the Rise, had Stan turned in the other direction, he would have seen his daughter still wrapped in Tommy's arms.

Phyllis had been keeping up an act to hide her tiredness and when she'd left for work she hadn't seen her daughter either. She was just relieved that she was out of sight of anyone now and her steps slowed. The thought of the cleaning waiting for her at the factory was almost more than she could bear, and when her shift finished she still had Winnie to sort out. As her steps faltered, Phyllis wondered again what was wrong with her. She didn't feel ill and wasn't in any pain. It was just so hard to stay awake and on her feet.

'Watcha, Phyllis, long time no see. You'd think we lived miles apart instead of a few streets.'

The voice startled her, but she recognised it, thinking that it was as though talking about her cousin had conjured her up. 'Rose,' she said, her voice clipped. 'I can't stop to chat. I'm on my way to work.'

'Yeah, me too. My stint behind the bar starts at seven.'

'Then like me, you'd best get a move on,' Phyllis said, not waiting for a reply as she hurried past Rose. As children they had played together and attended the same school. They'd been bridesmaids at each other's weddings, but in those days Rose had been a nice woman. She was far from that now though, yet when the gossip had first started Phyllis had tried to warn her cousin that she was ruining her reputation. She'd told Rose that losing her husband during the war was no excuse for her behaviour. Other women had suffered the same loss, but they still remained respectable.

Rose refused to listen, and the final straw had been when she had an affair with a married man. Of course it gave credence to the local gossip that she'd go after anything in trousers, and if Mabel was right, Rose was at it again. Ashamed to be associated with her, Phyllis wanted to avoid her cousin like the plague.

Phyllis's thoughts about Rose abruptly ended when she arrived at the factory, the other cleaner, Joyce Brewster, turning up at the same time from the other direction. The walk, though not long, had exhausted Phyllis and it was as much as she could do to carry on through the yard to the entrance. 'I . . . I'm just going to the toilets,' she tiredly told Joyce once inside, 'and as I'll be in there, I might as well make a start on them.'

'Yeah, all right,' Joyce agreed. 'I'll do the manager's office before we both have a go at the factory floor.'

Phyllis just nodded, but no sooner had she gone into the toilets than her head began to swim. With nowhere else to sit she managed to open a cubicle door and with the lid down she sat on the toilet, leaning forward until the dizziness passed. Tears filled her eyes. What was wrong with her?

'Phyllis, are you all right?'

She looked up at Joyce and found herself blurting out, 'I . . . I'm so tired.'

'If you ask me, you should get yourself to the doctor's.'

Phyllis nodded. Perhaps Joyce was right, maybe she should get herself checked out. She stood up and swayed, grateful that Joyce squeezed into the small space to give her a hand. 'Thanks. I . . . I'll be fine in a minute, and then I'll get on with the cleaning.'

'I think you should go home,' Joyce advised.

'No, I can't afford to do that. I'm already skint, but at least it's payday tomorrow.'

'I'll cover for you. Go home, have an early night, and if you still feel rough tomorrow, get yourself to the doctors.'

'I can't leave you to clean this place on your own.'

'I'll manage, skimp on a few things, and with any luck nobody will notice.'

'Thanks, Joyce,' Phyllis said gratefully as she doubted she could even pick up a broom at the moment.

'You'd do the same for me,' Joyce said brusquely. 'Now off you go.'

With a small, weak smile, Phyllis left, but found that the short walk home felt more like miles.

At last she arrived to find the house in darkness. Amy was out with Tommy, and no doubt Stan was at the pub. She took off her coat, sat beside the banked-up fire and closed her eyes. Winnie wouldn't need sorting out for a couple of hours so she could have a little nap.

The warmth of the fire was comforting, and in minutes Phyllis was asleep.

At nine o'clock, after just walking along, with no particular destination in mind, talking, and stopping for the occasional kiss and cuddle, Amy could see that Tommy was tired. She insisted that they make their way back home and outside her door, as she kissed Tommy goodnight, he asked, 'Can I see you again tomorrow night?'

She smiled happily as she looked up at him. 'Of course you can.'

They kissed again, and then with one last hug, Tommy left her to walk up the Rise. Amy watched him for a moment, then went indoors to find her dad out and her mum asleep in a chair.

After her cleaning job and then getting Winnie to bed, her mum wasn't usually home much before ten. Puzzled, Amy gently nudged her arm, but there was no response.

'Mum, Mum,' she urged.

'Wh . . . what?' she muttered as her eyes fluttered open.

'Are you all right?'

Her mother blinked, shook her head and then sat up, looking up at Amy to ask, 'What's the time?'

'It's nine fifteen. Did you finish work early?' Amy asked.

'Err . . . err . . . yes,' she said, rubbing her eyes and then lowering them as though to gather her thoughts before continuing. 'Joyce was in a hurry to get home so we skimped a bit. I was back about half an hour ago and must have dozed off for a while. I'd best pop round to Winnie's and get her to bed.'

Since she'd fainted on Monday her mum said she was fine, but looking at the dark circles under her eyes, Amy wasn't so sure. She had done all she could to help her mum, taking on the ironing and a few other tasks, along with washing up after dinner every night, yet looking at her now it didn't seem to have helped. 'I could give you a hand with Winnie,' she offered.

As her mother stood up she said, 'There's no need. I won't be long.'

Amy tried again, but her mother still refused to let her help. It was too early for bed, so Amy sat down, her thoughts turning to Tommy. It had been wonderful to see him and she had almost melted in his arms.

Moments later the door suddenly flew open and her mother cried frantically, 'Amy, Amy, run down to the tele-phone box and ring for an ambulance.'

'Why? What's happened?'

'It's Winnie. She's sitting in her chair and I can't wake her up. I . . . I think she might be dead!'

'Dead!'

'Get a move on in case I'm wrong! I'm going to fetch Mabel.'

Amy ran then, as fast as she could, hoping that by the time the ambulance arrived it wouldn't be too late.

Chapter Seven

When the ambulance turned the corner, its loud bell piercing the air, it proved that Mabel wasn't the only nosey person on Lark Rise. A lot of people came outside to see what was going on. Of course it was mostly curiosity, mainly women who soon formed into small groups, talking in low voices while their eyes took in the comings and goings at Winnie's house.

'Look at that nosey lot,' Mabel commented as they hurried outside. 'They can't wait to find out what's going on.'

If it hadn't been such a tragic and traumatic event, Phyllis might have laughed at the irony. Mabel was worse than any of them, but her words proved to be correct when Daphne Cole hurried up to them. 'What's going on? Is Winnie all right?'

Neither had time to answer because the ambulance men had left the vehicle, and Phyllis urged them inside, unaware that Mabel firmly closed the door behind them, leaving Daphne hovering outside.

Amy was still inside, pale faced and Phyllis now wished that she'd kept her daughter away. She stood beside her while the ambulance men quickly checked Winnie, expecting them to confirm what she and Mabel already knew.

Instead, one of them said, 'I think I can feel a weak pulse.'

'Right, let's get her into the ambulance,' the other one said, before turning swiftly from Winnie to ask, 'Are you relatives?'

'No, we're just neighbours,' Phyllis said, finding her voice. 'I . . . I've been looking after Win . . . Mrs . . . Mrs Morrison.'

'Has she got any relatives?' he asked as they managed to lower Winnie onto a stretcher.

'Yes, a daughter, but she lives in Devon.'

'Right then, you'll need to come with us. Once we get Mrs Morrison to hospital, they might need to know a bit about her medical history.'

'I don't think I can tell them much, but I still want to come,' Phyllis said. Winnie was still alive and she didn't want to leave her.

Moments later she was following the ambulance men outside again, but not before saying, 'Amy, tell your dad what's happened. I'll see you when I get back. Thanks for your help, Mabel.'

With that Phyllis climbed into the ambulance, inwardly praying that Winnie was going to be all right. Guilt swamped her. She'd noticed that Winnie had been quieter than usual that day, her food hardly touched, but she had been so tired herself she hadn't made a fuss when Winnie said she was fine.

Now it looked like Winnie was at death's door, and Phyllis feared it was her fault.

Amy left Winnie's house with Mabel and locked the door. She saw Carol with her mother and they rushed up to her. Mrs Povis though just huffed and hurried into her own house, for once seeming to relish keeping what she knew to herself.

'Amy, is Winnie all right?' Daphne asked.

'My . . . my mum said she . . . died.'

'Oh, poor Winnie, but come on, you're shivering. Let's get you home,' Daphne said.

Amy found herself ushered into her own house, and urged onto a chair while Daphne said gently, 'No wonder you look so pale. It's never easy to see anyone who has passed away.'

'No . . . no . . . Mum was wrong. Mrs Morrison's alive. The ambulance men found a weak pulse.'

'Did they? Well, that's good news,' Daphne said.

'You still look a bit shaky though, Amy,' said Carol.

'I . . . I'll be all right. It was just a bit of a shock seeing her like that, and well . . . I . . . I really thought she was dead.'

The door opened and Daphne said, 'Here's your dad now.'

'What's going on?' Stan said, looking worried as he surveyed the scene.

'Winnie has been taken ill, but we'll leave Amy to tell you all about it,' Daphne said. 'Come on, Carol.'

'Bye, Amy,' Carol said, giving her a hug. 'See you in the morning.'

'Yes, all right,' Amy said, and with her dad waiting expectantly, she told him all that had happened.

He listened, then said, 'If Winnie was that bad, I can't see her making it.'

'Oh, Dad, don't say that.'

'Facts are facts. What hospital did they take her to?'

'I don't know. It all happened so quickly and I didn't think to ask.'

'Whichever one it is, let's hope your mum isn't there half the night.'

Amy hoped so too, but by midnight there was still no

sign of her mum. 'I wonder why she isn't home yet,' she said, stifling a yawn.

'Go to bed, love,' her dad said. 'I'll wait up for your mum.'

There was a knock on the door and Amy jumped up to answer it. 'Mum!' she exclaimed as her mother staggered in, looking exhausted and close to tears. 'What's wrong?'

'I was flippin' stranded and I'm worn out,' she said, heading for the fire and flopping onto a chair.

'What do you mean? How did you get stranded?' Stan asked.

'I didn't have any money for the fare home so I had to walk.'

'Oh Mum, I should have realised that you hadn't taken your purse,' Amy cried, appalled that it hadn't even crossed her mind.

'It wouldn't have made any difference if you had. There's nothing in it,' she said bitterly.

There was a moment of silence, but then Stan said, 'You should have told someone at the hospital, one of the nurses or something. They might have been able to sort something out.'

'I was in too much of a state to think. I sat around for ages, but then they came to tell me that Winnie had passed away soon after we got there. I was then bombarded with questions. They wanted information about her next of kin too, and all I could tell them was her daughter's married name and that she lived in Devon, Tiverton I think. After that, all I wanted was to get out of there and come home.'

'Oh, Mum, you must be really upset,' Amy said.

'Yes, I am, but make me a hot drink, love, cocoa if there's any left, and then we should all go to bed. I've got to be up at five in the morning.'

Amy went through to the kitchen, wishing as always that

her mum didn't have to get up so early to go out cleaning. She had said that her purse was empty, but her dad, as always, had enough money in his pocket to go to the pub. She made the drink, took it to the living room, tight lipped with indignation on her mother's behalf as she found herself blurting out, 'Here you are, Mum. It isn't right that you had to walk all that way, not when some people have got money for booze.'

There was a moment's silence and then her dad asked, 'What's that supposed to mean?'

Amy couldn't believe she'd spoken out like that, and hastily kissed her mother on the cheek. 'I'm going to bed. Goodnight, Mum,' she said, her dad's question unanswered as she turned on her heels and hurried upstairs.

They were quiet for a minute or two after Amy left the room, but then Stan said, 'I don't know what's come over Amy, but I suppose that was aimed at me.'

Phyllis's reply was clipped. 'She shouldn't have said that, but if the cap fits, wear it.'

'Now listen here, I give you a fair whack of my wages.'

Phyllis gulped down her cocoa and then rose to her feet, only saying, 'Not now, Stan. I'm tired and I'm going to bed.'

With that she went upstairs, and confused, Stan locked up before following her. He found Phyllis already in bed, the room so cold that he quickly threw off his clothes to climb in beside her, and said, 'I don't know why you're being funny with me. How was I supposed to know that you didn't have the fare home?'

'I didn't mean to snap at you. It's just that I'm upset about Winnie, and that long walk almost knocked me out. Now please, I've got to get up at the crack of dawn and need some sleep.'

Mollified, Stan said, 'All right, love,' and as his wife turned away from him he threw an arm around her waist, nestling close to her back.

Stan could tell by her breathing that Phyllis was soon asleep, while he remained awake, his thoughts turning. He wasn't going to stand for Amy having a dig at him. Phyllis had never complained about the money he gave her and thinking back, he realised that things had been fine until she started looking after Winnie. It had worn her out, and though it wasn't a nice way to look at it, he was relieved that the old girl had passed away. Things could get back to normal and Phyllis would be able to cope with her cleaning jobs.

Chapter Eight

As usual, when Amy got up at six thirty on Friday morning her mother was still at work. She had to make her dad's breakfast, and with only one egg left she decided to fry it. He came down ten minutes later to find her in the kitchen, just about to pour boiling water into the teapot. She offered him no greeting, and instead went on to spread margarine on a couple of slices of toast.

He went back to the living room where soon after Amy took his breakfast through, still saying nothing as she turned to walk away.

'Sit down, Amy,' he commanded sternly.

Amy could guess what was coming and her heart began to thump. Her father was rarely angry, with her, or anyone else, but she had spoken out last night and he was obviously still annoyed. Well she was too, and she wasn't sorry for what she had said. Defiantly she replied, 'I'm going to get my bowl of cereal and then I'll sit down.'

'Fine, do that,' he snapped.

Amy poured some cornflakes, but with only a little sugar in the bowl she left it for her mum and just added a little milk. She then carried it to the table and sat down, waiting for what was to come.

'Right, my girl, from what you said last night, you seem

67

to think it's my fault that your mother had to walk home from the hospital. Is that right?'

'Yes,' she agreed.

'Well let's get a few things straight . . .'

Amy listened as her father spoke. All right, he may not have known that her mother didn't have the fare home, but he still had money for beer on a Thursday night while her mother was broke. It gave Amy the courage to speak. 'Mum's worn out. Instead of going to the pub nearly every night, you should give her a bit more housekeeping money and then she could give up at least one of her jobs.'

His face suffused with anger and he snapped, 'You don't know what you're talking about. Your mum's been doing too much because she chose to look after Winnie. It's got nothing to do with money.'

'But if she could just give up one of her jobs . . .'

'That's enough!' he thundered.

Amy had never seen her father in such a temper. She lowered her head, saying no more, and found that her throat was so constricted with nerves that she couldn't eat. She picked up her bowl and went back to the kitchen, relieved when shortly after she heard the front door slam as her dad left for work.

When Phyllis finished her early morning cleaning job, she arrived home and found as usual that her daughter was just about to leave for the shoe shop. Amy smiled weakly, but Phyllis could tell that it was forced and concerned, she asked, 'What's the matter?'

For a moment Amy hesitated, but then she blurted out, 'I've upset Dad.'

'How did you manage to do that?'

'I told him that instead of going to the pub, he should give you more housekeeping money.'

Her mother's small frame seemed to stretch as angrily she said, 'I won't have you speaking to your father like that. You have no idea what he puts up with. He came home from the war wounded, feeling less than a man, reduced to doing a job he hates for low wages, and though his leg still gives him pain, he never complains.'

'I didn't know that,' Amy said, sounding contrite.

'That's because he always puts on a cheerful front. As for him going to the pub, it's his only pleasure and I'm not complaining, so you . . .'

A knock on the door interrupted Phyllis, along with Carol's voice shouting through the letterbox, 'Amy! Amy, are you ready for work?'

'Go on, just go,' Phyllis snapped.

Amy looked stricken, about to say something, but instead she grabbed her coat and hurried out.

No sooner had her daughter left than Phyllis sat down, rubbing both hands over her face. She shouldn't have lost her temper, not when this was all her fault; Amy falling out with her father because she thought Stan kept her short of money. It wasn't true. With what he gave her, plus Amy's keep and her cleaning jobs, she'd managed fine until she'd taken on looking after Winnie. She had been worried about Winnie's frailty and ensured that she gave her a good breakfast, a nourishing lunch with fresh fruit, along with plenty of meat on her plate for dinner.

Everything had been fine, Phyllis realised, until she'd fainted. Amy had spoken out in her concern for her, and as a now-familiar wave of exhaustion washed over her, Phyllis knew that she couldn't go on like this. It was time to see the doctor.

'It's only me,' Mabel called as she came in through the back door and into the living room. 'I collared Stan when he left for work, and though he didn't seem in the best of moods, he told me about Winnie.'

Phyllis wasn't in the mood for talking, but there'd be no getting rid of Mabel until she heard the whole story. 'Yes, she passed away soon after we arrived at the hospital.'

'I can't say I'm surprised. Winnie looked as though she was gone before the ambulance turned up.'

Phyllis voiced her feelings. 'I should have seen earlier that something was wrong. By the time I did it was too late.'

'Don't be daft. You told me yourself that Winnie's been going downhill for some time now. If you ask me it was more old age than illness, her heart giving out or something like that.'

Mabel's words made sense, and Phyllis clung to them as she said, 'They wanted to know about Winnie's next of kin so I told them what I could about Susan. It wasn't much. I didn't know her full address, but with her married name and the area she lives in, I expect they'll find her.'

Mabel tossed her head, saying in disgust, 'Susan didn't do anything for her mother, but when she's told I bet she'll be down here like a shot to see what she can get her hands on.'

'Winnie hasn't got much. Her furniture is old and worn, and I think she only had her bit of pension.'

'Well then, Susan will probably have to pay for her mother's funeral,' Mabel said, smiling with satisfaction.

Phyllis glanced at the clock and said, 'Mabel, I'm sorry, but can we talk later? I've decided to see the doctor and I want to get there before the waiting room fills up.'

'Is it to do with that fainting spell you had?'

'Yes, but I don't suppose it's anything to worry about. I just thought I should get it checked out.'

Mabel rose to her feet. 'Right then, I'll be off, but let me know how you get on.'

Phyllis agreed, and in case the doctor wanted to examine her, as soon as Mabel left she went upstairs to have a wash.

Celia Frost was still angry. Thomas had gone out for over two hours last night and returned looking cold and tired. He'd gone straight to bed, while Celia had been left fuming. If he now had a setback it would be Amy Miller's fault. She should have seen that Thomas wasn't fully recovered and sent him home, but no, the girl had kept him out walking in the cold for far too long.

She had looked in on Thomas at eight o'clock that morning, and seeing that he was asleep had quietly closed the door again. That had been an hour ago, so she decided to check on him again. If he was awake, she'd prepare his breakfast.

However, just then Celia heard footsteps coming down-stairs, then Thomas walked into the room, saying cheerily, 'Morning, Mum.'

'Thomas, you should have stayed in bed. I was about to make your breakfast and bring it up to you.'

'There's no need. I'm all right now; fit enough for work if I hadn't overslept.'

'Don't be silly. Work can wait until you're fully recovered.'

'I've had enough time off, and though Dad hasn't said anything, I know he's busy.'

'He can manage, and if you rest over the weekend you may be well enough on Monday.'

'I'm fine now, and I'm seeing Amy again tonight.'

'I don't think that's wise,' she said, thinking quickly. 'You

71

were over-tired when you came home last night. If you really want to return to work on Monday you must stay in and take it easy until then.'

'There's no need for that, Mum. I told you I'm fine so please stop fussing.'

Celia thought Thomas sounded just like his father and annoyed she said, 'When you're ill, it's me who has to look after you, running up and down stairs, wearing myself out to cater for your every need. You don't call it fussing then.'

Thomas blinked, looked surprised by her outburst, but then said, 'I'm sorry, I didn't mean to sound ungrateful. I am.'

'Then don't accuse me of fussing when I'm just trying to make sure you don't do too much before you're fully recovered.'

'I shouldn't have said that, and I'm sorry,' Thomas said, apologising again.

Mollified, Celia said, 'You're forgiven, but I don't want you to go out on Saturday night. I've invited the Willards to dinner and as Melissa is coming too, it would be nice for her to have someone of her own age to talk to.'

'I'd rather go out with Amy.'

'You'll have seen Amy for two nights by then, and as I've already told Melissa that you'll be here, it would look very rude if you went out.'

'You could invite Amy too.'

Celia was appalled and made an excuse. 'I'm afraid I can't do that. It would upset the numbers, and the dining table only seats six.'

'But . . .'

'Thomas,' Celia interrupted, doing her best to look upset, 'I'm really looking forward to this dinner party, so please don't ruin it for me.'

'Oh, all right. I suppose I can see Amy on Sunday.'

'Thank you, darling. Now, what would you like for breakfast?'

'A boiled egg would be nice.'

Celia went through to the kitchen, smiling that she had got her own way.

At eleven o'clock, Phyllis at last took her turn to see the doctor. There had been quite a lot of people in front of her when she'd arrived, and at first she'd been tempted to leave, but the walk to the surgery had worn her out so she'd sunk gratefully onto an empty seat.

'How are you, Mrs Miller?' the doctor asked, indicating a chair to the side of his desk while taking out her scant notes.

Phyllis wasn't surprised that there was little for him to read. She was rarely ill and couldn't remember the last time she'd seen Dr Trent. 'I'm not feeling too well. I fainted recently, and I feel tired all the time.'

'Have you any other symptoms, shortness of breath, chest pains?'

'No, nothing like that.'

He leaned forward to pull down her lower eyelid and then said, 'You may be anaemic. Take off your coat and top please. I'll examine your chest.'

Phyllis felt embarrassed, but did as Dr Trent asked. When she was ready he turned to look at her and frowned. 'You look severely underweight. Have you got a cough and if so, have you coughed up any blood?'

Startled, Phyllis wondered if he thought she had tuberculosis. Her voice trembled as she replied, 'I haven't got a cough, so no.'

Nevertheless he put his stethoscope to his ears and moved

round to her back, telling her to breathe in and out naturally. He did the same at the front, removed the stethoscope and then pinched the skin on her forearm between his finger and thumb. 'Get dressed and sit down again, Mrs Miller.'

Phyllis found her hands shaking so much that she had difficulty fastening her buttons. Tuberculosis, no please, not that, she inwardly prayed.

At last she was dressed and as she sat down again Dr Trent said, 'Your chest is clear, but you're anaemic and from what I can see, severely undernourished.'

'I . . . I haven't got TB?'

'No, Mrs Miller, we can rule that out. However, I'm concerned about your weight. Have you got a problem with your digestion, pain when you eat?'

'No, I haven't.'

'Any vomiting or diarrhoea?'

Once again Phyllis said no, and Dr Trent leaned back in his chair, studying her for a moment, before saying, 'Mrs Miller, are you actually eating anything?'

'Yes, yes, of course.'

'Well, clearly not enough,' he said. 'You look like you've been deliberately starving yourself. That isn't the case is it?'

'Of course it isn't,' she said indignantly.

'Is it that you can't afford to eat properly?'

'Well, I must admit I've been a bit short lately, but things have changed and I'll have a bit more money now.'

'I'm glad to hear it, because continued undernourishment can lead to serious problems,' he said, before scribbling out a prescription. 'Take these pills for your anaemia and come back in a month. By which time I want to see that you've put on weight. '

'Yes, doctor,' Phyllis said, feeling a huge sense of relief

as she left the surgery to walk home. Deep down she'd been worried about her tiredness, had thought she had something seriously wrong with her, but it was just lack of proper food and anaemia. She would only tell Stan and Amy about the anaemia and say that the pills would soon put her right. Her daughter could stop worrying, and tonight she'd try to be the peacemaker between Amy and her father.

'Amy, cheer up,' Carol said at work during a quick break mid-morning. 'All right, you fell out with your dad, and your mum had a go at you, but it's not the end of the world. They dote on you so all you've got to do is apologise when you get home and it'll be over and done with.'

'I hope so,' Amy said.

'Is your mum in a state about Winnie Morrison?' Carol asked. 'Come to that, are you?'

'It was awful to see her like that, and I was at first, but I'm all right now. She was a nice old lady, but I didn't really have that much to do with her. Mum was really upset though and now I've gone and made things worse.'

Fed up of hearing about Amy's fall out with her parents, Carol changed the subject. 'The week has dragged, but it's Friday at last and tonight I'm going out to dinner with Roy.'

'And I'm seeing Tommy,' Amy said, at last smiling.

'Where is he taking you?' Carol asked.

'I don't know, probably just for another walk but it won't be a long one. Tommy's a lot better, but he tires quickly.'

Carol thought it sounded boring. A walk, no thanks, it wasn't for her. She'd rather go dancing or to the pictures, but tonight was something different again. They were going out to dinner, and not only that, Roy had a car!

'Carol, Amy, you've had a fifteen-minute break, and we have customers.'

'Coming, Miss Winters,' Carol called, reluctantly going back into the shop to assist a woman who was waiting to be served.

'Have you got those in a size six?' the woman asked, pointing to a flat, brown shoe on display.

'I'll have a look for you,' she said politely, while glancing outside to see if she could see Roy on the other side of the road. There was no sign of him, but it didn't matter. She'd be seeing him tonight and she had the perfect dress to wear, one that made her look older and sophisticated.

Carol smiled as she went to the stock room, hoping that this date with Roy would be the first of many, unaware then that Roy had something entirely different on his mind.

Chapter Nine

Amy was ready with her apology when she arrived home from work, and as soon as she saw her father, tears welled in her eyes. 'Dad, I shouldn't have spoken to you like that. I was wrong, and I'm sorry.'

He looked at her for a moment and Amy held her breath, but then his arms opened. As she walked into them he said, 'You were worried about your mum, and it's understandable. I shouldn't have lost my temper and I'm sorry too.'

'Well you can stop worrying,' Phyllis said from the kitchen doorway. 'I went to see the doctor today and there's nothing much wrong with me. He said I'm tired because I'm anaemic, that's all. The pills he prescribed will soon sort me out.'

Amy smiled, happy that her dad had forgiven her, and happier still to hear that her mum was going to be all right. She looked at her now and puzzled, said, 'I can't believe the pills have worked that quickly, but you look so much better already.'

'Yeah, well, I haven't got Winnie to look after so I had a little nap this afternoon and it made all the difference. Now dinner's ready, so change your clothes and I'll dish up.'

Amy ran up to her room. She had been fretting all day, but Carol was right, she'd soon been forgiven for her outburst. She hoped her friend would enjoy her date that evening, especially as she'd had to listen to her going on and on all week about Roy taking her out to dinner, along with the fact that he had a car.

It might be nice to have a boyfriend with a car, Amy thought, but it didn't matter to her that Tommy didn't have one. She'd be seeing him later and once changed, she ran back downstairs, smiling happily at the thought.

Carol had previously told her mum that she didn't want any dinner and after calling a quick hello, she went upstairs to get ready. She was meeting Roy at eight and wanted to make sure she looked perfect.

It was seven thirty before Carol was satisfied with her appearance, leaving her only half an hour to get to Arding & Hobbs. She hurried downstairs and into the living room, saying, 'I'm off. See you later.'

'Hold on, my girl,' her dad called. 'Your mum told me you're going out to dinner with some bloke, but I want to know a bit more than that. Who is he? Is he a local, and where is he taking you?'

'Dad, if I don't leave now I'll be late.'

'You're going nowhere until you answer my questions.'

Carol could have screamed with frustration, but she knew she'd never get out of the door until she appeased her dad. 'His name is Roy, he's a shop fitter, doing up a place across the road from where I work. I'm not sure what restaurant he's taking me to, but I promise I won't be late home. Please, Dad, can I go now?'

He pursed his lips, but at last said, 'Yeah, I suppose so.'

'Thanks, Dad. Bye, Mum,' Carol said and grabbing her coat she dashed out, unable to run in heels as she hurried up the Rise and onto Lavender Hill. Thankfully she saw a bus coming and just managed to hop onto it, flopping down on the nearest seat to catch her breath. It was only a couple of stops to Clapham Junction, but it gave her enough time to compose herself. She got off, and was soon approaching the department store, disappointed to find that Roy wasn't there yet.

Carol hated standing around, but within minutes she heard a car horn and as he drew into the kerb, Roy leaned over to open the door, saying, 'Hop in.'

Carol was impressed. It was a big, black car, a saloon, though she had no idea what make it was. 'Hello,' she said, climbing in.

'You look nice,' he said.

'Thanks,' she replied, liking the compliment as they drove off, especially as he had yet to see her dress.

'Carol, I'm afraid I've come out without my wallet.'

'Oh,' was all she managed, hoping that Roy didn't expect her to pay for dinner.

'Not to worry. I've booked a table for eight thirty and as the restaurant isn't far from where I live it'll give me plenty of time to pop in and get it.'

'That's good,' she said, relaxing now and enjoying the drive. She glanced at Roy, thinking that he looked nice too in a dark blue suit and tie. They continued to chat easily, finding that they shared the same taste in music, and Carol hardly took note of the journey as she continued to glance at Roy, thinking that he was a real catch.

It was some time later when Roy turned into a side street in Tooting and pulled up outside a terraced house. 'I'll just get my wallet,' he said. 'It won't take long, but you're welcome to come in for a minute. I could do with a woman's view on my new decor.'

Curious to see his flat, and flattered that he wanted her opinion, Carol said, 'Yes, all right.'

As soon as Roy opened the door, she could see that the house had been divided into two flats, and she followed him upstairs. He used a Yale key to open a door at the top of the stairs, and she saw a tiny hall before they went into a room that wasn't a bad size, though part of it was screened off to serve as a kitchenette. The decor in her opinion was awful, in various shades of brown, the carpet old and feeling sticky beneath her feet. Not only that, there was a stale smell of tobacco, mingled with cooking fat.

'Well, what do you think?' Roy asked.

'Err . . . err . . .' Carol hesitated.

'It's all right, I can see by your face what you think,' he said, chuckling, 'but I haven't done anything with this room yet. My wallet's next door so come and see that.'

He led her back to the tiny landing, and flinging open another door, she stepped inside to find herself in a bedroom. She barely had time to notice the equally bad decor before Roy pulled her into his arms. For a moment Carol froze, but then feeling a frisson of fear she tried to push him away. 'Stop it, Roy.'

'Come on,' he husked, tightening his hold, 'don't bother playing hard to get. As soon as you agreed to come in, we both knew what was going to happen.'

'No, no,' she protested. 'I just came to look at your flat.'

'It isn't mine, but as my mate was good enough to leave it clear for us, we might as well make the most of it.'

As Roy tried to kiss her, Carol turned her head away, struggling against his arms. 'Let go of me!'

Powerless against his strength, Carol found herself thrown on the bed with Roy holding both her wrists above her head with one hand, while he frenziedly used the other to lift up her clothes. She tried to fight him off, kicked out with her legs, but he pinned her down. What happened next made Carol cry out in pain and distress, but Roy ignored her frantic cries for him to stop.

When at last it was over, Carol was left sobbing, while Roy looked at her dispassionately and said, 'Act your age, you daft mare. I don't know what all this fuss is about.'

Anger rose then to almost choke her, her voice a croak as she said, 'You're not getting away with this. I . . . I'm going to tell the police that you raped me.'

Roy's eyes narrowed, but then his smile was mocking. 'Go on then, but when I tell them my version of the story, who do you think they'll believe?'

'What . . . what do you mean?'

'Think about it. You're twenty-three, an adult, and they're not going to see you as an innocent when only half an hour after meeting me you willingly came up to this flat, knowing we'd be alone. Any bloke would take that as a signal and yours was loud and clear.'

'But I wasn't giving you a signal and I'm only seventeen.'

'What! That means you're underage,' Roy yelled, his face suffused with anger. 'You lied to me and if you don't keep your mouth shut I could end up inside.'

'You shouldn't ha . . . have done it. I said no, tried to fight you off, but you wouldn't stop.'

Roy looked agitated now and rubbed a hand around his chin before saying, 'I just thought you fought a bit because you like it rough. After all, I've known other women who do. If you drop me in it I'll make sure a mate of mine on

81

your local paper gets to hear about it. I'll tell him that seventeen or not you're a tart, and when I wouldn't pay for it, you got your own back by accusing me of rape. I bet your parents would love to see that splashed across the newspaper.'

Carol felt bile rising in her throat, utterly humiliated as she scrambled off the bed, wanting only to get away from Roy. She still had her coat on, and as she straightened herself out, Carol felt soiled and sullied with shame.

Her shoes had come off in the struggle, and shoving her feet into them she hurried from the room, her mind and emotions in turmoil.

Roy did nothing to prevent Carol from leaving. He couldn't believe that he'd got it so wrong. When she'd agreed to come up to the flat, knowing she'd be alone with him, he'd taken it as read that she was as keen for sex as he was.

Of course there'd been a bit of a struggle, but he'd seen that as part of the game. It had come as a shock to find that Carol was a virgin, but of course by then he'd been too far gone to stop. He groaned, still unable to believe that he'd misread the signals. Carol didn't look seventeen, nor had she acted like a virgin, with all the flirting and flaunting she'd done to attract his attention in the first place.

Roy hoped that the act he'd put on, the confidence he'd displayed that the police wouldn't believe her, along with the threat of being splashed across the local paper would be enough to stop Carol from reporting him for rape. If she still did, Roy thought, at least she had no idea where he lived, or his surname. That bit of hope was soon quashed when Roy realised that Carol knew where he worked, and though the job was finished, he could still be traced through his firm.

At last he left the flat, desolate, knowing that his only chance was that he'd said enough to stop Carol from going to the police. It wouldn't be long before he found out one way or the other, and in the meantime he would have to put on a front, act like he didn't have a worry in the world.

It was half an hour later when Roy pulled up outside his small, terraced house. He got out of the car and went inside, fixing a smile on his face as he said to his wife, 'Hello, darling.'

She rose to waddle towards him, heavily into the pregnancy, but still so beautiful that she took his breath away. Her ankles were badly swollen due to high blood pressure and she'd been advised to take it easy. Roy dreaded to think what would happen if it all came out; the hurt and stress it would cause.

Worse, it would probably mean the end of his marriage. Roy cursed his weakness for illicit sex, and vowed that it would never happen again as he gently took his wife into his arms.

Though Roy didn't know it, he had no need to worry. In turmoil, Carol had eventually found the main road and a bus that would take her to Clapham Junction. She was now walking along Lavender Hill, her head bowed in shame.

Close to the top of the hill she would have to pass the police station, and a part of her inwardly screamed out in her need to make Roy pay for what he had done. Yet upon reaching it, Carol didn't pause to go inside. It wasn't just that the police might not believe her – worse was her fear of Roy's threat if she accused him of rape, the lies he would tell his friend on the local newspaper.

She'd be branded a tart and imagining her parents' reaction, Carol trembled with fear and shame. They must never find out! Never!

It wasn't yet ten o'clock when she turned the corner onto Lark Rise and she fought to compose herself. She had to pretend that nothing was wrong, and as Carol arrived home, she somehow managed to hold herself together.

'Hello, you're early,' her father said.

'Yeah, I know. The bloke I went out with was a bit boring so I made an excuse to leave,' she lied. 'Where's Mum?'

'She's round your gran's again. Since the day your gran got a television I reckon your mum got hooked on it. She's always going on about some programme she likes to watch a few nights a week, but I'm no mug and I know what she's up to.'

'What do you mean?'

'She thinks that I'll get fed up with her going to your gran's and I'll buy our own television. It's working, I'm saving up, but it'll be a month or two before I've got enough,' he said, glancing at the clock. 'She should be home soon, but keep it to yourself. I want the new television to be a surprise.'

'All right. I'm a bit tired so I think I'll have an early night. Tell Mum I said goodnight.'

'Will do,' he said. ''Night, love.'

Carol hurried upstairs. She had got away with it, yet she still felt filthy, sullied and going into their tiny bathroom she washed herself over and over again.

At last Carol went to bed, but found sleep was impossible

as behind closed lids she couldn't stop the scene from replaying in her mind. She felt Roy's hands on her again, the fear, the shock and the pain. She hated Roy, loathed him, but along with that came feelings of self-disgust, shame, her mind tortured until at last, Carol fell asleep.

Chapter Ten

March came, heralding spring, and by mid-May there was clement weather. Amy had watched her mother carefully since Winnie had passed away, and was pleased to see that she no longer looked tired. There was colour in her cheeks again, but as the concern for her mother diminished, she became worried about Carol.

Her friend had been vivacious, outgoing and confident, but now Carol's love of music and dancing was a thing of the past. Carol was now eighteen and the days when they had talked about everything had gone as her friend became withdrawn, though when questioned Carol continued to insist crossly that nothing was wrong.

It was Sunday afternoon and Amy would be seeing Tommy later, but now as she helped her mother with the washing up she told her, 'Lena Winters is being transferred to a larger branch. We'll have to get used to a new manageress soon.'

'I'm sure she'll be fine.'

Amy hoped so, but her mind drifted back to Carol and she voiced her concerns again. 'Mum, I wish I knew what was wrong with Carol.'

'Maybe she's mooning over a boy or something.'

'No, I don't think so. The last date Carol had was back

in February and she said that was a washout. She hasn't mentioned anyone since.'

'In that case, maybe Carol's seeing someone she doesn't want you to know about.'

Amy mulled that over, but she couldn't see why Carol would keep a boyfriend a secret from her . . . unless? Surely not, Amy thought – but if that shop fitter Carol had been out with was a married man, it was the only thing that made any sense. Carol had certainly been very keen on him, and maybe she was still seeing him, perhaps unhappy now because he wouldn't leave his wife?

'You've gone quiet, Amy. Do you think I'm right?'

'No, I don't. Carol has never hidden anything from me, so I think it must be something else,' she replied, keeping her suspicions to herself.

'That's the washing up done,' her mother said, tipping the water down the sink and then helping Amy to put the dishes away.

Other than her concern for Carol, in all other ways Amy was happy. Her mother was her old self again, and Tommy had been fine since his last bout of bronchitis. If only Carol was happy too, then everything would be perfect, but if her friend was really going out with a married man, Amy feared it would all end in tears.

Celia was moaning again, and George was fed up with it. She'd obviously had plans for Thomas and Melissa, but they had come to nothing. Now, after having dinner in the Willards' home last night, she had another bee in her bonnet.

'I could have screamed when Libby went on and on about that chap that Melissa is seeing now. Did you notice that supercilious smile on her face when she was bragging about him being a trainee accountant with wonderful prospects?'

'No, can't say I did,' George replied, wishing that Celia would give the subject a rest.

'Libby didn't actually say the words, but she was obviously letting me know that she doesn't think Thomas is good enough for her daughter.'

'I don't know where you get your daft ideas from – I didn't get that impression. If you ask me, you're just peeved because your bit of matchmaking didn't come off.'

Celia glowered at him, but then Thomas came downstairs, dressed to go out and she turned her attention to him. 'I suppose you're seeing that girl again,' she snapped.

'If by *that girl*, you mean Amy, then yes,' Thomas replied stiffly.

'I don't know what you see in her. She's as common as muck.'

'She is not!' Thomas protested.

'Yes she . . .'

'Shut up, Celia,' George growled. 'Come on, son, let's get out of here. I need a bit of air so I'll walk down the Rise with you.'

'Go then, George,' Celia said, 'leave me on my own, as usual.'

'You might as well get used to it, Celia,' he snapped, and as they walked outside, George took a deep breath. He had done it again, shot his mouth off, and this time in front of Thomas. Yet did it really matter? Everything was in place now, and he'd ensured that Thomas was skilled enough in handling glass to take over the business. With Thomas's other skills, George was sure that the firm could generate enough income to support both him and his mother. In fact his son would probably do far better than he ever had.

'Dad, what did you mean by that?' Thomas asked as they began to walk down the hill.

'By what, son?' he asked, playing for time.

'That parting shot about Mum getting used to being alone.'

'Oh, that . . . well . . . it's just that when she gets on her high horse it drives me out, and it's something your mum's been doing a lot lately.'

Thomas didn't look convinced and, anxious to change the subject, George said, 'You've been seeing a lot of Amy. Are things getting serious?'

'I like her, Dad. I like her a lot and yes, I'm serious about her.'

Would it lead to marriage? George wondered, baulking at the thought. It was something he hadn't taken into consideration. He'd been so wrapped up in himself, in his own wants and needs, but if Amy *was* the girl for Thomas, he would one day want to marry her. His son would then have to support a wife and eventually a family, with the added burden of his mother. How could he do that to him?

With a feeling of despair, George saw his dreams slipping away. He desperately tried to cling on to them, and clutched on to the thought that his son could be very astute. There had been signs of his mother's ambition in Thomas and on more than one occasion he'd suggested ways to expand the business. Of course, George thought, he'd always dismissed his son's ideas, but if he was left to get on with it, Thomas could put them in practice, and surely he'd make them succeed.

'See you later, Dad.'

George had been so deep in thought that he hadn't realised they'd reached the Millers' house. 'Yeah, see you, son,' he replied, walking on as Thomas knocked on the door.

At the bottom of the Rise, George turned the corner. All the final arrangements for tomorrow had been made so he wasn't seeing her today, yet, still fretting about the ramifications of what he was going to do, George didn't feel like returning home either.

George thought about some of Thomas's suggestions to expand the business and at last, after trudging for half an hour he smiled, his guilt assuaged by the realisation that if he stayed, all he'd do was hold his son back. Thomas would make a huge success of the firm, while he'd start up again somewhere else, keeping it to a one-man band that he could cope with.

George thought about the new life he'd be starting tomorrow. He hadn't made the same mistakes and had been honest from the start. She knew his problem and wouldn't be like Celia, with her constant complaints about his lack of ambition. It was like a huge weight had been lifted from his shoulders. From now on his life would be a simpler one, alongside a woman that he truly loved.

'Winnie's place has been empty since her daughter cleared her stuff out, but that could be about to change,' Mabel said to her husband. 'I still can't get over how Susan gave all her furniture and stuff to that junk man. There were a few nice bits and the least she could have done was to offer them to Phyllis.'

'Hmmm,' was the only sound Jack made.

For all the notice he took, Mabel felt she might just as well talk to herself, but she continued. 'Phyllis looked after Winnie for all that time, but she didn't even get a thank you. The funeral was a paltry affair too, with Susan shooting back to Devon more or less as soon as her mother was put in the ground.'

'Hmmm.'

'Jack, are you listening to me?' Mabel said loudly.

'What . . . yes . . . of course I am.'

'What did I just say then?'

'Err . . . something about Winnie's place.'

'I saw the agent showing it to a young couple yesterday. If it's anything like this place, with a leaky roof and damp, I doubt they'll want it. Nobody else has.'

'You're probably right,' Jack agreed and Mabel knew she had lost him again as he stuck his nose back in his book.

She looked around the living room, thinking that if anyone was shown this place they'd probably turn their noses up too. 'Jack, don't you think it's time we thought about redecorating? We haven't had new wallpaper and paint for years.'

With a huge sigh he looked up. 'What's the point? You just said yourself that these places are riddled with damp.'

'Some new furniture then; a sofa and armchairs to replace these tatty ones.'

'Why waste money? Anyway, I like my chair. It's comfortable and fits me like an old glove.'

Mabel gave up. Jack had never liked spending money, preferring to save it for a rainy day. Sighing, she walked to the window. She had seen George Frost walking past and had wondered where he was going. The pubs were shut, and other than kids playing outside, there weren't many people to be seen on a Sunday afternoon. Only five minutes later, as though to disprove Mabel's theory, Amy Miller had walked past, arm in arm with Tommy Frost, the two of them so wrapped up in each other that they hadn't spotted her looking out of the window.

Young love, Mabel thought, sighing now. There had once been a time when Jack had looked at her like that, with adoration. Nowadays though, she was lucky if he looked at her at all. She turned to gaze at her husband now, seeing that although he was only in his mid-forties, he looked more like he was fifty. Jack was balding, growing tubby around the middle, but there were still remnants of the good-looking young man she'd fallen in love with. They had let themselves go, Mabel decided, both looking older than their years in comparison to Daphne and Frank Cole.

Mabel scowled. At forty-six, Daphne was two years older than her, yet she looked years younger. Of course she wore fashionable clothes and make-up, so that helped, yet the stuff she plastered on her face was light in comparison to Phyllis's cousin, Rose. There was still gossip going round that Rose was seeing a married man, but as yet nobody had put a name to him. Mabel felt sorry for the man's wife, and she glanced at Jack again, thinking that at least she didn't have to worry about her husband straying.

Tommy was holding Amy's hand, happy to be with her as they headed for Battersea Park. The funfair had opened again when Easter fell at the beginning of the month and once he'd paid for them to get in, he was planning to take Amy for a ride on the big dipper.

After chatting for a while they walked in companionable silence, Tommy's thoughts drifting to his father. He'd been acting strangely, sitting back and giving him more responsibility at work. They had taken it in turns to go out on repairs or replacements, but it had never made sense to Tommy that they didn't have two vehicles. It would have doubled the amount of work they could take on. He'd suggested it many times, along with other ways they could expand, but his father had always dismissed his ideas.

Tommy hadn't understood why until just recently, when

he'd at last been allowed to look at the books. Once again he felt a surge of pity for his father, and remained amazed that he'd hidden the truth for so long. The books were a mess, his father's handwriting almost illegible, and there were numerous mistakes in accounting. His father was an intelligent man, and a craftsman when he handled glass, but it was obvious the paperwork involved in running a firm was beyond his capabilities. No wonder he hadn't wanted to expand. More work, perhaps taking on a council contract, meant sending written quotes, proper invoicing and accounting.

'I love the funfair,' Amy said excitedly as they walked through the park gates.

'Me too,' Thomas agreed. He'd have a word with his dad; suggest taking on the paperwork permanently. By doing that they could expand the business and with it would come a rise in pay. If Amy agreed to marry him that meant it wouldn't have to be a long engagement before they could afford to get married.

It was a wonderful thought, but as they approached the funfair, Tommy was unaware that his father had other plans – ones that would have a profound effect on his future.

Chapter Eleven

Celia woke up on Monday morning to find the bed empty beside her. She threw on her dressing gown, expecting to find George downstairs, but instead saw two letters propped on the mantelshelf.

Puzzled, she picked up the one with her name on it, and after managing to decipher the dreadful handwriting she stood frozen in shock; stunned. George had gone! He'd left her for another woman!

At last, after reading the contents again, Celia came to life and, grabbing the other letter, she hurried back upstairs and into her son's room. 'Thomas! Thomas! Wake up!'

When he didn't respond, she shook him. 'Thomas! Come on, wake up!'

His eyes slowly opened, he blinked, and as they cleared she cried, 'Thomas, your father has left me.'

'Wh . . . what?'

'Your father has gone! Here, he left you this letter.'

Thomas shook his head as though to clear it and then sat up, taking the letter from her hand. He ripped it open, his reaction when he managed to read it the same as his mother's at first. 'I can't believe this,' he finally murmured, after the initial shock had sunk in. 'He . . . he's handed over the business to me.'

'To you! What about me? What about your brother?'

'There's no mention of you, and Jeremy isn't here to run the place.'

'Give that letter to me,' Celia demanded.

Thomas passed it to her and said, 'Mum, let me get dressed then I'll come downstairs and we can sort this out.'

'Yes, yes, all right,' she agreed.

It wasn't long before Thomas walked into the living room, but by that time Celia was sitting with his letter clutched in her hand. It was bad enough that George had gone off with another woman, but he had also left her financial future in the hands of their son. 'Did you know about this?' she snapped, waving the letter.

'Of course not.'

'Surely you noticed something, had some inkling.'

'Not really, though Dad's been giving me more responsibility at work, sorting the books and things. I didn't realise that he had a problem until then. Did you know?'

'Yes, of course, but he would never accept my help,' Celia said as her stomach began to churn. George had left her! Why hadn't she seen the signs? They had been there, she now realised, thinking about how George had been going out more lately, but she had never suspected that he was seeing another woman. Her emotions were on a rollercoaster; first there had been shock, then anger, but now the tears came – tears she couldn't stem, and her body shook with emotion. Thomas tried to comfort her, but she pushed away from him.

'Mum,' he said, 'you can't go on like this. I'm going next door to get Libby.'

'No! No, don't do that,' Celia cried, unable to bear the shame of it, the gossip that would fly when it became known that George had left her. With a supreme effort she fought to calm down, able to say at last, 'I'm all right now.'

'Are you sure?'

'Yes, yes, I'll make us both a cup of tea and then we'll have to work out what we're going to do,' she said, wiping the tears from her cheeks as she went through to the kitchen. Anger and bitterness rose again to replace her tears. She had given George the best years of her life, and two sons, but he had left her for another woman. Well, whoever she was, she was welcome to him, Celia decided, determined not to let this beat her. But her bravado didn't sustain her for long and she had to choke back a sob.

Rose looked around her small, dank flat for the last time, happy to leave it. She had fallen on her feet at last, even if she knew some would be scandalised when it came out – including her cousin Phyllis.

When there was a ring on her doorbell, Rose went to see who it was, hiding her impatience when she saw it was the woman who lived upstairs. Lydia was nice enough, but always looking to borrow something, and it soon became obvious she was at it again.

'Rose, I'm sorry to ask, but my youngest won't eat his porridge without sugar. Can you spare a couple of spoonfuls?'

Rose had left not only sugar, but a few other bits and pieces in her larder and said impulsively, 'Yes, of course I can. Come in, Lydia.'

'I can't stop. I've got to get the kids off to school,' she said while following Rose to the kitchen.

'Here,' Rose said, as she began to place the bag of sugar, along with a tin of corned beef, spam, and other bits and pieces into Lydia's arms.

'What are you doing? I only wanted a bit of sugar.'

'I know, but I'm leaving so you might as well have what's left in my cupboard.'

'Leaving? Where are you going?'

'This flat is riddled with damp and when another place came up I talked the landlord into letting me have it,' Rose lied.

Lydia's neck stretched with indignation. 'I don't think that's fair. My flat is just as damp and as I've got kids he should have offered it to me.'

'Tell that to the landlord.'

'I've only had dealings with the agent so how come you got to speak to Mr Jacobs? I don't even know how to get in touch with him.'

'Where there's a will there's a way,' Rose told her.

'Give me his address or phone number then,' Lydia demanded.

'I don't think he likes it bandied about, but you could try asking the agent.'

'I will. You can be sure of that,' Lydia said stiffly, but she kept hold of the food that Rose had given her as she marched out.

Rose was too happy to care. No more bar work at the Park Tavern, she thought, no more putting up with the owner's groping hands. She hadn't told him she was leaving. He'd find out soon enough when she didn't turn up for work, and until they found a replacement his fat, lazy wife would have to do a bit of work for a change.

With a final look around, Rose picked up her suitcase. It was time to go – time to start her new life.

Amy was in the stock room with Carol. She tried to draw her friend out, but Carol didn't want to talk. Amy felt as though she had lost her friend; the chatty, funny, vivacious girl she'd known was so different now that it was like trying to talk to a stranger. She still tried, saying now, 'Did you go out over the weekend?'

'No,' was the short reply.

'Tommy took me to the funfair in Battersea Park.'

'Lucky you.'

There was a hint of sarcasm in Carol's tone and struck by a thought, Amy said, 'Are you annoyed with me because I'm still dating Tommy and we don't see much of each other outside of work now?'

'No. Why should I be?'

'I know you don't approve of him.'

'Amy, I take back everything I said about Tommy. From what you've told me, he's a decent bloke and believe me, as they're few and far between you should hold on to him.'

'Carol, you sound so bitter. Has someone hurt you? Let you down?'

'Questions, questions! I'm sick of your questions,' she said, her voice rising.

'I'm sorry,' Amy said quickly. 'It's just that I hate to see you like this and if I can, I want to help.'

The hard mask slipped, and looking as though she was about to cry, Carol said, 'You can't help me, Amy. Nobody can.'

'What is going on out here?' Mrs Jones, their new manageress, asked in a sharp voice. 'I heard raised voices.'

'Nothing, Mrs Jones,' Amy said, drawing the woman's eyes to her while Carol quickly looked down at the stock list. 'I slipped a bit on the ladder, that's all, and sort of yelped a bit.'

'Well, be more careful in future and Carol, we have customers so I need you in the shop,' the manageress said.

As the two of them left the stock room, Amy could have screamed. She had managed to get Carol talking at last, but now the moment had passed.

The rest of the day passed with little opportunity for her to speak privately to Carol again, but as they left work at five thirty, Amy knew she'd have a chance as they walked home.

'Amy, I've got to go somewhere. I'll see you tomorrow morning,' Carol said, turning to quickly head off in the other direction.

Startled, and with no time to say anything, Amy was left to wonder where Carol was going, but came up with no answers. She walked home alone, going over and over in her mind what Carol had said that morning in the stock room. She had said that nobody could help her, but what did that mean?

When at last Amy turned into Lark Rise, an awful thought had begun to form. No, it couldn't be that. As far as she knew Carol hadn't been out with a boy for ages – but all thoughts of Carol were driven from her mind when she drew level with Tommy's house and he came running out of the door to speak to her.

'Amy, I'm sorry, but I can't see you tonight.'

His face looked drawn and worriedly she said, 'It's all right, I don't mind, but what's wrong?'

'I'm not supposed to say anything, but I know I can trust you to keep this to yourself. It's my dad. He's left my mum and she's in a dreadful state. She's been up and down all day, one minute angry; the next in tears.'

Tommy looked so upset, and laying a hand on his arm, she said, 'Don't worry, he's sure to come back soon.'

'I doubt that. He's gone off with another woman.'

'Oh, Tommy, no wonder your mum's in a state.'

'I'll have to get back to her, but if I can, I'll see you tomorrow.'

Amy stood on tiptoe to kiss him, and giving her a swift

hug, Tommy went back inside. She thought she saw the lace curtains twitch, as though his mother had been watching them, yet for once she felt sorry for her. Amy sadly walked the rest of the way home.

'Why the long face?' Phyllis asked her daughter when she arrived home from work.

Amy hesitated for a fraction of a minute, but then said, 'I can't tell you unless you both promise to keep it to yourself?'

'Keep what to ourselves?' Phyllis asked.

'Promise me first,' Amy urged.

'All right, all right, I promise,' Phyllis agreed.

'Dad?' Amy asked, looking at him.

'I'm not interested in women's gossip, but yeah, all right.'

Amy hesitated for a moment again, but then said, 'Tommy's dad has gone off with another woman. He said his mum's in a terrible state.'

Phyllis's stomach turned as she asked, 'What woman?'

'I don't know,' Amy said.

To Phyllis's surprise, it was Stan who voiced her thoughts. 'I can guess,' he said. 'I reckon he's gone off with Rose.'

'Auntie Rose?' Amy exclaimed, her eyes widening with surprise.

'I know I told you to call her auntie when you were a child, but you can drop it now. She's your second cousin,' Phyllis said. 'But, Stan, what makes you think she's gone off with Tommy's dad?'

'I've seen her flirting with George when he's in the Park Tavern,' Stan told her.

'That doesn't mean anything. My cousin flirts with anything in trousers,' Phyllis said, though inwardly felt she was clutching at straws.

'Yeah, that's true,' Stan conceded. 'But if she isn't behind the bar this evening, I reckon I'll be proved right.'

Phyllis looked at her daughter and saw that the ramifications hadn't sunk in yet. She dreaded to think how Celia Frost would react when she found out that her husband had run off with a member of their family. Amy had looked so happy lately, but now, thanks to Rose, all that was likely to change.

Chapter Twelve

Frank Cole arrived home from work that same evening, hungry and ready for his dinner, but walked into a silent house. Daphne wasn't in the kitchen, and he was puzzled to find that she wasn't upstairs either. He was annoyed that she hadn't left a note to say where she was going, but at least Carol would be home soon and she might know where her mother was.

When over half an hour passed with no sign of Daphne or his daughter, Frank began to worry. He hurried to the Millers' house, saying when Amy opened the door, 'Did Carol walk home with you?'

'Err . . . no. She said something about having to go somewhere.'

'Did she say anything about meeting up with her mother?'

'No,' Amy said, shaking her head.

'All right, thanks,' Frank said, suddenly struck by an idea. Perhaps Daphne's mother was ill and they were both round there.

He hurried off and it didn't take him long to reach his mother-in-law's house, where he rang the doorbell. Daphne had been an only child, a late one, and his mother-in-law, Edna Newman, was in her seventies now. She looked a bit surprised to see him, but without preamble he asked, 'Is Daphne here?'

'No she isn't and I haven't seen her all day. Some daughter she's turned out to be.'

Frank thought Edna must have gone senile. 'Leave it out. Daphne's always around here.'

'That's only because she prefers my company to yours.'

Frank's jaws clenched, but he ground out, 'What about Carol? Is she here?'

'You must be joking. I haven't seen her for ages. Now I've got things to do, so bugger off.'

With that the door slammed shut, leaving Frank both angry at the old witch's attitude, yet bewildered too. Where the hell were his wife and daughter? He couldn't think of anywhere else to try, so he returned home.

It was after nine thirty in the evening before one of them turned up; by that time Frank was so out of his mind with worry that he was about to go to the police station.

'Where have you been?' he yelled at his daughter when she walked in.

'Out with a mate,' was Carol's terse reply.

'Where's your mother?'

'I don't know. Isn't she here?'

'No, she flaming well isn't. Have you got any idea where she might have gone?'

'She's probably round Gran's house.'

'I've checked there and your gran said she hasn't seen your mother today.'

'That doesn't make sense. Mum's always round there.'

'Your gran might be going batty, but it doesn't change the fact that your mother wasn't there,' Frank said, running both hands through his hair in agitation.

'Mum can't have gone far; she's sure to turn up soon.'

103

'She'd better,' he growled, then turning his anger on his daughter, 'and as for you, my girl, what are you playing at? You went straight out from work and I had no idea where you were either. I'm not having it – in future I don't want you disappearing without telling me where you're going!'

'Yes, all right,' Carol said meekly. 'Dad, I'm sorry, but I'm tired. I think I'll go to bed.'

Frank frowned, noticing for the first time that his daughter looked a bit washed out and pale. 'Yeah, yeah, all right, but aren't you worried about your mother?'

'No. Not really. As I said, she's sure to be home soon, but in that mood you're bound to have a row. I don't want to stay up to listen to it.'

With that, Carol went upstairs while Frank sat down again. Yes, his daughter was right. When Daphne showed her face, he'd have a few things to say to her – and he wouldn't be doing it quietly.

Carol was curled up in bed, hating what she'd done. Yet what choice had there been? She was sure that if she'd waited any longer her parents would have seen the tell-tale bump that was starting to show. They'd have gone mad, but at least this way they would never know anything about it.

It had been awful to go to that woman's house – terrifying to endure what had been done to her, but at least it was over now. The woman had said that there'd be pain later, but so far Carol felt fine, though she was mentally and emotionally exhausted. She closed her eyes, and at last drifted into a troubled sleep.

Carol had no idea how long she had slept, but she awoke with agonising pain ripping through her stomach. She drew up her knees and clenched her teeth, fighting the need to cry out. At last it abated, but soon after it started again and perspiration soaked her body.

She bore wave after wave of pain that grew in intensity until at last, in fear and agony, sure that something was wrong and she was dying, Carol couldn't stand it any more. 'Mum! Mum!' she yelled. 'Help me!'

Her bedroom door flew open, but it was her father who turned on the light as he dashed into the room. 'What is it! What's wrong?'

'Mum! I want Mum!'

'She isn't here.'

Agony again came tearing through her and Carol screamed, barely aware of her father rushing to her side as she felt something slithering from her body. She flung back the rumpled sheet, looked down, but saw only blood, soaking the sheets, unable to do anything but stare, transfixed, as the stain spread.

Her vision dimmed and she felt strange, her head swimming, but then Carol knew no more as darkness enclosed her.

Frank was barely able to comprehend what his eyes saw, but acting on impulse he bunched up the top sheet, frantically trying to stem the blood that was flowing from his daughter's body.

Carol was unconscious, her face ashen and, sure that he could see her lips turning blue, Frank knew he had to get help. He fled the room and headed for the nearest telephone box, his hands shaking so much he could only just manage to dial the emergency service.

'Ambulance,' he cried when the call was answered.

He then gave the address, begged that they hurry, before he ran home again, relieved to find that though Carol was still unconscious, she was breathing.

Though almost overwhelmed with anxiety, Frank was no fool and could see what had happened. He just couldn't believe it – couldn't comprehend that Carol had just had a miscarriage.

Every minute felt like an hour as Frank waited in Carol's bedroom for the ambulance to arrive, his mind reeling. He needed Daphne, his daughter needed her mother, but she wasn't there and somehow he had to deal with this alone.

Frank went to the window over and over again until at last he saw an ambulance turning onto Lark Rise. In the early hours of the morning the bell was silent as it pulled up outside. He ran downstairs to let them in, urging the men to Carol's bedroom where he watched their every move until his daughter was being carried to the ambulance. After a momentary hesitation, he climbed in too.

The ambulance sped off, and when they reached the hospital Carol was unloaded, still unconscious and deathly pale, her skin almost translucent. Frank looked up at the night sky and felt like howling his distress to the full moon, but instead he followed behind as they entered the hospital, his shoulders slumped like those of an old, broken man.

When Amy's father had come home from the pub, he'd said that Rose hadn't turned up for work. She had seen the look that passed between her parents and at last realised what would happen when Celia Frost found out that her husband had run off with Rose, a member of their family.

Amy had gone to bed, not only fearing Celia's reaction, but Tommy's too. She had lain awake for ages, finally drifting off to sleep after midnight, and woke to the sound of her father's voice.

'Come on, Amy, it's time to get up.'

'Wh . . . what?' she murmured.

'Amy, I'll have to leave for work soon and you haven't made my breakfast.'

Amy blinked her eyes, and at last her mind cleared. Not long after that she was downstairs and working as quickly as possible, finally putting her father's breakfast in front of him. 'Sorry, Dad, I had a bad night.'

'Yeah, something disturbed me too. I heard what sounded like a car, doors banging, voices, but I managed to go back to sleep.'

'I didn't hear any of that,' Amy said as her father quickly demolished his food.

He then gulped down his tea and rose to his feet. 'Right, I'm off. See you later,' he said, grabbing his coat before hurrying out.

Unusually, her mother hadn't come home from her cleaning job by the time Amy was ready to leave, and she wondered what was holding her up. She hurried out to find her mother outside Mrs Povis's house, the two of them deep in conversation. Was her mother telling her about Tommy's dad and Rose? Amy hoped not, because once Mabel got to hear about it the gossip would spread like wildfire.

'Amy,' her mother said as she approached, 'there's no point in waiting for Carol. She isn't in, nor is anyone else. We don't know what's going on, or who has been taken ill, but Mabel was disturbed in the early hours of this morning and got up just in time to see an ambulance pulling away. She knocked on the door fifteen minutes ago to see if they needed anything, but there was no answer.'

Amy's heart skipped a beat as she recalled that Carol's dad had been looking for her, and then he'd asked if Carol was with her mother. It had seemed a bit of an odd question, but with other things on her mind, Amy hadn't given it much thought. It still didn't make much sense, nor did it help to work out who had been taken so ill that an ambulance had been called. Amy didn't know what to do. She'd be late for work if she didn't get a move on, yet she couldn't leave without knowing what had happened. 'Mum, I think I'll run to the telephone box. If I ring our local hospitals, one of them will be able to tell me if they admitted Carol or her parents, and if they're all right.'

'You haven't got time to do that, and anyway, as you aren't a relative I doubt they'd tell you anything. Go to work, love, and if there's any news I promise I'll ring the shop.'

Amy was about to protest, but then saw Frank Cole walking down the hill. All three of them went to meet him, and seeing that he looked dreadful Amy asked anxiously, 'Mr Cole, what happened? Who was taken ill?'

'Carol, but she's going to be all right,' he said.

'What's wrong with her?' Mabel asked.

'I've been up all night and I'm in no mood for questions,' he said tersely, brushing past them.

'Well, that's nice ain't it,' Mabel complained. 'I only asked out of concern for Carol.'

Amy doubted that, but kept her opinion to herself, only saying, 'Carol's mum must still be at the hospital, and maybe I'll be allowed to visit her this evening.'

'Yes, I'm sure you will, love, but you'd best get a move on now or you're going to be very late for work.'

'All right, see you later,' Amy called as she hurried up the hill thinking about her friend. If Carol had been suffering an underlying illness for some time, it explained why she hadn't been herself lately. Poor Carol, but at least her dad said she was going to be all right.

She passed Tommy's house, tensing as she imagined his mother flying out to confront her about Rose like a dragon breathing fire. Nothing happened, but for how long? How long before both Tommy and his mother found out the truth?

Chapter Thirteen

At first, Carol had barely been aware that she'd undergone emergency surgery to stop the bleeding, nor did she know that her father had refused to leave the hospital until he knew that she was going to be all right.

It was late afternoon before Carol fully realised that she had nearly died, yet when questioned she had refused to tell the doctor who had performed the abortion. She knew they were illegal and that no doctor would have performed one – it had been her choice to go to the woman, and though warned of the risks, she had paid the fee; sure that she had no other option. Carol had sensed the doctor's annoyance, and though most of the nurses were kind, there was one who showed her obvious disapproval.

Carol still felt drained as she absentmindedly scanned the ward she'd been moved to, avoiding eye contact with any of the other occupants. They were all women, some pregnant, but she had no idea why they had been admitted. In one bed a young woman was crying softly, but Carol was too preoccupied with her own unhappiness to care.

Time dragged, but at last it was visiting time. She watched the door, looking out for her mother, but behind a stream of other visitors, she saw only her father. He looked dreadful;

dishevelled, pale, and when he came to stand by her bed she blurted out, 'Where's Mum? Isn't she with you?'

'No, she ain't.'

'Dad, I can understand why she's angry with me,' Carol said as tears threatened. 'She's probably furious, but I was hoping she'd come so that I could explain why I did it.'

He pulled up a chair, sat down and said tersely, 'You can explain it to me.'

Carol felt her father's animosity and gulped, but she managed a stuttering start. He listened in silence until she got to the part about going up to Roy's flat, but then his face reddened with fury. 'You did what?' he yelled, drawing looks from all over the ward.

'Dad, please, I . . . I know it was stupid, but I didn't expect him to . . . to rape me.'

'He did what?' he yelled again, this time jumping to his feet. 'Where is he? I'll kill him!'

'I . . . I don't know. He lied to me and the flat wasn't his.'

'Mr Cole,' a nurse said as she hurried up to them. 'I must ask you to keep your voice down. You're disturbing the other patients and visitors.'

'Yeah, yeah, sorry, nurse,' he said, sitting down again, though his legs shook with suppressed agitation.

'Dad, when . . . when I found out that I was pregnant, I didn't know what to do. I knew you and Mum would go mad, and not only that, I . . . I couldn't stand the thought that I was having his . . . his . . .' Unable to carry on, Carol buried her face in her hands as tears now streamed down her cheeks.

She became aware of her father stroking her head, his soft murmurs that he understood, until at last she was able to stifle her soft sobs. 'Dad, will . . . will you tell Mum what happened, tell her I'm sorry and . . . and ask her to come to see me?'

'I can't, love. Your mum's gone and she left before we both came home from work. She doesn't know that you had an abortion, or that you're in hospital.'

'What do you mean?' Carol asked, confused. 'Where has Mum gone and when is she coming back?'

He ran both hands over his face, and then said, 'After you went to bed last night, I found a letter from your mother on the mantelpiece. It had fallen behind the clock, but I saw the edge of an envelope sticking out. Here, you might as well read it.'

Carol took the letter, frowning as she read.

Frank, I'm sorry. I am leaving you. I've been nothing but a wife and mother for so many years, but the children are adults now and no longer need me. I'm sick of just being used and want to make a new life for myself. Please don't try to find me as it would be pointless. Nothing will persuade me to come back, but please tell the children that once I am settled I will write to them.

Carol expected more, but the letter was brief, unsigned, the words somehow cold and clipped. She looked at her father, saw the pain and hurt in his eyes as her hand reached out to grasp his. 'I don't know what Mum means by just being used, but she'll come back, Dad. I'm sure she will.'

'Maybe, I don't know, but I'll have to tell your brothers. Knowing those two, they'll be more upset that your mother won't be around to do their washing and ironing.'

Carol felt tired, emotional, and sank weakly back onto

her pillows. 'Dad, I'm sorry I let you down, but please, don't tell the boys what happened to me, or about the abortion. I feel so ashamed and I don't want them, or anyone else to know.'

For a moment he said nothing, but then he sighed. 'All right, love. We'll do our best to keep it a secret, but we'll need a cover story. Amy collared me this morning along with her mum and that nosey cow Mabel. We'll have to come up with something to put them off the scent.'

'I'm sorry, Dad, but maybe you could say it's my appendix or something,' Carol suggested, fighting to keep her eyes open.

'I'm not sure you'll be in hospital long enough for that, but we could try something like food poisoning.'

'Yes, good idea,' Carol said wearily, her eyes closing.

Carol felt her father stroking her hair again as he said, 'I can see you're tired and I think it's time I left. I'll see you tomorrow.'

Somehow she managed to open her eyes a slit, even managed a small smile, and seeing her father's sad face she wanted to reassure him again that her mother would come back. She opened her mouth to speak, but he placed a finger over her lips, saying softly, 'It's all right. Everything is going to be all right. Just go to sleep, love.'

Unable to fight it, Carol did.

Frank left the hospital again, his feelings still all over the place. He had been shocked, angry, then despairing after reading Daphne's letter, but all those emotions had been overshadowed when he'd been in fear for his daughter's life. He had spent the night at the hospital and it had been morning before a doctor told him that Carol was going to be all right. But, unable to see her, he had been advised to go home.

On Lark Rise, in no mood to speak to Amy, her mother, or that nosey mare Mabel he'd brushed them aside. Once inside his empty house Frank had drawn the curtains against the outside world and broken down, clutching the letter again. There had been no warning, no signs that Daphne was unhappy, yet everything around him had obviously been an illusion, his marriage nothing but a farce.

Unable to face turning up late for work, Frank had remained indoors all day as his mind twisted and turned, first dwelling on Daphne and then his daughter. Carol had been pregnant, then she'd gone to a back-street abortionist and it had nearly killed her. He had thought his daughter perfect, untouched, but that had turned out to be false too. Well that was it, Frank had decided. Like her mother, Carol could bugger off too – and good riddance to both of them.

By visiting time that evening, Frank's mind was well and truly made up and he'd intended to tell Carol that he never wanted to see her face again, yet all that had changed when he'd heard his daughter's story. She'd been raped, a bastard taking her innocence. He vowed that he'd find the bloke, and when he did, he'd make him suffer. Frank's hands balled into fists at the thought.

Until he got more information about the bloke from Carol, it would have to wait, but in no mood to go home to an empty house, Frank decided to see his sons. He would have to tell them about their mother and might as well get it over with.

He went to their flat on Lavender Hill, and his elder son Paul opened the door when he arrived. 'Well this is a surprise. Come on in, Dad.'

Frank followed his son into their living room, where

Davy, his younger one, looked equally surprised to see him as he almost spilled a pretty red-haired girl from his lap. 'Dad! What's up?'

'We need to talk, and in private,' Frank said, looking pointedly at the redhead.

'Sorry, Gloria,' Davy said as he pushed the girl to her feet. 'You'll have to get lost for a while.'

She pouted prettily, but then shrugged, saying nonchalantly, 'Fine, I'll leave. See you around.'

Dave followed the redhead out of the room, but he was soon back, smiling with amusement as he said, 'Gloria pretends she doesn't care, but she can't get enough of me.'

'We've got more important things to talk about than your love life,' Frank snapped.

Dave's eyes widened, but he only said, 'All right, so sit down and tell us what this is all about.'

Frank took a seat, his sons too, before he said abruptly, 'Your mother's left me.'

'What?' Paul exclaimed. 'No, I don't believe it.'

'Believe it or not, but I'm telling you she's gone,' Frank said as he pulled the letter from his pocket and handed it to Paul. 'You'd better read that.'

'What does it say?' Dave asked.

Paul read it out, and both looked stunned. There was a pause, as though they needed time to take it in, but then Davy said, 'So Mum just left, leaving this letter, and we're supposed to wait until she gets in touch with us?'

'That's about it,' Frank said.

'There must be more to it than this. Did you have an argument or something?' Paul asked. 'If you did, once Mum has calmed down she's sure to come back.'

'There was no argument. Just that letter,' Frank said wearily as exhaustion now hit him. 'There's one other thing.

115

Carol was admitted to hospital with food poisoning, but she's fine. She might be allowed home tomorrow so there's no point in going to visit her.'

'What did she eat to cause that?' Dave questioned.

'She isn't sure, but it was probably a bit of dodgy fish,' Frank lied. 'Anyway, I'm bushed, so I'm off now.'

For the first time, he heard concern in Dave's voice. 'Dad, with Mum leaving like that, it must be hard on you. Are you all right?'

'Yeah, I'll cope.'

'Have you tried Gran's? Mum might be there,' Paul suggested.

'She isn't. It's the first place I checked.'

For the first time Paul echoed his brother's concern. 'If you need anything, or any help to find Mum, just ask, Dad.'

'You read her letter. Your mother doesn't want to be found, and to be honest, that suits me fine.'

'You don't mean that, Dad.'

'Yes I do, son,' Frank said and after saying goodbye, he tiredly made his way home. He had meant what he said to his son. After walking out on him like that, leaving just a blunt letter, he wasn't going to run after Daphne. She was looking for a new life, so let her find one. She wouldn't find it easy without a man bringing home a wage, and with few skills, he doubted she'd get much of a job.

With a grim sense of satisfaction, Frank imagined his wife living in a grotty one-room flat, probably beginning to miss him and the decent life he'd worked hard to provide her with. She'd eventually come crawling back, he decided, and he would enjoy shutting the door in her face.

With that thought still in his mind, Frank arrived home, and despite his bravado, he hated walking into an empty house. Still, it wouldn't be for long. Carol would be home again soon and the two of them would jog along nicely.

Frank went to bed, his last thought that he'd keep his daughter safe and close to him. From now on he'd make sure that no other man ever laid a finger on her again.

Chapter Fourteen

Amy was in bed on that Tuesday night too, unable to sleep as her mind twisted and turned. Any hopes she'd held that Rose hadn't run off with Tommy's dad had been quashed. Her mother had been to Rose's flat on her way home from work and found it empty.

Added to that, Amy was concerned about Carol and after a restless night she woke on Wednesday, hoping to find out how her friend was before she left for work. When her mother arrived home from her early morning cleaning job, Amy was ready to leave and said, 'I'm going ask Mrs Cole how Carol is.'

'All right, love,' Phyllis said as she kicked off her shoes. 'Let me know what she says.'

Amy hurried out, surprised when instead of Mrs Cole, Carol's father opened the door. 'Err, hello, Mr Cole, I thought you'd be at work.'

'I've got a couple of days off.'

Amy wondered if it was to do with her friend and asked worriedly, 'Is Carol all right?'

'Yes, she's fine. It was food poisoning.'

'Can I go to see her this evening?'

'There's no point. She'll probably be allowed home later today, or if not, tomorrow morning.'

Amy hadn't seen Mrs Cole since Carol had been taken ill, so asked, 'Is your wife ill with food poisoning too?'

There was a momentary hesitation, but then he said, 'Yeah, a touch of it and she's in bed. That's why I'm taking a couple of days off.'

'Oh dear, can I do anything to help?'

'Thanks for the offer, but we're coping. It didn't hit Daphne as hard as Carol, and as I was just about to make her a cup of tea I'd best get on with it.'

The door closed before Amy could say anything else and turned to see Mabel Povis on her doorstep, arms folded across her chest.

Amy tensed, dreading that the news had broken out about Tommy's dad and Rose, but instead Mrs Povis asked, 'Well, did you manage to get anything out of Frank Cole this time?'

Relieved, Amy said, 'Yes, Carol has food poisoning, but she's getting over it now, and though Mrs Cole wasn't as bad, she's been in bed with it too.'

'She can't be much of a cook then,' Mabel said sarcastically. 'Still, it explains why I haven't heard a peep out of Daphne Cole for a couple of days. Sometimes her voice is loud enough to hear through my walls.'

A door opened on the other side of the road, and moments later, tubby, middle-aged Edna Price scurried over to join them, her hair still in curlers and slippers on her feet. 'Amy, I saw you talking to Frank Cole. What did he have to say?'

'I'm sorry, I must go or I'll be late for work, but Mrs Povis will tell you.'

'Well, Edna,' Mabel began.

After hurrying indoors again to tell her mother what she had found out, Amy walked briskly up Lark Rise, deciding that rather than be late, she'd get a bus to work. She hadn't seen Tommy since he'd told her that his dad had left, and though she hoped he was all right, when she reached his house, Amy didn't have the courage to knock on the door.

Maybe he'd come to her house that evening, Amy hoped; but once again she feared that when the truth came out, Tommy would never want to see her again.

Celia's head was still spinning with all the ramifications she'd had to face since George had left two days ago, not least that Thomas now owned the business. Celia had seen a change in her son's personality almost overnight – he had taken over the running of the business with a maturity that surprised her. Already that morning, over breakfast, Thomas had said he was going to employ another glazier. It would mean buying another van, but he seemed confident that it would be money well spent.

It had been such a short time since he had taken over and Celia felt that Thomas was moving too fast. She tried to caution him, but he'd dismissed her concerns as though her opinion counted for nothing.

Alone in the house now, Celia sat unmoving, uncaring that she was still in her dressing gown and the housework untouched. George had left her and Celia's emotions were raw. Where was he? And who was this other woman? Was it someone she knew? Tears filled her eyes. She had thought her marriage perfect, her home one to be proud of, and had enjoyed her social standing, but now her life was never going to be the same again.

The doorbell chimed and Celia stiffened. She didn't want to see anyone, and hoped that whoever it was would go away. The bell rang again, followed shortly after by the rattle of the letterbox as something was pushed through, then, thankfully, silence.

Celia went into the hall, saw the envelope and bent to pick it up. It was addressed to both her and George and was from Libby Willard – a formal invitation to attend a reception to celebrate her daughter's engagement. To add to her misery, the reception was to be held in the Conservative Club. Celia sank onto the bottom of the stairs, covering her face with her hands.

Libby obviously didn't know yet that George had left her, but it was sure to come out eventually. When it did, and even if the invitation still stood, Celia knew that she would never be able to walk into the Conservative Club on her own. She could just imagine the looks of disdain or pity on the other women's faces and she couldn't stand the thought of that.

Self-pity could have swamped Celia, but she was a proud woman and that pride sustained her now as she rose to her feet. She had done it once, dragged herself out of the slums, and there was no way she was going to let people look down on her now. George had shunned her offer to help him with the business, the paperwork that he found impossible, but she wouldn't let that happen again. She'd insist that Thomas allowed her to be involved, and together they'd expand the business. With her help it would be a success, and she'd be a rich woman, able to hold her head up high.

Until then, if anyone dared to upset her, she'd swat them away like flies.

Mabel had told Edna Price about Carol and the food poisoning, adding that Daphne Cole was in bed with it too. In return she had been passed a bit of juicy gossip. It peeved her that Edna had heard about it before her, and she went to see Phyllis, saying indignantly as she stepped inside, 'Here, Phyllis, why didn't you tell me about your cousin, Rose? I had to hear it from Edna Price.'

'I promised Amy I wouldn't say anything and for her sake I was hoping that nobody would make the connection. Yet as they left on the same day, I should have guessed there was little chance of that. To ruin one marriage was bad enough, but to run off with George Frost, well, I could kill Rose, I really could.'

'She's done what?' Mabel gasped, astounded.

Phyllis looked confused. 'But . . . but you just said you heard about it from Edna Price.'

'She didn't tell me that! All she said is that Rose has been given another flat, and according to the woman who lives upstairs, she probably got the agent to re-house her by lying on her back.'

Phyllis groaned as she rubbed her eyes. 'That sounds bad enough, but the truth is far worse.'

'Rose, and George Frost! If I hadn't heard it from you, I'd never have believed it.'

'Mabel, promise me you'll keep it to yourself. If people think that Rose just left because she's been re-housed, there's a chance that Celia Frost won't hear the truth.'

'What do you take me for? Of course I'll keep it to myself,' Mabel snapped, still peeved that Phyllis hadn't confided in her. After all, they were supposed to be friends, and she was quite capable of keeping her mouth shut.

However, later that day, Mabel forgot her promise when she was chatting to Edna Price. The woman was going on about Rose and the agent again as if she was the font of all knowledge, and annoyed, Mabel took delight in putting her straight.

* * *

Tommy had been glad to leave for work. He felt sorry for his mother, but he just couldn't cope with the emotional state she was in. One minute she was angry, the next she was crying, and clinging to him so much that he felt stifled.

When his father had left, Tommy had been stunned, unable to comprehend that he'd gone off with another woman. He wasn't blind, and had heard the many arguments between his parents, but hadn't expected it to come to this.

Once over the initial shock, Tommy knew he had to think clearly. He had no idea if his father would ever come back, but as the business had been handed over to him he was now responsible for their finances. His whole future depended on him making a success of the business and he'd been anxious to get started.

He *had* to build it up to ensure that the profits would eventually be sufficient to support two households; his mother's, and when he got married, his own. He could have shied away from the burden, but though his health might be weak, Tommy's mind was strong. There was a lot of potential for growth in the business, and already the labour exchange had sent him a man to interview.

Tommy liked Len Upwood on sight and was pleased with the man's qualifications. He had a round, friendly, open face below light brown hair and Tommy only had one reservation – Len was in his late thirties and he might not take kindly to being given orders by a twenty-one-year-old. Yet even as that thought crossed his mind, Tommy realised that the man's age and experience could work to his advantage. If the business took off and he could employ more staff, with his qualifications, Len would make an excellent foreman.

He decided to give Len a try to see if they could work well together and said, 'At the moment this is a small business, passed on to me by my father. I'd like to expand and to eventually employ more staff, however, for now, if I offer you the job it would just be the two of us. How do you feel about coming to work for me on a trial basis? Let's say for a month, and if it works out I'd be happy to make it a permanent position. I can match your previous wage, and though I can't guarantee it on a regular basis, there will be the opportunity for overtime.'

'That sounds fine to me, Mr Frost. I'd like to take the job.'

'Good, and call me Tommy. There's only one other thing. When can you start?'

'How about tomorrow?'

'Great,' Tommy said, reaching out to shake the man's hand. 'For now, until I can get another van delivered, I'll do the in-house glass cutting and you can go out on installations. There are several jobs lined up for tomorrow, so I'll see you at eight o'clock sharp.'

'I'll be here on the dot and thanks, Mr Frost.'

'Tommy.'

'Yeah, sorry, Tommy,' Len said, and both standing up, they walked together to the unit's exit door.

Tommy was glad to have the man on board. It was the first time he'd had to interview anyone for a job, and he just hoped that in Len, he'd made a good choice.

Carol had awoken that morning feeling better, at least physically. Her mental state was another matter. At first, her only thought had been to get rid of the baby, one that had been conceived from rape instead of love. Now though, seeing other women in the ward in varying stages

124

of pregnancy, she was beginning to feel a sense of loss; that the baby she'd been carrying hadn't just been Roy's, it had been a part of her too.

Her feelings seemed to be echoed by the young woman who was continually crying, and later that day Carol felt worse when the sour-faced nurse told her that, though the young woman was desperate for a baby, it had been her fourth miscarriage. Carol had closed her eyes against the disapproval on the nurse's face as she attended to her – she could guess what the nurse was thinking; that she had taken a life, killed her baby, while that poor woman longed to have one.

When the doctor began his rounds, Carol hoped he'd discharge her. She wanted to go home, to get out of this ward, but he insisted that she remain another day. A dark cloud of depression now hung over her, and she escaped into sleep, spending most of the day dozing on and off until visiting time.

'Hello, love, how are you feeling?'

Carol looked up at her father and as he put the pillows behind her back, she sat up. 'I want to come home, Dad. I pleaded with the doctor and he said I can leave tomorrow, so can you bring me some clothes in the morning?'

'It'll have to wait until the evening. I can't take another day off work.'

Carol felt tears flooding her eyes and said, 'Please, Dad, you could drop them off early, before you go to work and if you bring my purse too, I . . . I can get a taxi home.'

He looked about to protest, but then his hand reached out and with one finger he gently wiped a tear from her cheek. 'All right, I'll do that then, but with your mother gone, you'll be coming home to an empty house. As far as anyone knows, you had a bout of food poisoning, your mother too, so nobody has twigged yet that she walked out. Make sure that if you see anyone, you keep to that story for now.'

'I will, but have you heard from Mum?' Carol asked, still unable to accept that her mother had left and sure that she'd come back at any moment.

'No, not a word,' he said then adding softly, 'Come on, don't start crying again. It may be just the two of us now, but we'll be all right. You've had a rough time, but can stay at home and forget about work for a while.'

'Yes, all right,' Carol agreed meekly. All she wanted was to get out of this ward and to be at home. For now, she couldn't think any further than that.

Chapter Fifteen

On Thursday, Mabel was on the look-out as usual when she saw a taxi pulling up next door. She shot outside in time to see Carol climbing out and hurried up to her, saying, 'So you're home. How are you? You still look a bit pasty.'

'I'm fine,' Carol replied tersely and almost throwing the fare at the driver she said no more before going indoors.

Mabel shook her head at the girl's abrupt manner, but with a bit of news she went to pass it on to Phyllis. 'Carol just turned up in a taxi. She said she's fine, but I'm not so sure. She looked like death warmed up to me.'

'Food poisoning can be nasty, but if they discharged Carol she must be all right. I'll tell Amy when she comes home from work; no doubt she'll be round there like a shot.'

'Has Amy seen anything of Tommy?'

'No, not yet, but she's hoping to see him this evening.'

Mabel felt a bit sick. She'd promised to keep it quiet about Tommy's dad and Rose, but now she'd spouted her mouth off and gossip was sure to have spread. The only thing she could do was bluff, insist that it hadn't come from her, so keeping up the pretence she said, 'It's funny that he hasn't been to see her since his father ran off.

Maybe he and his mother have heard that he left with your Rose.'

'With the story going round about her being re-housed, I don't see how. Anyway, she isn't *my* Rose and what she did has nothing to do with Amy.'

'If she gets to hear the truth, I doubt Celia Frost will see it that way.'

'Thanks, Mabel, you're making me feel a lot better.'

'Now then, I'm only warning you, that's all. I've heard that Celia Frost can be a nasty piece of work.'

'It's not Celia Frost I'm worried about, it's Tommy. Amy thinks the world of him, but this could break them up.'

Mabel pursed her lips in thought and then said, 'If he blames Amy, then she'd be better off without him.'

'Yes, I suppose you're right,' Phyllis agreed. 'But she's still going to be upset.'

'Amy's young, she'll get over it – as the saying goes, there are plenty more fish in the sea.'

'That may be, but I could still kill Rose, I really could.'

'I should think you'll be able to leave that to Celia Frost,' Mabel said and after chatting for a while longer, she returned home to put a glass to the wall and pressed her ear against the end. It served to magnify the sound of voices through the thin walls. If Carol had got over the food poisoning, surely her mother was up and about by now.

Though she kept listening for some time, not a sound could be heard and Mabel was puzzled. She couldn't put her finger on it, but something odd was going on next door.

Amy missed Carol at work. She'd told Mrs Jones that Carol was ill and in hospital, but couldn't say how long she'd be absent from the shop. Mrs Jones had been unsympathetic and said that in order to keep Carol's job open she would need an official sick note.

With no one to cover for her, Amy had agreed to work her half day off. The time dragged and Amy was glad when it was time to go home. She was missing Tommy, but as she walked up Lavender Hill, a van pulled up beside her. 'Amy, hop in and I'll give you a lift.'

'Tommy!' she exclaimed, happy to see him and relieved that he looked equally pleased to see her.

'I'm sorry I haven't been able to take you out,' he said after leaning across to kiss her. 'With my mum in such a state, along with my father passing the business over to me, I've been up to my eyes in it.'

'It's all right. I understand,' Amy replied, welcoming another kiss.

He smiled softly. 'I've missed you.'

'And I you,' Amy told him.

'I should be able to see you tonight, and as I've now got my dad's van, we can go for a drive instead of a walk.'

'I'd like that,' Amy said.

'It was a shock to be handed the unit, but now that I've got my head around it, I've got big plans to expand the business.'

Amy hardly took any of this in because now that she was with Tommy, she was beginning to feel the strain. When the gossips put it all together and Tommy heard about it, he would soon work out that she must have known that his dad had gone off with Rose. He'd realise that she had kept it from him and it would only make things worse. Though it might be the end of their relationship, Amy couldn't keep silent any longer. 'Tommy, can you pull over again? I . . . I need to tell you something.'

He glanced at her, a worried frown creasing his forehead,

but he did as she asked, only then saying, 'Amy, you aren't going to give me the elbow are you?'

'When you hear what I have to say, I think it might be the other way round.'

'Unless you're going to tell me that you're seeing someone else, I can't see that happening.'

'Of course I'm not,' Amy said, her mouth so dry that she ran her tongue over her lips before continuing. 'Tommy, I . . . I don't know if you've heard about my mum's cousin, Rose?'

'I know about her reputation,' Tommy said when she hesitated, 'but if that's what's worrying you, it doesn't matter to me. It's you I'm going out with, not your mum's cousin.'

Amy had to tell him – had to get the words out, and in a rush she blurted, 'But she's the one your dad went off with.'

'What!' he exclaimed. 'Rose?'

Amy could only nod, and when he said nothing else, her stomach churned. They sat in silence, until, unable to wait for the words she dreaded to hear she opened the van door, saying, 'I . . . I'm sorry, Tommy.'

'Don't go, Amy,' he said, taking hold of her arm. 'I was a bit stunned for a while, but you can't be held responsible for what your mum's cousin does. There's no need to apologise.'

Amy felt a surge of relief, but her smile was tremulous and the next moment Tommy shuffled over to pull her into his arms as she said, 'I . . . I thought you wouldn't want to see me again.'

'Don't be daft. I love you, Amy.'

'I love you too, but . . . but there's your mother and when she hears about Rose . . .'

'She won't blame you either,' he interrupted assuredly.

Amy wasn't so sure that Celia Frost would see it like that, though for now she was content to be held in Tommy's arms.

Frank arrived home to find Carol asleep on the sofa. She still looked pale, and so vulnerable that he cursed the two people who had nearly cost his daughter her life. There was the man who had raped her, and he'd like to get his hands on him, along with the crone who had performed a botched, back-street abortion.

He was hungry, but realised that there was little food in the house. Carol would want something to eat too, so with little choice Frank decided to pop along to the fish and chip shop. 'Carol,' he said, gently shaking her, 'wake up, pet.'

Her eyelids fluttered, then lifted, and blinking the sleepiness away she sat up. 'Dad, you're home.'

'Yes, but I'm just off to the chippie. What do you fancy?'

'I'm not hungry,' she said listlessly. 'I'll have something later.'

'You'll be lucky. The cupboards are practically bare.'

'Maybe just a few chips then,' she said as there was a knock on the door.

'Whoever that is I'll get rid of them,' Frank said, finding it was Amy when he opened the door.

'Hello, Mr Cole. My mum said that Carol's home. Can I see her?'

'Not now, Amy, she's asleep.'

'Oh, right, perhaps I could call back later?'

'Yes, do that,' Frank said, anxious to get rid of her. He wasn't sure that Carol was up to answering any awkward questions at the moment, and though he'd put it around that Daphne had food poisoning too, he wasn't sure they'd be able to keep that story going for much longer.

131

'I don't want to see anyone, not even Amy,' Carol said as he closed the door.

'I won't be able to fend her off for long, but before you see her we need to work out what we're going to say about your mother.'

'She's sure to come home soon.'

'We'll talk about it when I come back,' Frank said.

Head down, he walked to the chippie, thinking that unlike Carol, he wasn't so sure that Daphne would come home. Not that he wanted her to. He still felt bitter that she had walked out on him, with little explanation other than she wanted a new life.

As he joined the queue in the fish and chip shop, Frank began to realise that though he didn't want Daphne back, he couldn't go on like this. He wanted a proper meal when he came home from work, his clothes freshly washed and ironed, and the house looking like it used to, instead of every surface covered with dust. There was only one answer, he realised, whether Carol liked it or not.

As Phyllis expected, when Amy came home from work and heard that Carol was home, she had immediately dashed out again. However she'd soon returned, saying that Carol was asleep and she'd try again later.

They were now in the kitchen where Amy said, 'Mum, I've got something to tell you. Tommy gave me a lift home in his dad's van, well, it's his now as he's taken over the business.'

'That's a lot for him to take on.'

'Yes, I suppose so, but . . . well . . . I told him about his dad and Rose.'

Phyllis almost dropped the saucepan she was holding and exclaimed, 'Why on earth did you do that?'

'Because it's bound to come out eventually and I didn't want Tommy to think I was keeping it from him.'

'The gossip going round is that Rose has been re-housed, that's all.'

'Yes, but for how long?'

Phyllis sighed. 'I suppose you're right, but how did Tommy take it?'

'Surprisingly well, but I doubt his mum will feel the same.'

'If she's got any sense, Celia Frost will realise that none of this is your fault.'

'I hope so, Mum, but I dread facing her.'

'Well if she's funny with you, let's hope Tommy puts her straight. If he doesn't stand up for you now, he won't in the future and you'd be better off without him.'

Amy said nothing in reply, but Phyllis hoped she had marked her words as she finished plating up the dinner.

Tommy had arrived home too, finding that though it was early days yet, his mother looked more like her old self. She was dressed, with her hair tidy and even managed a small smile as she said, 'Hello, Thomas. How was your day?'

'It was fine and I took on another glazier.'

'Are you sure you know what you're doing, Thomas? You're inexperienced at running a business and there's a lot to learn. You'll have profit margins to deal with, over-heads, and of course the accounts.'

'I know all that, Mum,' Tommy said; a little irritated that his mother was already questioning his abilities. He'd seen the mess his father had made of the books, and there'd been numerous cases of under-quoting which wouldn't happen now that he was in charge.

'I'm not criticising you, darling. It's just that I'd like to help. If I take over most of the paperwork, such as the accounts, wages and invoicing, you won't be tied up with office work.'

'There's no need. I can manage.'

'Don't be difficult, Thomas. You're father is intelligent, but he could never grasp arithmetic and was treated like a dunce at school, so much so that he was ashamed and tried to hide his problem. I of course found out about it and had he accepted my help, the business would have been more successful.'

'I haven't got his problem and I'm perfectly capable of handling the office work.'

'I'm sure you are. It's just that I want to be involved with building up the business and I insist that you accept my help.'

'No, Mum. Thanks for the offer, but it won't be necessary,' Thomas said firmly but then seeing her face suffuse with anger, he quickly back-pedalled, adding, 'at least, not at the moment. If my plans to expand are successful and I take on more staff, then yes, your help will be invaluable.'

She looked a little mollified and said, 'Very well, we'll leave it for now, but bring the account books home tomorrow and I'll take a look at them.'

'There's no need for that. Everything is up to date.'

'Don't argue with me, Thomas. I said bring them home and I meant it. Now, no doubt you're hungry so I'll see to your dinner.'

Thomas wasn't happy and felt that unless he stood up to his mother, she would end up trying to take over the business. He wasn't going to put up with that, but at the moment she was still too vulnerable for him to make a stand. Not only that, he still had to tell her about his father and Rose.

He ran both hands over his face and decided to leave it for a couple of days. It might be cowardly, but for now he was in no mood to put up with any more of his mother's histrionics. At the moment she was calm, her old bossy self, but once told, it was sure to set her back – and that wasn't something he was looking forward to.

Chapter Sixteen

On Friday morning Mabel did a bit of housework, upstairs and down, occasionally putting a glass to the wall. Though she had heard Frank Cole's voice, along with Carol's before he left for work, since then there had been nothing but silence.

At eleven she went to see Phyllis to voice her suspicions and she was now a bit miffed that her friend was laughing at her. 'I'm telling you, when Carol was in hospital, Frank kept his curtains drawn. He was acting strangely, keeping out of sight as though he was hiding something.'

'That doesn't mean that he's done his wife in,' Phyllis said, chuckling.

'You may think I'm daft,' Mabel said indignantly, 'but I'm telling you there's something funny going on. All right, maybe I've let my imagination run riot, but nonetheless, I still haven't seen, nor have I heard, a sound from Daphne Cole.'

'Mabel, she's ill so that's hardly surprising.'

'Carol was worse but she's all right now.'

'I don't think she's fully recovered. Amy went to see her when she came home from work yesterday, but Carol was asleep and still was an hour later. Amy would have tried again, but Tommy arrived to take her out.'

'Carol's still able to speak – I heard her this morning, but her mother seems to have been struck dumb.'

'Daphne has probably got something else along with the food poisoning, perhaps tonsillitis.'

'It's possible I suppose, but as Carol's home, you could go along to see her and at the same time ask how her mother is,' Mabel wheedled.

'Why me? Why don't you go?'

'Because Daphne Cole hasn't got any time for me, nor has her daughter; I doubt I'd get over the doorstep.'

'As it happens, now that Frank has gone back to work, I was going along later to see if Daphne needs anything, a bit of shopping maybe.'

'Good, and once you find out what's going on, you can pass it on to me.'

'Yes, all right, if only to prove to you that nothing sinister has happened. Oh, and by the way, Amy told Tommy about his dad and Rose.'

'She did! Did he go potty?'

'No, not at all, and he doesn't blame Amy, though he's decided not to tell his mother for a couple of days. Apparently he thinks she's still too fragile.'

'Fragile! Celia Frost! Huh, that'll be the day.'

'Her husband went off with another woman, and that's enough to knock anyone for six.'

'It wouldn't bother me. With my Jack being so quiet I'd hardly miss him.'

'You don't really mean that, Mabel.'

'Maybe you're right, but it isn't something I'd ever have to worry about. Jack would rather read a book than go in for a bit of slap and tickle, with me, or another woman.'

'Here, have another cup of tea,' Phyllis said as she picked up the pot.

137

'I won't say no, but then I'd best be off,' she replied, and it wasn't long before Mabel was in her own house again with a glass pressed to the wall. Still nothing from the Coles' house – not a sound.

Mabel's lips tightened. Laugh at her or not, if Phyllis didn't get to see Daphne Cole that day, she was going to take her suspicions to the police.

At one time, the thought of staying at home every day, doing nothing but housework and cooking, would have horrified Carol. Now though, when her father had suggested it last evening, she had listlessly agreed.

She had got up that Friday morning, but had done nothing, not even bothering to wash and dress. She was so depressed that the thought of doing anything was too much of an effort and the dust remained on every surface. It didn't matter. Nothing mattered any more.

When there was a knock on the door, Carol didn't get up to answer it. But whoever it was wouldn't go away, the knocks becoming more persistent, and then the letterbox lifted, a voice calling, 'Daphne, Carol, are you there?'

Carol recognised the voice – it was Amy's mum. As she called out again, it was obvious that Phyllis wasn't going to go away. 'Daphne, Carol, are you all right?'

Sighing, she got up and partially opened the door, following her father's instructions as she said, 'My mum isn't here. She's gone to look after a sick relative.'

'Oh, dear, is that your gran?'

'No, it's a great aunt who lives in Kent,' she lied.

'Carol, are you all right?' Phyllis asked gently.

'I . . . I'm fine,' she said, yet Phyllis's concerned expression was too much and she was unable to stem the tears that flooded her eyes.

'Please, love, let me come in.'

At first Carol was going to refuse, but for some reason she found herself standing back and allowing Phyllis to walk in. 'I can see you still feel rough,' Phyllis said, 'and as you're not dressed, I hope I didn't get you out of bed.'

Carol didn't reply and returned to the sofa, wiping the tears from her eyes. She felt it dip beside her as Phyllis sat down too, her voice once again soft as she touched her arm and said, 'You're upset. Is there anything I can do to help?'

'I . . . I don't want to talk about it.'

'All right, I won't pry, but you look so pale and I'm worried about you.'

Like a dam bursting, Carol broke then, and with a sob she flung herself into Phyllis's arms. Nothing was said as she cried, Phyllis's soft arms holding her, until at last, limp, her head pounding, Carol was able to say, 'I . . . I'm sorry. I'm all right now.'

'Are you sure?'

Carol nodded, but Phyllis said, 'I don't think you are, and listen, if you need me I'm only a couple of doors away. I know Amy is anxious to see you. Can I tell her to call in when she comes home from work?'

Carol managed a small nod, but knew she would never be able to tell anyone that she'd been raped and had an abortion – not even Amy. Self-loathing and shame swamped Carol again. If anyone found out she'd be ostracised, treated like a dirty tart, and it would be no more than she deserved.

'I'm going shopping soon,' Phyllis said. 'Is there anything I can get for you?'

'No . . . No thanks,' Carol managed to say. Her dad had said the cupboards were bare, but she didn't have the energy to think about what they might need.

'I don't like to think of you being on your own all day. I'll come back later to see how you are.'

Carol wanted to be left alone and said, 'No, don't do that. I'm fine.'

'Well, if you're sure,' Phyllis said, 'but don't forget I'm only a couple of doors away if you need anything.'

Carol nodded; glad when Phyllis then left. She picked up a cushion to clutch to her chest, lying down again. With so much time to think, Carol went over it all again, despising herself. She had lied about her age, told Roy she was twenty-three, and as she'd gone up to that flat no wonder he hadn't seen her as an innocent. Roy had raped her, but she had asked for it, and worse, she had aborted the consequences – killed her baby!

Unable to stand the agony of thinking about it any more, Carol closed her eyes and once again escaped into sleep.

Celia forced a smile when Libby called to see her, but it was knocked off her face when the woman spoke. 'Celia, my dear, I'm so sorry. I must have appeared so insensitive when I sent that invitation to Melissa's engagement party, but honestly, I had no idea that George has left you.'

'How . . . how did you find out?'

'I was in the grocers and heard two women gossiping. I was of course shocked to hear that they were talking about George and the fact that he went off with someone called Rose Bridges. It seems she's a common barmaid and one of Amy Miller's relatives . . . her mother's cousin apparently.'

Celia felt her face flame with both embarrassment and anger. She felt sick, humiliated, found she couldn't speak, though Libby was obviously waiting with relish for some kind of response.

'It must be dreadful for you, Celia. Of course my husband would never do such a thing so I can't imagine how you must feel, but if there's anything Tim and I can do . . .'

Once again Celia's pride came to her rescue and standing stiffly she said, 'I'm perfectly all right, thank you. Now if you'll excuse me, I'm rather busy.'

Libby's eyebrows shot up, but Celia ushered her to the door, where after saying a swift goodbye, she closed it firmly as soon as the woman stepped outside. Anger swamped Celia now. It was bad enough that George had left her, but for a common barmaid – and one who was related to the Millers!

She'd make George pay for this; for her loss of standing, her humiliation. As sickening as it was, at least she had a way to find him now and Celia stormed out of the house to march down Lark Rise, determined to get the information she wanted.

Mabel had collared Phyllis as soon as she appeared outside of the Coles' house.

'Well,' she asked, 'did you see Daphne?'

'Carol said she isn't there,' Phyllis said as Mabel followed her home and they walked inside. 'She's gone to Kent to look after a sick relative.'

'I don't believe it. One minute Daphne Cole was supposed to have food poisoning too, and the next she's gone off to Kent? I reckon Carol's lying.'

'Now why would she do that?' Phyllis asked impatiently, too worried about Carol to listen to any more of Mabel's daft ideas.

'All right, maybe that's what Frank told her and Carol *thinks* it's the truth.'

Both women then jumped when someone pounded on

her door. It sounded urgent and Phyllis's first thought was that something was wrong. Fearing that something had happened to Stan or Amy, she rushed to open it, only to be thrust aside as Celia Frost stormed in.

'Oi, you've got no right to barge into my house!' Phyllis protested.

'Where is she?' Celia snapped.

'Where's who?'

'Don't act the innocent,' Celia snapped. 'You know perfectly well who I'm talking about. That tart! Your cousin! Now, where is she?'

'I've no idea.'

'You're lying!'

Phyllis was shaking, but she wasn't going to be intimidated by Celia Frost and stretching her neck she said, 'Now listen here. I've had nothing to do with my cousin for years and I won't have you calling me a liar. I don't know where Rose is, and what's more I don't want to know. Now get out of my house!'

Celia stood her ground, eyes blazing. 'You must know that she's gone off with my husband and I'm not going anywhere until you tell me where they are!'

'I don't *know* anything!'

'Don't give me that! Everyone is talking about it, though I only got to hear about it this morning. My neighbour took great delight in telling me that my husband has left me for a tart from this family!'

Phyllis's stomach turned and she shot a look at Mabel before saying to Celia, 'If that's what you've heard, it's just rumour, gossip, and so far unsubstantiated.'

Celia's eyes narrowed into slits, her tone venomous as she hissed, 'You would say that. After all, it's one tart defending another.'

Phyllis had tried to hold her temper, but now she lost it and though the door was still open she threw it wider. 'I'm not standing for that! Get out of my house before I throw you out!'

'Don't worry, I'm leaving,' Celia snapped, 'and keep your daughter away from my son! She's another tart and I won't have him tainted by the likes of her.'

Phyllis erupted then, but Mabel grabbed her before she managed to land a blow. 'Stop it, Phyllis! She isn't worth it,' she said before shouting at Celia, 'Go on, bugger off while you've got the chance.'

'You sound as common as muck, just like her,' Celia said scathingly as she strode out the door.

Phyllis struggled to get free from Mabel, but she held her fast, and still fuming, she turned on her friend. 'It was you, wasn't it? You must have spread the gossip!'

'I only told Edna Price.'

'Get off of me!' Phyllis yelled, and she continued her tirade as Mabel let her go. 'I was mad to trust you, and in future stay away from me. You'll never be welcome in my house again!'

'Oh, Phyllis, don't say that.'

'Just get out! You're no friend of mine.'

'But I haven't done any real harm,' Mabel protested. 'You said yourself that Amy has already told Tommy and he'd have passed it on to his mother.'

'In a few days, yes, but that isn't the point,' Phyllis said bitterly. 'You couldn't have known that when you told Edna! I've always defended you in the past, made excuses for your poisonous tongue, but never again! Now as I said, get out!'

'Fine, please yourself!' Mabel snapped.

As the door closed behind her, Phyllis slumped onto a

chair, unable to believe that in one morning she had told two women to get out of her house. As her temper cooled, Phyllis wondered if she had been a bit harsh on Mabel, but there was no getting away from the fact that she would never be able to trust her again.

Chapter Seventeen

On Friday afternoon, Tommy was pleased with how the day had gone. He was happy with Len's work and the two of them got on well together. However, as soon as he walked indoors after work it was like being confronted by a mad woman instead of his mother – and the smile instantly dropped from his face.

He was unable to get a word in as she ranted and raved, though when he did get the chance it wouldn't be to put up with her demands.

'Did you hear me, Thomas? I said you're not seeing that girl again!'

'I could hardly *fail* to hear you,' he replied. 'But unlike you, I don't blame Amy for Rose's behaviour and I *will* be seeing her again. In fact, I'm taking her out tonight.'

'You are *not*!'

'I'm not a child that you can dictate to now. I'm a grown man and I can see who I want, go where I want to, and even find a place of my own.'

Shocked, his mother stared at him, blinked, and then came the tears. 'You're going to leave me . . . just . . . just like your father.'

Tommy found that though he was able to stand up to his mother when she was in a temper and making demands,

145

he was hopeless when she started crying. 'Mum, I didn't say that. I was just pointing out that if I wanted to leave home, I could.'

'I . . . I couldn't bear it if you left me too,' Celia said in a small voice.

He could have told his mother that when he got married he'd want a place of his own, yet knew she wasn't ready to hear that yet. He began to wonder if she ever would. For now though he had to make a stand and said, 'I don't want to leave home, but you've got to accept that I'm not going to stop seeing Amy.'

The handkerchief came out and she wiped her eyes, silent for a while, but then at last she drew in a breath. 'It seems I'll have to, but don't expect me to welcome her into my home.'

'You haven't so far, so that won't make a lot of difference,' he said, only just managing to keep the sarcasm from his tone. 'Now I'm going to have a wash and change my clothes.'

With that Tommy left the room, glad again to get away from the rollercoaster of his mother's emotions.

Celia was left feeling that she'd been blackmailed by her own son. The threat had been there; if she tried to stop Thomas from seeing Amy, he'd leave home. She'd been left with little choice, at least for now, but one day in the future she hoped to find a way to come between that tart and her son.

Amy's mother was just as bad, Celia thought, lying when she said she didn't know where her cousin was. Of course she knew, and no doubt Amy did too. Well, that was something she'd talk to Thomas about. At least he'd be able to get that information from Amy and when he did, she'd be able to confront George. She needed to vent her feelings, to tell George just what she thought of him, and that tart he'd left her for would feel the sting of her hand across her face.

That thought made Celia feel a little better, and when her son came downstairs to find his dinner ready and on the table, she had a story in place. She waited until they were both seated and then said, 'Thomas, I don't feel I can move on with my life until I can ask your father for a divorce.'

'Don't you think it's too soon to think about divorce? Dad might realise he's made a mistake and come home.'

'I'd slam the door in his face! After leaving me for that common woman, I'd never take him back!' Celia snapped.

'Are you sure, Mum? Divorce seems so . . . so final.'

Celia took a deep breath, endeavouring to sound calm. 'Yes, I'm sure, Thomas. The problem is, I don't know how to contact your father. As he left with a cousin of her mother's, Amy must know where they are, so when you see her tonight, would you ask her for their address?'

'I can ask her, but I doubt she'll know.'

'At least try,' Celia urged.

Thomas agreed and then tucked into his food, while Celia just picked at hers. After all she had faced that day she had no appetite, and no matter how hard she tried, she couldn't get George's betrayal out of her mind. It was then she remembered something and asked, 'Thomas, did you bring the account books home?'

'No, sorry, I forgot, but as I told you they're up to date, so you don't have to worry about them.'

'It isn't that I'm worried. I just need something to do, something to take my mind off your father. It will at least help me to *feel* that I'm of some use.'

Thomas quietly ate his food, but at last he said, 'All right, Mum. You can take over the accounts, but there's little for you to do yet.'

'Thank you, darling,' Celia said. It was a start, but in the future she hoped to gain control of all their finances.

Amy arrived home a little later than usual, and as dinner was ready she'd have to eat it before going to see Carol. Now though, she was listening to her mother, aghast as she continued, 'Not only did the woman barge in demanding to know where Rose is; she called me a liar and a tart!'

Before Amy could react, her father said angrily, 'I'm not going to let her get away with that.'

'It's all right, Stan. I dealt with it. I chucked her out.'

'She called you a tart and deserves more than that. If Celia Frost was a man I'd knock her off her feet.'

'Well she isn't, and as I said, I dealt with it. Now come on, Amy, give me a hand in the kitchen.'

Amy shared her father's anger that Celia Frost had called her mother a tart, and as she followed her into the kitchen, she said, 'I didn't think it would be long before the truth came out. Tommy wasn't going to tell his mother yet, but now that the gossip has reached her she had no right to barge in here like that.'

'You're right, but the fact that it got out is my fault, Amy; well, partially. I'm sorry, love, but when Mabel heard some gossip about Rose I assumed it was about her running off with George Frost. As I thought Mabel knew I started talking about it, but it wasn't what she'd heard. Of course, it was too late then, but Mabel promised to keep it to herself. I should have known better – Mabel couldn't keep her mouth shut and broke that promise, but I'm finished with her. I told her that she'll never be welcome in my house again.'

'Mum, you've been friends for years; there was no need for that. I told Tommy the truth and he was going to tell his mum. She just got to hear about it a bit earlier, that's all.'

'Mabel still betrayed my trust.'

'She thrives on gossip and you must have known she wouldn't be able to keep it to herself,' Amy pointed out.

'I don't want to talk about Mabel any more. There's something else I need to tell you, but it's not for your father's ears. You saw how he reacted when I said that Celia Frost called me a tart, well he'd go potty if I owned up that she called you a tart too. Not only that, she told me to keep you away from her son as she doesn't want him tainted by the likes of you.'

Amy was dumbfounded and once again she found herself gawking at her mother. 'I . . . I'm supposed to be seeing Tommy tonight.'

'If his mother's got anything to do with it, you won't be, and if you ask me it's probably for the best.'

'I can't stand her, but I . . . I really like Tommy.'

Her mother sighed, 'That may be, but as your dad and me have said before, you should think long and hard about what sort of future you'd have with him. You could end up with Celia Frost as your mother-in-law, and do you really want that? Now, dwell on what I've said and in the meantime take your dad's dinner through to him. I'll bring ours.'

Amy did think about it while she was eating. She had sensed that Celia Frost didn't like her and had been intimidated by her haughty and superior manner, but now it was as if the worm had turned and Amy was angry.

Celia Frost had called her mother a tart, had labelled her as one too, and at last Amy came to a decision. If Tommy came to take her out later she would have a few things to say to him. It tore Amy up to think it might be the end of their relationship, yet she had to speak her mind.

'Amy, I went to see Daphne Cole and Carol today.'

'Are they all right?' she asked, her thoughts turning swiftly to her friend.

'Daphne wasn't there. She's gone to look after a sick aunt, but I'm worried about Carol. She still looks really ill, and upset about something, though she wouldn't tell me what the problem is. Maybe she'll talk to you.'

'I'll go along to see her,' Amy said and, anxious about Carol, she bolted down the rest of her dinner.

Frank Cole was a worried and angry man as once again he had to go out to buy a takeaway meal. He was sick of fish and chips, and this time decided on a longer walk to the pie and mash shop. He'd arrived home to find his daughter dozing on the sofa, still in her nightclothes and the house-work untouched. He'd left her the money to get some food in, but she hadn't been outside the house and at first he'd done his nut, only to backtrack when Carol had curled into a ball, sobbing.

He didn't know what to do, how to cope with her, and just hoped she'd pull herself together soon. Frank decided that what he needed was a stiff drink, and breaking his journey he called in at the Park Tavern. There were several men in there, all still in their work clothes and obviously having a couple of drinks before they headed home.

'Watcha, Frank,' the landlord said. 'What can I get you?'

'A pint of bitter, please.'

'Coming up,' he said, pulling the pump. 'I don't suppose you know of anyone looking for a bit of bar work do you?'

'No, sorry.'

'Well if you do, head them in my direction. I've been left in a fix since my barmaid, Rose, went off with George Frost.'

'You're kidding! This is the first I've heard about it.'

'It's a fact, though I only found out why Rose really left when the gossip reached me,' he said, then moving away to serve another customer.

Frank took a long drink then wiped the back of his hand across his mouth. He had too many problems of his own to show any interest in Rose and George Frost.

Still, he thought, at least it would keep the gossips busy and with any luck they'd be too occupied to question the story that Daphne had gone to look after a fictitious aunt in Kent. It would keep them at bay for now – yet for how long?

Amy could see why her mum was worried. Carol looked awful and had obviously been crying. She was in her night-clothes, her hair lank, and sitting next to her, Amy could smell her body odour. She said that her dad had gone out to get them something to eat, and worriedly Amy said, 'Carol, I don't think they should have let you leave the hospital. You still look really ill.'

'I'm all right.'

'You don't look well enough to come back to work, but Mrs Jones won't be able to keep your job open unless you've got a sick note.'

'I'm not coming back. I'm handing in my notice.'

Shocked and upset, Amy asked, 'But why?'

'My mum's gone to . . . to look after a sick relative and until she comes back, I'm needed at home. There's the housework, cooking and . . .' Carol's voice trailed off as though she didn't have the energy to carry on.

'I know you'll hate being stuck at home. Is that why you've been crying?'

'No . . . Yes . . . Oh, please, Amy, stop asking me questions.'

'I'm sorry. It's just that I'm worried about you.'

'Well don't be. I've had food poisoning that's all, and it's left me a bit drained. Now, my dad will be back soon so I'd better lay the table,' Carol said as she slowly, but pointedly rose to her feet.

Though Amy could see how pale her friend looked, Carol's tone felt like a dismissal and she reluctantly stood up too. 'All right, but if you need anything . . .'

'I'll let you know,' Carol finished for her.

'I'll call in again to see you tomorrow.'

'Don't do that. There's no need,' Carol said, her eyes dull and her tone cold.

Amy's stomach lurched. They had been friends for so long, shared so many confidences, but now it felt as though Carol was treating her like an unwelcome stranger. Like her mother, Amy felt that there was more to Carol's state of mind than food poisoning and she tried again. 'Carol, I know you're still ill, but if there's something else worrying you, please, let me help.'

'I'm sick of this. I said I'm fine and I don't need you pestering me. Go away and leave me alone.'

'Carol, you can't mean that!'

There was no reaction to Amy's plea, just cold words as Carol said, 'And shut the door behind you.'

Too choked to speak now, Amy reluctantly left. Yet no

matter what Carol said, or how many times she tried to dismiss her, Amy wasn't going to give up. Something dreadful must have happened to turn Carol into this cold stranger, and when she was ready to talk about it, Amy was going to be there for her friend.

Chapter Eighteen

Stan had been deep in thought and he'd hardly listened when Amy came back from seeing Carol, although she and Phyllis had yammered on about it for ages.

Now though Phyllis was at work, and Amy was upstairs getting ready to go out with Tommy. When the young man turned up Stan was determined to have his say and only five minutes later there was a knock at the door. He let Tommy in, and with Amy still upstairs, Stan said sternly, 'Now then, Tommy, I'm not happy about your mother barging in here earlier today and insulting my wife.'

'She did what?' he asked, looking shocked.

'You heard me. Your mother wanted to know where Rose is, and when my wife couldn't tell her she called her a tart. I'm not putting up with that.'

'Mr Miller, I'm sorry, but this is all news to me. I arrived home to find my mother in a terrible state because she had found out about my dad and . . . and Rose, but she didn't say anything about coming here.'

'Yeah, well, she did, and if it wasn't for my wife I'd have been up at your place giving your mother a piece of my mind.'

'I'll speak to her,' Tommy said quickly. 'I'll see it doesn't happen again.'

'If you ask me, your mother's a law unto herself and I can't see her listening to you. She'll be turning on Amy next and I'm not going to stand for that. In fact, now that there's bad blood between your mother and us I want you to stop seeing my daughter.'

'Dad!'

Amy had come downstairs and Stan turned to look at his daughter. He saw by the shocked expression on her face that she must have overheard, but he wasn't going to backtrack. 'I'm doing this for your own good,' he said to her, his attention then returning to Tommy when the young man spoke.

'Mr Miller, please, you can't blame me for what my mother said and did.'

Stan was about to answer him, but it was Amy who spoke first.

'Tommy,' she said softly, 'I was going to talk to you about this later, but to ease my dad's mind I might as well get it over with now. I don't blame you for your mother's actions, but nevertheless she barged in here and insulted *my* mum. Unless your mother apologises, I'll never speak to her again – though I doubt that would bother her. She doesn't like me, I know that, and now that this has happened, maybe we should stop seeing each other.'

'No, Amy, don't say that. If she dares to insult your mother again, or you, I'll walk out and find a place of my own.'

Stan looked at Amy, loving her loyalty towards her mother, but impressed by Tommy's response too. In the light of this, he decided that it was up to Amy now. If she wanted to go on seeing Tommy, he wouldn't stand in her way.

'Do you really mean that, Tommy?' Amy asked.

'Yes, I do.'

'In that case,' she said smiling at last, 'where are you taking me tonight?'

Stan saw the delight on Tommy's face, but then the young man sobered and said, 'Is that all right with you, Mr Miller?'

'Yes, I suppose so,' he answered, straight-faced, hoping as the two of them left that his daughter had made the right decision.

Celia was waiting up when Thomas arrived home after seeing Amy, and she immediately asked, 'Well, did you find out where your father is?'

'No,' he said sternly, 'but I did find out that you barged into Mrs Miller's house and insulted her.'

'It wasn't like that,' Celia protested. 'Phyllis Miller's cousin went off with your father and I have every right to know where they are. She refused to tell me and then demanded that I leave her house.'

'Was that before or *after* you called her a tart?'

'Thomas, I was upset; angry that she was lying.'

'She wasn't lying, and I'm telling you now, Mother, if you don't apologise, Amy will never have anything to do with you again.'

Celia almost laughed – that suited her just fine, yet she knew tears were the best defence for her behaviour and wailed, 'I know I haven't been myself since your father le . . . left me, that I've been acting irrationally, without thought, but I . . . I can't seem to stop myself, Thomas.'

'Mum, please, don't cry,' he said worriedly.

'I . . . I can't help it,' Celia sobbed. 'I almost went out of my mind when I heard about your father and that . . . that woman, and I was hysterical when I went to see Amy's mother. Surely you can understand that? And as women,

156

you'd have thought that Amy and her mother would make allowances for my behaviour too.'

'Mum, I'm sorry. I can't speak for them, but I should have realised how hard this has been for you.'

Celia felt a surge of triumph. She'd shown that Amy and her mother were lacking in understanding, a seed planted that she hoped would grow. She'd water it well – put more doubts about Amy in her son's mind, and hopefully when the plant came into full bloom, that girl would be out of her son's life for good.

On Saturday morning, Mabel wasn't at her usual post, looking out of the window. Instead, Jack had gone to work a shift and she was sitting in a chair, still deeply hurt about the way Phyllis had spoken to her. All right, she *had* opened her mouth to Edna, but it hadn't been the end of the world. Celia Frost was going to find out anyway, so there had been no need for Phyllis to get on her high horse. They'd been friends for years, but that had counted for nothing when Phyllis virtually chucked her out of the house.

Mabel shifted in her seat, feeling hard done by. What she needed was a distraction, but she'd heard on the grapevine that the young couple had turned down Winnie's place. That meant there'd be no removals van turning up, nothing to ogle as it was unloaded, and as her mind turned to Phyllis again, she was unable to stem the tears that flooded her eyes. Maybe she should go and talk to Phyllis, try to sort things out, but it was Saturday and Stan would be at home.

On the other hand, Mabel thought, sniffing, why should she be the one to do the running? She had tried to help Phyllis when Celia Frost had turned up, stopped her from laying into the woman, only to have Phyllis's temper turned on her.

Mabel sniffed again. It should be Phyllis who apologised, not her, and until she did, then sod her! Agitated, Mabel stood up as she decided to put her case to Edna, sure that she was right and the woman would come down on her side. She hadn't really had a lot of time for Edna in the past, thinking her slovenly, but now with nobody else to spout off to, Mabel had no choice.

It was then that Mabel heard the sound of a raised voice next door so she quickly grabbed a glass and put it against the wall, her ear pressed to it. She heard Frank Cole yelling, and though it was a bit muffled, his words were clear enough. Mabel frowned. He was ordering Carol to pull herself together, to take over doing the housekeeping now that her mother had gone and wouldn't be back.

Mabel reeled away from the wall. As she'd suspected, all that talk of Daphne Cole going to look after a sick relative had been a pack of lies, something that Frank Cole had come up with to put people off the scent.

Feeling vindicated, Mabel decided to act. She put on a jacket, picked up her handbag and instead of going to talk to Edna, marched out of her house, heading for Lavender Hill and the police station.

'Dad, I will do the housework,' Carol said when her father at last calmed down. 'It's just that I don't feel up to it yet.'

'Go and get some grub in then and at least cook us a decent meal.'

'I . . . I don't want to go out.'

'Why not? A bit of fresh air will do you good.'

'Dad, I don't think I can walk very far.'

'You're just making excuses.'

'I'm not. I really don't feel well.'

With a frown on his face, Carol saw her dad studying

her, and then he said, 'Maybe I should get the doctor to take a look at you.'

Carol didn't want to see a doctor. She just wanted to be left alone. 'No, Dad, I just need a bit more rest, that's all,' she protested, 'and the doctor will only say the same thing.'

'All right, we'll leave it until Monday, but if you're no better by then, I'm calling him out. In the meantime I suppose it's down to me to get a bit of shopping in, but I haven't got a clue what to buy or how to cook anything.'

Carol struggled to make an effort. 'I'll write you a list and if you get something simple, like sausages, I think I can manage to cook them with a bit of mash.'

'Well I suppose that's a start,' he said, looking marginally happier as he went to find a pen and paper.

When the list was done and her father left, Carol sank back on the sofa. Not only was he pushing her to do things around the house, he was constantly on at her about Roy. He wanted to find him, but she couldn't tell him where the flat she'd been taken to was, making it impossible for him to go there to question the real owner. Nor could she tell him who Roy worked for. All she knew was that it was a shop fitting company and now Carol closed her eyes, thinking back to that dreadful night when she'd been raped. She found that her anger had gone, and her need for revenge was dead – as dead as the baby she had carried. All she felt now was disgust that she had put herself in that situation; that she hadn't fought harder. If she'd really tried she could have kicked Roy where it hurt, and that would have stopped him. Her weakness had resulted in a baby – and what had she done! She had taken her child's innocent life. Guilt returned to overwhelm her.

When there was a knock on the door, Carol didn't go to open it, instead just willing whoever it was to go away.

'Carol, it's me,' Amy called through the letterbox.

Despite telling Amy to leave her alone, to stay away, she had come back time and again, but Carol didn't want to see her – to talk to Amy or anyone else. When the letterbox lifted again and Amy shouted through, Carol at last sat up and yelled, 'Go away! I'm busy!'

There was silence then, and relieved, Carol once again put her head back onto the cushions. She closed her eyes, wanting only to escape into sleep again, and remained like that, dozing, until her father returned.

Mabel left the police station, satisfied that at last, after repeating her story to an officer in CID, she had finally been taken seriously. Though she felt it was her duty to report a murder, she'd also been frightened of the repercussions. After all, she was living next door to a killer – and who knows what Frank Cole would do to her if he found out that she'd been the one to dob him in.

However, assured that when they questioned Frank Cole they wouldn't reveal the source of their information, Mabel walked home feeling happier, though she still scuttled past Frank Cole's house and into the safety of her own home.

Jack was still at work, and unable to settle, Mabel paced nervously, wondering when the CID would knock on Frank Cole's door. What she needed was someone to confide in, but how could she tell anyone that she'd been to the police to accuse Frank Cole of murdering his wife? Gossip was rife around here and it would soon get back to him, the thought of that making Mabel's knees go weak. She'd be safe as long as Frank Cole was arrested, but what if he wasn't? What if they couldn't find any evidence?

Mabel would never know how she got through the rest of that day, and she was constantly looking out of her window to see if the CID had turned up yet to question Frank. So far there was no sign of them and Mabel began to wonder if she'd been mistaken, that instead of taking her seriously, she had just been patronised. She should have felt angry, but instead found herself relieved. Maybe she was wrong, maybe Daphne Cole really had gone to look after a sick aunt – yet even as this thought crossed her mind, Mabel still felt it was highly unlikely.

By the time Jack came home Mabel had managed to cook his dinner, and after greeting him they ate in virtual silence. When the meal was over Mabel carried their plates through to the kitchen, unaware that at that moment, a black, unmarked car had pulled up outside the Coles' house.

Frank had tried Daphne's mother again, but the old girl insisted that she hadn't seen or heard from her.

He'd returned home and at dinner time done his best to get through a plate of burned sausages, lumpy mash, and equally lumpy gravy. Carol had barely touched hers, her head down as she toyed with the food on her plate. She looked terrible; drab and scruffy. It was hard to equate her to the vivid, beautiful and vibrant daughter he'd been so proud of just a short time ago.

'Look at the state of you!' he said. 'When I get my hands on the man who did this to you he'll be sorry he was born.'

As though his words had lit a fuse, Carol cried in anguish, 'My baby wasn't born. I killed it, Dad. I killed my baby.'

For a moment Frank was too surprised to react, but as Carol shook with sobs he quickly stood up to go to his daughter's side. At first he just stroked her head, but then Carol surged up and into his arms. He felt helpless, unable to understand why his daughter was in this state. She must have been only about twelve weeks pregnant, maybe less.

'Come on, girl. You didn't kill a proper baby. It would've been little more than a blob.'

'A blob!' she cried, pulling away from him. 'How can you say that?'

Frank had never been much good with words of comfort and it was with some relief that he heard a sharp knock on the door. He rose to open it and seeing two men he asked, 'Yeah, what do you want?'

'Mr Cole. I'm Colin Foreman, CID, and this is my colleague. Can we come in?'

'What for?' he asked, puzzled.

'We'd like to ask you a few questions.'

'What's this about? What sort of questions?'

'They concern your wife.'

Frank paled and stood back, asking anxiously as the men walked in, 'Has something happened to her?'

'That's what we're here to find out, Mr Cole.'

Both men saw Carol, and seeing the state she was in, Frank wasn't surprised that their eyes widened imperceptibly. He said quickly, 'This is my daughter, Carol. She hasn't been well, but what's this about my wife?'

'We'd like to see her. Is she here?'

'No, she . . . she's gone to look after a sick relative.'

'What relative?'

'A . . . an aunt.'

'I see, and where does this aunt live?' Foreman asked.

'Err . . . in Kent.'

'At what address?'

Frank swallowed and stalled by asking, 'Why are you here asking me questions about my wife?'

'All in good time, Mr Cole. Now as I said, I'd like this relative's address.'

'I haven't got it.'

162

'So you're telling me that your wife has gone to look after a sick aunt, but you don't know where this relative lives.'

'Yeah, that's right.'

'Do you have any means of contacting your wife?'

'Err . . . no.'

'When do you expect her to return?'

'I'm not sure. As soon as her aunt recovers I expect, but what's with all these questions?' Frank asked yet again.

'We're investigating certain allegations that have been made, Mr Cole, and as I'm not satisfied with your answers we're going to have to take them seriously.'

'Allegations! What allegations?'

'They're regarding the fact that your wife seems to have disappeared, and as I think this matter now needs further investigation I'd like you to accompany us to the station.'

'What for? I haven't done anything,' Frank protested, but then he paled as the penny dropped. 'Wait! Surely you don't think I've done my wife in?'

'Have you?'

'No, no, of course not! If someone is accusing me of doing that they must want their head examined.'

'Dad, tell them the truth. Show them the letter Mum left for you,' Carol urged.

Frank's mind was reeling. Yes, Daphne's letter, but where had he put it? He hurried to the mantelpiece, searching, but there was no sign of it. 'I can't flaming well find it!'

'What's this about a letter, Mr Cole?' Foreman asked.

'It's one my wife left when she walked out on me.'

'So now you're saying that she *isn't* looking after a sick relative.'

'Yeah, that's right. The truth is she left me.'

Foreman's eyes narrowed with suspicion as he asked, 'So why concoct the story about a sick aunt?'

163

Frank ran a hand through his hair in agitation. 'Look, my wife walked out the same day that my daughter went into hospital and I was in a bit of a state. I just said that to keep the gossips at bay for a while, that's all.'

Foreman didn't look convinced, but Frank saw a spark of the old Carol as she said sharply, 'My dad isn't lying. I saw the letter and read it.'

'Did you recognise your mother's handwriting?'

Once again Carol flared as she snapped, 'Of course I did!'

Foreman didn't react, unperturbed by Carol's outburst as he said, 'Nevertheless, I'd like to see this letter, Mr Cole.'

Frank began searching again, finding it down the side of his fireside chair and with relief he was at last able to hand the letter to Colin Foreman. The man read it, passed it to his colleague, who so far hadn't uttered a word and still didn't as Foreman said, 'It seems you're telling us the truth this time, Mr Cole. It would have saved us a lot of time if you had done that in the first place.'

'My dad hasn't done anything wrong and whoever made the allegation is the one who wasted your time,' Carol said angrily. 'Was it Mabel Povis?'

'I'm not at liberty to say, but I think we can say this matter is closed now.'

With nods of goodbye both men left, and as Frank was still too stunned to react it was Carol who said as the door closed behind them, 'He didn't say it was Mabel, but I bet it was and I'm not letting her get away with it.'

Frank looked at his daughter, thinking that at least the visit from CID had served to snap Carol out of her lethargy. 'Leave it, love. No harm's been done and we can't say for sure it was her.'

'I can't believe you're so calm. You've been accused of murder yet you say no harm's been done!'

'It hasn't, though it was a bit sticky there until I found your mum's letter. The CID are satisfied, they left, and I'm just relieved to see that you've got your old spark back.'

'Oh Dad. I wish Mum would come home.'

'Now don't go all maudlin on me again. She might and she might not, I don't know.'

'I'm surprised that Davy and Paul haven't been round to see us.'

'I told them you had food poisoning and knowing those two, they're waiting until they think you're fully recovered before turning up, expecting to be fed.'

'Well they can think again,' Carol said indignantly.

Frank looked at his daughter, sure that she was going to be all right now. She'd be able to look after this place and hopefully her cooking would improve. As for Mabel Povis, if she was the culprit she was probably shaking in her shoes now expecting him to retaliate, and it served her right. He'd prolong it – leave her to stew until he was good and ready to sort her out.

Chapter Nineteen

It was now mid-June and Tommy was pleased with the way business was going. Though initially reluctant to let his mother take over the books, she kept the accounts efficiently, leaving him more time to concentrate on building up custom. Profits were already up and he'd just gained a contract to supply all the windows for a new build of twenty houses that were near completion.

His mother hadn't apologised, but thankfully Amy hadn't mentioned it again. He hoped that one day there could be some sort of relationship between Amy and his mother, but at the moment any mention of apologising or inviting Amy to the house caused hysterics. Tommy knew he was taking the coward's way out, but until his mother's emotions were less raw, he was leaving things as they were.

Since his father had left they hadn't heard from him; not a letter, or a phone call, and with the business to run Tommy was relieved that he'd only had a couple of mild asthma attacks. If he had a bad spell that kept him in bed, at least he now felt confident that Len would be capable of handling things until he was on his feet again. However, Len would need help for the installations and after a hectic day on Thursday, he said to his mother, 'I'm going to employ another couple of glaziers, along with buying two more vans.'

'It'll make a huge dent in our profits. Can't you manage with one man and a van?'

'Not with this new contract. As it is, Len and I are already at full stretch.'

'Very well, I'll allow it, but if nothing else comes up by the time the work is finished, you'll have to dismiss them. I'm not paying out wages for men to sit around doing nothing.'

Tommy was close to the end of his tether. He'd been patient, had let his mother handle the accounts, but she was overstepping the mark lately and he had to put a stop to it. 'Mother, I don't need your permission to employ men, nor do you pay their wages.'

'How dare you speak to me like that! I'm your mother and I have every right to have a say in the running of the business. I make up Len's pay-packet, handle his tax and insurance, and therefore I know just how much extra staff will affect our profit margins.'

Tommy only just managed to stem his temper but he couldn't hold back the barb. '*Our* profit margins? I think you're forgetting that Dad handed the business over to me.'

'That's it, rub it in, add to my humiliation by pointing out that I have to rely on you to support me,' she cried, tears imminent now.

'Mother, that wasn't my intention. I appreciate that you keep the accounts, and we agreed on a monthly salary. I also quite rightly pay you for my keep so I don't feel that I'm supporting you.'

She sniffed, but her eyes were still moist and she dabbed at them delicately with a lace-edged handkerchief and said croakily, 'I'm glad to hear that.'

Tommy sighed. He wanted to say more, to tell his mother that she had to let him run the business his way, without interference, but he'd never been able to handle her when she was tearful.

He'd leave it for now; and anyway, it was Amy's birthday next week and when he told his mother what he intended to do, she'd probably have another bout of histrionics.

Amy hadn't given up on Carol, and when it came out that her mother had walked out, it went some way to explaining – along with her illness – the state Carol had been in.

As the weeks had passed Amy still saw Carol as often as she could, though she now felt the widening distance between them. They had once been so close, like sisters, but Carol now seemed far older than her eighteen years.

As she wasn't seeing Tommy that night, Amy was with Carol now and where once they had talked about boys, fashion, and the latest music, these days Carol's only conversation seemed to be about cooking and housework. Of course she still ranted occasionally about Mabel Povis, but the once-nosey woman was a shadow of her former self and was rarely seen peeping through her curtains these days.

As though aware of Amy's thoughts, Carol said, 'People round here don't like snitches, and after what Mabel Povis did to my dad, she's been ostracised. Your mum's the only one who has any time for her now.'

'I think my mum feels sorry for her.'

'Well she shouldn't. That woman accused my dad of murder and he could have ended up in prison.'

'I know and I'm not sticking up for her. I think my mum's mad too, but she's so soft-hearted and when Mabel Povis turned up at our door, crying, she let her in.'

'She came here too, trying to say she was sorry, but unlike your mum, my dad slammed the door in her face,' Carol snapped.

They had been through all this so many times, and hoping to change the conversation, Amy said, 'When I finish early on my half days off, I sometimes bump into Lena Winters.'

'How come she isn't at work? I thought she'd been transferred to another branch.'

'Yes, that's right, in Streatham, but apparently because it's a larger shop she's got an assistant manageress. It allows her to take every Thursday off. She seems so different now that she isn't our boss, and I think she must be lonely as she usually invites me to join her for a coffee and a chat.'

'I always felt her cold and distant,' Carol commented. 'Anyway, let's get back to Mabel. As I just said, my dad slammed the door in her face, and since then when I see her, I make my feelings plain. I even spat at her feet the other day.'

Not Mabel again, Amy thought as she once again tried to divert Carol, asking, 'Have you seen anything of your brothers?'

'Since I told them I wasn't going to do their washing and ironing, we hardly see them.'

'Has your mum been in touch?'

'No,' Carol said, her face saddening.

Amy noted that as usual now, Carol's face was void of make-up. Her hair was shiny though and looked newly washed, but it hung without any attempt at styling below her shoulders. 'Carol,' she said, 'I liked Linda, the girl who was taken on to replace you and we became friends, but I was shocked when she was caught fiddling the till. She's been sacked so there's a job going; I'm sure Mrs Jones would take you on.'

'No thanks. I was sick of smelly feet and anyway, I'm needed here.'

'Don't you get fed up with being stuck at home all day?' Amy asked.

'Not really. I've discovered that I like cooking and I enjoy trying out new recipes. I made a lovely meat pie with suet pastry today and my dad loved it. At least he's still eating, but I'm a bit worried about him. He's drinking heavily and goes to the pub every night.'

'So you're mostly on your own,' Amy said, feeling sorry for her friend.

'It doesn't bother me,' Carol said, nodding towards the recently acquired television. 'I've got that for company now and I'm happy enough.'

Amy found it hard to believe. Just a short while ago the thought of making a cake or pie would have had Carol in fits of laughter, and she wouldn't have been happy stuck indoors every night in front of a television.

It didn't seem possible that in such a short time she had changed so much. Had the old Carol gone forever? Amy was beginning to think so and the thought saddened her.

Frank finished his pint, wiped the back of his hand across his mouth and went to the bar to order another. He wasn't in the mood to chat and once served, he went back to the table to sit alone with his thoughts. At first he'd believed his daughter's story, but it was so sketchy that it didn't really add up. She didn't know the bloke's full name, who he worked for, nor where the flat was in Tooting. It didn't ring true, and he'd come to the conclusion that Carol wasn't as innocent as he'd thought. She'd been caught out though, made a mistake and found that she was pregnant. The bloke had probably buggered off, leaving her little choice than to get rid of the baby. If the abortion hadn't been botched, he wouldn't have known anything about it, but it had gone wrong so Carol had to come up with a story, using rape as her only defence.

His stomach churned. Until all this happened he'd seen Carol as his perfect, untouched daughter, but he was now seeing her in a different light. And it didn't help that she looked so much like her mother. Frank knew that he was sick, that the feelings he'd until now stifled were unnatural, but every night, lying alone in his bed now, the urges grew and one day he feared he'd act on them. He gulped his third drink, determined to get drunk. That way he'd return home incapable of anything other than passing out again, sleeping it off until his alarm woke him in the morning.

Frank had downed his fourth pint when the door opened and Terry Price walked in. He was a big, bullish-looking bloke, a bouncer who was handy with his fists. His wife, Edna, was another one like Mabel Povis, a nosey bitch who loved to gossip. 'Watcha, Frank. How are you doing?' Terry asked.

'Fine,' he slurred. 'How's your missus? Still busy on the jungle drums no doubt.'

'What's that supposed to mean?'

'That she's got a big mouth,' Frank said, inciting what he knew would be coming.

'I can see you're drunk, but I ain't standing for that. There's nothing wrong with my missus.'

'Yes there is. She's a fat, ugly, old cow,' Frank slurred, sure that he had gone far enough now. With the sick thoughts in his head he deserved a good kicking.

Frank didn't offer any resistance as Terry hauled him to his feet and dragged him outside.

*　　*　　*

Stan could see what was about to happen, and limped outside, with about five other men following behind him eager to see the fight. They watched the blows landing, but when it became obvious that Frank Cole was incapable of defending himself, Stan became fidgety. Maybe he should wade in, but Terry Price was a huge bloke and unless the others joined in to help, he was likely to come off as badly as Frank.

When Frank no longer had a wall at his back he fell to the ground and Terry laid into him with his boots. Like a pack of animals scenting blood there was baying, but Stan couldn't watch it any more and stepped forward, shouting, 'He's had enough, Terry.'

The man's head shot round, eyes wild as he growled, 'I ain't even started yet.'

'Leave it out. You can see he's drunk,' Stan said, incensed as Terry continued to put the boot in.

The kicking stopped as once again Terry fixed him with cold, gimlet eyes. 'He wasn't too pissed to insult my wife, but if you want to take his place, come on then, I'm waiting.'

Terry stood with his fists raised, ready, and Stan swallowed, but he limped forward, only to see the man drop his arms as he said, 'You're a cripple, Stan, but the only one with the guts to take me on. It wouldn't be a fair fight, so forget it.'

'That wasn't a fair fight either,' Stan pointed out, nodding towards Frank who was still lying on the ground. 'Are you going to leave him alone now?'

'He deserved a kicking, but yeah, I'm done. It was no fun when he didn't fight back.'

Now that the fight was over the other men trailed behind Terry as he walked back into the pub, while Stan hurried over to Frank. He crouched by his side, and urged, 'Come on, mate. Let's get you home.'

'Nah . . . nah . . . neesh a drink,' he said through a nasty split lip.

'I think you've had enough,' Stan said, seeing that as well as the split lip, Frank's eyes were puffy, which meant he'd probably have a couple of black eyes. 'Can you stand up?'

'Yesh . . . I think so,' but on trying Frank curled on the floor, clutching his ribcage.

'Frank, maybe I should call an ambulance,' Stan said, worried about the damage Terry's boots had inflicted on Frank's body.

'No . . . no . . . I'm all right. Jush gi . . . give me a minute,' he said, and then after a couple had passed he raised an arm. 'It . . . it's agony when I take a breath, but if you give me a hand . . .'

Stan did, though it wasn't easy, and then came an unsteady walk home as he did his best to support Frank's weight. 'You daft sod. If you'd kept your mouth shut about Terry's wife, this wouldn't have happened,' he admonished.

'Gl . . . glad it did,' Frank gasped painfully.

Puzzled, Stan managed to take Frank's keys and open his door, saying as they staggered inside, 'How can you be glad about taking a beating.'

'Ke . . . keeps me out of mischief,' Frank said as he collapsed onto the sofa.

It made no sense to Stan, but the room was in darkness, which meant that Carol was probably in bed. 'Are you sure you're all right? Or do you want me to get Carol up to give you a hand?'

'Nah . . . nah, thash the last thing I want. You go, I'll be fine.'

Stan didn't argue. He'd done his bit, but the extra weight

of holding Frank up had put a strain on his damaged leg. His limp really bad now, Stan put the man's keys on the table and left, putting the puzzle from his mind.

What Frank said or did was none of his business, but from the state the man was in, Stan doubted he'd be fit for work in the morning.

Chapter Twenty

Carol woke earlier than usual on Friday morning. She'd heard the commotion downstairs the night before, guessed her dad had come home drunk again and though she felt sorry for him, she dreaded the thought of facing his hangover. Since Mabel Povis had tried to get him done for murder, he'd become uncommunicative, had taken to drink, and Carol seethed on her father's behalf. She would never forget the day the CID had turned up, her horror at the accusation that had somehow managed to snap her out of her own self-absorption.

She had been in a black pit, hating herself so much that she hadn't spared a thought to what her dad had been through. On the same day that her mum had walked out, she'd had an abortion and she knew her dad had feared that she might die. On top of that, he'd been questioned by the police and though able to prove his innocence, Carol knew there were some locals who would say there was no smoke without fire.

If anyone said anything to her, they'd get a mouthful, Carol thought, now fiercely protective of her father. In fact looking after her dad, seeing that he had nice meals to come home to and the house immaculate had become her penance. Unwilling to get up yet, Carol lay in bed, her thoughts drifting to the conversation she'd had with Amy the previous evening. They had once been so close, worked and laughed together but that seemed eons ago now. In reality it had only been around four months, yet Carol knew she had been a different person then. She'd been happy, thought only of fashion, music, dancing, and a part of her longed to turn back the clock so that she could become that innocent girl who had once loved life again.

Sadly Carol knew it was impossible and shaking these thoughts off, she climbed out of bed to get quickly washed and dressed before going downstairs, only to stand with her hand over her mouth in horror.

'Dad, Dad, are you all right?' she cried, dashing to the sofa and kneeling at his side, yet looking at his grotesquely swollen face the question seemed inane. Of course he wasn't all right. Along with the swelling on his cheeks, his eyes were like slits in a yellow mass of bruising and there was blood on his chin that had trickled from a nasty split in his lip.

'Wh . . . what?'

Carol rushed to the kitchen and poured water into a bowl before grabbing a clean cloth to go back to her father's side. She tried to dab the caked blood from the cut but he pushed her hand away and she felt helpless, useless to deal with his wounds. 'Dad . . . I think you need to see a doctor.'

One eyelid partially opened and he squinted up at her, moaning, 'No . . . no . . . but get me . . . get me a drink . . . water . . .'

She hurried to do his bidding, but as he seemed incapable of holding the glass, she lifted his head with one hand while holding the water to his lips with the other. He drank a little then tried to sit up, but groaning in pain he found it impossible and sank back. 'Dad, who did this to you?' Carol asked again.

'Ca . . . can't remember.'

Worriedly she repeated, 'I think you need the doctor.'

'No, I'm just a bit bruised and I'll be all right. Just find me a couple of pain killers.'

Unsure that her father was right, Carol nevertheless did as he asked. As the pain killers took effect his swollen face relaxed as he drifted off to sleep, and Carol went to quietly pour a bowl of cereal before returning to sit close by, ready to be there if her father needed anything when he woke up.

Mabel waited until ten thirty, then went along to see Phyllis. She didn't know how she'd have got through the last weeks without her and would be forever thankful that they were friends again. There were few people who spoke to her now, all of them disgusted or angry when it came out that she had accused Frank Cole of murdering his wife. Of course he'd been the one who had put it about, and though he hadn't actually used her name, everyone had pointed the figure at her.

It had shaken her to the core that Frank had been found innocent, and when the nastiness started she only had Jack to turn to. Instead of being sympathetic, he had been furious with her, and said that in future she should keep her nose out of other people's business.

'Watcha,' Mabel said as she walked into Phyllis's house.

It was obvious that Phyllis was now subject to the occasional bit of gossip too as she said, 'Hello. Have you heard about Frank Cole?'

'No,' Mabel said, stiffening. 'What about him?'

'He got beaten up last night.'

'Well I hope people aren't blaming me for that too,' Mabel said nervously. 'Who did it?'

'Terry Price. Apparently Frank was drunk again and insulted Edna.'

'How did you find out about it?' Mabel asked. 'Did Edna tell you?'

'No, it was Stan. He saw it happen and helped Frank home.'

'I suppose people will say it's my fault that he turned to drink,' Mabel said. 'Yet I've been thinking about it lately and in all fairness, if Frank had told the truth about Daphne leaving him in the first place, my suspicions wouldn't have been aroused.'

Phyllis was prevented from answering by a knock on the door, but her voice was loud when she opened it. 'Rose! You've got a cheek showing your face here.'

'Why? What have I done?'

'You know full well what you've done,' Phyllis said indignantly. 'You ran off with George Frost.'

'I flaming well didn't,' Rose said.

'Yes you did!'

'I did not, but I'm not standing on the doorstep arguing with you, so let me in and we can sort this out.'

Mabel stood up as Rose walked in and said, 'I'll go.'

'No, I'd prefer you to stay,' Rose said. 'No doubt you've heard this rubbish too and I want to set the record straight.'

'Phyllis?' Mabel asked, hoping she'd agree. 'Is that all right with you?'

'Yes, yes, sit down, Mabel.'

Mabel did, looking at Rose who was dressed respectably in a well-cut suit. She wore less make-up and her hair was beautifully styled, showing her to be a very attractive woman.

'Right,' Rose said. 'What's this about George Frost?'

'There's no need to act the innocent,' Phyllis snapped. 'He walked out on his wife and as you both left on the same day it was easy to put two and two together. What's happened? Didn't it work out and that's why you're back?'

'Now listen here. I may have left, but it wasn't with George Frost. If you must know I'm living in Bethnal Green now, with Samuel Jacobs.'

'What! Our landlord?' Phyllis gasped.

'Yeah, that's right.'

'We haven't seen him in years,' Mabel said. 'He got a bit past it and started using an agent, so how did you meet him?'

'He came in the Park Tavern one lunchtime, and though you're right, he doesn't do much now, he still keeps an occasional eye on his agents. We got talking and well, he asked if he could see me again.'

'Ain't he a bit old for you? He must be in his late seventies by now.'

'Mid-seventies, but I prefer older men,' Rose said.

'As long as they're rich,' Mabel returned, unable to keep the sarcasm out of her tone.

'Think what you like, Mabel, but I must admit that Samuel is a *very* wealthy man,' Rose said, smiling with satisfaction.

'There's no fool like an old fool,' Mabel couldn't resist saying.

Phyllis had been standing stiffly, with her arms folded, but they dropped to her side as she said, 'So you didn't run off with George Frost?'

'That's what I've just said, isn't it?' Rose replied.

'Well he went off with someone,' Phyllis told her.

'Yes, but now you know it wasn't with me can I sit down?'

'I suppose so,' Phyllis said grudgingly, she too taking a seat.

Mabel did the opposite and stood up. 'I'd best be off, Phyllis.'

'Yes, all right. I'll see you later.'

Mabel said a curt goodbye to Rose, and then went home. Now she knew that Rose hadn't gone off with George Frost, she had another candidate in mind. She had dates to work out before voicing her opinion, but then Mabel berated herself. After what happened the last time she'd voiced her suspicions, it would be better to keep her big mouth shut.

Rose drank the tea her cousin had made and then said, 'Well, Phyllis, now that we've sorted out that misunderstanding I can tell you why I came to see you.'

'Go on then.'

'I'm here to invite you to my wedding.'

'What? Samuel Jacobs asked you to marry him?'

'Yes, he did, and soon.'

'No doubt you're marrying him for his money,' Phyllis said with obvious disapproval. 'What about his family? What have they said about it?'

'His wife died ten years ago, and they were childless. There are distant relatives, second cousins or something like that, but they're hardly in a position to put up any opposition. They only pay Samuel a token visit once a year to keep him sweet, but he's no fool and knows they're only after his money,' Rose told her.

'As I just said, you are too,' Phyllis retorted.

'And as I just said, Samuel is no fool. He knows what he's doing,' Rose replied, again smiling with satisfaction. She knew exactly what she was doing too, that in hopefully not too many years she would be a very wealthy widow and one who owned this, her cousin's house, along with a lot of others on Lark Rise and the surrounding streets. Samuel was an astute businessman, buying up property during the war when other people wouldn't take the risk of bomb damage. He'd purchased a lot in Bethnal Green too, and though in both areas some of them had been destroyed in the Blitz, a great many had survived.

Phyllis frowned and said, 'Surely Samuel Jacobs is a Jew – I can't see him marrying you unless you convert to Judaism?'

'He isn't a practising one and has agreed to a registry office wedding.'

'Rose, I haven't had much to do with you for years, so why invite me?'

'Because you, Amy, and of course Stan are the only family I've got,' Rose said and decided it was time she spoke her mind. 'I know why you haven't had any time for me, but when the gossip had flown around you never once asked me if any of it was true. Instead you appointed yourself as my judge and jury, once telling me that I was ruining my reputation. Most of what you heard was a load of old tosh, but you chose to believe the nasty-minded gossips, finding me guilty; just as you did this time with this rubbish about me going off with George Frost.'

'You can hardly blame me for that. It wouldn't have been the first time you've broken up a marriage.'

'Once, Phyllis, I made a mistake once, and that was because I was daft enough to believe the bloke when he told me his marriage was all but over.'

'More fool you then,' Phyllis said.

'Yeah, and though I must admit I went off the rails a bit when my hubby died, I've never been the tart I was made

181

out to be. I was lonely and wanted a man in my life again, but I only slept with a few of them.'

'A few! Stan's the only man I've been with.'

'That's easy for you to say. Stan's still alive, but what was I meant to do when I lost my husband? I was still young, but maybe you think I should've become a nun, or spent the rest of my life alone.'

Phyllis just looked at her for a moment, but then she said, 'I suppose I should apologise for thinking that you went off with George Frost.'

'If you're going to sound that grudging, don't bother,' Rose said. 'I must be mad coming here to invite you to my wedding and expecting you to be happy for me.'

'Rose, you're marrying an old man for his money. I don't see how you can expect me to approve of that.'

'Why not? Instead of being a lonely old man, ending his days unloved and uncared for, I've brought a bit of happiness into Samuel's life. He knows I don't love him, but I make him laugh, take care of him and it's given him a new lease of life.'

'I hadn't thought of it like that,' Phyllis said as she poured them both another cup of tea. She then began to giggle. The giggle turned to a laugh, then she was almost crying with mirth, until able to gasp, 'I . . . I don't know about a new lease of life, Rose. If . . . If you're at it too much you're more likely to give him a heart attack that finishes him off.'

Rose laughed too, but at last they sobered, Phyllis then saying, 'I'm sorry, Rose, I really am. I don't know when I turned into a prude, but somewhere along the way I did, and you're right, I shouldn't have judged you – then, or now. Mind you,' she added without malice, 'those low-cut tops and the make-up didn't help.'

'You should try one out on Stan. It might give him a new lease of life too.'

Phyllis chuckled, winked cheekily and said, 'Fortunately he doesn't need one.'

They laughed together again, and it was as though the closeness they had once shared was slowly creeping back. Rose hoped it would deepen, but only time would tell.

Chapter Twenty-One

Though Tommy told his mother that Rose hadn't been the woman his father left her for, it did little to change her attitude towards Amy.

Tommy wasn't going to let this stand in his way, and on the twenty-second of June, the night before Amy's birthday, he was on his way to the pub where he knew he'd find Amy's father, determined to do things properly and ask his permission to propose.

The stench of tobacco stung his nostrils as Tommy walked into the bar at seven thirty and the smoke from many cigarettes was thick. He coughed, hoping he didn't have to resort to using his inhaler.

Stan Miller was at the bar, men on each side of him, and Tommy swallowed nervously before saying respectfully, 'Mr Miller, I hope you don't mind, but can I have a private word with you?'

Stan raised his eyebrows, but said, 'Of course you can, but first, what are you having to drink?'

'Err . . . just a half of mild ale, please.'

'Coming up,' Stan said and after it was poured, he picked up his own pint of beer and indicated a vacant table.

They sat down and dry-mouthed, Tommy took a gulp of ale, finding that the words he had so carefully prepared were stuck in his throat. Another gulp of ale didn't help, and he just sat, unable to say a word.

'Come on, Tommy, spit it out. What's this about a private word?'

'I . . . wanted to ask your permission to propose to Amy.'

'Yeah, well I guessed as much,' Stan said, taking a swig of beer before continuing. 'Right then, lad, I'll tell you how I feel about it. I've got nothing against you, Tommy, but I can't say the same about your mother. I can't see her being happy about it and I don't want her making my Amy's life a misery.'

'Don't worry, she won't. I'll see to that,' Tommy assured him.

'I suppose with your dad gone, your mother relies on you financially. How are you coping with running his firm?'

'It's *mine* now, Mr Miller, and I'm doing well. I've already expanded the business and profits are well up.'

'That's good, but if you marry Amy you'll have two homes to support. Now I hate to say this, but I know you've got a weak chest. What happens when you go down with bouts of bronchitis? Who's going to look after things then?'

'I've got a bloke working for me who's capable of running things in my absence,' Tommy assured him.

Stan Miller took another swig of beer, his face closed, but then he said, 'All right then, but of course it's up to Amy. If she wants to marry you I won't stand in your way.'

'Thanks, Mr Miller,' Tommy said, smiling at last.

'It wouldn't have made much difference if I'd refused. With Amy being eighteen tomorrow and you twenty-one, you don't need my permission.'

'I know, but I wanted to do things properly.'

'I still think you're both a bit young, so I hope it's going to be a long engagement.'

'I don't know, Mr Miller, not too long I hope.'

'When are you going to propose?'

'Tomorrow night,' Tommy replied, 'and as I've got something special planned I'd rather Amy doesn't know about the proposal in advance.'

'Don't worry, I won't say a word.'

'Thanks, Mr Miller. Now can I buy you another drink?'

'Yes, a pint of bitter.'

Glad to have got it over with, Tommy went to the bar, and he remained in the pub chatting to Amy's dad for another hour before making his way home. He still had to break the news to his mother, but he'd wait until after he'd proposed to Amy.

When Tommy left, Stan was about to go back to the bar when Frank Cole came up to the table. The man had looked awful after his beating and there were still livid bruises around his eyes. 'Stan, did you hear that I lost my job?'

'Yeah, but you're sure to get another one.'

'In the meantime I'm skint so will you buy me a pint?'

'Yeah, all right,' Stan agreed, though he wasn't happy about it. Broke or not, it didn't stop Frank from coming to the pub every night and scrounging drinks.

'Thanks, and did I just see you talking to Tommy Frost?'

'Yeah, that's right,' Stan replied, keeping shtum as he'd promised and saying instead, 'Did you hear that Tommy's father didn't go off with Rose?'

'Yeah, Carol told me,' Frank replied.

'Yeah, well, the gossips got it wrong.'

'They get a lot of things wrong, Stan, and I should know.'

Stan nodded as they walked up to the bar, where after buying the man a drink he later saw Frank cadging another one off someone else. By nine thirty, Stan could see that the man was getting drunk, while he decided it was time to go home.

He called his goodbyes and stepped outside, his thoughts returning to Tommy as he limped to Lark Rise. He'd say nothing to Amy, but he'd tell Phyllis that a proposal was imminent.

Celia was beginning to feel isolated and missed the social life she had once enjoyed. She wasn't invited to the Willards' for dinner now, and though she had been a member of the Conservative Club, since George left none of their acquaintances had been in touch. It was as though she'd been ostracised and it stung badly.

All she had left was her son, and Celia was relieved that he had come home before nine, a lot earlier than she'd expected. Thomas had only told her that he'd been to see someone to discuss business, and though she had pressed him, he had refused to be drawn. Celia had found that Thomas could be stubborn and forceful, traits that she hadn't been aware of before he had taken over the running of the business. In such a short time he had increased profits and trade, but she still worried that he was moving too quickly, though any attempts she made to point this out were dismissed as though her opinion counted for nothing. It angered her, but she was determined not to give up, to become more involved in the running of the business and if necessary, prevent Thomas from expanding any further in this current financial year.

An hour had now passed, but there was little conversation. Thomas was reading a book on business management, but Celia saw that he had hardly turned more than a couple of pages. She was sure he had something on his mind, and said, 'Is there something worrying you, darling?'

'No,' Thomas replied, looking up. 'What makes you think that?'

'You seem rather withdrawn.'

'I'm reading, Mother.'

'Not from what I've seen, but if you don't want to talk about it, at least we can discuss something else. I'm alone too much, Thomas, so when you *are* at home it would be nice if we could have some sort of conversation.'

'After a busy day at work and then going out earlier, I'm tired, Mother, and all I want to do is relax.'

'You're not too tired to see Amy several nights a week, and when was the last time you spent a Sunday at home with me?'

His expression hardening, Thomas said, 'Had you apologised to Amy, I'm sure if invited she would have joined us for dinner on occasional Sundays, and at other times.'

'Thomas, as I pointed out before, I wasn't myself then, and I thought Amy would be more . . . more forgiving. I . . . I'm still deeply hurt that your father left me for another woman, and . . . and . . .' Celia stuttered, forcing tears to her eyes.

'Mum, please, don't get upset again.'

'I . . . I think I'll go to bed,' Celia said as she stood up. As always, Thomas couldn't bear to see her crying; the weapon a useful one. She had won again and as she didn't want that slut of a girl in her home, nothing would induce her to apologise. She'd planted another seed against Amy, showing her to be unforgiving, and one day soon Celia hoped all her barbs would come to fruition.

Amy had finished sewing the hem of a skirt that had come loose and Phyllis said, 'With Rose getting married at the end of August, we'll have to sort out something to wear.'

'Mum, you never had a good word to say about Rose. What changed your mind?'

Phyllis sighed. She wasn't proud of herself, and was determined that in future she wouldn't be a prude, or listen to gossip. 'I jumped to the wrong conclusion about Rose and Tommy's dad, and about a lot of other things too. She's not as bad as she's been made out to be, but no doubt the gossips will be tearing her to shreds now that she's going to marry Samuel Jacobs.'

'He *is* a bit old for her, Mum.'

'Yes I know, and rich, but he knows that Rose doesn't love him so it's not as if she's making a monkey out of him. He was lonely, but now Rose takes care of him and it's given him a new lease of life,' Phyllis said, but then recalling her conversation with Rose she giggled. Old or not, it seemed that Samuel Jacobs was still capable of having an active sex life, but it wasn't something she could tell Amy.

'What's so funny?' Amy asked.

'Nothing . . . nothing, love,' Phyllis said, relieved then that Stan walked in.

'Hello, my lovelies,' he said, grinning.

'You're drunk,' Phyllis said.

'No, I'm not. If you think that you should see Frank Cole. When I left he could hardly stand up.'

'Carol's worried about him,' Amy said. 'He's so hungover every morning and since losing his job he hasn't tried to find another one.'

'Well, I don't know what they're going to do for money then,' Phyllis said. 'It's a crying shame. The man's gone to pieces since Daphne left him.'

Stan walked over and perched himself on her lap, saying with a grin, 'I'm so irresistible that I don't have to worry about you walking out on me.'

'Don't kid yourself and get off me, you daft bugger,' Phyllis appealed. 'You weigh a ton and you're squashing my legs.'

'A ton! Now you've offended me,' Stan said.

'I'll do more than offend you if you don't move.'

'Give me a kiss and I might.'

'Oh, all right,' she said, kissing him on the cheek.

'I suppose that will have to do for now,' Stan said as he stood up.

Phyllis looked at Amy, saw that her daughter was grinning, and said, 'I don't know what's so funny.'

'You two are,' Amy said. 'The way you carry on at times is hilarious, but I'm off to bed now.'

'Not before you kiss your poor downtrodden dad too.'

'I'll give you downtrodden,' Phyllis threatened.

'See what I mean. I married a dragon,' Stan said, appealing to Amy.

It didn't work, and with a swift kiss on her father's cheek she shot upstairs, her laughter trailing behind her.

'Right, Stan, what's this about a dragon?' Phyllis asked.

'You know I was only joking, and now that Amy's out of the way, I've got something to tell you.'

Phyllis listened, and though she had suspected that if Amy continued to see Tommy this would eventually happen, her stomach turned over. 'Oh, Stan,' she whispered. 'I wasn't expecting this yet.'

'I know, love, I know, but it's sure to be a long engagement so we aren't losing our daughter yet.'

His words made Phyllis feel marginally better and soon after they went to bed where she found a measure of comfort in her husband's arms. She thought about warning Amy that Tommy was going to propose, that it would give her daughter time to think long and hard about her answer – yet even if she did, Phyllis knew that Amy would still say yes.

There was no denying that Tommy and Amy loved each other, and when they eventually got married, at least there'd be something to look forward to. Grandchildren, Phyllis thought, smiling a little now as she at last drifted off to sleep.

Chapter Twenty-Two

Amy woke up on Saturday morning, her eighteenth birthday, wishing that she didn't have to go to work. At least the shop would be busy, and she'd made friends with Doreen, who'd been taken on when Linda had been sacked. Doreen was funny and they shared a few laughs when they got the chance, so with any luck the time would pass quickly and then tonight she would be going out with Tommy. Though it wasn't a big occasion like a twenty-first birthday, Tommy had told her earlier in the week that he had planned something special.

After yawning and stretching out her arms, Amy got out of bed. Her parents didn't work on Saturdays, but when she went downstairs Amy found that they were both up and seeing her, they smiled.

'Happy Birthday,' her mother said, giving her a hug, which was followed by one from her father.

Amy was then given a birthday card and a flat box tied with a ribbon. She eagerly opened it, smiling with delight when she found a pretty silver bracelet inside. 'I love it. Thanks Mum, thanks Dad,' she said, kissing them both.

'I'm glad you like it,' her mum said.

Amy then read her card, misty-eyed at her parents' words of love. Breakfast followed, and they had only just finished eating when there was a knock on the door, her mum letting Mabel in.

'Happy Birthday, Amy,' she said, passing another envelope and package. 'I wanted to catch you before you left for work.'

'Oh, thank you,' Amy enthused, quickly reading the nice card and then opening the package to find a manicure set in a small tapestry case. 'This is lovely and just what I need,' she said, hugging her.

'That's good,' Mabel said, 'but I'd best be off.'

'Thanks again,' Amy called as the woman left. It was all a rush then to get ready for work, and after her parents hugged her again, Amy hurried out of the house, only to hear a voice calling her. She turned to see Carol, still in her nightclothes as she beckoned from her doorstep.

'Happy Birthday,' Carol said as Amy hurried up to her. 'I'm sorry, but now that my dad has lost his job, money's really tight and I couldn't afford to buy you anything. Unless he finds another one soon, I'll have to be the one who goes out to work.'

'I don't think we need anyone at the shop, but I could still ask the manageress if you like.'

'Yes, all right,' Carol agreed.

'I'll let you know what she says, but I've got to run or I'll be late.'

'Thanks,' Carol called as Amy rushed off.

Though she liked Doreen, Amy still missed working with Carol, but doubted there were any vacancies. She hurried to the top of Lark Rise and then decided to hop on a bus to the Junction.

Thankfully Amy made it just in time and arrived to see the manageress opening the shop. She waited until they were inside and said, 'Mrs Jones, my friend used to work here and she'd like to come back. Are there any jobs going?'

'Not at the moment, I'm afraid,' she said as the door opened and the Saturday girl arrived.

Amy was disappointed, but it was the start of what turned out to be a busy day, and as Amy had hoped, time flew as she ran to the stock room again and again to find mainly summer sandals.

Amy measured a lot of children's feet too, sandals in demand again, but at last the working day came to an end and Amy was on her way home.

Frank Cole was in a foul mood. What he wanted was another drink, the need gnawing at him, but he'd only been able to cadge one pint at lunchtime. With no money, the regulars at the Park Tavern were fed up with buying him drinks. When there was a knock on the door he left Carol to answer it and after chatting to someone for a minute or two she closed it again.

'Who was that?' Frank asked.

'It was Amy. She came to tell me that there aren't any vacancies in the shop.'

'Who asked her to find out?'

'I did,' Carol said. 'You haven't been looking for another job so I thought I'd go back to work to bring some money in. In the meantime I suppose we could find a few things to pawn.'

'There's no need for that. I'll find a job next week.'

'Dad, even if you do, unless you stop drinking so heavily you'll never get up for work in the mornings.'

'Yes I flaming well will,' Frank said, annoyed when there was another knock on the door. 'Whoever that is you can tell them to sod off!'

Carol opened it, but then stood aside to let Davy and Paul in. Frank calmed down instantly. Both his sons were working so he should be able to tap them for a few bob. 'Hello boys. How about taking your dad out for a couple of pints?'

'Sorry, Dad, we've got plans for tonight,' Dave said. 'We've been up the King's Road and only popped in on our way home to see how you're doing.'

'If you're after a meal, forget it,' Carol said. 'There's hardly any food in the cupboards.'

'Why's that?' Paul asked, frowning.

'Dad lost his job.'

'I haven't managed to find another one yet, so is there any chance of a few quid to tide me over?' Frank asked.

'Yeah, all right,' Paul said taking out his wallet, and Dave did the same.

Frank eagerly took the proffered notes. 'Thanks, boys. I'll pay this back as soon as I can.'

'There's no hurry,' Paul said and Dave nodded in agreement.

Now that he had money, Frank was inwardly willing them to leave. He couldn't go to the Park Tavern though, as after scrounging from the regulars they'd expect him to return the favour when they saw he had funds. There was a way round that though. He'd go to a different pub, and with a good few quid he'd be able to afford a few whisky chasers.

'Have you heard anything from Mum?' Carol asked her brothers.

'No,' Dave said shortly then adding that they had to leave.

'You've hardly been here for five minutes,' Carol protested.

'Yeah, I know, but we've got to get ourselves togged up for tonight.'

They had no sooner left than Carol said, 'Dad, can I have some of that money? I need to get some food in.'

'The shops are shut now so it can wait until Monday. Now I'm off out,' he told her, and before Carol could say another word he left, heading for a pub on Lavender Hill.

At the top of the Rise, Frank recalled Carol saying that they could pawn some stuff. He hadn't liked the idea at first, but now realised that it could raise a good few bob. He was hardly in to watch it so he could sell the television too, ensuring that when this money ran out, he'd have plenty more.

Amy was in her bedroom, almost ready and wearing a pretty, blue flowered summer dress that flared at the waist and ended just below her knees. She was just putting on her make-up when she heard a knock on the front door, and after hurrying to apply a shade of pink lipstick, she ran downstairs to find that her mother had let Tommy in.

'Hello,' he said, smiling when he saw her. 'Happy Birthday, you look nice.'

'Thanks, but as I don't know where you're taking me, I wasn't sure what to wear.'

'That's fine,' Tommy said.

'Phyllis, do you remember what you were wearing when I . . .'

'Shut up, Stan.'

'Oh yeah, right, sorry.'

Amy looked at her parents, puzzled by this exchange and her father's shamefaced expression, but she didn't have time to dwell on it as Tommy said urgently, 'If you're ready, let's go.'

'I'm ready,' she smiled, saying goodbye to her parents.

Tommy opened the van door, and as she climbed in he said, 'I wish I could take you out in a nice car, but one day I hope to own one.'

'This is fine and far nicer than walking,' she replied and

when Tommy got in behind the wheel she asked, 'Are you going to tell me where we're going now?'

'No, not yet, but you'll soon see.'

Amy was puzzled as Tommy drove off, but it wasn't long before she saw Battersea Park ahead of them. 'Are we going to the funfair?'

'Yes, and I hope that's all right with you.'

'It's fine,' Amy replied. She hadn't known what to expect, and though she loved the funfair, it was the last place she'd thought about when Tommy said he was taking her somewhere special. He turned his head to smile at her, and she smiled back, thinking that she really didn't mind. She was with Tommy and that was all that mattered.

Once parked, they walked along a path, the bright lights of the funfair clear in the night sky. Soon they were going through the funfair's turnstiles and inside, where Tommy urged her towards the big wheel.

'Let's go on this before it's replaced by the new one,' he urged, saying something then to the man operating that Amy failed to hear. Moments later the wheel stopped and they climbed on, sitting side by side, with a bar put across the rocking seat which Amy thought nervously was to prevent them from falling out.

As the wheel began to turn, soon reaching the top, Tommy held her hand and Amy was enchanted by the views of the funfair stretched out below them. On the descent, Amy's stomach did a little flip, but around they went and up to the pinnacle again. The wheel came to a stop then, Amy finding it a little frightening to be suspended so high up, and when the seat they were in swung, she was unable to stifle a little yelp.

'Don't worry, you're safe,' Tommy said, placing an arm around her.

'I'm all right,' she said, laying her head on his shoulder. 'It's wonderful up here, Tommy. It feels like the two of us are alone on the top of the world.'

'See those stars, Amy,' he said, pointing up to the sky. 'I can't bring one down to slip on your finger, but I can give you this instead. Will . . . will you marry me?'

Amy could barely see the box that Tommy had flipped open with one hand, but even if it had contained a plastic ring her answer would have been the same. 'Oh, yes, Tommy. Yes please,' she said, flinging herself into his arms.

The seat rocked, but this time Amy didn't scream and Tommy's lips met hers.

'I love you, Amy,' he husked.

'And I love you,' she said as they began to move on a downward descent again.

They drew apart and Tommy smiled ruefully. 'I asked the chap who operates the wheel to stop it for a minute or two when we were at the top, but I didn't expect it to scare you.'

'I was only nervous for a moment. It was a wonderful place to propose, so romantic, magical, and something I'll never forget,' Amy said and meant it. She was eighteen, engaged to be married, and for Amy at that moment, everything was just perfect.

Chapter Twenty-Three

By the last week in August Carol was near the end of her tether. Almost everything of value had been pawned, but her dad spent most of the money on booze. With no sign of him ever getting a job she had gone back to work, and had just arrived home from the paint factory on Friday to find her dad eagerly waiting. It was payday and she knew what he wanted – but he'd have a long wait if he thought she was going to just pass over her wages again.

'Come on, Carol,' he urged, 'give me your pay-packet.'

'No, Dad,' she argued.

'Do as you're told,' he snarled in her face.

She reeled back from the stench of his breath and unwashed body, finding the father she had known almost unrecognisable. He was a hopeless drunk now, and though she felt partly to blame, Carol knew that with rent to pay and food to buy, she had to hang on to her wages. 'Dad,' she said, hoping appeasement would work as she opened her handbag to pull out a ten bob note, 'here, take this.'

With hands shaking in his need for alcohol, he snatched it from her, and as though unable to wait a moment longer to get to the pub, hurried out.

Carol's shoulders slumped with relief, yet she knew that

as soon as the money was spent her father would be back for more. Her stomach rumbled, and going through to the scullery she looked for something to eat, finding just a couple of slices of bread and a small piece of cheese, enough to make a sandwich. It would have to suffice, but Carol was determined to go shopping in the morning, to get more food in while her dad would still be in bed sleeping the booze off.

With no television to watch now, by seven thirty Carol was bored. There was housework to do, but after being at work all day she wasn't in the mood, and anyway, Carol decided, she had the weekend to tackle it.

When there was a knock on the door she was actually pleased to see Amy and let her in with a smile. 'Hello, aren't you seeing Tommy?'

'No, he's swamped with work and as we're both taking the day off tomorrow to go to Rose's wedding, he'll be working late tonight.'

Carol had once thought that Amy's life was boring, but now, compared to her own it seemed interesting. 'What will you be wearing?'

'A yellow dress and jacket,' Amy said.

'Is the dress plain or patterned?'

'It's got a pattern of small, white flowers, but the jacket is plain. With so few people going to the wedding there won't be a bit of a do afterwards, but we're going for a meal in a restaurant.'

Carol felt a stab of envy. Amy had got engaged to be married last month, her life moving forward, while Carol knew that hers had stagnated. It was as though since the loss of her baby, she'd given up on life too, but now for the first time Carol felt a longing to live again. Even the quiet wedding sounded better to Carol than being stuck at home every weekend, but at least the evening passed quickly as they continued to chat. They spoke more about Rose and her marriage, Carol musing, 'I suppose Rose is living in clover now.'

'We haven't seen Mr Jacobs' house yet,' Amy said, 'but when Rose comes to see us she always turns up in a taxi. She wears lovely clothes now too, sort of classy.'

'I bet that makes the curtains twitch, though the gossips are probably green with envy.'

'I don't envy Rose,' Amy said. 'He may be rich, but I couldn't marry an old man like Mr Jacobs.'

'I'm not sure I could either, but good luck to Rose. When he kicks the bucket she'll inherit the lot.'

'Yes, I suppose so,' Amy said, then changing the subject, 'I know you didn't like working in the paint factory at first. Is it any better now?'

'Some of the women are a laugh so that helps, and at least I don't have to work Saturdays.'

'Talking of Saturdays, I'd best be off. We'll all have to be up early in the morning to get ready for the wedding.'

'Have a nice time,' Carol said, sighing when Amy left. There'd be no nice time for her tomorrow, she'd be spending the day doing housework. For now though, not wanting to be up to see her father rolling home drunk, Carol decided to go to bed.

An hour later, Carol was in the throes of a terrible nightmare and her eyes snapped open in the dark. Someone was on top of her, hands groping – but then she screamed in terror. This wasn't a nightmare; she was awake, and desperately she fought to throw the man off whilst crying out, 'Dad! Dad, help me!'

'Shut up!'

Her mind reeling, Carol froze for a moment, unable to

believe it, yet the voice was his, along with the stench. 'No! No, Dad! It's me, Carol!' she cried frantically. 'Stop it!'

Still it continued, her father deaf to her cries, and almost out of her mind, Carol hit out in the darkness, punching, yanking his hair, and when he yelled she found a surge of strength, enough to throw him off her body.

Frantic to get away from her father, Carol scrambled from the bed and fled downstairs where, grabbing an old raincoat from the hook, she ran from the house.

Carol flung the coat on as she headed for the one place where she knew she'd be safe, protected. Her chest heaving, she only paused occasionally to draw breath, aware of nothing around her but her need to get there, until at last she arrived and thumped frantically on the door. Nobody came, nobody opened it, and sobbing she sank down onto the doorstep.

With no idea of the time, Carol didn't know how long she sat there, her mind in turmoil at what her father had tried to do, until at last her brothers turned up. Carol rose unsteadily and almost fell into Paul's arms.

'Carol, what's wrong? What are you doing here? Are you hurt?' he asked urgently.

'No . . . no,' she croaked, feeling her legs crumbling beneath her.

Paul lifted her up, carried her inside and laid her gently onto the sofa, while Davy said, 'Carol, you've got nothing on your feet and they're bleeding. What the hell happened?'

'I . . . he . . . he . . .' she stammered.

'A man did this to you?' Paul growled. 'Who was it? When we get our hands on him we'll kill him!'

Carol couldn't take any more – couldn't bear to relive what had happened again and her mind closed down. Exhausted, she closed her eyes and sank into darkness.

*   *   *

Paul looked down at his sister the following morning. She was still asleep, and seeing the dried blood on her feet again, his lips tightened in anger. Until Carol woke up it was hard to make sense of what had happened, but sick at the thought that she'd been raped, he said to Dave, 'Look at her. She's still in her nightdress, so whoever did this must have broken into the house.'

'But where was Dad?' Dave asked.

'We don't know what time it happened, so maybe he was out.'

'Yeah, that's probably it, but surely he'd have seen that she wasn't there when he came home?' Dave pointed out.

'He might have assumed she was in bed.'

'True,' Dave agreed, 'but he's going to notice that she isn't there this morning.'

'If Carol's up to it we'll have to take her home, but if she's been raped Dad's going to do his nut.'

'No! No, I don't want to go home!' Carol cried, suddenly sitting up.

Surprised Paul said, 'I thought you were still asleep.'

'Please,' Carol begged. 'Don't make me go home.'

It she'd been attacked in her own bed, no wonder she was too scared to go back, Paul thought. 'All right, stay here for now. Dave can shoot down to tell Dad where you are.'

'No! No, he mustn't tell him I'm here!'

Confused, Paul asked, 'Why not?'

'Be . . . because he . . . he tried . . . in my bed . . . I . . . I fought him off, got away,' Carol sobbed, her words disjointed.

'Flaming hell,' Dave said. 'Surely you're not saying that Dad tried it on?'

Carol nodded, tears rolling down her cheeks, but Paul

203

couldn't believe it, didn't *want* to believe it and said, 'Dad wouldn't do that. He was probably drunk and stumbled into your room instead of his own.'

'He . . . he might have been drunk, but I woke up to find him on . . . on top of me and his hands were . . . were all over me.'

Paul felt bile rising in his throat and unable to stand the sound of his sister crying, he strode to the kitchen. He put water in the kettle and then placed it on the gas before taking three cups from the cupboard.

'What are you doing?' Dave asked as he appeared in the doorway.

'Ain't it obvious?' Paul snapped. 'I'm making us a drink.'

'You must be kidding. Carol just told us that Dad tried it on with her, and all you're doing is making tea.'

'Oh, I intend to do more than that. First though Carol probably needs a drink and her feet need to be sorted, bathed.'

'Then what?'

'Then you and I are going to take a walk to Lark Rise,' Paul growled.

Mabel had been disturbed by the yelling soon after she'd gone to bed last night, but she'd vowed to keep her nose out of anyone's business now, especially the Coles'.

Yet here it was, just after nine in the morning, and while they were eating breakfast, the Coles were at it again. It even disturbed Jack this time and he looked up from his morning paper to say, 'I don't know what's going on next door, but they're making a hell of a racket.'

Something thumped loudly against the adjoining wall, and Mabel jumped. 'It sounds like someone's throwing furniture around.'

'Yes, it does,' Jack agreed. 'Maybe I should go and see what's going on.'

'No, don't do that. It's none of our business,' Mabel said, 'and anyway, if there's some sort of fight going on, I don't want you getting involved in it.'

'All right, I'll stay put,' Jack agreed.

There was more shouting, but then abruptly, blissfully, it all went quiet. 'Well I don't know what that was all about,' Mabel said.

'Me neither,' Jack replied, but then went back to his newspaper.

For a moment Mabel wondered if she should go next door to check that everyone was all right, but then decided against it. Frank Cole would only slam the door in her face again.

Mabel ruminated, wondering again if she was right, that instead of Rose, it had been Daphne Cole who had gone off with George Frost. The dates matched, but once again she had kept her suspicions to herself.

Mind you, maybe it wouldn't hurt to tell Phyllis. After all, no doubt it would come to light one day, these things always did – and then, Mabel thought, smiling smugly – she'd be proved right.

Unaware that anything untoward had happened in the Coles' house, Amy was sitting beside Tommy in the registry office, fiddling with her engagement ring. She loved the diamond solitaire, and though she knew Tommy would have liked the stone to be a bigger one, Amy was happy with his choice. On her small, thin finger the diamond appeared large, and now, looking up, Amy had to smile at the scene of Rose standing beside the rotund, grey-haired Samuel Jacobs as the two of them listened to the registrar's words. Rose looked lovely in a pale pink, shot silk suit, her hat pink too and delightfully frivolous with its tiny veil.

'My feet are killing me,' her mother hissed from Amy's other side. 'One of the straps on these sandals is cutting into my big toe.'

'I've got a plaster in my handbag,' Amy hissed back, thinking that though her mother was complaining, she looked lovely too in a beige suit and hat, the brim trimmed with white ribbon which matched her bag and sandals. It had been hard to find suitable outfits that didn't cost a fortune, but they'd been lucky when they found a ladies' dress shop that was shutting down. With a bit of bargaining, her mother had got her hat thrown in too, but Amy didn't think that any she tried on suited her, so had decided not to wear one.

It had been a lovely surprise to find that Rose had arranged a car to pick them up, so they had arrived in style, but now Amy looked at the other guests, two dour-faced middle-aged couples. They had hardly acknowledged them when they turned up, and Amy wasn't looking forward to sitting with them in the restaurant. She felt it might be a bit strained, but then to her surprise it was suddenly all over. It had happened so quickly, but Rose and Samuel Jacobs signed the register, and then shortly afterwards they were all outside.

'Congratulations,' her mother said to Rose and Mr Jacobs.

'Yes, from me too,' said her dad, shaking the old man's hand.

'Thank you,' he said, smiling.

The other two couples said nothing but Amy stepped forward to kiss Rose on the cheek. 'You look lovely,' she enthused, and meant it. 'Congratulations.'

'You look lovely too,' Rose said. 'The table is booked for two so I think we should make our way to the restaurant.'

One of the dour-faced men stepped forward then and said, 'Samuel, we won't be coming. Rachel is rather tired.'

'I see, and what about you, Sidney? Will you and Helen be joining us?'

'We've got a long drive home, so no.'

'Right, goodbye then,' Samuel said shortly.

'They don't like me,' Rose said as they walked away.

'It's the thought of losing my money they don't like. Now come, my dear, let's get to the restaurant.'

'Phyllis, the car is still waiting for you so we'll see you all there,' Rose called.

The drive only took about ten minutes, and as soon as they walked into the restaurant they were led to a table. It looked lovely, with a white, crisp linen tablecloth, beautifully folded napkins and sparkling glasses. There seemed to be so much cutlery, several knives and forks laid out at each setting and Amy looked at them worriedly. She glanced at her mother, saw that she looked intimidated too, but then Rose hissed, 'I was the same at first, but don't panic. Just watch me and do what I do.'

They both smiled gratefully, and no sooner were they all seated than a waiter poured them a glass of what Amy supposed was champagne. To her surprise she saw her father rise to his feet to offer up his flute in a toast, 'To Samuel and Rose.'

'To Samuel and Rose,' the rest of them chorused as Amy noticed that despite her mum's best efforts, her dad's old suit that he'd had for years still looked shiny. There had been no money left for a new one, but he hadn't complained, happy for them to buy new clothes.

The meal began, and watching Rose, Amy was able to

pick up the right cutlery for each course. Samuel Jacobs was charming, amusing, and Amy liked him. Her mother had always called their landlord an old skinflint, but she seemed to have warmed towards him too.

'Rose has told me that you two are engaged,' Samuel said. 'Have you set a date for your wedding?'

'Not yet,' Amy replied.

'When you do, and if you need a house to rent, just let me know and I'll see what I can do.'

'That's jolly kind of you, sir,' Tommy enthused.

'Samuel, you must all call me Samuel, or Sam. After all, we're family now.'

'Here's to that,' Rose said, lifting her glass.

As Amy smiled at Tommy, she was unaware that her mother had had a sudden idea, or that she'd soon be in league with Rose to make sure that if possible, it would come to fruition.

Though they'd been over it before, Paul found himself talking about it again. 'I was fuming, ready to lay into Dad, to pulverise him, but he was so pathetic that I couldn't touch him.'

'Yeah, I was the same,' Dave said, 'and I took my temper out on the furniture instead.'

'What did he say about me?' Carol asked anxiously, looking ridiculous in a pair of Dave's rolled-up jeans and a shirt that came down to her knees.

'That he was sorry, and sickened by what he'd done. He was drunk, Carol, and staggered into your room by mistake. He was so full of booze that the poor sod thought you were Mum.'

'Yeah, he was crying like a baby,' said Dave.

'Yes, yes, you've already told me,' Carol snapped, 'but I

don't care what excuses he made, I'm not going home. Dad gets drunk every night and he might make the same mistake again.'

'I don't think he will. I think you'll be safe now,' Dave said.

'You *think* I'd be safe! What good's that?' Carol said bitterly.

Paul realised that his sister was right. Carol had fought their dad off this time, but if the same thing happened there was no guarantee that she'd be able to again. 'You're not going home,' he said firmly. 'You're staying here.'

'Oh, thank goodness for that,' Carol said, visibly slumping with relief. 'If you'd refused to let me stay, I would've been stuck with asking Gran to take me in.'

'That'd be a barrel of laughs,' Paul said. 'You'll be all right here. Dave can share my bedroom and then you can have his.'

'I dunno about that,' Dave complained. 'What about when I bring a girl home?'

'Don't worry about it. We'll work something out,' Paul told his brother.

'I'll need my clothes,' Carol said, 'and my other things, make-up and stuff.'

'Right then, come on, Dave. If we want to try out that place in Old Compton Street tonight, we'd better get Carol's stuff now.'

'What place?' Carol asked.

'It's a coffee bar, called the 2i's. A skiffle group called The Vipers perform there and we've heard they're good.'

'Paul, will you do something else for me? If I write a quick note, would you give it to Amy? If there's no one in, just shove it through the letterbox.'

'Yes, all right,' Paul agreed, and soon he and Dave were

on their way to Lark Rise. He wasn't looking forward to seeing his father again, unable to believe that the man he'd looked up to had turned into a pathetic drunk; one who was so out of his mind on booze that he'd almost raped his own daughter.

Chapter Twenty-Four

As Tommy had feared, his mother had reacted badly to his engagement. There had been more histrionics and tears, but he'd stood firm and she had lapsed into sullen silence. That had been over four months ago, and his mother had calmed down since then, the subject never mentioned – as though by burying her head in the sand she thought it would go away.

Tommy had left it like that, but nothing was going to stop him from marrying Amy and he'd put all his energies into expanding the business. It was now the end of October, and the contract to supply windows on the housing development had been completed on schedule. On the strength of recommendations from the builder Tommy hoped to acquire another large one. In the meantime other, smaller jobs were flowing in so he'd kept the men on, and when on full stretch he often worked late, cutting glass ready for the next day's work. It was something else his mother complained about, but he wasn't late when he arrived home at five on Friday, his chest heaving from another asthma attack.

'If you aren't careful you'll go down with bronchitis again. You're working too hard, doing too much,' his mother warned, rushing to his aid until at last, his breathing came under control.

Tommy knew she was right and hated his weakness, but too drained to discuss it now, he closed his eyes. If he got another contract, along with the work that was coming in now, the only answer would be to take on more men, but that would entail buying more vans too. He'd have to look at the accounts to see if that was a viable option. For now he was too tired to think and with his breathing easier, his mind closed as he drifted off.

'What . . .' Tommy said, blinking as his mother's voice intruded.

'I said it's after seven and you haven't had anything to eat yet.'

Tommy rubbed his eyes, hardly aware that he'd gone to sleep as his mother continued, 'Now you're awake I'll reheat your dinner.'

'All right, thanks,' he said, sitting up. He hadn't seen Amy since Tuesday and was missing her, and though they were going out tonight he would have to get up early in the morning to get to the yard. Tommy knew he couldn't let up on the work. He didn't want a long engagement; he wanted to marry Amy as soon as possible, and to make that happen he'd graft for seven days a week if necessary.

'There's been a right old carry on today,' Phyllis told her daughter when she came home from work.

'What do you mean?' Amy asked.

'Frank Cole has been evicted.'

'No, but that's awful. Why?'

'Because he hadn't paid his rent for ages and on top of that his place is in such a filthy state that it's infested with rats. Mabel found one in her kitchen and went absolutely barmy.'

'It's still awful that he's been chucked out. Couldn't Rose

212

have done something? She must've known him from when she worked in the Park Tavern.'

'She tried, but Samuel is a businessman and when his tenants don't pay the rent for that length of time, they're out. At least Frank has got somewhere to go. He'll probably turn up on his sons' doorstep, so Carol's going to be stuck with him again.'

'Yes, I suppose so,' Amy said.

Phyllis frowned. 'Frank fell apart when Daphne left. He's turned into a dirty, smelly drunk, scrounging off everyone, but like you, I still feel sorry for him. Did I tell you that Mabel now thinks that it was Daphne Cole who ran off with Tommy's dad?'

'Yes, but I hope she's not spreading it around. There's been enough trouble caused by gossip.'

'Mabel has learned her lesson. She only told me, but has Carol heard from her mother?'

'She's never mentioned it, so I don't think so,' Amy replied.

'Does Carol still like living with her brothers?'

'Yes, and she's got a new job as a receptionist in a hairdressing salon. Paul and Davy take her out with them and she's like her old self again, into the latest fashions and music.'

'That's good, but here's your dad so I'd better get our dinner sorted out,' Phyllis said as she hurried through to the scullery. She had something else to tell Amy and Stan, and though she had made a tentative decision, she was still a bit unsure.

Stan seemed unsurprised when they told him about Frank, and though sympathetic, he said that the man had turned into such a scrounger that he'd been barred from the Park Tavern. When they were seated at the table, Stan

213

lightened the atmosphere by joking around, pretending his chop was too tough to cut. 'What's this,' he asked, 'the sole off an old shoe?'

'Mine's all right,' Amy said.

'Your dad's is too,' Phyllis said. 'Stan, stop being a silly bugger and listen. I haven't said anything until now, because I've been thinking about it since Rose came to see me.'

'Thinking about what?' Stan asked.

'Rose isn't happy in Bethnal Green so she's persuaded Samuel to buy a place here in Battersea. They've already found a house close to the park, and Rose wants me to work for them.'

'Doing what?' Stan asked.

'I'd be a sort of housekeeper-cum-cleaner.'

'Can't Rose do her own cleaning?' Stan asked.

'Of course she can, but Rose has gone up in the world now. She's got used to having a cleaner, but the one they've got now won't want to travel this far.'

'How big is the house they've found?' Amy asked.

'It's got six bedrooms, two receptions, a dining room and study, two bathrooms and a kitchen.'

'Flaming hell, why do they want a house of that size?' Stan exclaimed. 'There's only the two of them.'

'It's about the same as the one in Bethnal Green,' Phyllis said. 'Anyway, Rose has offered me a third more pay than I'm earning now.'

'That sounds good,' Stan said.

'Yes, it does,' Amy agreed, 'but how many hours would you have to do?'

'From nine till two, five days a week.'

'That's not much different to your combined jobs, so why are you thinking about it?' Stan asked. 'It's more money, without an early start, or going out to clean that factory in the evening.'

'I know, but it's . . . well . . . it's the thought of being Rose's cleaner. What if she lords it up over me? I'm not sure I could take that.'

'I can't see Rose acting all high and mighty,' Stan said. 'She's always struck me as being pretty down to earth.'

'Is Rose any different when she comes to see you?' Amy asked.

'No, of course not, but that's different,' Phyllis replied. 'She visits me as my cousin, but if I take the job I'd be her employee.'

'Why don't you give it a try?' Stan suggested. 'If it doesn't work out and Rose becomes a proper madam, you can soon tell her where to stick her job.'

Phyllis smiled at Stan's turn of phrase, but he was right and she made up her mind to take the job. No more getting up at the crack of dawn, no more factory floors to clean – and for Phyllis, that sounded like heaven.

Mabel had kept out of the way during the eviction. In truth, she was glad that Frank Cole had been chucked out. He hadn't confronted her yet, but every night when he'd rolled home drunk her nerves had jangled, expecting him to come banging on her door to lay into her for dobbing him in to the police. She'd watched Frank going downhill over the past few months, but it wasn't her fault, Mabel decided. It was down to Daphne Cole for walking out on him and it was no wonder that Carol had left home too.

When she'd found a rat, it gave Mabel the ammunition she needed to get rid of Frank Cole. Of course nobody knew it, but she'd complained to the agent, hinting that the infestation was coming from Frank's house. When the agent gained entry he'd come out looking green and had thrown up in the gutter. With that and the rent arrears, it had ensured Frank's eviction and good riddance to bad rubbish, Mabel thought. She could relax now, and as the sun set she turned on the living room light just as Jack arrived home.

'Hello love, things have been happening today,' she said, going on to tell him about Frank Cole.

'He used to be a decent bloke,' Jack said, 'but only last night he collared me on the way home to tap me for money.'

'Did you give him any?' Mabel asked.

'Certainly not. I told him to get a job and earn his money like the rest of us. For that I got a load of foul language and insults aimed at you.'

'That doesn't surprise me, and between you and me, Jack, I'm glad he's gone. It's just us and the Millers sandwiched between two empty houses now, and with Frank's house needing more than just fumigating, it could be for some time.'

'Has the agent arranged to do anything about the rats?' Jack asked.

'Yes, he's getting poison put down,' Phyllis told him, shuddering at the memory of finding a big, dirty grey rat in her kitchen. 'I just hope we don't get any more coming in here.'

'I'll put some stuff down too just in case,' Jack said. 'Now, I'm going to get washed and changed.'

'Yes, all right,' Mabel said, knowing that once he'd done that Jack would want his dinner. She walked into the scullery, her eyes darting everywhere as she turned on the light. If she'd seen another rat it would have sent her out screaming again, but thankfully there were none to be seen.

Mabel knew there was another quiet evening ahead, with Jack's nose stuck in a book, but at least now that Frank Cole had left the Rise, things were looking up and her life could get back to normal. Or so she hoped.

Chapter Twenty-Five

Amy was looking out for Carol as she walked along Lavender Hill after work on Saturday. They came from opposite directions, and often bumped into each other, Amy now waving an arm as she saw Carol walking towards her. 'Hello,' she said as they met up. 'Your hair looks nice.'

'I'm going out with the boys tonight, and though the salon was busy one of the stylists quickly put it up for me.'

'How's your dad? It must have been awful for him to get chucked out of his house like that.'

'It was his own fault,' Carol said without any sign of sympathy. 'He should have got a job and paid the rent.'

'I suppose he's living with you and your brothers now?'

'No, he isn't with us. He turned up looking for money last night, and once he got his hands on a few bob he buggered off, which is just as well because there's no way I'd live under the same roof as him again.'

Amy supposed it was because Carol's father was a drunk, but it still seemed so hard and she asked, 'So where is he now?'

'I've no idea, though I'd guess that he's sleeping rough somewhere with the rest of the down and outs.'

'But that's awful,' Amy exclaimed. 'Aren't you going to try to find him?'

'No, I'm not, and if you knew what my father did to me, you'd understand why. Now I've got to go, so bye for now,' Carol said, abruptly walking off towards her brothers' flat.

Amy was left bewildered. She knew that Carol's dad had turned into a drunk, but now it sounded as though something else had happened to turn her against him. With no idea what he had done, Amy was left to wonder as she continued on her way home.

Carol stomped upstairs to the flat. Her brothers were at home, only working overtime on the occasional Saturday, and Paul cocked his head as he looked at her, asking, 'What's got up your nose? I can see by your boat race that you're in a strop.'

'I bumped into Amy, and because you insisted that I kept my mouth shut about what Dad did to me, she looked shocked that I don't give a damn about him being evicted.'

'Give it a rest, Carol,' said Dave. 'It happened months ago, but you keep going on about it. We've told you over and over again that Dad was drunk, that he didn't know what he was doing and like us, you should give him the benefit of the doubt. We're worried about him since he shot off yesterday, and though we've been having a scout round we can't find him. We'll give it another go tomorrow.'

Carol was still sick with worry, fearing that her dad would one day blurt it out – that he'd tell her brothers about the abortion. Not only that, the thought of having him anywhere near her was more than she could bear. 'If you find him, don't bring him here. You weren't there that night! I was and I'm still having nightmares. I screamed at Dad, yelled at him, told him it was me, Carol, but it didn't stop him. He may have been drunk, but he wasn't deaf!'

'You never told us that,' Paul said sharply.

'Yes I did. I must have done,' Carol protested.

'No, you didn't,' said Dave. 'You just said he came into your room and that you had to fight him off.'

'Dave, do you know what this means?' Paul asked.

'Yeah, that Dad lied to us. He must have known it was Carol, but the filthy pig told us he thought she was Mum,' Dave said, his features now tight with anger.

'Well that's it. He can rot in hell,' Paul growled, 'and he'd better not turn up here again.'

Carol hadn't realised that she'd left out some of what had happened that night and felt a huge sense of relief that her brothers believed her now. If they had found their dad and taken him in, she would have been forced to leave, but that wasn't going to happen now. She loved living with Paul and Davy – loved it when they took her out with them. Her bad mood lightening, she said, 'Come on, let's forget about Dad. We're going to the 2i's coffee bar tonight and I wonder who'll be performing.'

'Another lot of hopefuls I should think,' Paul said. 'Since that Tommy Hicks was spotted and signed up with Decca, the place is buzzing.'

'He's just had a record released called *Rock with the Caveman*, but he's changed his name to Tommy Steele now,' Dave said.

Carol hadn't thought much of the small coffee bar when her brothers had first taken her there, the live music played in the basement, but now it had become the in place to be.

It was great to be a part of a new, emerging music scene and now Carol felt that she was really living again.

*   *   *

Rose was excited. They'd already exchanged contracts on the new house in Battersea and as it was an empty property, they'd soon be moving in. 'If it's all right with you, I'll pop down to see Phyllis in the morning. I want to find out if she's made up her mind about coming to work for us.'

'My dear,' Samuel said, 'you don't have to ask my permission every time you want to go out.'

'I know, but I don't like leaving you on your own for too long. You could come with me.'

'No, Rose. As you know, I've just evicted one of my tenants on Lark Rise and feelings might be running high among his neighbours.'

'I suppose it's possible,' Rose said, wondering if as Samuel's wife, she'd take some stick too. 'I did try to dissuade you, but you wouldn't listen to me.'

'Rose, I run a business, not a charity, and I can't allow my tenants to accrue rent arrears that they'll never be able to repay.'

'I know, I'm not criticising you.'

'I'm glad to hear it. Now you go along to see Phyllis in the morning and don't worry about me. I'm not so doddery that I need constant care. You're my wife, Rose, not my nurse.'

Rose grinned, 'I'd say that what we got up to last night proves you don't need nursing.'

'My father never did,' Samuel said. 'He lived into his late eighties and was comparatively healthy until the day he died.'

'That's wonderful,' Rose managed to enthuse, though inwardly thinking that if Samuel lived that long, it would be many, many years before she became a rich widow. Still, as things were at the moment she wasn't complaining. Samuel was generous, her extensive new wardrobe proved that, along

221

with her weekly allowance. He'd also recently suggested driving lessons so that she could have her own car.

She had soon adapted to living in luxury, Rose thought, and when she went to visit her cousin now the contrast in their lifestyles was starkly obvious. Though she knew she could help her cousin financially, Rose also guessed that Phyllis would be too proud to accept handouts. At least in offering her the job as their cleaner, Phyllis would be earning more money, and that was a start.

She'd just have to be devious, Rose decided, in finding other ways to help Phyllis, if not financially then in other areas. She looked around the sitting room and an idea came to mind, one that would serve them both. She'd have to get around Samuel, but she'd already found that as long as he was in the right mood, it wasn't too difficult.

Rose smiled. When they went to bed, she knew just how to make Samuel amenable to her suggestions. She glanced at the clock – it was far too early to retire yet, but later she would get her own way.

At ten thirty that evening, after going to the cinema with Tommy, Amy was snuggled up to him in his van, parked outside her house. The summer was over and the autumn evening chilly, but in the van they were protected from a fall of light rain.

'Sorry,' Tommy said after yawning widely.

'You're tired, and with the hours you're working I'm not surprised.'

'I'm fine and as it's Sunday tomorrow I can have a lie in,' he said.

Amy placed her hand gently on his cheek, saying softly, 'That's something I suppose. At least you aren't working seven days a week.'

'If it could bring the date of our wedding forward, I would.'

'We haven't discussed a date,' Amy told him.

'If business continues to go well, and if I get a nice big contract again, how do you feel about next spring . . . perhaps April?'

'I'd love that, but what if you don't get a large contract?' Amy asked as she drew away from Tommy. 'I know we're not going to have a big wedding, but we'd still need a firm date to book the registry office.'

Tommy bit his lower lip in thought and then said, 'Do you think Rose's husband meant it when he said he'd rent us one of his houses?'

'Yes, I'm sure he did.'

'Well then, new contract or not, if we start off in something small, maybe a one-bedroom flat, the rent would be low.'

'We'd have my wages too,' Amy pointed out.

'I don't expect you to work when we're married.'

'Tommy, there's no need for me to stay at home just to clean a one-bedroom flat.'

'I still don't like the idea, but we can talk about that another time. For now, come here and give me a kiss,' he said.

Amy went willingly into his arms, melting as their kisses grew deeper, until aware of Tommy's rising passion, she breathlessly pulled away. 'I . . . I'm sorry, Tommy. I want to wait until we're married.'

'I know,' he groaned, and though obviously frustrated he added, 'I do too, so let's make a firm date for the second Saturday in April.'

Amy willingly agreed and soon after she slipped out of the van to go indoors, still smiling with happiness.

*　　*　　*

Stan had just come in from the pub, followed shortly by Amy, and seeing the look on her daughter's face, Phyllis said, 'You look chuffed about something.'

'I am,' Amy said, her eyes sparkling. 'We've set a date for the wedding.'

'What! Already!' Stan exclaimed.

'It's all right, Dad. It won't be until next year . . . in April.'

'But you've hardly been engaged for five minutes,' he protested.

'It's been four months, and by next April it will have been ten.'

Unlike Stan, Phyllis was happy about the date, and said, 'That gives us six months to sort out all the arrangements.'

'Mum, I've already talked to Tommy and we've decided on a small, registry office wedding.'

'No, Amy,' Phyllis protested. 'I want to see my daughter walking down the aisle in church, wearing a beautiful, flowing white gown that's fit for a princess.'

'I'm sorry, but it isn't what we want.'

'Tommy might want a simple wedding, but I can't believe it's what *you* want, Amy. Every girl dreams of a huge white wedding.'

'But don't you see, Mum, it wouldn't be huge. There's just us, Rose and Samuel, along with a few friends. On Tommy's side of the church, if his mother refuses to come, the pews would be virtually empty too.'

'She's got a point, love,' Stan said.

Phyllis didn't want to admit it, but Amy was right – a church wedding would be a very spartan affair. As for Celia Frost, it made her fume that she still chose to ignore Amy and she hoped the woman would end up alone and lonely as she deserved. Pushing Tommy's mother from her mind, Phyllis said, 'Fine, a registry office it is, but I still want it to be a special day, Amy, with you in a lovely dress, and flowers, lots of flowers.'

'All right, Mum, whatever you say, and afterwards we could sort of copy Rose and go to a restaurant.'

Phyllis was happy with that, and with something she knew that she was keeping as a surprise. Unbeknown to Amy, Rose had already had a word with Samuel, but he hadn't been happy about the length of time that could be involved. Now though, with the wedding only six months away, Phyllis hoped her plan could come to fruition. If it did, everything would be just perfect, and Stan would be over the moon too.

Celia had made Thomas a cup of cocoa before they retired for the night, and after drinking it he said, 'Mother, before we go to bed I have something to tell you. Amy and I are going to marry next year and we've decided on April.'

She stared at him in horror. 'No, Thomas, you can't mean that!'

'I'd hardly say it if I didn't mean it.'

'Next April! No, I can't believe it.'

'I don't see why. We're engaged and you must have known the wedding would follow.'

'I didn't want to think about it.'

'I know . . . you buried your head in the sand, but you've got to face up to it now. Amy is going to be my wife, *your* daughter-in-law and you've got to accept that. You've also got to stop slighting Amy. It's gone on for long enough.'

'I haven't *got* to do anything,' Celia snapped.

Thomas reacted angrily, his voice rising. 'Fine, but if that's your attitude, think about this. When I marry my loyalties will be to my wife – and I won't be visiting you if Amy isn't welcome too.

Celia's stomach churned with a mixture of anger and fury. Thomas had made his feelings clear. If she didn't accept Amy, she'd lose him too. It rankled, but there really was no other choice and she said, 'Thomas, you know I couldn't bear that. All right, invite Amy to join us for dinner tomorrow and I'll do my best to make her welcome.'

The anger drained from his face as Thomas said, 'You won't regret it, Mum. Amy is a sweet, kind person and I'm sure that like me, you'll grow to love her.'

Celia felt like telling her son that hell would freeze over before that happened, but Thomas stood up, leaned over to kiss her and said he was going to bed. She bade him good-night, and watched him leave the room, while she was left still inwardly fuming.

Thomas had chosen Amy over her, and now he had the audacity to virtually blackmail her into accepting the common slut too. While words of vitriol against Amy poured into her mind, Celia grabbed a writing pad, putting them all down on paper, along with everything that had happened since George walked out.

When it was finished, Celia found an envelope and the last address she had for her son Jeremy. He had probably moved on by now so might never receive it; but if he did, Jeremy would at least know what a terrible life his mother now suffered, Celia thought.

Chapter Twenty-Six

Phyllis looked around her living room, smiling, despite the cold and wet Thursday December morning. When Rose had moved into her new house, she'd insisted on some new furniture, and as always Samuel had given in to her.

To save her the hassle of getting rid of it, Rose had begged her to take some of the furniture from the Bethnal Green house off her hands and Phyllis had been happy to oblige. The suite may be old, but to Phyllis it was beautiful, the fabric a plush rose brocade that showed hardly any signs of wear. It was a bit large for her small living room, but Phyllis didn't care, and though she'd only been able to make use of one pair of the matching, pinch pleat curtains, they made the room look warm and inviting, if a little crowded. The Christmas tree didn't help; though only a small one it took up one side of the hearth, one of the chairs in front of it hiding the lower branches. She'd forgone any other decorations, just putting ornaments on the tree, and it did look rather nice, Phyllis thought, smiling at the very old, homemade angel on the top.

Of course Phyllis knew her home was still nothing in comparison to her cousin's, but she didn't envy or begrudge Rose her change of fortunes. Instead she was growing ever closer to her cousin and looked forward to going to work every day. With that in mind, Phyllis put her coat on, grabbed her umbrella and hurried out. The scaffolding was still up outside the house, along with Mabel's and the empty ones on either side of them, though in this weather Phyllis doubted the roofers would be working that day.

Phyllis was glad she didn't have to worry about the weather. It was lovely and warm in Rose's house and any worries she'd had that her cousin would lord it over her had soon been dispelled. In fact, Rose insisted that they do the housework together, which meant it took a lot less than five hours, leaving them loads of time to spend in the kitchen, chatting over cups of tea.

With the wind buffeting her umbrella, by the time Phyllis arrived she was soaked. Rose took one look at her and urged her to the kitchen where her coat was swiftly removed, a towel handed to her and dry slippers offered for her feet.

'You should have stayed at home,' Rose chided. 'I could have managed without you.'

'It'll be Christmas soon and with saving for Amy's wedding too, I didn't want to lose five hours' pay.'

'You silly mare, I'd still have given you your full wage,' Rose protested as she poured two hot drinks. 'Here, get this down you and you can dry off before we start work.'

'I feel guilty enough without letting you pay me when I don't turn up,' Phyllis said, voicing her feelings.

'I don't get it. What have you got to feel guilty about?'

'Rose, even if I did it on my own, it wouldn't take five hours a day to clean this house. Most of the bedrooms aren't used, and with just you and Samuel living here the rest of the house is so tidy that it hardly needs one pair of hands, let alone two to keep it nice.'

'Leave it out. There's polishing, hoovering, along with the laundry and ironing.'

'They'd still get done if you cut my hours.'

'No, I don't want to do that,' Rose said, shaking her head emphatically.

'You must,' Phyllis insisted. 'I'm not daft and though I really appreciate what you're doing, it's making me feel like a charity case.'

'Now hold on, you've got it all wrong. Our last cleaner did the same hours as you, and this house is about the same size.'

'Yes, but did you help her to clean it?'

'Well, no, but I enjoy doing it with you,' Rose answered. 'We have a laugh, and if you must know I don't want to cut your hours because I love having you here every day. Samuel isn't one for conversation, at least not women's talk, and I'd go potty if I only had him for company.'

'I thought you were paying me for five hours' work because you think I need the money.'

'Phyllis, I don't know where you got that daft idea from, but now that we've sorted it out, get that drink down you and we can make a start on the living room. Oh, and by the way, I've got a nice dinner service put by for Amy.'

'Rose . . .' Phyllis warned.

'Now don't start again. It isn't charity; it's one the last people who lived here left behind and I found it boxed up in the cellar. With the amount of china I've got already, I haven't got room in my cupboards for another one, and anyway, it isn't as nice. There are lots of other bits and pieces down there too, but if you're going to turn funny every time I offer stuff I was going to chuck out anyway, I won't bother again.'

'I'm sorry, Rose. I know I can be a bit touchy.'

'A bit! Now that's an understatement,' Rose said, chuckling.

Phyllis pushed her playfully on the arm and for the next hour they worked companionably together, chatting. During a pause Rose asked, 'How is it going with Celia Frost?'

'It isn't going anywhere. As you know we were invited to dinner, but the woman acted as though she's related to royalty and it got right up my nose. It was worse when I returned the invitation and she actually inspected her knife and fork before using them. For Amy's sake I managed to keep my mouth shut, but the less I see of that stuck-up cow the better.'

'So you won't be spending Christmas together as a family then?'

'You must be joking. No thanks.'

'I know it's only twelve days to Christmas and it's a bit late to suggest it, but how about coming here?'

'Or you could come to us,' Phyllis said.

'No offence, love, but it'd be a bit of a squash.'

'None taken, and anyway, you're right,' Phyllis agreed.

'So you'll come here?' Rose urged.

'Yes, we'd love to.'

'Smashing, but maybe you should run it past Stan and Amy first.'

'Stan gets on really well with Samuel and I know he'll agree, and as I doubt Celia Frost will invite Amy to spend Christmas with her, I should think she'll be happy to come here too.'

'That's settled then,' Rose said as they carried on cleaning. She broke off occasionally to spend a little time with Samuel, and then at twelve thirty they all shared lunch together, something else her cousin had insisted on from the day that Phyllis started working for her.

Samuel picked up the second half of his sandwich, but

before biting into it he said, 'Phyllis, my agent has told me that the work on your house and the others is near completion.'

'Thank you, Samuel. It'll be lovely for us not to have leaky roofs.'

'Yes, well, though it's costing me a lot of money, Rose pointed out that I've been a bit remiss in keeping my properties in good repair.'

When Rose winked at her, Phyllis hid a smile. They'd been complaining for years without result, but Rose had worked wonders in such a short time. Samuel may have been a skinflint in the past, but it seemed he was putty in Rose's hands.

Rose now said, 'Samuel, it makes sound business sense. If you don't maintain your properties, they'll end up only fit for demolition.'

'Yes, yes, but it'll take a long time to recoup the cost of the work in rent payments.'

Phyllis was hardly listening as she felt a surge of excitement at something else that Rose had achieved. Once the repairs were done and the house decorated, she'd pass on the news, but for now she was keeping it a secret – a lovely one that she'd enjoy revealing.

It was Amy's half day. It had been raining when she left for work that morning, forcing her to get a bus to work, and it was still teeming down now. She swiftly put up her umbrella as she left the shop, deciding that bad weather or not, she had to buy her Christmas presents, and then nearly bumped headlong into Miss Winters.

'Isn't this rain awful?' the woman said. 'I think it's going to ease off soon, but in the meantime why don't you join me for a cup of coffee?'

Amy would rather get on with her shopping, but seeing the appeal in Miss Winters' eyes she agreed and they dashed into Arding &Hobbs, hurriedly folding their umbrellas. The Christmas decorations looked lovely, festive and cheerful, but they hardly paused as they made their way up the elevator to the tea room.

Once seated, with Miss Winters insisting on buying them both a cake to have with their drinks, she said, 'How are you, Amy?'

'I'm fine, thank you.'

'How is your young man?'

'His business is doing really well and . . . and we're getting married next year.'

'Oh, that's wonderful, Amy. Have you set the date?'

'Yes, the second Saturday in April.'

'A spring wedding, how lovely. What church are you getting married in?'

'It won't be a church wedding. We're getting married in the registry office,' Amy said, thinking that on the odd occasions when she saw her, Miss Winters showed a keen interest in her life, almost as if she didn't have one of her own to talk about. She had always thought her lonely, and felt sorry for her former manageress. Impulsively, she asked, 'Are you spending Christmas with anyone?'

'Err . . . yes . . . a friend.'

Amy hoped this was true, that Miss Winters wasn't going to be alone for the festive season. They continued to chat for a while, but then Amy said, 'I'm sorry, I've got to go now. I want to buy some presents.'

'Yes, me too, but I think I'll finish off this pot of tea first,' Miss Winters said. 'It was lovely to see you again, my dear, and maybe we'll bump into each other again soon.'

Amy said goodbye, feeling sorry again for her former

boss as she left the table and took the elevator again to the ground floor. However, with a limited amount of money, her mind was soon elsewhere as she searched the store for presents.

Mabel was on the look-out for Phyllis and finally saw her arriving home. She waited five minutes and then popped next door, huffing as she said, 'I suppose you're going to tell me that you're too busy for a chat again.'

'Now look, I only said that once and it was on Monday. I didn't get home until after two thirty and I still had my laundry to do.'

'I'm not surprised. You seem to spend all your time with Rose.'

'Mabel, I work for her.'

'It's more than that. The pair of you are as thick as thieves now.'

'I admit we've grown close, become friends, and Rose has been good to me.'

'Yeah, but she's buying your affection.'

'That isn't true,' Phyllis protested. 'I don't know what's come over you lately, Mabel, but it seems to me you're jealous. Rose has only given me things that she was going to chuck out, and that's hardly buying my affection.'

Mabel slumped onto a chair. 'All right, I'll admit it, I am jealous, but it's not about the stuff Rose has given you. It's just that since you got back in with her I feel like I've lost my best mate.'

'Don't be silly, of course you haven't,' Phyllis protested.

'You've just said you and Rose are close now, friends as well as cousins, so that leaves me out.'

'No it doesn't and I don't know where you got that daft idea from.'

'It isn't daft. Rose has taken you away from me.'

'She's done no such thing!' Phyllis snapped. 'I haven't dropped you, nor do I intend to, but it sounds like you think I can only have one friend.'

'I don't think that,' Mabel said, backtracking. She was making herself sound childish and realised that now. 'It's just that you're the only friend I've got.'

'No I'm not. You're friends with Edna, and that woman who lives in number twelve. Then there's . . .'

Mabel broke in, 'None of them have spoken to me since that business with Frank Cole.'

'Maybe you should make the first move, talk to them. I should think you'll find that it's all water under the bridge now.'

'Yeah, maybe I will,' Mabel said, thinking that it might be nice to get chatting to Edna and the others again. She could open the conversation by hinting that she knew a lot about Rose and Samuel Jacobs, which was sure to pique their interest.

Since Frank Cole had left, Mabel's appetite for gossip had returned, and it would be nice to find out what was going on locally. Her decision made, she decided to make a start on her overtures in the morning.

Chapter Twenty-Seven

Celia saw Amy carrying bags of shopping as she hurried past her window, and her lips tightened. She managed to put on a front when Amy came to the house now, but it was one that hid her true feelings. Her opinion hadn't changed – she still felt that Amy was socially inadequate and totally unsuitable for Thomas, but all her attempts to undermine the girl had failed. Thomas had found it charming that Amy had been tongue-tied the first time she was invited to dinner, and he didn't seem to notice the girl's dreadful etiquette.

Amy's parents were just as bad, when at Thomas's insistence Celia had invited them to dinner. Stanley Miller had slurped his soup, and then to her horror he had lifted the bowl to drink the last dregs. Celia had been disgusted and wanted as little to do with them as possible, but there had been a return invitation. It was, of course, a disaster, and with so little in common Celia hoped her feelings were reciprocated. Now, as the months passed, she was running out of ideas to undermine Amy.

Celia saw a taxi pulling up outside and gasped as a familiar figure climbed out. With a cry of delight she hurried to open the door, uncaring of the rain as she ran to his side. 'Jeremy! Oh, Jeremy! You've come home!'

'Hello Mum,' he said, grinning then pulling out two suitcases before paying the driver.

Celia ushered him inside and then threw her arms around her son. 'I can hardly believe you're here,' Celia enthused. 'Leave your cases there for now, darling, and come into the living room.'

Jeremy smiled when he walked into the room, his eyes coming to rest on the tree. 'It's just as I remember it, though there wasn't a Christmas tree in view when I left.'

'Considering it was in July, that's hardly surprising. Please, darling, tell me that you're home for good.'

'Mum, I've only just arrived and I don't know what my plans are yet.'

'At least say you'll be here for Christmas?'

'Of course I will.'

'That's something,' Celia said, hoping that Jeremy would decide to stay for a lot longer than that. 'Sit down, darling. Are you hungry?'

'I wouldn't say no to a sandwich,' Jeremy replied.

Celia was almost crying with happiness and dashed a tear from her eye as she looked up at her son. Jeremy had left little more than a boy, but had returned a man and a very handsome one too. She made him a sandwich and then listened as Jeremy told her about his travels; the places he'd been, the jobs he had done, all of which had been transient. It sounded as though her son had been living the life of a nomad, and she felt it was time he settled down in one place. If she had anything to do with it, Celia decided, that place would be here, by her side.

'I was still in Greece and got your letter,' Jeremy continued. 'I had found work harvesting olives, but you sounded a bit desperate so I decided to come home.'

'I'm so glad you did,' Celia told him.

'Have you heard from Dad since you wrote to me?'

'No, not a word, and I have no idea where he is.'

'It was a bit of a surprise to hear that he handed his business over to Tom. How is he coping with it?' Jeremy asked.

'I prefer Thomas, but I suppose calling him Tom is all right. Anyway, he's done well; increased trade and pays me a salary for keeping the accounts. However Thomas has made it clear that I'm to have no say in the running of the business, and of course I don't get a share of the profits.'

'What sort of money are we talking about?' Jeremy asked.

Celia rose to her feet and finding the account books, she showed them to her son. 'When your father ran the firm it was just a one-man band. He made enough money to see that we were well provided for, and employed Thomas, but refused to expand. In the short time since Thomas took over he's already gained new contracts, employed more glaziers and purchased new vans. Despite that expenditure, as you can see,' Celia said, pointing to the latest figures, 'Thomas has hugely increased profits.'

Jeremy whistled through his teeth and then said, 'He's done well, but by rights, surely the firm should be yours.'

'You'd have thought so, but as your father made sure that everything was done legally there's nothing I can do about it,' Celia said sadly.

'Well morally I think it's wrong and when I see Tom I'll tell him that the least he can do is to offer you a half share in the firm.'

'As the elder son, you should have a share in it too, but Thomas will never agree. He's changed and hardly listens to a word I say; especially when it comes to that common slut he's going to marry. I told you about her in my letter and I'm frightened that once they're married, Amy will persuade Thomas that he doesn't have to employ me, and . . . and if that happens, I . . . I'll end up destitute,' Celia sobbed, putting on the tears.

Jeremy moved to her side and placed an arm around her shoulder. 'Mum, stop worrying. You've got me now and I'll deal with Thomas.'

Celia sniffed, but inwardly she was smiling. She had someone on her side now, and at last the future looked brighter.

Though around seven years had passed since he'd last seen his brother, when Tommy walked into the living room, he recognised him instantly. 'Jeremy,' he gasped, 'I can't believe it.'

'It's good to see you, Tom. What were you, about thirteen or fourteen when I left home?' Jeremy asked as he stood up.

'Yes, about that.'

'You've grown up, but you're still a skinny runt,' Jeremy said, his grin taking any malice out of the words.

As they hugged awkwardly, Tommy noted that his brother was still taller than him, his body muscular, and with his dark hair and vivid green eyes, he was strikingly handsome. Jeremy had been his idol, the older brother he'd looked up to, and it had been gut-wrenching when he left home. Now he was back, and Tommy hoped it was permanent as he asked, 'Is this just a visit, or will you be staying?'

'I'm not sure yet, it depends.'

'On what?'

'This and that, what prospects there might be for me here, that sort of thing,' Jeremy replied.

'Thomas, it's wonderful to have Jeremy home again and I hope we can find a way to persuade him to stay.'

'I hope so too, Mum.'

'Jeremy and I have been chatting for so long that I've got behind with preparing dinner. I'll get on with it now and leave you two to catch up.'

As their mother left the room, Tommy coughed and sat down. He felt rough and had spent the day shivering or sweating in equal measures. Mild, familiar symptoms had started a couple of days ago, signalling the onset of bronchitis, but as he was too busy to take time off he'd have to work through it. Jeremy took a seat too, and Tommy managed to rally, saying, 'From your letters, I know some of the places you've seen, but I'd be interested to know more.'

'Well now, as I told Mum, I made my way home from Greece, but I went to so many countries that it would take a long time to describe them all,' Jeremy said, going on to talk about one or two.

As Tommy listened, he felt that in comparison to his brother he'd hardly seen or done anything. Yet even so, he'd never had a yearning to travel, preferring all things familiar. The thought of having to find any menial sort of work in a foreign country to earn a crust, as Jeremy had, didn't appeal.

'That's enough about me,' Jeremy said. 'What about you? Mum tells me that you're getting married.'

'Yes, that's right.'

'I'm twenty-five and don't fancy settling down yet. Don't you think you're a bit young for the marriage game?'

'No, I don't. Amy is the girl for me.'

'She must be pretty special.'

'She is,' Thomas enthused.

'In that case, when am I going to meet her?'

'This evening if you like,' Tommy suggested, though in

truth all he wanted to do was to crawl into bed. He couldn't give in though, and if his mother saw that he was under the weather she'd start mollycoddling, something he didn't want. 'Amy only lives at the bottom of the Rise so we can pop down there after dinner.'

'You're on,' Jeremy agreed.

'Thomas, I don't think you should take Jeremy to meet Amy this evening,' Celia said. 'Surely it can wait. With all that travelling to get here, he must be tired.'

It was Jeremy who answered, 'I'm fine, Mum.'

'Well don't be long. It's bound to catch up with you and I think you need an early night.'

'We won't be out for more than an hour or so,' Tommy assured her.

'Make sure you aren't.'

'Yes, Mummy,' Jeremy mocked, affecting the voice of a child.

'Oh you,' she said, yet smiling as she went back to the kitchen.

With a wry grin Jeremy said, 'Mum's already making me feel like a ten-year-old again. Is she always like this?'

Tommy nodded, relieved that his mother was too focused on Jeremy to worry about him. 'It's worse if you're ill. You've only got to sniff and she wants to confine you to bed, though with a business to run I can't take time off unless I'm really rough.'

'Yes, we'll have to talk about *your* business,' Jeremy said, 'but it can wait for now.'

Tommy frowned, but then Jeremy said he was going upstairs to freshen up before dinner, leaving him to wonder about his brother's enigmatic remark.

* * *

Though he hadn't said as much, Jeremy had grown tired of travelling. He'd already been thinking about returning home when his mother's letter arrived, and reading her impassioned words had set the seal on his decision. What he hadn't thought about at that time was his father's piddling little business, but that had changed when his mother had shown him the accounts. He was interested now – very interested, and somehow he was going to make sure that as the elder brother, he rightfully got his share.

A little later, over dinner, his mother looked at Thomas and said, 'You look a bit flushed. Are you all right?'

'Yes, I'm fine. It's just a bit warm in here, that's all.'

Jeremy wasn't so sure. Out of their mother's sight he'd seen Tom use his inhaler a few times and had heard him coughing. However, soon after they had finished eating, Tom said, 'Right, Jeremy, are you ready?'

'Yes, let's go,' he replied.

'Don't be long. You look exhausted, Jeremy.'

'I must admit it's catching up on me, but it's still far too early to go to bed. See you later, Mum.'

She called goodbye and shortly after he and Tom walked out into the cold night air. Jeremy shivered, stuffed his hands into his pockets and picked up his pace. They were halfway down the Rise when Tom started coughing again, bending over and holding a hand against his racking chest.

'Tom, are you all right?' Jeremy asked, worried that his brother seemed to be struggling for air.

'Yes . . . yes . . . just give me a minute.'

Jeremy wondered if they should turn back, but then Tom rallied and they began to walk again until they came to some houses with the fronts partially obscured by scaf-folding. Tom knocked on one of the doors and because the light was behind her, Jeremy could barely see the young

241

woman who opened it, though he did notice that she was tiny.

'Tommy, I wasn't expecting you, but come in,' she invited, stepping back.

As they went inside, Tom said, 'Amy, my brother has just returned home from his travels and I've brought him to meet you.'

As Amy closed the door and then smiled up at him, Jeremy found himself riveted. She was indeed tiny, but beautiful, with curly blonde hair, a cute little nose and wide, cornflower blue eyes.

'Amy, this is Jeremy,' said Tom, jolting him out of his daze.

'Hello,' she said, a little shyly, 'it's nice to meet you.'

'It's even nicer to meet you,' Jeremy said, putting on the charm. 'Tom didn't tell me that you're absolutely gorgeous.'

Amy flushed prettily and Jeremy was smitten, unable to believe that his mother had described this fantastic girl as a common slut. In all his travels he'd never met anyone who'd had this shattering effect on him, and he was sickened that she belonged to his brother.

Jeremy's gaze was pulled away from Amy as Tom introduced him to her parents, and they were invited to take their coats off. He was again polite and charming, while noting furniture that looked absurdly large and grandiose in such a pokey room. He was asked to sit down by Amy's mother, while noting that Tom was still standing with an arm around Amy. She was looking up at him with obvious affection and Tom was smiling down at her.

'As you can see, they're a right pair of lovebirds,' Amy's mother said. 'Come on, you two. Can't you take your eyes off each other for a minute and sit down?'

'Sorry,' Tom said, reluctantly taking a seat, but then a heaving cough hit him again.

'Tommy, are you all right?' Amy asked worriedly as she perched on the arm of his chair.

'Yes,' he said, recovering. 'Don't worry. It's just a touch of asthma.'

Jeremy wasn't so sure, but then Amy's father spoke to him, asking, 'Have you been to many interesting places?'

Once again Jeremy talked about his travels, embellishing some of his adventures, but he failed to catch Amy's attention for long. She was too wrapped up in Tom, and Jeremy wasn't used to being ignored in favour of a runt. He knew he was good looking, and was used to girls throwing themselves at him in their willingness to share his bed.

Amy was different and he found her a challenge – his first one. It was a contest he was looking forward to winning.

Chapter Twenty-Eight

Tommy awoke in the night, his body drenched in perspiration as coughs violently shook his body. He sat up, gasping for breath as his bedroom door was flung open. The light went on and he saw his mother in her thick blue dressing gown, wearing a ridiculous pink hairnet, but to Thomas at that moment, she appeared a ministering angel.

As the coughing fit passed, she plumped up the pillows behind him, put his inhaler in his hand and then scurried off to return with a bottle of medicine. 'This should help a little until I can get the doctor to you in the morning,' she said softly.

He dutifully swallowed the foul-tasting liquid, then croaked, 'Thanks, Mum, but there's no need to call the doctor.'

'Don't be silly,' she said, laying a soft palm on his brow, 'you're burning up.'

Tommy didn't get a chance to argue because his mother hurried off again, this time returning with a bowl of water and a cloth. She bathed his brow, the cool relief feeling wonderful, and at last, exhausted, he drifted off. For the rest of the night Tommy slept fitfully, a painful cough frequently awaking him, but every time he opened his eyes he found his mother by his side.

Morning light filled the room when Tommy became fully

awake again and he blinked, shocked to see that his bedside clock showed that it was after seven thirty. He sat up, flung back the blankets, and swung his legs round to get out of bed, only to be struck by a wave of dizziness. He felt awful, shivery, yet hot, but he had to get to work.

'Hold on, Mum said you're not to get up,' Jeremy said as he walked into the room.

'I don't think I can,' he had to admit weakly, lying back down.

'Mum's going to ring the doctor as soon as the surgery opens.'

Tommy struggled to sit up again. 'I'll have to make a call too. My foreman needs to know that I won't be able to make it today, and though he can manage without me, I want to speak to him about a couple of urgent jobs.'

'I can do that for you. Just tell me what you want this foreman of yours to do.'

With his head swimming, Tommy doubted he could make it downstairs, so he gratefully sank back again. 'My foreman's name is Len Upwood,' he said, going on to explain what work needed to be given priority.

'Right, leave it to me,' Jeremy said confidently. 'I'll sort everything out.'

'You just need to pass on what I've told you to Len. He's a good bloke and he knows what he's doing.'

'So do I, Tom. I know just what I'm doing,' Jeremy said as he left the room.

As far as Tommy knew, his brother knew nothing about the glass trade and he doubted he'd ever fitted a window. Still, Jeremy only had to pass on the message, so feeling that he had nothing to worry about now, Tommy relaxed, only to be hit by another fit of coughing that left him gasping for breath.

This wasn't a mild bout of bronchitis, Tommy worried. It was a bad one and maybe it was just as well that his mother was calling the doctor. At least a course of antibiotics would get him back on his feet, and sooner rather than later.

Jeremy rang Len Upwood, but he wasn't going to leave it at that. He was going to take a look at the business and after breakfast he said, 'Mum, with Tom laid up I think I'll drive to the unit. There's a saying that while the cat's away the mice will play, so I want to make sure there's no slacking.'

'All right, dear,' she said. 'I'm sure Thomas will appreciate that.'

'Where does he keep the van keys?'

'On the hall table,' she said, 'but have you got a licence to drive?'

'Of course and I'll see you later,' Jeremy said, glad to get out of the house and onto the road. Of course he didn't have a driving licence. He'd never stayed in one country long enough to get one. Thankfully his mother was too distracted by Tom and his bronchitis to realise that, and anyway, he *had* learned to drive. He just hadn't passed any sort of test.

It didn't take Jeremy long to get a feel for the van, and soon he was pulling up outside the unit, finding only two men in sight when he went inside and asked, 'Which one of you is Len Upwood?'

'That'd be me,' said a round-faced man of around thirty, who was in the process of cutting a sheet of glass. 'What can I do for you?'

'I'm Jeremy Frost. We spoke on the telephone earlier.'

'Oh, right, you're Tommy's brother.'

246

'Yes, and I'm here to make sure that things are running to schedule in his absence.'

'Well you can tell him they are, including the jobs he wanted prioritised,' Len said as he bent over his work again.

'It doesn't look like it to me. There are only two of you working. Where are the rest of the men?'

Len's head snapped up again. 'Where do you think? They're where they should be, out in their vans working on repairs and installations.'

Jeremy felt a fool and didn't like it. Nor did he like Len Upwood's derogatory tone. He'd spent too many years working as a menial; being shown little respect, and he'd had enough of that. For now though he had to make a dignified exit and said, 'Right, that's good. I'll report back to Tommy and if you come across any problems, give me a ring.'

Len just looked at him, saying nothing, and Jeremy left the unit, jaws grinding as he got into the van. If he'd been the boss, Len would have shown him some respect, deference, and now it infuriated him that the business belonged to his brother. Tom was a weakling, always had been, but he had the life that Jeremy wanted, along with the girl.

Jeremy drove off, his grip tight on the steering wheel, determined to find a way to usurp his brother.

Mabel was in Edna's house, and as she looked around the untidy living room she was trying to hide her distaste. Edna was dishevelled as ever; her hair greasy and unwashed, her body odour foul.

'Well, I must say I was surprised when you knocked on my door,' Edna said, as she puffed on a cigarette, two fingers stained a yellowish brown from the nicotine.

'Yeah, well, I thought you might be interested to hear about Rose and Samuel Jacobs.'

'What's to know? It's common knowledge that Rose married him, no doubt for his money.'

'Yeah, and she persuaded him to buy a big house close to Battersea Park.'

'I've heard about that too, *and* that Phyllis is working for her. From what I've seen, what with that posh furniture being delivered, Phyllis has done all right for herself too.'

'It was only stuff Rose didn't want any more.'

'What about you getting your roof repaired?' Edna said sarcastically. 'I've been on about mine for years, but I'm not one of the favoured few like you.'

'I had nothing to do with it,' Mabel protested. 'From what Phyllis tells me, ours aren't the only ones that are getting repaired. Yours might be next.'

'It'd be about time.'

'I couldn't agree more,' Mabel said, hoping to overcome Edna's slightly hostile manner. 'It's about time Samuel Jacobs did something about our complaints. After all, he's had enough rent out of us over the years. He's been living in luxury on the money he's raked in, while we've been living in squalor.'

'Yeah, that's right. Would you like a cup of tea, Mabel?' Edna asked.

Mabel smiled. The ice had been broken and she said, 'Yes, please.'

'I've got a bit of juicy gossip to tell you, but I'll put the kettle on the gas first.'

Mabel fidgeted with expectation while the tea was made, but it turned out to be worth it and her eyes rounded in surprise. 'I don't know why I'm shocked. After all, it's no more than I'd expect from the likes of her.'

'I only found out about it recently,' Edna continued. 'A friend of a friend's daughter was in there at the same time, but I don't get to see her very often. Mind you, as the two of them were such good mates, I should think Amy knew about it.'

'If she did, she never said a word,' Mabel said, wondering if Amy had kept it from Phyllis too. Well she'd soon remedy that. Phyllis had refused to hear a bad word about that girl, but at last Mabel had been proved right. She was looking forward to seeing Phyllis later and pointing that fact out.

'No, Mum, I don't believe it,' Amy said. 'It sounds like Mabel is back to her old ways, and this is just nasty, wicked gossip.'

'I thought the same, and I gave her a mouthful, but I've had time to think about it since then. I'm not so sure now. When you look back, Carol was supposed to have had food poisoning, but don't you remember the state she was in when she came out of hospital? We were both worried sick about her.'

'Yes, but then we found out that it was because her mother had walked out.'

'I'm beginning to think there was more to it than that. If you remember, you were worried about Carol *before* she went into hospital. You said she'd become moody and withdrawn.'

'That doesn't mean she was pregnant, or that she had an abortion,' Amy said indignantly.

'I'm only saying it's possible that the gossips have got it right.'

'No they haven't!' Amy argued. 'They're just a bunch of nasty-minded women who seem to enjoy ruining people's reputations. I dread to think how Carol is going to feel if she hears about this.'

'Maybe you should warn her.'

Amy was about to reply when there was a knock on the door and she went to open it, surprised to see Tommy's brother. 'Jeremy?'

'Tom asked me to tell you that he can't see you tonight. I'm afraid he's stuck in bed with bronchitis.'

'Oh no,' Amy cried, all thoughts of Carol at that moment flying from her mind. 'Do you think it would be all right if I pop up to see him?'

'I don't see why not.'

'Mum, Tommy's ill,' she said, grabbing her coat from a hook by the door.

'Amy, your dinner!'

'I'll have it when I come back,' she said, hurrying out and asking Jeremy as they quickly walked up the hill, 'How bad is it?'

'He's pretty rough, but he's been put on antibiotics so that should sort him out.'

The wind was biting and Amy pulled her collar up, almost halting in her stride when Jeremy put an arm around her to draw her closer. 'You're cold,' he said softly and with what sounded like concern.

Amy didn't know how to react. She felt awkward to be this close to Jeremy and to have his arm around her, but if she pulled away it would look churlish. Confused, she just carried on walking and was glad when they arrived.

However any relief she felt was wiped away when Celia saw her, the woman saying, 'Amy, what are you doing here?'

'I . . . I've come to see Tommy.'

'*Thomas* is in bed, and as I've told you before, it wouldn't be proper for you to go up to his bedroom.'

'Leave it out, Mum,' Jeremy protested. 'They're engaged.'

'Nevertheless, it wouldn't be right,' Celia argued.

'The days when couples needed chaperones have well gone, but if you're going to be prissy about it, I'll take Amy upstairs and act as one.'

'Oh, very well, but only for five minutes. Thomas is ill and needs his rest.'

'Thanks, Jeremy,' Amy whispered gratefully as they went upstairs.

'I didn't realise my mother was such a prude.'

Any comment Amy might have made died on her lips when they walked into Tommy's bedroom. He looked awful and she flew to his side. Tommy tried to smile, and tears filled Amy's eyes. This was the first time she'd seen him like this, and it was heartbreaking to hear when he began coughing, his chest heaving and perspiration beading his forehead. 'Oh, Tommy,' she cried, feeling utterly helpless.

'I . . . I'll be all right,' he gasped. 'Sorry about tonight.'

'Don't be silly, it doesn't matter.'

'I . . . might be stuck in bed for a good few days.'

Amy felt it would take longer than that and said, 'Don't try to get up before you're fully recovered.'

'I've got a business to run,' he croaked.

'Don't worry,' Jeremy said, speaking for the first time. 'I can keep an eye on things for you.'

'No . . . no need,' Tommy said, but Amy looked sideways to see that Jeremy was leaning casually against the door frame and she smiled at him gratefully. He winked and she flushed, turning to see that Tommy's eyes had closed. Softly she kissed his cheek, but he didn't stir, and after just sitting beside him for another couple of minutes, she indicated to Jeremy that they should leave.

Celia was waiting for them at the foot of the stairs, and Amy wondered if she'd been timing the visit. 'As you saw, Thomas is very ill and he needs lots of rest.'

'Would it be all right if I just pop in for a few minutes each day?'

'Yes, of course it will,' Jeremy agreed before his mother got a chance to answer. 'That's all right, isn't it, Mum?'

Celia hesitated, but then said stiffly, 'Yes, I suppose so.'

'Thank you,' Amy said. 'I'll go now, but I'll call in after work tomorrow.'

'I'll walk you home, Amy,' Jeremy offered.

'There's no need,' she said hurriedly.

'I insist,' he said.

'Jeremy, you heard her,' Celia snapped. 'There's no need.'

Before he could respond, Amy pulled open the street door, calling a swift goodbye before hurrying out, relieved that Jeremy didn't follow her. There was something about Jeremy, a sort of dangerous magnetism that made her nervous and she was glad to get away from him.

Chapter Twenty-Nine

Carol had done her Christmas shopping and had put a small tree in front of the window, adding fairy lights and baubles. It was Sunday morning, so she had wrapped the presents chosen for her brothers and placed them under the tree. She hoped the hint would work, that some would be added for her, but more than anything she longed for her mother to get in touch. It had been around seven months now without a word, and when she'd been to see her gran, the old lady still insisted that she hadn't heard from her either. Carol didn't believe it. Before she left her mother had been to see her gran every day, and it didn't make sense that she hadn't at least been in touch to make sure that the old woman was all right.

Not only that, if Gran hadn't been in contact with her mother, she wouldn't know that the house on Lark Rise was now empty, and if she did come back it would be a bit of a shock. Thoughts of the recent past, the things that had happened in that house, suddenly crowded Carol's mind. It was too painful to think about, so when there was a ring on the doorbell, Carol was glad of the distraction.

Even though there had been no sign of her father, Carol still looked out of the window to make sure it wasn't him at the door, and was thankful to see that it was Amy. She ran downstairs to let her friend in, but Amy said, 'Are you on your own? I've got something to tell you, but it needs to be in private.'

'It's all right, my brothers aren't in. Come on up,' she said and when they sat down in the living room, Carol could see how tense Amy was. 'What's wrong? Why do you need to talk to me in private?'

Amy swallowed as though nervous, but only said, 'Tommy's got bronchitis and he's really rough.'

'Oh, no wonder you look upset.'

'Tommy's brother has come home too. Jeremy is older than Tommy and has been away for about seven years. He seems all right, and he's really good looking.'

'Is that what you've come to talk to me about? Do you fancy him or something?'

'No, of course not,' Amy protested.

'Then what is it?'

'I . . . I was going to tell you about this yesterday, after work, but I saw your brothers arriving home and I didn't want to talk to you in front of them. That's why I came today, hoping they were out . . .'

Amy's voice had trailed off and worried that she was in some kind of trouble, Carol urged, 'You're safe, we're on our own, and if I can help you know I will.'

'This . . . this isn't about me. It's about you. I hate to tell you this, and of course it's all lies, but there's some nasty gossip going round and I thought I should warn you.'

Carol's stomach clenched. Surely it hadn't come out after all this time? She dreaded what was coming, but had to ask, 'What are they saying about me?'

'They're saying that you . . . well, you had an abortion.'

Carol lowered her head and ran both hands over her

face as she groaned, 'Oh God, if this reaches Paul and Davy they're going to go mad.'

'Maybe they should,' Amy said. 'If they sort the gossips out, it might put a stop to them.'

'No, no, you don't understand,' Carol cried. 'It's me they'll sort out, probably chuck out me of this flat. Oh, Amy, what am I going to do?'

Amy looked bewildered for a moment, but then as though the penny had dropped she gasped, 'Are you saying it's true?'

Carol nodded, and then it all came out in a rush as she told Amy what had happened; about Roy, the rape, the abortion, sobbing when she came to the end.

Amy had tears in her eyes too as she said, 'If I'd known I might have been able to help, or at least be there for you.'

'I was too ashamed to tell anyone, and if the abortion hadn't been botched, nobody would have needed to know.'

Amy moved to her side to put an arm around her, and at her friend's show of sympathy tears ran, unchecked, down Carol's cheeks. 'Oh, Amy, I dread to think what's going to happen when my brothers find out.'

'If you tell them your side of the story before they hear it from anyone else, I'm sure they won't be angry with you, or throw you out. None of it was your fault, and like me, they'll realise that.'

Carol clung to Amy, hoping she was right, but deep down she doubted it.

Jeremy thought Amy looked upset when she called in to see Tom, and she didn't look any better when she left. So far the antibiotics hadn't made any difference and Tom was still rough, with his mother insisting that Amy's visit was a short one.

He couldn't understand why she was so against Amy. From what his mother had said in her letter he'd expected a hard-faced, common, gold-digger, but from what he'd seen Amy was far from that. As they walked into the living room he said, 'Mum, I don't know why you don't like Amy. I think she's rather nice.'

'Nice! I thought you'd have more sense, but it seems you're as blind as your brother. You've been taken in by her innocent act, but as I told you before, when Amy marries Thomas she'll take control of the money and I won't see a penny of it.'

'Amy doesn't seem that type of girl,' Jeremy argued. 'From what I've seen you easily intimidate her and I don't think she'd dare go up against you.'

'You hardly know her, but she's just the type, a consummate actress who has already pulled the wool over your eyes. Amy has a good teacher in one of her relatives too, a tart who married an old man to get her hands on his money.'

Jeremy's eyebrows rose. 'Really? I didn't know that.'

'Here's something else for you to think about. We talked about having a share of the business, but if Amy's got anything to do with it that's never going to happen.'

Jeremy didn't like the sound of that. Was his mother right about Amy? He didn't know, but it wasn't something he was prepared to risk. 'In that case, Mum, we're going to have to put our heads together and do something about it.'

'Don't you think I've tried? I've done everything I can, but Thomas is so besotted with Amy that he won't hear a word against her.'

'Let me think about it. Maybe I can come up with something,' Jeremy suggested.

'Very well. Anyway, with the roast nearly ready I'll need to cook the vegetables.'

By the time she returned, Jeremy had come up with a

plan that would serve him well. 'Mum, I've got an idea, but to make it work I need to spend more time with Amy,' he said, going on to explain what he had in mind, and was pleased when she readily agreed.

'There's only one thing,' she said. 'Don't you think Amy would find it a bit odd if I suddenly change my attitude towards her?'

'Yes, she might,' Jeremy conceded. 'Right then, we'll have to take it slowly.'

'If this works, it'll be worth it,' his mother said.

'Oh it'll work, I'll see to that,' Jeremy said confidently. It might take a little longer to achieve his ultimate aims – ones he had kept from his mother to ensure her cooperation, but in the end he'd have everything he wanted.

'I still can't believe that Carol had an abortion. The poor girl, she must have been through hell,' Phyllis said.

They had been talking about it for some time, her mother sympathetic, and Amy nodded, deeply sad for her friend. She couldn't imagine the horror of being raped, nor of being left pregnant, let alone having a back-street abortion. 'Yes, she's been through hell, and now, thanks to the gossips, it's all been dragged up again.'

'I know,' Phyllis agreed, 'and Mabel has already felt the length of my tongue.'

'Hello my lovelies,' Stan said, grinning as he walked in. 'I hope my dinner is ready 'cos I'm starving.'

'With all that beer in your belly it's a wonder you've got room for anything else,' Phyllis chided.

'I only had a few pints,' he said, but then Amy saw her father's face straighten as he looked towards her. 'What's up, love? Are you still upset about this garbage that's flying around about Carol?'

'I went to see her this morning,' she said, going on to tell him what had happened, but then shocked by her father's response.

'Well now,' he said, 'that explains it. With his wife walking out on him, and his daughter getting herself knocked up, it's no wonder Frank Cole turned to drink.'

'Carol didn't get herself "knocked up", as you so crudely put it. The poor girl was raped!' Phyllis snapped.

'So she says, but if you ask me women are too fond of leading blokes on and then crying rape.'

'My God, all these years and I've only just realised that I married a Neanderthal.'

Amy didn't want to hear any more and dashed upstairs. She couldn't believe her father's attitude, and if he was anything to go by, no wonder Carol was dreading telling her brothers.

Carol was trying to pluck up the courage to do just that, but so far her nerves were failing her.

'Come on, Carol, what's up?' Paul asked. 'You've had a gob on you since we came home and you've hardly said a word.'

'It's probably a woman's thing,' Dave commented. 'She always gets a bit moody around this time of the month.'

'Is that it, Carol? Is your belly giving you a bit of gyp?' Paul asked.

'No, no, it . . . it's just that I've got something to tell you.'

'Go on then.'

'You're going to be furious and I'm scared,' she said, wringing her hands.

'Has Dad been round? Is that it?' Paul asked sharply.

'No, I haven't seen him.'

'What's wrong then?' Paul asked.

Carol began hesitantly, her voice quivering, but when she got to the part about being raped, Paul's face reddened with anger. 'Who was it? I'll kill him!'

'Yeah, me too,' Dave growled, 'but I'll castrate him first.'

'You won't be able to find him,' Carol said, her voice still quivering as she continued.

'So Dad knew about this,' Paul snapped, finally stopping his pacing when she came to the end.

'Yes, he . . . he called the ambulance and while I was in hospital, he told everyone that I had food poisoning.'

'Yeah, I remember that,' Dave said. 'That was at the same time he came round here to tell us that Mum had walked out. He should have told us about this too and between us we could have found the bastard.'

'Yeah, he should've,' Paul hissed angrily. 'Carol got raped, had an abortion and he didn't say a bloody word.'

Carol couldn't look at her brothers and had her head down as she said, 'I asked him not to tell you. I . . . I was so ashamed and I thought you'd go mad.'

'Yeah, we're going mad all right,' Dave shouted.

It had started, and fearing her brothers' tempers, Carol was shaking, but then Paul yelled, 'Shut up, Dave. Can't you see the state she's in?'

'Yeah, sorry,' Dave said, 'but you can't blame me for doing my nut.'

Paul sat down beside her and Carol tensed, only to slump with relief when her brother said softly, 'You shouldn't feel ashamed and though we're furious, it isn't aimed at you. It wasn't your fault. You were raped, and I don't blame you for getting rid of the baby. The only thing that puzzles me is why you've decided to tell us about it now?'

'Because it's all come out and the gossips are having a field day.'

'Don't worry about that. We'll soon sort them out.'

Carol didn't want to stir up any more trouble and said, 'Leave it. I wouldn't want to give them the satisfaction of thinking they've upset us, and anyway, once they find someone else to gossip about it'll all die down.'

Paul went quiet for a moment, but then said, 'All right, if that's what you want, but if they don't shut up about it, they're going to be sorry they were born.'

Carol laid her head on Paul's shoulder, glad that her fears had proved ungrounded. Amy had been right she thought, her brothers hadn't turned on her, instead, as always, they were being protective.

Her mother had run off, her father had gone out of her life too, but she still had her brothers and at last, Carol was able to smile again.

Chapter Thirty

Tommy was a lot better on Tuesday when Amy called in to see him on her way home from work, and she was grateful that Celia Frost allowed her to stay a little longer, this visit extended to half an hour. Of course Celia insisted that Jeremy remain in Tommy's room the whole time, but Amy found her less stiff and formal when they returned downstairs.

'Amy, I think the antibiotics are helping. Thomas had a less restless night,' Celia said.

'Oh, that's good.'

'With Jeremy coming home so unexpectedly and Thomas being so ill, I'm afraid I've been rather lax in inviting you to come to join us for dinner on Christmas day.'

Amy was taken by surprise. She hadn't expected this invitation and had already agreed to spend Christmas at Rose's, hoping that Tommy would join them in the evening. 'Err . . . thank you, but I'm afraid I've made other arrangements.'

'Oh come on, Amy,' cajoled Jeremy. 'I don't know what you and Tom had planned, but it's only a week away and I doubt he'll be fit enough to go out.'

'Jeremy is right,' Celia said. 'If you can't join us, I'm afraid Thomas will be very unhappy that he won't be able to spend any time with you. Can't you possibly change your arrangements?'

'Well, yes, I suppose I could,' Amy said, yet though she wanted to be with Tommy, she wasn't so sure about spending Christmas day with his mother.

'That's settled then,' Celia said brusquely.

'I must go. My mother will be wondering where I am,' Amy said at Celia's sudden change of tone, glad of an excuse to leave.

Thankfully Jeremy didn't press to walk her home this time, something he had taken to doing despite her initial protests. It didn't take Amy long to walk down the hill and into her house, where she said as soon as she went in, 'Mum, you're not going to believe this, but Celia Frost has invited me to join them for Christmas dinner.'

'But you've already agreed to come with us to Rose's.'

'I know, but do you think she'll mind if I bow out?'

'I shouldn't think so. Rose is easy-going and takes it as it comes, but I'm not sure how *I* feel about it. We've always spent Christmas together, but now you're getting married I suppose this is the shape of things to come. How do you feel about it, Stan?'

'It's all right with me.'

'All right, Amy, go to Celia Frost's then,' Phyllis said, although she still sounded a bit peeved. 'I've been keeping your dinner hot so get changed. If you don't eat it soon it'll be ruined.'

Amy was soon sitting at the table, thoughtful as she said to her mother, 'It's odd really. Celia Frost always seems to resent any time that Tommy spends with me, so I don't know what made her invite me to dinner on Christmas day.'

'It's obvious. Celia has got her other son home again, so it's made her less clingy and possessive of Tommy.'

'Of course, I hadn't thought of that,' Amy said. She was still nervous in Jeremy's company, but if his being there softened Celia's attitude towards her, Amy wanted him to stay.

Mabel was seething. She'd told Phyllis about Carol, proving her point that the girl was a tart, but Phyllis refused to believe it and all she'd got in return was a mouthful of abuse. She'd tried to tell Phyllis that she was just trying to protect Amy from having such an unsuitable friend, yet it hadn't made any difference, she'd still been shown the door. Well that was it; Phyllis could stew in her own juice from now on and Rose was welcome to her.

Jack was on a late shift and wouldn't be home until nine that evening, so with nothing else to do Mabel was doing her best to look out of her window, hating the dark, winter evenings. The scaffolding obscured her view, and seeing as the work was finished she was annoyed that it was still up. There was a lack of street light too, as one of the lamps was out, but nevertheless Mabel saw someone lurking about next door. The Coles' house was empty, so it seemed a bit suspicious to Mabel, but unable to get a better view she had no choice but to go to her front door. Opening it cautiously Mabel peered round it, surprised to see a policeman, bent double as he looked through the letterbox. 'You're wasting your time,' she called. 'That house is empty.'

The copper stood up, put his helmet back on and walked up to her. 'I'm looking for any relatives of a Mr Frank Cole.'

'You won't find any in there,' Mabel said. 'His sons and his daughter live someone along Lavender Hill.'

'Do you have their address?'

'No, but you can try next door,' Mabel said, indicating Phyllis's house.

'Thank you,' he said.

'Hold on, what has Frank Cole done now?' Mabel called.

She was ignored and as the copper knocked on Phyllis's door, Mabel swiftly closed hers. Phyllis had called her a nasty-minded, malicious gossip and Mabel wasn't going to give her more ammunition. Instead she rushed back to the living room and pressed her ear to the wall. If Phyllis let the copper in, she might find out why he wanted to find Frank's relatives.

When the policeman left, Carol found her feelings were all over the place. He was dead! She had hated him; loathed what he tried to do to her, but other memories now flooded her mind. Childhood ones, happy ones; of being spoiled, of laughter when they were all together as a family. The man she remembered from those times had been different, a good man and not the stinking drunk who had come into her bedroom . . .

'I just can't take it in,' Dave said, interrupting her thoughts. 'Dead, found in the filthy basement of a bombed-out building, and now they want us to identify him.'

'I'm not looking forward to it,' Paul said, 'but according to that copper, if they hadn't found an old letter in Dad's pocket with his name and address on it, he might have remained unknown.'

'Yeah,' Dave said bitterly, 'and there was no sign of foul play. He was just another frozen, drunken down and out that nobody gives a shit about.'

'Shut up!' Paul shouted. 'I feel bad enough that I didn't try to find him, without you rubbing it in.'

'I'm not trying to rub it in,' Dave argued. 'I feel rotten about it too, but if you remember, after finding out what he did to Carol, neither of us wanted anything to do with him.'

'He was still our dad!' Paul yelled.

Carol knew that Paul was more sensitive than Dave and this was hitting him badly, his grief manifesting in anger. 'I . . . I suppose you think I should've given him another chance,' she said, tears welling in her eyes as she looked up at him.

Perhaps it was seeing her distress, Carol didn't know, but the anger seemed to drain from Paul as he shook his head. 'No, we couldn't risk that, but if me and Dave had looked for him, maybe we could've got him off the booze and back on his feet.'

'It's no good dwelling on *if's* and *maybe's*,' Dave said. 'We've got to live with the choices we made, and anyway, we weren't Dad's keepers.'

'I suppose you're right,' Paul agreed, and as though grateful to find things to assuage his guilt he added, 'If anything, everything went pear-shaped for Dad when Mum left him.'

'I still can't make sense of why she walked out, nor why we haven't heard from her since,' Dave mused. 'We didn't try to find Dad, but we could try looking for her.'

'Let's get Dad sorted out first,' Paul said. 'We've got to identify him and then we've got to collect his belongings from the police station.'

'What's the point? All he probably had were the stinking clothes he was found in.'

'I know, but there might be some small thing we'd like to keep, perhaps his wedding ring.'

'He probably flogged it for booze ages ago,' Dave said.

'Maybe, but it might be something he hung on to, and then there's the funeral to arrange.'

'Mum should be there,' Dave argued.

Paul heaved a sigh. 'I doubt we'd find her in time . . . if at all.'

'We should still give it a try.'

'All right, but we can't do anything tonight. Not only that, the copper said we should go to the morgue in the morning so before we do anything else, we'll need to get that over with first.'

Carol closed her eyes against her brother's words. Morgue, they were going to the morgue, where in her imagination they would see her father laid out on a cold slab. It hit her then. Her dad was dead. She began to cry – not for the man who had almost raped her – but for the father she had loved.

Chapter Thirty-One

The scaffolding was being taken down outside when Amy left for work on Wednesday morning, a little earlier than usual. The men's wolf-whistles and cheeky comments followed her as she hurried up the hill, but Amy was too worried about Carol to pay them any mind.

She feared that something dreadful must have happened to Carol's dad and walked as fast as she could, arriving at the flat on Lavender Hill out of breath. Carol let her in, eyes red-rimmed and her face pale as she told Amy that her father was dead.

Amy was shocked, and stammered, 'Oh, Carol, I'm so sorry.'

'None of us are going to work today,' Carol said as Amy followed her upstairs. 'Dave and Paul are going to arrange the funeral, but I doubt it'll take place before Christmas.'

The brothers nodded a greeting as Amy walked into their living room, where she said again, 'I . . . I'm so sorry to hear about your dad.'

'At least this'll give the gossips something else to talk about,' Carol said bitterly. 'Paul wants to invite Dad's old mates to the funeral, ones he worked with or drank with in the local pub, so the news will soon spread.'

'I'll come, and I'm sure my parents will too,' Amy said.

'Thanks, I'd like that,' Carol said, her composure wavering as she blinked back tears.

'Is there anything I can do to help?' Amy asked.

'I don't think so, but it's good of you to offer,' Carol croaked.

As the conversation died out, Amy felt awkward, and inadequate. She didn't know what to say, how to offer any words of comfort. They had just lost their father and must be inconsolable. Paul flopped onto the sofa, put an arm around Carol and she leaned against him.

Amy felt that her presence was intrusive and said softly, 'I'd better go or I'll be late for work.'

Carol nodded, and telling them not to get up, Amy let herself out, her heart heavy with sadness.

Celia carried a tray up to Thomas and placed it across his lap. 'Jeremy has gone to the unit again. He left half an hour ago.'

'I've told him there's no need.'

'Darling, he's just keeping an eye on things for you . . . making sure the men don't slack while you're away.'

'Len Upwood is a good foreman and if needed, which I doubt, he's perfectly capable of keeping them in line.'

'I know, but I think Jeremy is getting restless and it gives him something to do.'

'Well, as long as he doesn't get in the way, I suppose it's all right,' Thomas said. 'Anyway, I feel a lot better today so I think I'll get up.'

Celia decided that it was time to start acting on Jeremy's plan and said, 'The living room has barely warmed up yet so eat your breakfast and stay there for a while. It'll be nice for Amy to see that you're up when she calls in, and Jeremy won't have to be a chaperon any more. Not that he minds, he'd do anything for you, and Amy must like him as she seems to hang on to his every word. I think Jeremy finds it a little embarrassing, but it's been lovely of him to keep Amy company for you while you've been so ill.'

With that, Celia left the room, telling Thomas that she'd be back for his tray in a little while. She'd made her opening shot – and from the frown she'd seen on Thomas's face, it had hit the target.

'I'm sorry, Rose. It'll just be me and Stan on Christmas day,' Phyllis told her cousin when as usual, before starting the housework, they were sharing a cup of tea. 'Celia Frost has invited Amy to her place for dinner.'

'You don't look too happy about it.'

'I'm not. We always spend Christmas together and Amy should've refused.'

'I doubt it was an easy choice for her. Celia Frost is going to be her mother-in-law, and knowing the woman, no doubt Amy wants to keep on her good side.'

'Huh, I doubt she's got one. But changing the subject, we had a policeman knocking on our door last night.'

With eyes rounding, Rose asked, 'What did he want?'

'Well, it was a bit odd really. As you know, Frank Cole has got two sons and the copper wanted their address. We thought they might be in trouble, so we kept shtum at first, but then he said it wasn't a criminal matter,' Phyllis said, pausing to drink her tea.

'What was it then?' Rose asked.

'The copper wouldn't go into details, but we got the gist that it was something to do with Frank . . . that he might have had an accident or something.'

'Oh no, I hope it isn't anything too serious,' Rose said.

'Stan seems to think it must be. He said if Frank was capable, he'd have got in touch with the boys himself and there'd be no reason for the police to be involved.'

'Yeah, I think he's right,' Rose said. 'What a shame though. It seems to be one disaster after another for that family and it makes you count your blessings.'

'Yes it does,' Phyllis agreed, thinking that Rose had turned out to be one of hers. Rose had been so good to her and life was so much easier now that she was earning more money.

One of the best things was yet to come, and Phyllis thanked her lucky stars that Rose had come back into her life.

Paul and Dave left the morgue, both sickened by what they saw. Their father had once been strong, and handsome, but the life he'd been living had taken its toll and in death he looked like a withered old man.

They were now waiting to pick up his belongings, Dave moaning because he still thought it was a waste of time, and when they were handed the package, at first Paul had to agree. He didn't now though, and after reading the letter that had been found in his father's pocket, his grief was replaced by fury. They chucked the foul clothing in the nearest bin, while Paul spat out, 'I could kill him.'

'It's a bit late. He's already dead.'

'He should have told us, Dave.'

'You read the letter. She asked him not to and let's face it, you can understand why.'

'All this time, and this is the last thing I expected,' Paul said. 'Wait a minute, according to that date Dad got this letter in June.'

'Yeah, so?'

'Don't you realise what this means? She's still in there and we can visit her.'

'She might not agree to see us.'

'We could give it a try.'

'How do you think Carol's going to take it when we tell her?' Dave asked.

'Let's go home and we'll soon find out,' Paul said, thinking that it was a daft question. Carol was going to he shocked – as deeply as they were.

Jeremy returned from the unit at midday. Len Upwood had continued to be surly, and as it had been impossible to assert his authority, Jeremy had gone into the small office where he'd flicked through the papers and orders. When the telephone rang he'd answered it, writing swift notes, and then seeing Len in the doorway, he'd taken great satisfaction in telling the man to get back to work, the call none of his business.

He'd taken the notes and driven home, surprised to find Tom up. Jeremy felt pleased with himself as he told his brother about the possible contract, but got an unexpected reaction.

'Did you talk to Len? It's a big development and he'll know we need to get working on a quote.'

'He was busy, but don't worry, I can give you a hand.'

'Jeremy, do you know anything about glazing and the costs involved?'

'Well, no, but it can't be that hard.'

'There are a lot of factors to be taken into account; frames, glass supplies, manpower costs, and that's just a start. Show me those notes.'

Jeremy handed them over, and after a brief look at them, Tom said, 'These are useless. I told you that Len knows what he's doing and if he'd taken the call he'd have asked the right questions.'

'I was only trying to help.'

'This is just a hindrance, and in future stay out of things you know nothing about,' Tom snapped as he stood up. 'I'll have to ring Len and tell him to call the developer for more information.'

Jeremy was left inwardly fuming. Tom had been a stick-thin boy with asthma who was being bullied at school when Jeremy left home, and he hadn't looked much better on his return. He was still thin with a weak chest, but now Jeremy was seeing a different side to his brother, one he hadn't expected. He'd thought Tom would be easy to manipulate, that getting an equal share in the business would be a doddle – now though, he wasn't so sure.

Chapter Thirty-Two

Tommy was still working on the quote on Thursday morning. It was a larger development than the last one, and he really wanted to gain the contract. When he'd started the calculations, it soon became obvious that it would be impossible to keep to schedule with his current workforce. He'd have to employ another couple of installers, but as he was unlikely to hear if he'd won the contract or not until after the Christmas period, there was no immediate urgency. For now he just had to get the quote in, along with the recommendations he had from the last developer he'd worked with.

'Thomas, you've been working on that all morning. It's twelve thirty and I think you should take a break now,' Celia said as she put a cup of coffee and a sandwich beside him.

'It's nearly finished,' he said, stretching his upper body, feeling the release of tense muscles across his shoulders and lower back. Other than that he didn't feel too bad as this bout of bronchitis hadn't kept him in bed for as long as usual. 'Have you made up the men's pay-packets?'

'Of course I have, and I drew out the extra cash you asked for when I went to the bank. I'm not happy about it though, and still don't feel it's necessary to give the men a Christmas bonus.'

'They've earned it and I'll give it to them tomorrow when I go to the unit.'

'Jeremy can do that. You're not well enough to go out yet.'

'Yes I am, and talking of Jeremy, where is he? I hope he hasn't gone to the unit again. Len didn't say a lot, but reading between the lines, I think Jeremy has ruffled his feathers.'

'Jeremy has a way with people, so I doubt that. I'm not sure where he is, but he didn't mention the unit when he left, just saying something about going for a drive and that he'd be home by about two.'

'He took the van?'

'Well yes, I said he could use it until you need it again. Surely you don't mind?'

'No, that's fine,' Tommy said, biting into his sandwich.

'I'm worried, Thomas. Unless Jeremy finds something fulfilling to do, such as working with you, I fear he'll leave again.'

'Mum, I'd like to give him a job, but he knows nothing about glazing.'

'He could learn, and it would be a huge incentive for him to stay if you offer Jeremy a share in the business.'

'No, I don't think I can do that. At the moment Jeremy would just be a dead weight, adding nothing to the business, yet taking a share of the profits.'

Tommy saw his mother's face suffuse with colour and expected an outburst, but instead she took a deep breath and said with unexpected calm, 'That might be true now, but given time I'm sure that Jeremy would become an asset. For instance, he has charm, charisma and would make an excellent salesman. He'd be able to bring business in, but until then you could make it a condition that he doesn't receive any unearned profits.'

'I suppose that could work, but I still need to give it a lot of thought.'

'Very well, I'll leave you to it, but I'm sure you'll come to the right decision,' Celia said. 'In the meantime, I'd rather we kept this conversation to ourselves. Jeremy doesn't know anything about this and I wouldn't want to raise his hopes, only to have them dashed.'

When his mother left the room, Tommy mulled it over. He liked having his brother around and regretted his outburst yesterday. He'd apologised, but still felt a bit rotten about it. He knew that Jeremy was only trying to look out for him, something he'd always done when they were kids, but with no experience, he really didn't know what he was doing. His mother was right though, Jeremy could learn, and he'd offer him a job, though he'd be little more that an apprentice to start with.

When it came to a stake in the business, Tommy was unwilling to be rushed into such an important decision. A job first, and then if it looked like Jeremy had an aptitude for the business, he'd consider giving him a share.

For now though he had this quote to finish, and when it was completed Tommy put it into an envelope, ready to be sent off. Moments later the door opened and Jeremy came in with a flourish. Tommy was surprised to see that he had Amy with him, his brother smiling as he said, 'It was Amy's half day so when I saw her walking home I gave her a lift.'

Seeing them together, Tommy saw that Amy looked pink-cheeked, and she seemed to be avoiding his eyes, almost as though she felt guilty about something. His mother had said that Amy hung on to Jeremy's every word, but looking at his tall, strong, good-looking brother, Tommy couldn't help wondering if there was more to it than that. He didn't like the feeling, yet Tommy was unable to stem the surge of jealousy that made his stomach churn.

Amy walked over to him now, saying softly, 'You look even better today.'

'I am,' he told her, relieved when Amy kissed him on the lips and at last met his eyes.

'That's wonderful,' she said, smiling, and then whispered close in his ear, 'I love you, Tommy Frost.'

'I love you too,' he hissed back, feeling the tension drain from his body while giving himself a mental ticking off for doubting Amy. He knew why of course. He was skinny and weak, and had allowed his own inadequacies to rule his feelings. It wouldn't happen again, he'd see to that, and as Amy continued to hold his hand, he hardly noticed that they weren't the only people in the room.

For Amy it was different. She had wanted to see Tommy, but longed to be away from Jeremy and was aware of him every second that he was in the room. He'd insisted on giving her a lift, but now Amy wished she'd found an excuse, any excuse to refuse. It was getting worse, the intimate way he looked at her, the smile on his handsome face so inviting that she was becoming frightened of her own responses.

How could she feel like this when she loved Tommy, really loved him? What Jeremy aroused in her wasn't love, it was something else – something almost primitive that both repelled and attracted her.

'I'm going back to work tomorrow,' Tommy said, breaking into Amy's thoughts.

'Are you sure you're up to it?' she asked.

'You sound as bad as my mother,' he said, although smiling.

'We're only trying to make sure you don't rush things,' Celia said. 'Isn't that right, Amy?'

'Yes, it is,' she replied, still unused to Celia's kindly attitude towards her.

'Well you can both rest assured that I'm fine,' Tommy said.

'Did you get that quote sorted out?' Jeremy asked.

'Yes, I've just finished it.'

'Would you like me to pop it in the post for you, or I'd be happy to deliver it by hand. After that muck-up it's the least I can do.'

'Don't worry about it. You were only trying to help and as I said last night, I'm sorry for overreacting.'

'One apology is enough,' Jeremy said, grinning. 'You don't have to grovel.'

'Right, I won't and yes, you can take it to the post office.'

Amy couldn't make sense of this conversation, only relief that Jeremy was going out. He smiled at her and she looked away, determined that from now on she was going to stay as far away from him as possible.

Jeremy took the envelope and went into the hall, his mother saying as she followed him, 'I have a couple of last minute Christmas cards that need posting too. Come upstairs and I'll give them to you.'

He didn't know why she just couldn't bring them down, but the explanation became obvious when they stood in her bedroom and she said, 'I've had a word with Thomas about giving you a share in the business.'

'You shouldn't have done that. I've only been home for a short time and it's far too early to raise the subject.'

'I don't think it is. There's no guarantee that we can get rid of Amy, so we need to make sure you've got a stake in the business before Thomas marries her.'

'My plan is already working. I know Amy's attracted to me, and didn't you see Tom's face when I came in with her? It was obvious that he was jealous.'

'Yes, but I also saw that it could go badly wrong. Instead of turning on Amy, Thomas might blame you.'

'He won't be able to do that, not when he sees the evidence with his own eyes.'

'It could still turn Thomas against you and I think it's too risky. The safest option would be to go for a share in the business, sooner rather than later.'

Though Jeremy hated to admit it, he thought his mother was right. It was the business or the girl, but what he really wanted was both. He'd go along with his mother for now – concentrate on getting a stake in the business, but once that was achieved, Amy would be his for the picking.

Chapter Thirty-Three

Christmas came, and for the first time since her marriage, Phyllis wasn't in her own home; though with Rose's kitchen now just as familiar to her, she was happily helping her cousin to prepare the finishing touches to the meal.

They had exchanged presents with Amy before leaving home, and now she said to Rose, 'Amy loved her new cardigan, and she gave me a nice handbag.'

'What did you get from Stan?' Rose asked.

Phyllis chuckled, 'As usual, I got something for the kitchen. This time it's a new frying pan.'

'Flaming hell, I hope you hit him over the head with it.'

'I felt like it, but Stan has never had a clue when it comes to presents. It doesn't occur to him that I'd like something for myself, and to be honest he looked so pleased with himself when he gave it to me, saying that he'd noticed my old one is a bit worn out, that I didn't have the heart to do anything other than smile.'

'I certainly smiled when Samuel gave me this bracelet,' Rose said.

Phyllis would have too, but she still didn't envy Rose. Stan might be a bit thoughtless at times, but in other ways he was a good husband. They might not be rich but Stan always had the power to make her laugh, and that was something Phyllis thought more precious than gold.

She couldn't imagine life without Stan, yet during the past year two marriages in the street had fallen apart. Phyllis still couldn't believe the events were linked – that George Frost and Daphne Cole had run off together. It was Mabel's theory, and another nasty rumour she'd set in motion since Frank Cole's death. It sickened Phyllis. Poor Carol had been through enough, and she had now become distant with Amy, as though wanting nothing more to do with anyone who lived on Lark Rise.

Mabel had seen everyone leaving next door, Phyllis and Stan walking off in one direction and Amy in the other. She'd worked it out of course. Phyllis was going to spend Christmas day with Rose, while Amy went to Celia Frost's.

She could guess how Phyllis would feel about that, her precious daughter preferring to spend the day with her future mother-in-law instead of her, and Mabel smiled with grim satisfaction. She was still fuming that Phyllis had turned on her again when she'd told her about Carol's abortion. It wasn't as though she'd made it up, she was only speaking the truth, but Phyllis had gone on her high horse, ranting and raving about malicious gossip.

They hadn't spoken since, but that didn't bother Mabel. She had more interesting friends, ones who were happy to dish the dirt on those who deserved it, especially the likes of Carol Cole. Still, it had been a bit of a shock to hear that her father was dead, and some people had been invited to his funeral. Not her of course, or Edna, but as her husband had once given Frank a beating, it wasn't surprising. There'd been other news too. Celia Frost's other son had turned up, and though she regularly kept her ear to the adjoining wall, hoping to hear Phyllis and Amy talking about him, so far Mabel hadn't learned anything of interest that she could pass on.

It was steamy in the kitchen as Mabel drained the vegetables and then dished up their dinner. It was just for the two of them, and for a moment Mabel was saddened as she remembered previous Christmases spent next door with Phyllis, Stan and Amy. They'd had some good laughs, Stan a born comedian, and though Mabel hadn't expected an invitation this year, she had hoped that one of her other mates would issue one.

'Here you are, Jack,' she said, placing their plates on the table.

'Lovely,' he said, and that one word was it for the rest of the meal.

Mabel looked at the Christmas crackers she'd placed on the table, and a wave of sadness washed over her. She'd been mad to try to make this meal festive. The crackers only served to emphasise the fact that there was just two of them, when there should have been three.

Amy gave her present to Celia, hoping that it was all right. She'd chosen the silky scarf with care, selecting one in subtle shades of pink and lavender.

'Thank you, Amy, this is lovely.'

With a sigh of relief that Celia's appreciation seemed genuine, Amy gave Jeremy his last minute present, a pair of gloves, for which he thanked her. He'd been different for the last few days, not at all flirtatious, and Amy found the feelings he aroused in her had diminished. It was as though Jeremy had a switch that he turned on when he was flirting; a light in his eyes, a magnetism, that thankfully he'd now turned off.

'This is for you,' she said to Tommy as lastly she gave him his present, one she'd saved for, and it had been worth it to see the delight on his face.

'This is a fabulous watch,' he said, putting it on and then grinning, he kissed her.

'Well this is all very nice,' Celia said, 'but we don't usually exchange presents until after dinner.'

Amy flushed with embarrassment. 'Oh, I'm sorry, I didn't know.'

'Don't worry about it,' Tommy said. 'You can have your present now too.'

'Thomas, I'd rather we do things the proper way and I'm sure Amy is happy to wait.'

'Yes, yes, of course,' she said, wondering why exchanging presents after dinner was the *proper* way. As a child she had always woken early on Christmas day, running downstairs to see what had been left under the tree. It had been a long time before she found out that it had been her father, not Santa, who brought soot down the chimney in which she always saw footprints. How awful it would've been to be told she couldn't open her presents until after dinner, especially as even now she woke up on Christmas day with a sense of excitement.

'However, I don't think it's too early for a glass of sherry,' Celia said. 'Jeremy, will you do the honours, but just a small one for me.'

As Jeremy rose to pour them, Amy looked at Tommy and now had to force a smile. It was nice to be with him, but she was finding the restrained atmosphere difficult.

'Thank you,' she said when Jeremy handed her a glass, and though she wasn't keen on the taste Amy sipped it, while the others talked about politics, a subject she knew little about.

'The Suez crisis is over, but do you think Anthony Eden is going to survive politically?' Tommy asked.

'I hope so,' Celia replied. 'I rather like him and he gained us a large majority in the last election.'

Amy's thoughts drifted to Carol, unable to imagine how awful Christmas must be for her this year. She had called in to see her several times since her father had died, and though Paul had told her about the funeral arrangements, Carol had seemed unwilling to talk.

'Amy, I asked if you'd like another glass of sherry?'

Celia's voice snapped Amy back to the present and she said, 'No thank you.'

'Well I'll have one, Jeremy, and then I'll see to our dinner.'

'I'll give you a hand,' Amy said, used to being in the kitchen with her mother.

'I have everything under control, and really, Amy, it isn't the done thing to expect help from one's guests.'

'Oh, come on, Mum,' Tommy protested. 'Don't be so stuffy and there's no need to treat Amy like a guest.'

'I have my standards, Thomas, or would you prefer me to treat Amy like a kitchen maid?' she asked.

'Don't be silly and for goodness sake lighten up, Mum. It's Christmas.'

'Yes, come on, Mother,' Jeremy agreed. 'Here, drink another glass of sherry.'

'Thank you, dear,' she said, smiling at her elder son.

When Celia finished her drink she went through to the kitchen, and Amy didn't dare ask if she wanted any help again. Her feelings of being out of place grew worse when she saw the immaculately laid dining table, with pristine linen and not a Christmas cracker in sight.

It was all so formal when they sat down to eat, so correct, and Amy missed her dad's jokes, the groans at those found in crackers, and even the silly paper hats. It struck her then that this was her last Christmas as a single woman and though it was nice to be with Tommy, she now wished she had shared it with her parents.

Carol had mixed feelings. There was still her father's funeral to face, but only a month later there was something to look forward to. She still found it almost impossible to believe and said to Paul, 'It was awful to see Mum like that, but at least she'll be home soon.'

'Don't tell anyone where she's been, not even Amy,' Paul reiterated again. 'I'm not saying that she'd say anything, at least not intentionally, but it only takes one careless word and it would spread like wildfire.'

'Yes,' Dave agreed, 'and if that happened, for Mum's sake, we'd have to leave the area.'

'Maybe we should do that anyway,' Paul suggested. 'If we all find work in another borough, we wouldn't have to worry about it coming out.'

'Well I'm game,' Dave said. 'What about you, Carol?'

'I wouldn't mind.'

'Right then, after Dad's funeral we'll start looking around, but with jobs and a decent-size flat to find, it might take a while,' Paul said, then cutting into a roast potato. 'For your first go at a Christmas dinner, this ain't a bad effort, Carol.'

'Yeah, it's really tasty,' Dave agreed.

Carol sighed. For all her talk in the past of never becoming a servant to men, she'd ended up as cook and cleaner first for her father, and now her brothers. 'Well as I cooked it, you two can wash up.'

'What! You must be joking,' Dave said.

'No, I'm not. I work full time too you know, and it

wouldn't hurt the pair of you to do some of the cooking and housework.'

'Carol's got a point,' Paul said. 'We did it before she moved in.'

'Yeah, but we didn't have any choice then,' Dave argued. 'Anyway, Carol won't have to do it for much longer.'

'You're not lumbering Mum with everything when she comes home,' Carol said, shaking her head in exasperation. 'We're all going to chip in.'

'If you say so,' Dave said, but then turned the subject back to moving out of the area. 'What about going over the river to Chelsea?'

'It depends on how much a flat would cost,' Paul said.

Carol hadn't hesitated in agreeing to move away from Battersea, yet knew that had she been asked the same question a year ago her answer would have been different. She'd been young and carefree then, but now every time she saw Amy it only served as a reminder of what had been happier times.

Amy still seemed so fresh, so innocent, while Carol felt so much older and tainted. They seemed eons apart now, and with Amy getting married in four months, the old friendship they had shared would be forever changed.

Maybe it was time to sever all ties to Amy – to move on to where there'd be no memories of the past to haunt her.

Chapter Thirty-Four

'Mabel, it's been two months since your roof was repaired, but there's no sign of ours, or any others being done,' Edna complained.

'Yeah, I know, and what do you think about Winnie Morrison's place being done up on the inside? It's a bit funny if you ask me, especially as after fumigating Frank Cole's place it hasn't been touched.'

'Samuel Jacobs has never been known to decorate his houses before he re-lets them. It's usually a case of take it as you find it or leave it, so yeah, it's a bit odd,' Edna agreed.

'I've got my suspicions, especially as Rose can twist Samuel Jacobs around her finger, but I won't say anything until I'm sure. She's even paying for Amy's wedding reception.'

'You and Phyllis aren't talking, so how did you find out about that?' Edna asked.

Mabel chuckled, winked and said, 'Thin walls, that's how.'

'Yeah, they come in handy at times,' Edna agreed, gesturing to the left. 'You should have heard those two next door yesterday. Wilf lost a mint on the horses again and Pat was going ballistic.'

'I'm glad I'm not married to a gambler,' Mabel said. 'I don't know how Pat puts up with it.'

'Nor me, or a drinker.'

'They're just as bad,' Mabel agreed, nodding sagely. 'Look what happened to Frank Cole.'

'Yeah, and I'd like to know what happened to Carol. She wasn't in the hairdressers when I went to have a perm. They said she'd left, moved away, but that was all the information I could get. Have you heard anything?'

Mabel was waiting for this and was pleased with her little snippet. 'I've had my ear to the wall and it's not only Carol who moved away, her brothers have gone too.'

'Really? I wonder why?'

'I know why. I heard Amy talking to Phyllis and it seems it's down to the nasty gossip that's been spread around about Carol,' said Mabel, knowing that Edna had been the one who set it in motion.

'Well, all I can say is good riddance to bad rubbish,' Edna said defensively. 'I don't like to speak ill of the dead, but my hubby had to give Frank Cole a hiding when he insulted me, and as for Carol, look how she turned out. Like mother like daughter, if your theory about Daphne running off with George is right.'

'I'm sure it is,' Mabel said, and as Edna poured her another cup of tea, they found a few more people to talk about.

Jeremy was aware of time passing too. It was now mid-February and though Tom had given him a job at the unit, he hated being treated like an apprentice. There was an uneasy truce now between him and Len Upwood, though it still annoyed Jeremy that Tom had taken the man's side. He'd expected that as Tom's brother, he'd be given some authority, but instead had been told that Len was the foreman and therefore the one who gave the orders.

On top of that, he'd done as his mother suggested and laid off Amy, but the more he saw her, the more his

287

obsession was taking a hold. He wanted her – but in eight weeks' time, Amy would be marrying his brother.

'Mum, we're getting nowhere,' he said that evening. 'There's no sign of Tom coming to a decision about giving me a share in the business, and we haven't even suggested that you should have a stake in it too.'

'He'd baulk at that, and for now we should just concentrate on you.'

'Yes, I suppose you're right, but once I'm on board I'll see that you get your share too,' Jeremy lied.

'I know you will, darling, and in the meantime I'll go on speaking to Tom on your behalf. I hope you can see now how difficult things have been for me since your father left. With Thomas in control of the business, I have no say in anything, and I have to rely on him for my finances.'

'You shouldn't have to dance to his tune. It isn't right, and though I've said nothing to Tom so far, maybe it's time I stepped in. It's Sunday tomorrow and we could sit him down for a family meeting. If you hint beforehand that I'm thinking of leaving the country again, it might make him a bit more amenable. If that doesn't work, with time running out, we'll have to go back to my first plan.'

'I still think it's too dangerous. You said you could discredit Amy; show her to be the tart she is, but if Tom sees you both in a compromising position, he might focus his jealousy and anger on you. If Amy convinces him that she's the innocent party, you'll never get a share in the business. In fact, any relationship you have with your brother will be over.'

Jeremy felt a surge of annoyance and frustration. All right, he'd carry on doing things his mother's way; but there'd come a time when he'd get his hands on Amy and there was no way she'd be able to resist him.

* * *

For Amy, the first part of the New Year had been painful. She had gone to Frank Cole's funeral with her parents, and though Carol had thanked them for coming, she seemed distant and cold. Worse was to come when she went to see Carol a few days later, only to be told that they were moving out of the area and with so much to arrange they were too busy for visitors. After so many years of friendship, for Amy it was like a slap in the face. She had kept her distance for over a week, but despite being given the cold shoulder, she didn't want to lose touch with Carol and had tried again.

Amy stared absentmindedly at the television, remembering her last visit to Carol and the final blow. Carol said they'd be moving soon, and when Amy had asked for their new address, there had been the lame excuse that she couldn't remember it, followed by an offhand remark that she would write when they were settled.

There was no point in calling again, Carol had said, but when they had said their goodbyes she had thawed a little. Carol had thanked her for being such a good friend, briefly hugged her, and Amy knew from that moment on that she would never hear from her again.

'You're miles away,' Tommy said.

'Sorry,' she said, pushing away her unhappy thoughts.

'It's all right, I know you're a bit preoccupied with sorting out the wedding.'

'There isn't much to do now, especially since Rose offered to lay on a reception. She told me to leave it all to her, though of course my mum is making sure she gets her say in everything.'

'Now that's not fair,' Phyllis protested. 'I just want to make sure that Rose gets it right, that's all. Take the cake for instance. She was going to have one made with four tiers. Now what's the point of that when there's only going to be about a dozen or so of us to eat it?'

Amy smiled and said, 'Rose certainly likes to do things in a big way. Take that dinner set she gave me. There's eight of everything, plus the vegetable tureens. I'll need a big kitchen with lots of cupboards to fit it in.'

'Talking of that, I'd better get on with looking for a flat,' Tommy said. 'I've been snowed under with work since getting this new contract, but I can't leave it any longer.'

'No!' Phyllis said sharply. 'Don't do that.'

'Why not? With the wedding only eight weeks away I've got to find us somewhere to live.'

With a sigh, Phyllis glanced at Stan and stood up. 'We're going to have to tell them.'

'Tell us what?' Amy asked.

In answer to her question, Phyllis went over to the mantelpiece, and taking down a vase, she tipped something into her hand. 'I wanted to keep it as a surprise, but of course I'm as daft as a brush and hadn't thought about Tommy trying to find a flat. Here,' she said, holding them out. 'These are the keys to your new home.'

Bewildered Amy asked, 'What new home?'

'The one next door.'

'What? Winnie Morrison's place?'

'It isn't hers any more, love, and it's been empty for a long time. Thanks to Rose and Samuel it's now yours, and don't worry, it's all been done up for you.'

Amy couldn't believe it. She was getting married, but she'd still be close to her parents and that was just perfect. She smiled with delight, grabbed Tommy's hand and said excitedly, 'Come on, let's go and take a look at it.'

* * *

Celia was less than happy when Thomas came home that evening, full of the newly refurbished house they'd be renting when they got married.

'I don't know why you're so pleased about it,' she huffed. 'It's a pokey place at the lower end of the Rise, and hardly suitable for a man of your standing.'

'My "standing"? I'm no better than anyone else.'

'Of course you are,' Celia said, thinking that Thomas sounded just like his father. 'You have your own business and you employ eight men now, not including your brother.'

'Yes, that's me. Another *employee*,' Jeremy said.

'Yes, Thomas, and we were going to discuss that with you tomorrow. However, as you're here now and as we're still up, we might as well talk about it now.'

'Mother, I don't think that's a good idea,' Jeremy protested.

'I think it is. Look at Thomas, he's as pleased as punch with his life, and it's about time he realised that we're not. He waltzed in here, full of his so-called good news, and didn't even notice that I'm dreadfully upset.'

Thomas frowned and sat down. 'No, I'm sorry, I didn't. What's wrong?'

Celia pulled out a handkerchief and dabbed her eyes for effect. 'Jeremy has just told me that after your wedding, he's leaving. He's going abroad again.'

'But why?' Thomas asked, looking at his brother now.

'Jeremy won't tell you why, but I will,' Celia choked emotionally. 'You need to put yourself in his place, imagine how it would feel if your brother owned a family business that should in part be yours.'

'As I've said to you before, Jeremy wasn't here when Dad left so he passed it on to me.'

'I know, but in all fairness you can redress that now,' Celia said.

'It's all right, Tom, I don't expect you to give me a share of the business,' Jeremy said. 'You took it on, built it up, and you deserve to reap the profits. It's just that I find it a little humiliating to be employed by my kid brother so decided it's time I left.'

Thomas lowered his head, saying nothing, and putting a finger to her lips, Celia indicated to Jeremy that he should be quiet. It had been clever of him to say that he didn't expect a share in the business, and from what she could see it had given Thomas food for thought.

At last he raised his head. 'It would break Mum's heart if you leave and I'd like you to stay too. If you do I'll give you a share in the business, but none of the financial profit for this coming year because you're right, they're down to me. However, despite what Mum thinks, I have been giving some thought to your role as a salesman. You'll have to learn more about the business to be able to give estimates, but next year you'll get a share of the profits too.'

'Thomas, that sounds wonderful,' Celia enthused. 'What do you think, Jeremy?'

'Well, it's certainly an incentive to stay,' he said, then stayed quiet for a moment, as if mulling it over. 'All right, Tom, I'm happy with your terms, and don't worry, once I've learned the ropes I'll bring in plenty of new business.'

'With a share in the company, I won't be able to sack you if you don't,' Tom said, though smiling.

'What sort of share are we talking about?' Jeremy asked.

'How about thirty-three per cent?'

'Thomas, it should be half,' Celia protested.

'No, Mother, I'm happy with that,' Jeremy said.

'Good,' Thomas said, 'but with the amount of work coming in at the moment, and my wedding looming, if you don't mind waiting we'll get the legal stuff sorted out after that.'

'Yes, that's fine,' Jeremy agreed.

Celia was less than pleased. She'd have liked the formalities dealt with before the wedding, but she'd learned that Thomas wouldn't be pushed, and if one tried he would stubbornly dig his heels in. That was something Amy would find out if she tried to put a stop to Jeremy getting a share of the business. Not that Celia was really worried, because despite the things she'd told Jeremy about Amy, in reality she saw the girl as weak, easily intimidated, and inferior.

Jeremy surreptitiously winked at her, and Celia wondered why he was content with less than fifty per cent of the business. It didn't take her long to work it out and she was pleased by Jeremy's cleverness, sure now that he could outwit Thomas. Given time Jeremy would ensure that she got a share in the firm, an equal one, and with sixty-six per cent between them they would gain control.

It was perfect, she thought, her financial future would be assured, and instead of Thomas lording it over them, he would have to dance to their tune.

Chapter Thirty-Five

Amy found time flying past. It was a lovely spring day, the weather clement, and things had changed at work. For the past month she'd had Saturdays off and had loved it, happy to forgo her Thursday half days. On her final half day off she had bumped into Miss Winters again, and had been persuaded to join her for a coffee. Once again Amy had felt sorry for her former manageress, feeling that she was lonely, and had impulsively invited her to the wedding. Miss Winters had graciously declined, but wished her every happiness before they parted, that being the last time Amy had seen her.

It was a Saturday morning now and Amy was waiting for the delivery van to arrive. Though the house had been newly decorated, they had to furnish it, so when Tommy could spare the time they chose everything from the G-plan range. When the van turned up Amy saw curtains twitching, but ignored them as it was unloaded and her new furniture carried inside.

'What do you think, Mum?' she said, standing back to admire the light oak cabinet, with black lacquered panels. It had open shelves, along with a built-in cocktail cabinet and a space for a television set.

'It's very modern, but it's nice, and that drop-leaf dining table set is lovely too.'

'The light oak matches the cabinet,' Amy pointed out.

'Now I like that,' Phyllis remarked as a pale green and black settee was carried in and uncovered, along with two matching chairs.

Amy had been worried that the room would look too full, but now that everything was in place, she thought it looked lovely. 'There's just the bedroom furniture to unload now.'

'Is that G-plan too?' her mother asked.

'Yes, Tommy insisted on it. He said it's good quality and made to last.'

'If he can afford this lot, that business of his must be making a fair few bob.'

'Yes, I think it is.'

'Does Tommy still want you to give up your job?'

'Yes, but I'm not sure. He works long hours, and I'm a bit worried that I might get bored if I'm at home every day.'

'I'd say make the most of it, because once a baby comes along there'll be no chance of that.'

'It's a bit too soon to be talking about a baby. I'm not married yet.'

'Well once you are, don't take too long about it. I can't wait to be a grandmother.'

'I'll do my best,' Amy said, yet she had no idea what that side of marriage was like. When she was in Tommy's arms, he aroused passionate feelings that left her wanting more, yet they had somehow managed to restrain themselves.

Not for much longer, Amy thought, there was just one week to go and then she'd be Tommy's wife.

'Mum, I know you haven't been before, but you should come and see our house now that the furniture has been delivered,' Thomas said when he came home that night.

Celia had no interest in seeing a pokey house at the bottom of the Rise, even if her son was going to live in it. 'I still think you were mad to rent it, especially as you'll be living next door to your in-laws.'

'That won't be a problem. I get on well with Amy's parents.'

'You won't think that once they start to interfere, especially Amy's mother.'

'She won't do that and we'll be fine,' Thomas said offhandedly.

'You always dismiss my concerns as though they count for nothing,' she snapped.

'We managed to take an hour off work today to have the final fittings on our suits,' Jeremy intervened. 'Of course, I fancied a light blue waistcoat and matching cravat to go with mine, but Tom vetoed that idea.'

'It'd be a bit much for a registry office,' Tommy said.

'If you'd chosen to get married in a church, Jeremy could have been your best man,' Celia complained. 'Instead it's this paltry little affair, but I'm not lowering my standards. I'm wearing an apricot coloured silk suit and matching hat.'

'Yes, I've seen your outfit and you'll knock them out,' Jeremy said.

'Thank you, dear,' Celia said, pleased, yet wondering now if she should have bothered. There'd be nobody of breeding to impress, either at the registry office or the reception, despite it being held in the cousin's huge house, one that she had persuaded her rich husband to buy.

Money couldn't buy class though, and Celia dreaded to think what food would be served, probably something like jellied eels. She shuddered at the thought.

* * *

Tommy was glad that Jeremy had placated their mother by changing the subject to their suits and her outfit. Jeremy had a way with her, and since he'd come home life had been a lot easier. With both her sons around her now, she'd become less possessive of him, Tommy thought, and she was a lot more amenable when it came to Amy.

Though still inexperienced when it came to the glazing business, Jeremy was learning and Tommy didn't regret offering him a share in the business. He'd baulked at the idea at first, thinking that he'd been the one who had built it up, but then decided he was being selfish and unfair. Jeremy was his big brother, and by rights the firm should have gone to him. It was great to think that by taking him on board, Jeremy would always be around now, the two of them eventually able to take the business to new heights. With new towns springing up out of London and vast swathes of houses being built, the possibilities of even larger contracts beckoned.

'When you get up to speed with calculating estimates, I think you'll be able to try your hand as a salesman,' Tommy said, with the new towns in mind.

'I'll look forward to that, though of course I'll need a car.'

'When you're ready you'll get one,' Tommy said, thinking that it was about time he got himself a car too. With the wedding looming it would have to wait for now, but the accounts were looking very healthy, despite the expenditure on furnishing the house.

One week, he thought, and then Amy would be his wife. When he looked at her, sometimes he couldn't believe his luck, but Amy had chosen him and he couldn't wait to spend the rest of his life with her.

*   *   *

Mabel wasn't so happy as she lay in bed, going over the events of the day. She'd seen the furniture van arrive that morning, and was still fuming that Amy had been given the house next door to Phyllis. As she'd told Edna, with the place being done up it smacked of favouritism, not that she begrudged that when it came to Amy – it was Phyllis getting everything that got on her wick. Thanks to Rose, Phyllis had the life of Riley now, a house full of posh stuff and a well-paid job too.

'Can't you stop tossing and turning?' Jack complained. 'I've got an early start in the morning and you're keeping me awake.'

'All right, keep your hair on,' Mabel snapped, but then the heart of the matter hit her and she felt tears flooding her eyes. She'd tried to deny it – tried to act as though she didn't care, but in truth Mabel was heartbroken that she wouldn't be at Amy's wedding. She'd watched the girl grow up and was fond of her, but now because of her big mouth neither Amy nor Phyllis would give her the time of day. It was her own fault, Mabel knew that – knew that because of her obsession with gossip she had lost her best friend.

Sleep wouldn't come, and as always a feeling of self-hate filled Mabel's mind. If she'd acted sooner, if she'd done something differently, her beautiful boy might have lived. Though she'd been told that nothing could have saved him, Mabel still thought she had been a terrible mother, and it was only when she could find someone to talk about – someone who was less than perfect too – that she could feel a little better about herself.

* * *

Carol was feeling bad about herself too, and unable to sleep, she got up to make herself a milky drink. The flat they were renting in Chelsea was on the fourth floor of a tall, terraced house in Tedworth Square, which was in an area that sat between the King's Road and Royal Hospital Road. She had found another job as a receptionist, the boys were working too, and they had all settled well.

'What's the matter? Can't you sleep?'

Carol was about to pour milk into a small saucepan and was startled by the voice. 'Oh, Mum, you made me jump.'

'Sorry, but I heard you getting up.'

'I didn't mean to wake you,' Carol said. 'I tried to be quiet and crept out of our room as quietly as I could.'

'Don't worry, I wasn't asleep.'

'Do you want a milky drink too?'

'Yes please, and I can guess why you're not sleeping. You've lost your dad, and it's going to take time to get over it.'

'It isn't Dad that's keeping me awake.'

'What is it then?'

'Amy is getting married next week and I should be there. I feel rotten about the way I treated her.'

'You were protecting me, I know that, but I feel awful that you were forced to move away.'

Carol shook her head. 'You shouldn't. We didn't move just for your sake. It was for mine too.'

'I don't understand. What do you mean?'

It was time, Carol decided – time to tell her mother the truth. 'I . . . I was raped and . . . and then I had an abortion. Nobody knew about it at first, only Dad, but then the gossips found out about it and soon everyone knew.'

'Oh, Carol, I can't believe you went through all that and I knew nothing about it. I'm sorry . . . so very sorry.'

'Mum, please, don't cry. Look at me, I got through it, and I'm fine now.'

'I thought you were all grown up, and I waited until I felt you didn't need me any more before I left. I was wrong, but I just couldn't stand it any more.'

'What couldn't you stand?' Carol asked. 'You still haven't told us.'

'I can't talk to you about it. You're . . . you're too young.'

'I'm not an innocent any more, though God knows I wish I still was. I've been raped, and Dad tried it on with me too. I had to fight off my own father – so don't tell me I'm too young.'

'What! Your father! Oh no . . . no, I'll never forgive myself for leaving now. I know he adored you and when you used to get dressed up with all that make-up on, I used to worry about something in his eyes when he looked at you, but I never thought for a moment that you'd be in any danger, that . . . he . . . he'd . . .' she sobbed, unable to go on.

'You used to nag me about my clothes and make-up. I thought it was because you were jealous of me.'

'Jealous! No, no, never that,' she protested.

'Mum, you still haven't told me why you walked out on Dad.'

Daphne dashed her hands over her face to wipe away the tears, and then said, 'When it came to se . . . sex, your father was like an animal. It was night after night, and he'd never take no for an answer. He'd hold me down, force me, and . . . and after years of what felt like torture, I just couldn't take any more.'

'Oh, Mum, I didn't know,' Carol moaned, horrified at what her mother had endured.

'When I left, I found a small bedsit out of the area in Putney, and a job in a bar. I was going to write to you and the boys, but then one of the customers grabbed me and I just lost it. I picked up the nearest thing to hand, a bottle, and hit him over the head with it. I didn't even realise what I'd done until I saw him lying on the floor, unconscious, and bleeding.'

'You told us this much before, but now you've told me about Dad I can understand why you reacted like that. It all makes sense, yet it must have been a nightmare when you were sent to prison.'

'I think I just shut down, switched off, and at least I didn't have to serve the whole nine months.'

'Your letter to Dad was found on him when . . . when his body was discovered. The boys got hold of it when they went to pick up his belongings. I'm just glad we found you before you got out. But what about Gran, did she know you were in prison?'

'Yes, when I wrote to your Dad, I sent her a letter too and I begged them both not to tell you or the boys that I was in prison. I hoped to serve my time and write to you when I got out, making some excuse for not getting in touch before.'

'You didn't need to hide it from us.'

'I was so ashamed, Carol.'

'You've got nothing to be ashamed of.'

'Neither have you. We're both victims.'

'I'm so glad we've talked like this, Mum. It's made me feel that I can move on – that I can put it all behind me now.'

'You're forgetting one thing.'

'Am I?'

'What about Amy? You said you feel terrible about the way you treated her, but you can do something about that. Go to see her, tell her you're sorry, and if I know Amy she'll forgive you in an instant.'

'I don't want to go back to Lark Rise or anywhere near it. One look at me and the gossips will be off again and if they find out about you . . .'

'If you feel so strongly about it, write to Amy. You could suggest meeting somewhere, even here. Amy doesn't have to know I've been in prison and if you think about it, neither does anyone else. I'll just tell her that I was unhappily married and on your father's death I decided to return home.'

'Yes, of course, why didn't I think of that before?'

'As I said, you and the boys were trying to protect me, but there's really no need. I'll tell Paul and Davy the same, and if anyone sees me when I go to visit your gran I'll hold my head up high, keep my mouth shut, and they can think what they like.'

'That'll drive them mad.'

'Good, but to be honest, even if they find out, words can't hurt me, or you – unless you let them. Those narrow-minded bigots haven't lived our lives so they're in no position to judge us,' Daphne said, then yawning. 'Well now, I don't know about you, but I think I can sleep now.'

'Yes, me too,' Carol said, happier now as she followed her mother into their bedroom. They hoped to find a larger flat, but for now this would do. They had single beds, and so did the boys, though Dave was always complaining about how loudly Paul snored.

Carol snuggled down in her bed. She'd write to Amy

tomorrow, and send her a present. It was doubtful that the parcel would arrive before her wedding, but after that they'd be able to meet up. Smiling at the thought, Carol at last drifted off to sleep.

Chapter Thirty-Six

Amy was thrilled when she opened the parcel that had been delivered that morning. It was from Carol and contained a lovely vase. She smiled, imagined it on her new shelving unit where it would look just perfect, and then put it to one side as she read Carol's letter. Firstly Carol apologised for her behaviour but more importantly, wrote that she had wanted to come to her wedding and was sad that she had left it too late.

Amy looked at the address, saw that Carol was living in Chelsea, and then carried on reading. It was lovely that Carol wanted them to meet, possibly after the honeymoon, and that made Amy smile. They were only going away for the weekend to a hotel in Brighton and then it was back to work for both of them on Monday.

'Has Carol told you where she is now?' her mother asked.

'Yes,' Amy said, giving her the letter. While her mother was reading it, Amy was deep in thought. She had the day off and wasn't seeing Tommy that evening so there really wasn't anything to stop her. It was just a matter of timing, but if she left it until after six Carol was sure to be there, even if she was planning to go out later that evening.

'I bet you're pleased she's got in touch,' Phyllis said, passing the letter back, 'but we'd best get a move on or we'll be late for our appointments at the hairdressers.'

Amy put her shoes on, and grabbed a jacket. Rose had insisted that her mother take the day off too, and soon they were leaving the house, only to pull up short when Mabel trotted up to them.

She looked a bit nervous, but thrust a parcel into Amy's hand. 'It's a little something from me and Jack. I've known you since you were a little girl, Amy, and I'm fond of you so please accept it.'

With that Mabel turned on her heels and shot back into her own house, leaving Amy looking wide-eyed at her mother and asking, 'Now what am I supposed to do?'

'I don't know, but I suppose you either give it back or write Mabel a thank you note.'

'I'll put it indoors for now,' Amy said and that done, they were soon on their way again. It seemed ironic that she'd just had a wedding present from Carol, and another from a woman who had torn her friend apart.

Remembering that, Amy wished she had thrown Mabel's present back in her face.

Jeremy was in the office with Tom, waiting for a nod of approval as his brother went over his figures. It was only a small estimate, nothing really to tax his brain, but he still hoped he'd got it right.

'Well done,' Tom said. 'This is fine.'

Jeremy felt like he was in front of a teacher instead of his kid brother, and it didn't sit well. 'It was a doddle, and I think I've got the hang of it all now.'

'Yes, you're nearly there,' Tom agreed, reaching into his pocket for his inhaler.

'Are you all right?' Jeremy asked, thinking that Tom looked a bit wan.

'My chest is a bit tight, that's all.'

'Is everything set for your big day tomorrow?'

'Yes, I've moved all my stuff into our house, and Amy has done the same,' Tom said, but then he began to cough, leaning over the desk with his hand on his chest.

'You sound rough,' Jeremy said when Tom was left gasping for air and reaching for his inhaler again. 'You're not going down with bronchitis again are you?'

'I hope not, it's the last thing I need. I'll take it easy today and I might leave a bit earlier than usual. In the meantime, would you mind taking the wages to the men on site?'

'Of course not,' Jeremy said, more than happy to get out of the unit for a while. Tom got the pay-packets out of the small safe and Jeremy stuffed them in his pocket before heading for the van. As he drove off, his thoughts turned to his coming role as a salesman and the car that would come with it. He'd love a Jaguar, but as he doubted Tom would agree to that, a decent Austin would do for now.

When he got to the site, Jeremy found all the men at work installing windows, and after giving them their pay-packets he checked their progress as if he knew what he was doing. 'Everything looks fine, and are we still on schedule?' he asked Dick Hutton, the man Tom had put in charge of the crews.

'Yes,' he said, nodding, 'but can I have a private word?'

'Of course,' Jeremy said, walking a distance away from the other men.

'Mr Frost always gives the pay-packets to me and I hand them out to the men at the end of the day.'

Jeremy shrugged. 'So, they got paid early. I don't see that as a problem.'

'You should do. With their pay-packets in their pockets there's always the danger they won't show up again after lunch.'

'If that's the case I'll see that they're sacked,' Jeremy said, annoyed at the man's implied criticism, 'and you can tell them that.'

Dick looked at him for a moment as if about to say something, but then he just shook his head, as though in disgust, before walking away.

Jeremy didn't go after him – instead he went back to the van, thinking that Dick Hutton was another one like Len who didn't show him any respect. They'd be sorry, both of them, and though they might try to suck up to him in the near future, it would be too late.

Amy was pleased with her haircut. She hated her curls, wished her hair was straight and sleek, but at least with a shorter cut, it looked tidier. It was five thirty and she was sitting on a bus on her way to see Carol, thinking as it crossed the River Thames that she knew little about other areas of London.

When she got off the bus in Chelsea, Amy had to ask directions twice before she found Tedworth Square and Carol's flat in one of the tall houses. For a moment she paused, hoping that Carol wouldn't mind her turning up unexpectedly, but then finding the right doorbell she pressed it firmly.

It seemed ages before the door was opened, but at last Carol was looking at her wide-eyed as she said, 'Amy, how . . . oh, you must have got my parcel.'

'Yes, I did and thank you.'

'Come in,' Carol said, 'but be prepared for a surprise.'

Amy followed Carol up what seemed to be flight after

flight of stairs, until at last they reached the top landing where she opened a door, calling, 'We've got a visitor,' before urging Amy inside.

Amy's jaw dropped and she gawked at the woman smiling at her. At last she found her voice, but it was high and sounded like a question. 'Mrs Cole?'

'Yes, it's me, Amy. I left because I was unhappy in my marriage, but I should have kept in touch with Carol and my sons. I didn't because I feared they'd never forgive me for walking out, but I was wrong of course. When the boys found me I was shocked to hear about what happened while I was away. They persuaded me to come back, and so here I am.'

'We're dead chuffed, Amy,' Carol said.

'I'm sure you are, but Mrs Cole, you should know that Mabel Povis thinks you went off with Tommy's dad.'

'George Frost! But that's ridiculous.'

'We didn't believe it and told her so.'

'I expect she's still spread it around though, but not to worry. When she eventually sets eyes on me Mabel Povis will have to eat her words.'

'Amy, it's lovely to see you, but what are you doing here?' Carol asked. 'Aren't you supposed to be getting married in the morning?'

'Yes, but it wouldn't be the same without you there. It isn't too late, you could still come, you too Mrs Cole, along with Dave and Paul.'

'Amy, I'd love to,' Carol said. 'What about you, Mum?'

'Well if you don't mind, Amy, I think I'll decline, but I can't speak for my sons.'

'Of course I don't mind, but if you change your mind, you'll be welcome.'

'I'll have to sort out something to wear,' Carol said worriedly, 'and what time have I got to be there?'

Amy told her, and about the reception, Carol's mum then wanting to hear all about Rose and Samuel Jacobs. Unlike some, she wasn't judgemental, and then Paul and Dave arrived home. Amy saw that they looked surprised to see her, but soon recovered when Carol explained that she'd given her the address. Amy invited them to the wedding, both thanking her but saying they were working overtime the next morning.

'Mum, we're starving,' Paul complained.

'I've made a stew and it only needs warming up,' she said, going through a door that Amy presumed led to the kitchen.

'Cor, Mum's stew,' Dave said, licking his lips. 'I can't wait.'

'Come on then, let's get cleaned up,' Paul said. 'She won't let us sit down until we do.'

Carol grinned, saying as her brothers left the room, 'As you can tell, they prefer Mum's cooking to mine.'

'I should go now,' Amy said, 'but I'll see you tomorrow at the registry office.'

'Yes, you certainly will,' Carol agreed.

Amy gave her a hug and then, telling her that she'd find her own way out, she left, smiling happily that her oldest and best friend would be there at her wedding.

Chapter Thirty-Seven

Tommy opened his eyes on Saturday morning and blinked blearily up at his mother.

'I heard you coughing in the night. Are you all right?' she asked.

It was a fight to draw breath and Tommy struggled to sit up. 'I don't feel too good,' he admitted, 'but I'll make it to the registry office.'

'I doubt that. You don't look capable of getting out of bed.'

Tommy's chest felt as if a band of steel was enclosing it and he reached for his inhaler, saying after using it, 'I'll be all right. I'm getting up now.'

With a huff his mother left the room. It was bronchitis, Tommy knew that, but nothing was going to stop him from getting married that morning. He got up, sat on the edge of the bed, but then his door opened again and Jeremy hovered on the threshold as he said, 'Mum said your chest is bad again.'

'It's a bit tight, that's all. I'm just off to have a bath.'

'Good idea, get in quick before Mum hogs it,' Jeremy said. 'See you when you come downstairs.'

Tommy was glad of the privacy as he slowly made his way to the bathroom, having to pause once to draw breath.

He turned on the taps and as the room filled with steam he found it helped, and after lying in the hot water for a while he was able to cough up some of the mucus, which made his breathing a little easier.

At ten thirty they were ready, Jeremy looking tall, ruddy and handsome in his new suit. In contrast Tommy felt weak and washed-out, but his mother said, 'Don't you both look nice.'

'You look great, Mum,' Jeremy said and she smiled at his compliment.

The car they had hired arrived, and Tommy had arranged another one to take Amy and her parents to the registry office. The wind was blustery as they walked outside, but it was only a few steps to the car and moments later they were on their way. 'Well, this is it, Tom, your last hour as a single man,' Jeremy joked.

Tommy was hit by a bout of coughing and had serious doubts that he'd be well enough to travel to Brighton for their brief honeymoon. He feared for their wedding night, hated the thought of letting Amy down, and looking at his strapping brother, Tommy felt less than a man.

When Amy arrived at the registry office she got out of the car, and seeing Tommy there waiting for her, she smiled with joy.

'Amy, you . . . you look lovely,' he said.

Amy had chosen a calf-length, semi-flared white dress, with an inset of lace at the neck. A band of small blue flowers sat in her hair, which matched her little bouquet. However, she hardly took in the compliment. Tommy looked ashen and she said, 'What's wrong? You look so pale.'

'It's just a bit of a bad chest again,' he said.

'It's more than that,' Celia snapped. 'I think it's bronchitis.'

'I'm fine,' Tommy insisted as he reached out to take Amy's hand. 'Come on, I think we should go inside.'

They were only a small group, Amy thought, her mother looking lovely in a matching dress and jacket of stiff cream grosgrain. Rose was in pale green silk, her suit immaculately cut, and her hat a large one with a brim which she was holding down as though worried that the wind would snatch it away. Celia was in apricot silk, and if Amy wasn't so worried about Tommy, she might have smiled at the way she and Rose were eyeing each other.

They were told that the registrar wasn't quite ready for them, and while waiting, Tommy started to cough. Thankfully it didn't last long and after using his inhaler he stowed it away in his pocket again, just as Carol dashed through the doors.

'Thank goodness I made it,' she said breathlessly. 'I thought I was going to be late. Oh, Amy, you look lovely.'

'Thanks, and you look nice too,' Amy said, liking Carol's red dress and short navy blue jacket with red piping around the lapels.

'Tommy, are you okay?' Carol asked. 'You look a bit rough.'

He was about to answer when they were called in, and Amy was aware of his laboured breathing as they walked into the room. There were chairs arranged in rows, and a highly polished mahogany desk in front of them, enhanced by a large vase of flowers.

The registrar greeted them, the formalities dealt with, but then everything seemed to happen so quickly. In what felt like such a short time, words were exchanged and she was suddenly Tommy's wife. She lifted her eyes to meet his and he bent to kiss her, softly saying, 'Hello, Mrs Frost.'

The name felt so strange to Amy, but then Tommy began to cough again, and she hated to see him struggling to breathe. When he recovered they signed the register, and then they were on their way outside again when her mother and Rose showered them with confetti. 'Congratulations,' they chorused.

As Amy laughed, and shook some out of her hair, she noticed a parked car a short distance away, the two occupants inside watching them. There was something odd about their appearance; the man wearing a hat with the brim bent low and the woman with a scarf tied around her head that partly shrouded her face. Despite the fact that they were trying to hide their identity, Amy thought she recognised them and her eyes widened. She turned to Tommy, about to tell him when he began to cough again, bent double, and the moment was lost as the car drove off.

'This wind is taking my breath away,' Tommy gasped.

'I'm not sure we should go to the reception,' Amy said worriedly.

'No, it's all right. I'll be fine.'

'I hardly think so,' Celia said.

'Mum, don't fuss,' Tommy said tiredly.

'Right then, let's get some photographs,' Jeremy suggested.

He had taken so many that Amy thought he must have used up a roll of film, but at last she and Tommy got into the car and sat holding hands. She smiled at Tommy and he kissed her, but his lips felt hot, as though he was feverish, and she said, 'Tommy, I don't think we should go to Brighton.'

'You said that about the reception, but this time I won't argue. I'm sorry, Amy.'

'Don't be. We can always go another time,' she said, and soon they were pulling up outside Rose's house.

Celia looked around the large drawing room and despite herself, she was impressed. She'd expected to find that Rose had furnished it with tacky modern furniture and garish ornaments, but instead everything was tasteful, down to the obviously expensive Persian rugs and the crystal chandeliers. Rose's outfit had been a surprise too, the suit obviously designer, along with her handbag, shoes and gloves.

'Champagne, madam?' a waiter asked pompously.

'Thank you,' Celia said, taking a fluted glass from the silver tray. Rose had certainly pushed the boat out, she thought, hiring waiters and caterers.

'Tom just told me that they aren't going to Brighton,' Jeremy said.

'I should think not. He's in no condition to travel.'

'Would you all make your way through to the dining room,' Rose said. 'Lunch is served.'

'I don't know who she thinks she is,' Celia hissed to Jeremy. 'Look at her, trying to act like a lady when everyone knows she's a tart.'

Jeremy made no reply and as they walked through to the dining room, Celia saw that again, it was beautifully furnished. There was a two-tier wedding cake on the centre of the long table, which everyone admired, and then finding their place names, they all sat down.

Celia had to endure toasts to the happy couple, a silly speech from Amy's father, but at last the food was served. Celia just wanted to get the meal over with and leave.

She had nothing in common with these people, but then, when they were nearly through the second course Thomas began to cough, so badly that he was unable to catch his breath.

Amy looked helpless and pushing back her chair, Celia said to Jeremy, 'Come on, I think we need to get Thomas home and into bed.'

'Mum, he doesn't live with us now. His home is with Amy.'

Celia saw that all eyes were on her and felt a fool, but she kept her dignity by saying, 'I am fully aware of that, but when Thomas is this ill he needs constant care.'

'I'll see that he gets it,' Amy said. 'I just need to get him home.'

'Take my car,' Samuel offered.

'I'll drive,' Jeremy volunteered.

Celia said quickly, 'I'll come with you.'

'There's no need,' Amy said. 'Please stay and finish your meal.'

'But . . .'

'Mum, we'll be fine,' Thomas interrupted; the coughing fit over though he sounded breathless. 'I'm sorry, Rose, you . . . you've gone to so much trouble and I hate to leave.'

'Don't be daft. The caterers did all the work. You get yourself home, and into bed. By the look of you, it's the best place for you.'

Thomas nodded, but then he began coughing again. 'Right, come on, let's go,' Jeremy said. 'I'll be back as soon as Tom's settled.'

'I'll save your pudding for you,' Rose called.

'Make sure you ring the doctor,' Celia demanded, fuming. She doubted Amy was capable of looking after Thomas, and though she hated the thought of having to go to their house, she'd call in to see him in the morning and whether Amy liked it or not, if necessary, she'd insist on taking over his care.

As though he'd been holding himself together, Tommy seemed to give in when they arrived at Lark Rise and got out of the car. Amy saw that he could barely walk and Jeremy had to hold him up as she unlocked the door to go inside.

'I'll get him into bed,' Jeremy said. 'You'd better ring the doctor.'

Amy was so glad now that Tommy had insisted on having a telephone installed before they moved in, but then realised that she didn't have the number. 'Tommy,' she said as they were about to go upstairs, 'who is your doctor?'

'Dr Trent,' he gasped.

Amy hadn't been to the doctor's for years, but the name sounded vaguely familiar. It might be the same surgery, but as she didn't know the number she rifled through the directory until she found it. At last she got through, only to be told that Dr Trent was unavailable until Monday; however, at Amy's insistence that it couldn't wait till then, she was told that a locum would be sent.

Replacing the receiver, she ran upstairs, embarrassed to see that Tommy was half undressed and perched on the side of the bed. Colour flooded her cheeks and she averted her eyes.

'Amy, don't just stand there, give me a hand,' Jeremy said.

She moved forward, trying to pull herself together. Tommy was her husband now and she had to get used to this, but still her eyes remained averted and fixed on his chest.

'If I help him to stand up, you can pull up his pyjama bottoms,' Jeremy said.

'No, no, I'll do it,' Tommy protested, suddenly aware of her embarrassment as he covered himself with his hands.

'Amy might as well see what she's going to get,' Jeremy said, grinning.

'Shut up,' Tommy said, though weakly. 'Amy, we'll manage. Can . . . can you get me a glass of water?'

'I'll help Jeremy first,' she said firmly.

It was done swiftly, and then Tommy was in bed. 'Thanks,' he gasped.

'I'll get you that water,' Amy said, running back downstairs. She found a glass, and was filling it up when Jeremy came into the kitchen.

'I think Tom was as embarrassed as you,' he said, chuckling.

'It isn't funny,' she said testily.

'No, I suppose not, and it isn't funny that you won't be enjoying your wedding night.'

'What do you mean?'

'Oh come on, Amy, surely you realise that Tom's too ill to get it up. Of course, I don't mind acting as a stand-in.'

'You're disgusting,' she snapped.

'Oh come on, don't look at me like that. I'm only joking, but I think I'll get back to the reception and your lovely friend Carol before you chuck that glass of water at me.'

'Yes, I think you should,' Amy said, glad when he left. Jeremy had said he was joking, but there had been something in his eyes that made her shiver. She went back upstairs to Tommy and held the glass to his lips while he drank, pushing Jeremy from her mind as she willed the doctor to arrive.

'Sorry, Amy, I rui . . . ruined the wedding.'

'No you didn't. We're married now, and that's all that matters,' Amy assured him.

Until now Amy hadn't mentioned the two people in a car near the registry office. Surely it couldn't have been them? She tried to conjure up their images again and doubts set in. Amy just couldn't be sure, and with Tommy so ill at the moment, she decided it was probably better to say nothing for now.

Chapter Thirty-Eight

'How is he?' Phyllis asked, almost staggering inside when Amy opened the door.

'Mum, you're drunk.'

'No, I'm just a bit tipsy,' she protested. 'It turned into a bit of a do – and I reckon with all that champagne flowing old frosty knickers got a bit inebriated too. Jeremy took her home about an hour ago.'

'What about Carol?'

'Jeremy was pestering her, but I don't think she was keen on him. I've no idea why, he's a lovely-looking chap, but she made her excuses and left long before us,' she said, hiccuping. 'Oops, sorry. I really have had too much to drink.'

'Yes, I can see that,' Amy said.

'It was a good day, and evening, but I'm knackered now. If Rose had her way we'd still be there now, but you still haven't told me how Tommy is.'

'The doctor's been to see him and said it's bronchitis. He's asleep now, but that rotten cough keeps waking him up.'

'What a shame. You've missed out on your weekend in Brighton too.'

'I don't mind. I just hope that Tommy doesn't get any worse.'

'I'm sure he'll soon be on the mend,' Phyllis said. 'Anyway love, it's gone ten thirty so I'd best be off. Your dad's had a lot more to drink than me so I'll have to make sure he made it up to bed. I'm only next door if you need me,' she said, staggering outside again.

'Yes, I know,' Amy said, thinking that her mother would probably fall asleep as soon as her head hit the pillow.

After closing the door, Amy went upstairs and undressed quietly. Tommy was still asleep, and after putting on her nightdress she slipped gently in beside him. It felt strange lying in the darkness with someone beside her. She'd never shared her bed with anyone before, and Amy lay stiffly on her back.

As though aware of her presence Tommy stirred and turned on his side to put an arm around her. 'Amy?'

'I thought you were asleep.'

'I was just dozing,' he said, running a caressing hand over her body.

Amy responded, nervous yet strangely excited too as his hand slipped under her nightie to touch her in places she had never been touched before. 'Oh . . . Tommy.'

Abruptly it stopped as he began to cough again and was left fighting for breath as he gasped, 'I . . . I'm sorry, Amy, can't . . . can't . . .'

'Shush, it doesn't matter. We've got the rest of our lives together, so all you've got to do now is to get better.'

'Lo . . . love you, Amy.'

'I love you too, now try to sleep.'

It wasn't long before Tommy was snoring gently, and unable to settle it was nearly midnight when Amy crept downstairs to make herself a cup of cocoa. She was about to go into the kitchen when someone tapped on the front door, and wondering who it could be she cautiously opened it. 'Jeremy!'

'I just popped down to see how Tom's doing,' he said.

'Don't you know what the time is? He's asleep.'

'You aren't, Amy,' Jeremy said as he pushed his way inside.

'You're drunk,' she said, smelling alcohol on his breath. 'I think you should leave.'

'You don't mean that, Amy,' he said, pulling her into his arms. 'It's you I've come to see. I've seen the signals, the way you look at me, and you'll be pleased to know I'm not *too* drunk.'

'Get off me,' Amy cried.

'Shush, you don't want to wake Tom,' he murmured as his hands sought to open her dressing gown.

Amy fought to get out of his arms, opened her mouth to scream, but his hand closed over her lips. What followed was a nightmare, but Amy was powerless against Jeremy's strength. She was pushed to the floor, and her mind cried against what was happening. She thrashed, but then there was pain, awful pain as he entered her. Amy crumbled, lying beneath him and praying for it to stop. When it did, she was left broken and sobbed, 'Tommy will kill you.'

'I don't think so, Amy. Tom couldn't kill a fly, and anyway, you aren't going to tell him.'

'Ye . . . yes I am.'

'How do you think Tom would feel? It would destroy him to find out that his lovely new wife gave herself to his brother on their wedding night.'

'I . . . I didn't. You forced me.'

'Did I? Are you sure about that?' Jeremy asked. 'You didn't put up that much of a fight; just a token one, and that was the green light for me. Anyway, it would be your word against mine. Think about it, Amy, either way Tom would be left a broken man.'

Amy scrambled to her feet, feeling sore and bruised as she backed away from Jeremy, but he smiled sardonically and said, 'Oh come on, don't pretend you're scared of me.'

'Amy . . . Amy.'

Hearing his voice coming from the bedroom, Amy cried, 'That's Tommy.'

'Take my advice. Keep your mouth shut,' Jeremy said as he headed for the stairs.

Amy hesitated, but went upstairs too, standing in the doorway as Jeremy switched on the light and said, 'Hello, Tom. I was on my way home and saw a light on downstairs. I was a bit worried so I knocked on the door to ask Amy if there's a problem.'

Tommy blinked against the sudden glare of light and croaked, 'Chest bad, hurts.'

'Yes, you don't look too good. Try to get some sleep and I'll call in again tomorrow.'

As Tom's eyes closed, Jeremy moved away from the bed, while Amy stepped hastily to one side. 'Get out!' she hissed.

Jeremy gave that sardonic smile again, but then he left. Amy stayed where she was until she heard the front door close, then flew downstairs and locked it, putting the bolt across the top too.

A sob escaped Amy's lips. She felt so filthy, so soiled that she scrubbed herself in the bathroom, until at last, spent, she slipped into bed again. What followed was a night of broken sleep, Tommy coughing and Amy reliving the horror of what had happened. Guilt swamped her mind. Jeremy had said she didn't put up much of a fight, and it was true, she *had* given in.

Tommy mumbled in his sleep and turned over, his arm curling round her waist. Amy tensed and almost threw it off, but then, instead, tears came, rolling unchecked down her cheeks. Amy knew then that she couldn't tell Tommy – she was too ashamed to tell anyone, and in the early hours of the morning she finally cried herself to sleep.

Jeremy had slunk home, cursing himself. He'd been mad, out of his mind, but he couldn't blame it on drink. He'd wanted Amy, and had allowed lust to overrule his common sense. If Amy opened her mouth, everything would be ruined. There'd be no shares in the business and no chance of gaining eventual control. For a moment of madness, he'd lose everything.

Amy had to keep her mouth shut – she just had to, and he hoped he'd said enough to convince her of that. Jeremy tossed and turned in bed, fearing what the next day would bring, but finally fell asleep, to be woken on Sunday morning by his mother's voice.

'Jeremy, I'm going to see Thomas.'

'What time is it?' he asked, feeling muzzy headed.

'It's just after eight o'clock.'

'Don't you think it's a bit too early to disturb them?' he protested, blinking against the light as his mother drew the curtains.

'Of course it isn't,' Celia said. 'I'll see you when I come back.'

Jeremy's head cleared and as his mother left the room, he groaned. He dreaded what the morning might bring. Had Amy told Tom? He'd find out one way or the other when his mother returned – and now the wait seemed interminable.

Amy woke with a start to the sound of someone knocking on the front door. She sat up, looked at Tommy and almost cried out with anxiety. He was asleep, but looked so ill. As the thumps on the door grew louder Amy jumped out of bed and, throwing on her dressing gown, ran downstairs.

'It's about time,' Celia said, glaring at her. 'How is Thomas?'

'He . . . he looks awful.'

'I'll go up to see him,' Celia said.

From that moment Celia took over and Amy felt useless as she watched her mother-in-law placing pillows behind Tommy's back to prop him up, but also felt grateful that she was there. As he woke and began coughing, Celia was there to help him to bring up mucus, and after giving him his inhaler, Tommy began to breathe a little easier.

'Amy, what did the doctor leave for him?' Celia barked.

'Some tablets, antibiotics I think, they're on the bedside table, and a prescription for more, but the chemist won't be open until tomorrow.'

'Has Thomas had a tablet this morning?'

'No . . . not yet.'

With a tut of impatience, Celia said, 'Then get him a fresh glass of water.'

Amy ran downstairs again, feeling like an admonished child, but then the memory of last night returned and she knew that her days of innocence were over.

Tommy managed to smile at her when she returned with the water, but it was Celia who was by his side and gave him his pill. 'Thanks, Mum,' he said tiredly.

'Try to get some sleep. I'll go now, but I'll be back soon.'

As Tommy's eyes closed, Celia stood up quietly to leave, and Amy followed her downstairs where she said to her quietly, 'Thank you. I wasn't sure what to do.'

'That was obvious, and in future see that Thomas remains propped up,' she said crossly. 'I'll be back in an hour, by which time I hope to see you dressed.'

When Celia marched out, Amy ran upstairs, and seeing that Tommy had dozed off she threw some clothes on.

Moments later there was another knock on the door and she hurried down again to let her mother in. It was to be the shape of the rest of the day. Rose called in, and Celia came back several times, but one thing helped Amy to cope.

Jeremy stayed away.

Chapter Thirty-Nine

Amy rang the shop on Monday to say she couldn't come to work, and the manageress had been less than pleased. Then, by midweek, Tommy's condition had gone from bad to worse and when Amy woke on Wednesday morning she was so worried about him that she decided to call the doctor again.

Jeremy had kept away, but when Celia arrived just as Amy went downstairs, he was with her. It all came flooding back and Amy felt sick. She couldn't bear to look at him and kept her eyes averted.

Obviously unaware of the tension, Celia asked, 'Is Thomas any better this morning?'

'No, he . . . he had a terrible night again, and now he's got a dreadful pain across his shoulder blades,' Amy said as they went upstairs.

'I don't like the sound of that,' Celia said sharply.

Tommy barely focused on them when they went into the bedroom, his eyes feverish, his cough weak and his breathing ragged.

'Amy, ring the surgery,' Celia ordered.

'I was about to when you arrived.'

'Then do it now. Tell them it can't wait until Dr Trent does his rounds. Thomas needs to see him now!'

Amy flew downstairs and made the call, afterwards turning to see Jeremy behind her. 'Go away,' she hissed.

'Amy, please, I've been going out of my mind. I'm so sorry, I really am. I was drunk, but that's no excuse and I swear it will never happen again.'

'Just leave me alone.'

'I'll stay away as much as I can, but it will look odd if I don't call in to see Tommy now and then. I've made all sorts of excuses to my mother up till now, but I've run out of reasons and as soon as Tommy starts to recover, he'll want to know that things are running smoothly at the unit.'

'You can tell him, but don't come near me again. Ever!'

'I won't, I swear,' Jeremy said, just as his mother came downstairs.

Celia's eyes narrowed and she looked suspiciously at each of them, but she only asked, 'Is the doctor on his way?'

'Yes,' Amy said abruptly. 'He should be here soon.'

'Good, and in the meantime I want a bowl of cool water and a cloth to bathe Thomas.'

'I'll do it,' Amy said. She could see that Celia was annoyed, but didn't care, only glad to have something to occupy her mind until the doctor arrived.

It was Celia who let the doctor in and after examining Tommy, he said, 'I'm going to call an ambulance, Mrs Frost. This could be pneumonia and your husband needs to be in hospital.'

Amy's head spun. Pneumonia – the word striking fear in her heart.

Mabel thought that Edna's front room looked as untidy as ever, and she was trying to hide her distaste when a weak cup of tea in a cracked cup was put in front of her.

'I suppose you've seen what's been going on over there, but have you heard anything?' Edna asked.

'Not much, only that Tommy's got bronchitis.'

'It's been like flippin' Piccadilly Circus with all the comings and goings. First the wedding, and now this. Celia Frost is in Amy's place every five minutes and when she ain't there, it's Phyllis. Of course it's all gone quiet since that ambulance turned up and took Tommy away.'

'Did you see him?' Mabel asked. 'You're opposite and get a better view.'

'I saw him when he was carried out, and if you ask me he was close to death.'

'Oh no,' Mabel said, aghast.

'Yeah, well, he's always been a weakling. Now the older brother, he's a bit of all right and I wouldn't say no,' Edna said.

Mabel let that pass, her thoughts elsewhere as she said, 'Poor Amy, she must be worried sick.'

'She chose the wrong brother, that's for sure, and now it looks like she's going to be a very young widow.'

'Oh, Edna, don't say that,' Mabel cried, feeling a surge of disgust. A bit of gossip was one thing, but Edna seemed to be relishing the thought of the pain and suffering Tommy's death would bring.

'What are you looking at me like that for?' Edna asked. 'I'm only speaking the truth.'

Those words echoed in Mabel's mind and she felt sick inside. She was as bad as Edna. She relished gossip, had spread it, and enjoyed other people's suffering. She was as nasty-minded as Edna, but this time they were talking about Amy, a girl she had watched grow up into a lovely, sweet young woman.

Amy didn't deserve to suffer and there was nothing to

relish in the thought. There was only a feeling of sorrow. Mabel knew what it was to grieve and had let it turn her into a twisted, bitter old woman. Now though she felt a deep need to help – but Mabel knew that after all she'd said, done, and caused, any support or sympathy she offered Amy would be spurned.

In that moment, an idea was born; one that would turn Mabel's life around. She may not be able to help Amy, but surely there were others that she could. Mabel didn't know how, but from now on, instead of relishing people's pain, she wanted to be able to offer them help and comfort.

Time passed in a blur for Amy. Her parents and Rose came to the hospital when they could and at those times she clung to her mother, glad of her support.

Celia was there for long periods, and Jeremy came too, but as she was so desperately worried about Tommy, Amy found herself impervious to his presence.

She was aware at times of Jeremy's eyes on her, the concern in his voice when he urged her to rest, which she brushed away. She would never forgive herself for what happened, but at the moment it seemed distant, buried in her concern for Tommy. He had to get better – he just had to. The thought of life without him was unbearable.

The doctor was with Tommy now and she was waiting outside the room with Celia while he was being examined. 'I think he looked a little better,' Celia said.

'Do you think so?' Amy asked, clinging to that seed of hope.

Amy felt light-headed with exhaustion, but rose to her feet as the doctor appeared, aware that Celia had done the same. The man's face was grave and Amy swayed, fearing the worst.

'Mrs Frost, your husband still isn't responding to treatment. However, his condition hasn't deteriorated so I hope to see some sign of improvement in the next forty-eight hours.'

'Does . . . does that mean he's going to get better?'

'If he responds to the treatment the prognosis will be more positive. Now if you'll excuse me . . .'

Amy was left bewildered as the doctor walked away. *If* Tommy responds to treatment, the doctor had said, not *when*. Did that mean there was a chance that he wouldn't? Unable to bear the thought, Amy was unaware that Jeremy was walking towards them as her knees collapsed beneath her and she flopped back onto the chair, burying her face in her hands.

Jeremy saw it happen and picked up his pace, running the last few strides. 'What's wrong?' he asked his mother. 'Has there been bad news?'

'There's no news one way or the other. Thomas is neither better, nor worse. Amy is just tired, that's all.'

'Now look, Amy, this can't go on,' Jeremy gently admonished. 'You've got to get some rest.'

'You're right. Take her home, Jeremy.'

'No, no,' Amy protested, 'I'm not leaving Tommy.'

'For goodness sake stop acting like a martyr,' Celia said crossly.

'I . . . I'm not,' she said, her eyes filling with tears.

Amy looked so vulnerable and Jeremy found that he wanted to hold her, to comfort her, but knew it was impossible. She'd probably react violently if he so much as laid a hand on her, and after what he'd done, Jeremy couldn't blame her.

'Well I've been here all morning and I want to go home

330

to freshen up,' Celia said. 'Jeremy, after you've been in to see Thomas, if Amy insists on staying, you can take me home instead.'

'All right,' he agreed, aware that Amy would never agree to get into the van with him. He hoped that Phyllis or Rose would be able to persuade her to get some sleep, because from what he'd seen, Amy was close to breaking point.

After seeing his brother, who barely knew he was there again, Jeremy drove his mother home, tensing when she asked, 'What's going on between you and Amy?'

'What do you mean? Nothing's going on.'

'I'm not a fool, Jeremy. You can't take your eyes off her, and seem more concerned about Amy than your brother.'

'That isn't true. I just think she needs to get some rest.'

With a snort of disbelief, she said, 'There's more to it than that, and it's got to stop. All our plans will be ruined if Thomas gets wind of it and I can't believe you'd risk that.'

'I'm not, and you've got nothing to worry about,' Jeremy insisted, thinking that Tom was in no fit state to get wind of anything at the moment.

An awful thought then crossed Jeremy's mind. Tom was critically ill and what if he didn't survive? He hadn't signed any shares over to him yet, and if he died any chance of gaining control of the business would be lost.

Chapter Forty

Slowly Tommy recovered, and after being sent for convalescence he finally returned home. It was Saturday afternoon, the third week in May, and for the first time since he'd been admitted to hospital, he and Amy were truly alone.

'Do you realise that we've been married for over a month?' he asked.

'Of course I do.'

'And we still haven't had our honeymoon.'

Amy flushed. 'It doesn't matter.'

'Once I know that the business is running smoothly, I'll rebook it.'

'There's no need. I didn't go back to work and I've been a lady of leisure. I've met Carol a couple of times and she's been worried about you too, but I think I might look for a part-time job now,' Amy said.

'You don't need to work,' Tommy said, 'but I'm going back on Monday.'

'Are you sure you're not rushing it?'

'I'm sure, Amy. I feel great,' Tommy said and meant it. It felt good to be alive, especially as when he'd been in intensive care he'd felt so close to death.

When someone knocked on the door he said with a wry

smile, 'Well, we had half an hour to ourselves, so that's something.'

Amy's mother walked in, smiling widely. 'Tommy, it's wonderful to see you looking so well, though you could do with putting on a bit more weight.'

'Don't worry, Mum, I'll feed him up,' Amy said.

'I'm sure you will, but I won't stop. I just popped round to say welcome home, but now I'm sure you two would rather be alone.'

'Thanks, I appreciate it,' Tommy said and when she left he wrapped his arms around Amy. She stiffened again and he was puzzled. Since he'd arrived home she seemed tense, nervy, but before he could ask her what was wrong, someone else was at the door, his mother this time.

'How are you, Thomas?'

'I'm fine and glad to be home.'

'Jeremy has been marvellous while you've been away. The business is running smoothly and he's managed to acquire another contract, quite a large one too.'

'That's good. I'll go over it with him on Monday and it'll be great to get back into the driving seat.'

'The accounts are very healthy, with profits well up on this period last year.'

'Great, I'll take a look at them too, but for now I just want to enjoy this weekend with Amy,' Tommy said, hoping his mother would take the hint, and she did, but not before reiterating how wonderful Jeremy had been in his absence.

'I'm sure you'll see for yourself on Monday,' she said, then at last leaving.

Tommy sighed, drew Amy into his arms and kissed her deeply as his hands roamed her body. She pulled away, the look in her eyes almost wild. The penny dropped then. They hadn't yet consummated their marriage, so of course

333

Amy was nervous. In all honesty he was a bit edgy too, worried about his own inexperience, yet was unable to quell his rising excitement. It was going to be hard to wait for tonight, but with the risk of being interrupted by someone else calling in to see how he was, Tommy knew he had no choice.

'That was quick,' Jeremy said when his mother returned to the house.

'I'm afraid Thomas made me feel that I was intruding and I've no idea why.'

Jeremy could guess why his mother hadn't been made welcome; Tom wanted to be alone with Amy. His guts churned. Since that night when he'd taken Amy's virginity, he had felt that she was his, and the thought of Tom laying his hands on her made his jaws clench in anger.

'I did manage to tell Thomas how well you've done in his absence. He said he's returning to work on Monday, and I'm sure he's going to be impressed.'

Jeremy left his mother to ramble on. He knew he had no right to feel like this. Amy was Tom's wife, yet his feelings for her continued to grow. It wasn't just lust, it was more than that, and Jeremy thought he might actually be in love. It was something he'd never experienced before, girls just there to be used for a bit of fun, with one following another, but this time it was different.

'Are you listening to me?'

'What? Yes,' Jeremy said.

'What did I just say then?'

'Err, something about Tom being impressed.'

'I also said that you'll have to start pushing him for those shares now.'

'Yes, yes, I will,' Jeremy said, and though he was desperate to get his hands on them, they were the last thing on his mind at the moment.

'I see that Tommy's home,' Mabel said as she returned from the shops to see Phyllis vigorously polishing her letterbox.

'Yes, that's right.'

'Amy must be over the moon.'

'Yes, she is,' Phyllis said. 'Have you heard anything yet?'

'No, I'm still waiting, but hopefully it won't be for much longer.'

'And is Jack still all right about it?'

'Yes, though it took him a while to come round to the idea,' Mabel said, her mind going back to when she'd found the courage to knock on Phyllis's door. The reception had been cold at first, but when Mabel had poured her heart out, saying that she wanted to turn her life around, Phyllis had finally thawed.

Mabel hadn't known how, or what to do to make a difference, and as they'd discussed her options, the suggestion from Phyllis had been the last thing she'd expected to consider. Now though, Mabel knew that with so much love to give it was perfect.

'I don't usually do my front on a Saturday,' Phyllis said, 'but with working for Rose all week I get behind with my own chores.'

'If Jack and I pass muster, I'll have a lot less time on my hands too,' Mabel said, smiling at the thought.

'It won't be so bad if you get one that's old enough to go to school.'

'I wouldn't mind one way or the other,' Mabel said wistfully.

'Don't worry, I can't see them turning you down,' Phyllis said, stretching her back as she completed her task.

'I saw Daphne Cole the other day. She was on her way to visit her mother and though she was a bit off with me at first, she warmed a bit when I apologised for thinking that she'd gone off with George Frost.'

'I didn't think she had, but you wouldn't listen to me,' Phyllis said.

'I know. I was a horrible gossip and I'm ashamed of myself.'

'You've changed, Mabel. You're not like that now, but no doubt Edna Price is still as bad.'

'Yes, she is, but I avoid her as much as I can now.'

'I doubt she likes that, but I'd best get on. I'll see you later,' Phyllis said as she gathered up her cleaning materials.

With a wave, Phyllis went indoors and Mabel did the same. She was finding it hard to wait for news, but felt reassured now that Phyllis didn't think she and Jack would be turned down. Surely they would hear soon and then if they were accepted, she wondered if her first foster child would be a boy or a girl.

That night, Amy undressed for bed, and climbed in beside Tommy, shaking with nerves. She couldn't get what happened with Jeremy out of her mind, the fear, the pain, and as Tommy reached out for her she went rigid.

'It's all right,' he soothed. 'I'm nervous too.'

'You are?'

'Of course,' Tommy said. 'This is going to be the first time for both of us.'

Amy knew that it wasn't the first time for her and she was terrified that Tommy would somehow know. It increased her tension, and though Tommy continued to try to soothe her, she cried out in pain when he entered her.

'I'm sorry, so sorry,' Tommy said, yet there was no stopping him now.

Amy tried to respond but found she couldn't, and lay unmoving beneath him, just wanting it to be over.

At last with an animal grunt, Tommy was spent and moved from her body. 'I know that wasn't good for you,' he said softly, 'but I expected that. It'll get better, I promise.'

'How do you know?' Amy asked.

'I . . . well, it's something I've heard talked about,' he said.

Amy tried to fight them, but tears of relief filled her eyes. Tommy hadn't realised that it wasn't her first time, but along with that came shame and guilt. She had betrayed him, but then found herself gathered into his arms.

'Don't cry, Amy. I love you and I'm sorry I hurt you, but it'll be all right next time.'

Amy doubted it ever would, but after a while Tommy began to slowly explore her body and she found herself responding. He was right, it was better, and Amy found she was able to give herself willingly, welcoming Tommy as their bodies merged as one.

When it was over Amy snuggled into Tommy's arms, feeling truly his wife now. She loved him so much, and knew that all she could do now to assuage her guilt was to make sure that she was a perfect wife.

As she closed her eyes and drifted off to sleep, Amy's last thought was that so much had happened in such a short time since their marriage, but now, at last, the future looked brighter.

Chapter Forty-One

'Come on, Peter, get a move on or you'll be late for school,' Mabel said.

'I've got a belly ache.'

'Don't try that one again. It won't wash this time,' Mabel said, trying to sound stern.

'I wanna stay here with you,' Peter said, large brown eyes wide with appeal as he looked up at her.

'I'm sorry, love, but you've got to go. Anyway, it won't be for long. At the end of this week school breaks up for the summer holidays.'

'Uncle Jack wouldn't make me go.'

'Oh yes he would,' Mabel said.

'Will he take me to the park again when he comes home from work?'

'I expect so, but only if he knows you've been to school.'

Peter quickly shovelled the rest of his breakfast into his mouth and then said, 'All right, I'm ready.'

Mabel smiled. Peter was seven years old and had been with them since mid-June, almost a month now, and though it had been a shock when they'd first seen him, he'd already wormed his way into their affections. She'd been warned that his placement would only be temporary and had tried not to get too fond of him, but he was such an adorable little lad that it was impossible. Once outside she took his hand and they set off on the short walk to the infant school. When they arrived she hugged Peter and said softly, 'Now be a good boy and I'll see you later.'

'Bye, Auntie Mabel,' he said, returning her hug and clinging on until she urged him into his classroom.

She then returned home, and knowing that Phyllis had a week off work, she knocked on her door. 'Any chance of a cuppa?'

'Yes, come on in,' Phyllis invited. 'How's Peter?'

'He didn't want to go to school again, and though he's denied it, I think he's being bullied. I'm going to have a word with his teacher when I pick him up.'

'I hope he isn't, but kids can be cruel and Peter's a bit different,' Phyllis said, before going through to the kitchen to make a pot of tea.

Peter was different all right, Mabel thought, obviously the result of a mixed-race relationship, with his tight, curly hair and coffee-coloured skin. She knew it made him vulnerable, had seen the looks adults gave him, let alone children, but that only made her more protective of him.

Peter was her first foster child, and already he'd changed her life, along with her once narrow-minded prejudice. He was just a little boy who hadn't chosen the colour of his skin, and one who had already melted Mabel's heart.

Amy stood sideways, pushed her baggy blouse close to her body as she looked in the mirror and knew she couldn't hide it for much longer. She was three months pregnant, but as the marriage hadn't been consummated until four weeks after they married, she could only admit to two. If she told Tommy the truth – that she was carrying his brother's baby, it would destroy him; their marriage too. That only left one choice, to pretend that the baby was Tommy's, and though Amy had agonised over this decision for so long, she still wasn't sure she could live with the deceit.

She'd been sick again that morning and felt drained as she went downstairs to the kitchen, just as her mother walked in through the back door. 'Hello, love. I see you've got your boiler on so can I shove a few towels in with yours?'

'Yes, of course you can,' Amy said.

'I don't know why it's always wash day on Mondays, but it's been the same for as long as I can remember. Mabel called in so I got a bit behind. It's amazing how much she's changed. She's like a different woman now, softer, kinder and she's become a proper mother hen.'

Amy felt her stomach lurch and swallowed bile, but her mother must have noticed and asked, 'Are you all right, Amy? You look a bit pale.'

'I've been sick again this morning, but I'm all right now,' she said and seeing her mother's eyes widen Amy wished she could bite back the words.

'Sick in the mornings! That could mean you're pregnant. Oh, Amy, are you having a baby?'

She nodded and then found herself wrapped in her mother's arms. 'This is wonderful. Wait till I tell your dad.'

'Mum, don't do that. I haven't told Tommy yet.'

'Why ever not?'

'I wanted to be sure.'

'How many monthlies have you missed?'

'Err . . . two,' Amy stammered.

'Well I think that makes it certain,' she said then running her hands over Amy's tummy. 'I can feel a bump already. I'm going to be a grandmother!' she cried, almost dancing with joy.

Amy sat down, fighting to hide her feelings. She wished she could share her mother's happiness, but all she felt was despair.

Tommy was a happy man as he sat back in his office chair. Not only had Jeremy worked closely with Len to secure a new contract while he'd been away, there was now another one in the pipeline. Business was booming and he said, 'Well, Jeremy, you've certainly proved yourself. The solicitor has just rung me to say the papers have been drawn up and all we need to do is to sign them, giving you your thirty-three per cent share in the company.'

'Thanks, Tom. It means a lot to me, and now we'll be a proper family business.'

Tommy grinned. Amy hadn't said anything yet, but he'd seen the signs. 'Don't mention this to Mum yet because it isn't official, but I think there's going to be another addition.'

'You're giving Mum some shares too?'

'No, that's not what I'm talking about. Amy hasn't told me yet, but I think she's pregnant.'

Jeremy looked stunned and asked, 'Are you sure?'

'Well, not really, but she's got a little bulge in her tummy.'

Jeremy lowered his eyes, quiet for a moment, but then said, 'Well, in that case, congratulations.'

'Let's not jump the gun, and as I asked, keep it quiet until I know for sure.'

'All right,' Jeremy agreed, but then said, 'Well, I'd better get back on the road.'

'Is the car running all right?'

'It's fine.'

'Mine's all right too,' Tommy said. 'I think we made a good choice in buying Austins.'

'When are we going to the solicitors?'

'I'm a bit snowed under today, so how about tomorrow morning?'

'Righto,' Jeremy said. 'I'm off then and I'll see you later.'

'Yes, see you,' Tommy said. He wondered when Amy was going to tell him that he was going to be a dad, but with a pile of paperwork on his desk to get through, he had to concentrate on the task.

Jeremy's grip on the steering wheel was tight. He didn't know much about women having babies, but if Amy already had a bulge in her tummy it could mean that the kid was his. Of course Amy would never admit to it, but he'd know for sure if the baby was born a month early.

If it was his, Jeremy knew there was only so much he could stand. Tom already had Amy, and the thought of him taking over his kid too made his teeth grind in anger. Without thought he drove to Lark Rise and uncaring if anyone saw him or not, he thumped on Amy's door.

When it was opened, he pushed his way inside, grinding out, 'It's mine, isn't it? The baby's mine.'

'I . . . I don't know what you're talking about.'

'Don't give me that. Tom told me that you're pregnant.'

'Tommy told you?' Amy said, paling.

'Yes, that's right, so don't try to deny it.'

'I'm not, but the baby isn't yours.'

'Are you sure?'

'Yes, I'm sure,' she said firmly.

Jeremy wanted to reach out – to drag Amy into his arms – to feel her body next to his again. God, he wanted her! She must have seen something in his eyes and began to back away.

'No! Don't come near me!'

Jeremy saw her fear and came to his senses He didn't want

Amy to be frightened of him. He wanted her to love him, but she only wanted one man, and that was his brother. 'It's all right. I'm going,' he said and quickly left, unaware that a curtain was twitching on the opposite side of the road.

Edna scowled as she watched the car driving off. There were only a few people who had cars on Lark Rise, but now the Frosts had two. Some people seemed to have all the luck. Amy had married a bloke with a good few bob, but at least it hadn't turned her into a stuck-up cow like Celia Frost.

Of course Tommy wasn't a patch on his brother when it came to looks, and Edna wondered why Jeremy had been to see Amy. It had only been a short visit, but she had seen the expression on his face when he left. The man actually looked to be in anguish, and it was odd.

There was no point in asking Mabel if she knew what was going on. Mabel had changed, becoming all high and mighty, with no interest in sharing a bit of tittle-tattle now. There was more activity over the road, with Phyllis leaving her house in a hurry to go into Amy's. Edna wished she could be a fly on the wall to hear the conversation between mother and daughter.

'Amy, I thought I heard you shouting and I just saw Jeremy driving off.'

Amy was still trembling, but gripped her hands together as she thought quickly. 'You must have been hearing things. Jeremy just called in to pick up some papers that Tommy forgot to take to work this morning.'

'Oh, right, but you look a bit pale.'

'I've been throwing up again,' Amy said.

'You poor thing. I had morning sickness with you, but it eases off when you get past three months.'

'That's something to look forward to,' Amy said, trying to sound calm.

'Yes, but then later you get heartburn,' Phyllis said, grinning.

'Thanks, Mum, you really know how to cheer me up,' Amy said, forcing a smile.

'It's worth it though and there's nothing like that moment when you first hold your baby in your arms. Anyway, as long as you're all right, I'll get on with giving my place a turnout.'

'You're supposed to be having a week's holiday.'

'I know, Rose insisted, but it's daft if you ask me. I can't sit around all day doing nothing. It would drive me up the wall, but I tell you what, we could go out tomorrow to look at prams and things.'

'Yes, let's do that,' Amy said, trying to sound enthusiastic and relieved when her mother left. She then flopped onto a chair and buried her face in her hands. It had already started, the lies, the deceit; but had she managed to convince Jeremy that the baby wasn't his?

Chapter Forty-Two

On a cold Monday morning in December, a fire blazing in her grate, Mabel stared at the woman in horror. 'But you can't take Peter away from us now. He's so excited about Christmas and . . . and he helped me to decorate the tree. I . . . I've got all his Christmas presents too.'

'Mrs Povis, it won't be immediate, but I did warn you that the placing would be temporary.'

'I know you did, but as he came to us when his mother died, I didn't think he had anyone else.'

'We've managed to trace Peter's father and he's applied for custody.'

'But he's never said anything about his dad. He's only ever talked about his mum.'

'Peter hasn't seen him since he was two years old.'

'That means it'll be like handing the poor kid over to a stranger.'

'That's one of the things I've come to discuss. We feel that it would make the transition easier for Peter if his father comes here just to visit him at first, perhaps on a regular basis for a few weeks. It will give Peter a chance to get to know him before he goes permanently into his custody.'

'I'm not sure about that. You're asking me to let a strange man who I know nothing about into my house.'

'He won't be alone. Myself, or one of my colleagues will be with him.'

Mabel's head sank down. She knew on applying to become a foster parent that this would happen, but this was her first time and it was heart-wrenching. With no other choice, Mabel knew she would have to let Peter go, and knowing he'd be upset too, she had to somehow make it easier for him. 'All right then, his dad can come here,' she agreed.

With a smile of approval the woman said, 'I'll make the arrangements and be in touch.'

As the social worker left, Mabel felt some consolation in knowing that Peter would still be with them for Christmas, yet tears flooded her eyes at the thought of losing him soon afterwards. Alone now, she let them flow.

Amy and Carol were sitting in a café on the King's Road. Carol always had Mondays off and they often met up for a chat.

'What are you doing for Christmas?' Amy asked.

'We'll just be staying at home, but my boyfriend will be joining us.'

Amy smiled, glad that Carol had met someone and said, 'It sounds like things are getting serious with Eddy.'

'It's early days yet, but yes, I think they are. Eddy passed muster with the boys and my mum likes him too.'

'How's your mum these days?' Amy asked.

'She's as happy as a lark. She works in Sloane Square now, in Peter Jones, the department store.'

'What about your gran? Is she spending Christmas with you?'

'No, thank goodness,' Carol replied. 'Mum goes to see her every Sunday, but I mostly keep away. She's such a miserable old cow and all she does is moan.'

'I can't believe Christmas is less than two weeks away. We're going to Rose's with my parents, though Tommy had to placate his mother by saying we'd spend Boxing Day with her. I'm not looking forward to that.'

'I suppose that's because Jeremy will be there.'

'Yes, and as much as I try to avoid him, Jeremy makes it impossible. He's in our house at least two evenings a week and it's driving me mad. You're the only person who knows the truth and if I hadn't found the courage to confide in you, I think I'd have gone out of my mind.'

'That's what friends are for.'

'I know that I can trust you, but sometimes I wish I'd had the courage now to have an abortion.'

'I'm glad you didn't,' Carol said. 'Mine was botched and I could have died.'

'But look at the size of me! I'm so huge my mum thinks I might be having twins. Oh Carol, how am I going to explain it when I give birth in January instead of February?'

'Stop worrying. It's rare to have a baby at the given date. Some come a bit early and others late.'

'How do you know that?' Amy asked.

'This hairdresser's no different to the last – you'd be surprised what I overhear when women are having their hair done.'

'This baby needs to be born late, yet even that won't be enough to convince Jeremy that he isn't the father.'

'When I met him at your wedding, good looking or not, I didn't like him. He was too full of himself, but in this case I still don't think you've got anything to worry about. Think about it. Jeremy can't claim the baby is his. If he does he'd have to admit to raping you.'

'Jeremy would never do that. He's more likely to say

that I threw myself at him, that it was consensual, and sometimes I still wonder if it was.'

'Amy, we've been over and over this, and I've lost count of the times I've told you that it wasn't. Just because you gave up fighting, it doesn't mean you wanted it to happen. He overpowered you and I know what that's like because the same thing happened to me.'

'We grew up together, went to school together, but it still seems unbelievable that we've both been raped.'

'I know. It angers me sometimes that Roy got away with it, but if I don't let it go it will be like he's beaten me, ruined the rest of my life and I'm not going to let him do that. You've got to put it behind you too and instead think about that gorgeous baby you're going to have.'

'But what if I can't love it, Carol?'

'The baby will be a part of you, and my biggest regret is that I had an abortion. I know that had it been born I'd have loved my baby, and you will too.'

Amy cupped her stomach, hoping and praying that Carol was right.

Celia was Christmas shopping, and looking at baby clothes. Since the day she had been told that Amy was pregnant, she'd felt left out. Of course with Phyllis living next door to Amy, she had a hand in everything, and anyone would think she was the only grandmother to be. Huffily she continued to look at baby clothes and when a white woollen pram set caught her eye, Celia decided to buy it.

'Celia, my dear. How are you?'

'Oh hello, Libby,' Celia said, faking a warm smile. 'I'm very well thank you.'

'I see you're buying baby clothes.'

Celia tried to avoid Libby as much as possible nowadays,

and living next door to her remained a trial. However, the smile remained fixed on her face as she said, 'Yes, it's rather fun shopping for one's coming grandchild.'

'It must be nice to have Thomas and his wife living so close, even if they are at the *bottom* of the Rise.'

The inference was there, but Celia managed not to bite. 'It's only a temporary measure. Thomas ploughed all our profits back into the business for expansion and we employ a large workforce now. As we've made such huge profits this year Thomas will soon be buying a property, and of course, in a far superior area.'

'How nice,' Libby said, 'but I must get on. I've still got so many presents to buy. Goodbye, my dear.'

Celia nodded a goodbye in return. Thomas wasn't going to buy a house, but because Libby had got her back up she'd wanted to wipe the sanctimonious smile off her face. Now though, if Thomas remained at the bottom of the Rise she'd be made to look a fool, and in due course no doubt Libby would find great satisfaction in rubbing that fact in her face.

'Everything's on track to move into the larger unit,' Tom said. 'We certainly need the extra capacity, and talking about size, Amy is absolutely blooming.'

'When did you say the baby is due?' Jeremy asked, though he'd already worked it out.

'Amy said around mid-February and then I'll be a dad,' Tom said, grinning.

She's clever, Jeremy thought. Amy had already knocked off about a week, but he knew the baby would arrive a lot earlier than that. Amy had denied it, but Jeremy was sure he was right. Amy was carrying *his* child, but he'd have no claim on it.

'I hope it's a boy, but on the other hand, a daughter might be nice,' Tom mused. 'I keep swinging from one to the other.'

'Can we get back to this quote now?' Jeremy said impatiently.

'You're in a bit of a mood this morning. What's up?'

'Nothing,' Jeremy said, but in truth when Tom was looking as chuffed with life as he was now, Jeremy hated it.

The baby was his; Amy should be his – but Tom had it all.

Chapter Forty-Three

In January, Amy had done all she could to take it easy and so far the baby was five days late. If she could just hang on for another week, she might get away with it, but that now seemed unlikely.

'Hello, love,' her mother said as she came in through the back door. 'You've got your feet up I see.'

'Yes, my ankles keep swelling.'

'What did the midwife say this morning?'

'Oh, nothing much, just that everything is fine,' Amy said offhandedly. In truth, the midwife said she was sure the baby's head was in position, which meant the birth was probably imminent.

'You look tired.'

'I am, and I think I'll have a little nap.'

'All right, I'll leave you in peace.'

Amy managed a smile and then her mother was gone, leaving her to feel sick at the lies she was forced to tell. Only half an hour later, the pains started, small twinges at first that didn't last long, but as they increased, Amy knew she was in labour. She cupped her tummy in despair. How was she going to explain that the baby, who wasn't supposed to be born until February, was about to be born now?

It was then that Amy was struck by an idea, and though she hated what she was going to do, it was the only thing she could think of. She stood up and moved to the bottom of the stairs, where after lying on the floor she forced herself to scream, and she kept screaming and shouting until her mother appeared.

'That was Amy's mother,' Tom said frantically as he replaced the receiver. 'Amy's had a fall and she might have gone into labour. I've got to go! I've got to get to the hospital!'

'You're in no fit state to drive,' Jeremy said. 'Come on, I'll take you.'

'Yes, yes, all right,' Tommy agreed, running from the office.

As they raced through the unit, Jeremy called, 'Len, we've got a bit of an emergency. You'll have to hold the fort and if we're not back, lock up.'

Tom seemed oblivious to everything as he ran to the car, and soon they were speeding off. 'Where have they taken Amy?' Jeremy asked.

'To St Thomas', and get a move on!'

'I'm going as fast as I can,' Jeremy said, screeching around a corner, as anxious as Tom to get to the hospital.

'Yes, sorry,' Tom said. 'It's just that I'm nearly going out of my mind! Oh, God, I hope Amy's all right.'

At last they arrived, and after parking up Jeremy found he was once again racing after Tom. Inside at the desk they were given directions, and found when they followed them that Amy's mother was pacing in the corridor.

'Phyllis, how is she? Where is she?' Tom asked anxiously.

'She's in there, but we can't go in. The doctors are with her and . . .'

Tom didn't wait for Phyllis to finish the sentence as he pushed open the door she had indicated and went inside, while Jeremy asked Phyllis, 'What happened? Tom only said something about Amy having a fall.'

Phyllis sat down on a chair and Jeremy perched next to her as she said, 'I . . . I hadn't long been with her and she was going to have a nap when I went home, but then about an hour later I heard this awful scream. I dashed back to Amy's and found her on the floor. She . . . she had fallen down the stairs.'

Phyllis was crying, tears rolling down her cheeks, and Jeremy had just placed a comforting arm around her when Tom came out of the room with a sheepish look on his face. 'I got chased out,' he said.

They both jumped to their feet, Phyllis asking, 'How is she?'

'They're making sure that Amy hasn't sustained any injuries from the fall, but the doctor said so far everything looks fine.'

'And the baby! What about the baby?' Jeremy asked.

'There don't seem to be any problems. They're going to closely monitor the birth, and once they've finished examining Amy, I can go back in.'

This proved to be true when shortly afterwards the doctor came out and echoed what Tom had told them, along with saying that Amy was in the early stages of labour.

'What does that mean?' Tom asked Phyllis when the doctor walked away.

'It means it could be hours and hours before the baby is born.'

'So we could be here for a long time,' Jeremy said.

Tom shook his head. 'There's no need for you to stay, Jeremy. I'll ring you and Mum, when there's any news.'

'All right,' Jeremy reluctantly agreed, though inside his guts were churning. He should be there. Amy was going to have his baby, yet Tom would be named as the father.

* * *

Amy was glad to have her mum there, but it was mostly Tom who sat by her side. As the hours passed, the pain increased to an intensity that had her yelling out, begging for it to stop. The doctor and nurses came in on regular occasions, listened to the baby's heartbeat and examined her, but they had just left when Amy felt something change. 'Tommy, quick, I think the baby's coming! Go and get the doctor!'

He dashed outside, soon returning, and as Amy felt another urge to push the nurse said, 'Mr Frost, you'll have to wait outside.'

'But I don't want to leave her.'

'Tommy, just go!' Amy cried, straining through clenched teeth.

Tommy reluctantly left, and Amy gave in to the urge that was impossible to ignore. The doctor's instructions came through a haze of pain as she pushed, and then again, grunting, yelling, until at last, with one final push, her baby was born.

Amy heard small cries, and then the doctor said, 'Well done. You have a baby boy.'

Amy sank back, her body and hair wet with perspiration, but shortly after that her baby was placed into her arms. She took one look at him, and all her fears dissipated as her heart swelled with love.

All too soon, the nurse said, 'I'll just clean you up a bit and then your husband can come in.'

The baby was taken from her, but it wasn't too long before he was back in her arms and Tommy was walking into the room. He moved to the side of the bed, gazing at the baby, and Amy saw tears of emotion form in his eyes. 'My son,' he choked.

Amy fought tears too; tears of guilt, but as she held the

baby up for Tommy to hold, she could see the love in his eyes – love for both of them.

Tommy looked so happy, so overwhelmed with joy as he looked down at the baby, and Amy knew she'd rather live with the agony of her lies than take that away from him.

Chapter Forty-Four

Phyllis was overwhelmed by her new grandson. Amy and Tom had chosen the name Robert, and though he'd arrived early he'd been a good weight and was thriving. Stan was over the moon too, and he'd taken to popping round to Amy's to see the baby the minute he arrived home from work.

Phyllis knew she was just as bad, but Bobby, as he was mostly called, was so adorable that she couldn't keep away. January turned to late February, and one Thursday, after work, Mabel collared her as she passed her door.

'Come in, Phyllis. I've got a bit of news.'

'All right, but I can't stay long.'

As she stepped inside, Mabel swiftly closed the door against the cold and said, 'I'm taking on another foster child on Monday.'

'Oh, that's good,' Phyllis said. She knew how hard it had been for Mabel and Jack to part with Peter. It had knocked them for six and she'd doubted they would put themselves through that again. Now though she'd been proved wrong, and Mabel looked happy at the prospect of having another child to care for.

'It's a girl this time, called Sandra, and she's nearly five years old. She's got a club foot and the poor kid's been in care for years with no sign of anyone wanting to adopt her.'

'Would you consider adoption?'

Mabel bit on her lower lip in thought and then said, 'I grew really fond of Peter, and if the same thing happens with Sandra, do you know, I just might.'

Phyllis suspected it would happen and they talked about it for a few more minutes before she was able to get away. She then went straight to Amy's, saying as she went in, 'How's my grandson?'

'He's fine, but I'm not so sure about Tommy. He didn't look too well this morning, but he still went to work.'

'Let's hope it isn't anything to worry about,' Phyllis said. Bobby was asleep, one little fist tucked under his chin, and with his thick head of dark hair, he looked adorable. He had brought so much joy into their lives, and she would be forever grateful that thanks to Rose, both her daughter and grandson were living so close to her that she could see them every day.

'You look a bit rough,' Jeremy said to Tom when he returned to the unit after seeing a building contractor.

'I wasn't so bad this morning, but it's getting worse now. How did you get on with the contractor?'

'If we can get the quote down by three per cent, I think it's in the bag.'

'All right, we'll go through the figures again to see if it's possible,' Tom said, but then he started coughing and was left gasping for breath.

'You should go home.'

'I think I might have to,' Tom said after using his inhaler. 'I just hope my boy hasn't inherited my asthma and weak chest.'

'I doubt that's likely,' Jeremy said, quickly covering the remark by adding, 'From what I've seen, Robert's going to be a proper bruiser.'

Tom smiled proudly. 'Yes, he's great isn't he, but I see Mum's still got you calling him Robert.'

'She thinks Bobby sounds common.'

'I like it,' Tommy said. 'It suits him and I can't tell you how amazing it is to be a father.'

Jeremy knew what it was like. From the moment he'd first held Robert the bond had been instantaneous and it had taken all his willpower not to shout that this was his son – not Tom's. Somehow he had managed to remain silent, but now every time Tom talked about *his* boy, or bragged about being a father, it ate at him, gnawed at his guts, until he could barely look at his brother without hatred in his eyes.

Tom was coughing again and then said croakily, 'It's four o'clock so I think I'll knock off early. If I'm not up to it tomorrow, you and Len can go over that quote again.'

'I'll pop down in the morning to see how you are,' Jeremy said, thinking it was the perfect excuse to see Robert again and of course Amy. The more he saw of them both, the more he wanted them, but knew his brother would always stand in his way.

Amy was thinking back to her chat with Carol on Monday. With a baby now and the hassle of getting a bus to Chelsea, Carol had agreed to meet in a café on Lavender Hill. Carol had arrived grinning like a Cheshire cat and after making a big fuss of Bobby, she had held out her left hand to show Amy her engagement ring.

Amy smiled at the memory, thrilled for her friend, but then the door opened and Tommy arrived home early from work. 'Oh, Tommy, you look awful,' Amy said as she stood up.

'My chest is bad again.'

'Why don't you go to the surgery and get the doctor to take a look at you?'

'I've already been to the surgery, poked my head into the waiting room, but it was packed. I didn't feel up to hanging around.'

'In that case I think you should go straight to bed and if you're no better in the morning I'll get the doctor to call in to take a look at you.'

'Yes, all right,' he agreed, just as Bobby began to cry.

'He's hungry,' Amy said, picking him up. She was breast-feeding and Bobby still woke in the night, but mostly he was a contented baby.

Tommy walked over and fondly stroked the baby's head, but then he moved away quickly as he began to cough, saying when he managed to catch his breath, 'It's been ages since my chest was as bad as this.'

Amy felt a frisson of fear as she recalled how ill Tommy had been with pneumonia. Bobby was wailing in earnest now and she urged, 'Go to bed, Tommy. I'll feed him and then instead of waiting till tomorrow morning, I'll ring the doctor to see if he'll call in when he's finished with his patients.'

Tommy didn't argue, which made Amy more anxious, and as Tommy went upstairs she sat down, unbuttoned her blouse, and as Bobby latched on, for the first time she waited impatiently for him to finish his feed.

Stan went to see his grandson shortly after arriving home from work, to find Amy with Robert in her arms and looking harassed as she let him in. 'What's up, love?'

'Tommy's ill. I rang the doctor ages ago but he hasn't turned up yet.'

'Calm down, he's sure to arrive soon,' Stan assured.

'I hope so, Dad,' she said, handing the baby to him. 'You can keep an eye on Bobby while I go up to check on Tommy.'

Stan was happy to do just that as he limped over to sit down by the fire, cradling his grandson in his arms. He was a little cracker and as he'd always wanted a son, Stan felt this was the next best thing. He gently stroked the baby's cheek, and though there was a way to go yet, he was looking forward to the time when Bobby could walk and talk.

There was the sound of a car drawing up outside, and Amy must have heard it too as she flew downstairs to open the door. 'Good evening, Mrs Frost,' the doctor said, nodding a greeting to Stan as he walked inside.

'My husband's chest is bad again,' Amy told him, ushering the doctor up to see Tommy.

Stan looked into the flickering flames of the fire, finding his mind drifting back to the past. There had been a time when he hadn't been happy about Amy courting Tommy – when he'd thought that with his weak chest and time off work, he'd never be able to support a wife. He'd been wrong about that. Tommy had made a great success of his father's business and even Celia, old frosty knickers, hadn't turned out to be too much of a problem. He still didn't think much of Celia though, and he knew Amy sometimes found her a bit of a trial, but on the whole, his daughter's future looked rosy.

For a moment he thought about George Frost, and wondered where he was. Did he know that he was a grandfather too? Somehow Stan doubted it, because if George had found out, surely he'd have turned up by now.

*　　*　　*

Jeremy didn't arrive home until six thirty that evening, and as soon as he told her that Tommy wasn't well, Celia went to see for herself. 'Why didn't you ring me?' she complained as Amy let her in.

'I thought I'd wait until the doctor had seen Tommy and I was just about to call you.'

'I see,' Celia said, doubting it was true, 'and what did the doctor say?'

'That Tommy's chest is very congested. He gave him two antibiotic pills immediately and a prescription for me to get in the morning.'

'I'll go up to see him,' Celia said.

'He's asleep so I'd rather you didn't wake him.'

'I won't do that,' she said impatiently. 'I'll just look in, but have you made sure that he's propped up?'

'Yes, of course, and you'll see that for yourself.'

'I should hope so,' she replied tersely, and upstairs she found that Thomas was indeed asleep, with pillows piled up behind him. At least Amy had learned something, Celia thought, before going down to the living room where she immediately went to look at her grandson.

Robert was asleep too, but it didn't stop Celia from picking him up. 'He looks so much like Thomas when he was a baby and I can see Jeremy in his features too.'

There was no reply and Celia glanced up to see that Amy looked a little flushed. 'I hope you're not annoyed that I picked Robert up. I haven't woken him.'

'No, it's fine.'

Celia sighed and gently placed Robert down again. 'I should go. Jeremy will want his dinner. I have a ten o'clock appointment with a chiropodist in the morning, but I'll ring to see how Thomas is before I leave.'

Amy just nodded, and Celia hurried out, thinking that

to see her grandson she had to make an effort with her daughter-in-law, yet still wishing that Thomas had found a girl of finer breeding to marry.

Amy was glad to close the door on Celia. She too had seen the resemblance to Jeremy in her son's features and dreaded they would always serve as a reminder of his conception. She hated it when Jeremy came to see them, though thankfully he always came in the evenings so they were never alone. If he held Bobby she always wanted to snatch him back, and she hated the way Jeremy surreptitiously looked at her. That wasn't all she had noticed. She had seen the resentment in Jeremy's eyes when Tommy was holding Bobby, sometimes a dark anger, and it frightened her.

'Amy!'

Tommy's voice jerked her back to the present and she ran upstairs. 'I'm here,' she said as she went into their bedroom.

'I'm sorry, but I'm thirsty. Can I have a glass of water?'

'Of course,' she said, going to his bedside table and pouring a glass of water from the jug.

'Oh sorry,' he apologised again. 'I didn't realise it was there.'

Amy saw that his eyes looked a bit glazed and his forehead was hot to the touch. So far the antibiotics weren't having any effect, but he managed to take the glass and after drinking, his eyes seemed to clear.

'Thanks,' he said, handing it back. 'How long have I been asleep?'

'Only for about an hour, but while you were your mum called in to see you. She'll be back in the morning.'

Tommy nodded, and laid his head back while Amy asked, 'Can I get you anything to eat?'

'I'm not hungry.'

'What about something light, if only a boiled egg?'

'No thanks,' he said, coughing, and breathless before he managed to speak again. 'I wouldn't mind a cup of tea though.'

'Coming up,' Amy said, but after going downstairs to make it, she returned to find that Tommy had fallen asleep again.

What followed was a restless night, Tommy waking, coughing, and Bobby waking twice in the night too. Amy snatched what sleep she could, praying that in the morning, Tommy wouldn't be any worse.

Chapter Forty-Five

Phyllis woke on Friday morning to find that Stan had his arms wrapped around her, and contented, she let her mind drift as she savoured the warmth of their close contact. She hoped that Tommy wasn't any worse that morning. With him being ill and a baby to look after, Amy had a lot on her plate, and at that thought, Phyllis decided to ring Rose to ask for the day off. She knew that her cousin wouldn't mind, and still thanked her lucky stars for the day that Rose had offered her the job. There had been a time when money was so tight that she'd half starved herself to make the food go round, but nowadays she hardly ever had to watch the pennies. In fact, Phyllis thought, she'd never been so well off – or so happy.

There was a snort and a grunt as Stan woke up, his arms tightening around her. Stan was ready for a bit of loving that morning and Phyllis was happy to oblige, so it was another half an hour before she got up to wash and dress before going downstairs to prepare his breakfast.

When he too came downstairs, Phyllis was ready to place a plate of eggs, bacon and fried bread in front of him. He licked his lips, grinned and said, 'Now that looks good enough to eat, but so do you. How about we go back to bed?'

'Don't be daft. You'll be late for work.'

'It'd be worth it,' he said, winking cheekily.

'Just eat your breakfast,' Phyllis admonished as she poured their drinks and sat down too, happy to munch on a piece of toast. When Stan left for work she'd pop round to Amy's and use her telephone to ring Rose. If Tommy was really rough, she'd volunteer to look after Bobby for the day, and the weekend if necessary.

Not that it was any hardship, she thought, smiling softly.

Amy awoke to the sound of someone knocking on the door. She looked quickly at Tommy, then Robert in his cot, saw that they were both still asleep, so quickly put on her dressing gown and hurried downstairs.

'Now there's a sight,' Jeremy commented when she opened it. 'I must have got you out of bed.'

'What do you want?' Amy asked bluntly.

'I'm on my way to the unit, but I thought I'd pop in to see how Tommy is.'

'He had a restless night and he's still asleep,' she said, but then heard Robert crying.

Jeremy must have heard him too because he pushed the door wider to step inside and Amy was fuming when he followed her upstairs. She picked Robert up to soothe him and saw that Tommy was waking up too.

'Hello, mate, how are you?' Jeremy asked him.

Tommy blinked and looked a bit confused to see his brother in the room, but then he began to cough again and it was Jeremy who moved forward to prop him up. 'That's it, Tom. Get it up.'

'Thanks,' Tommy gasped.

'I called in to see how you are, and you're certainly not fit for work today.'

'No, sorry, I'm not, but hopefully I'll be back on my feet soon.'

'Don't worry, Tom, until you are we can manage fine without you,' Jeremy said.

Robert was wailing again and Amy knew that he was hungry as well as needing a nappy change, but Tommy said, 'I need a drink of water.'

'It's all right, Amy. I'll see to Tom while you sort the nipper out,' Jeremy said.

Amy nodded, took Robert downstairs where she changed his nappy and then sat down to feed him. A few minutes later she heard footsteps on the stairs and quickly covered herself, flushing when Jeremy came near to look down on them. She hated his close proximity and hissed, 'I think you should leave now.'

'Tom wants a cup of tea and as you're a bit busy, I'll make it,' he said, his voice then lowering as he added, 'I also thought I'd take a look at my son.'

'He isn't yours! He's Tommy's,' Amy said, quietly yet forcefully.

'You know that isn't true,' Jeremy said, crouching down in front of her. 'I'm playing the role of his uncle, but I'm much more than that.'

'You *are* his uncle,' Amy insisted, though she couldn't meet Jeremy's eyes.

'You can deny it all you like, but it won't stop me loving my son. Or you.'

Fearful that Tommy would hear, Amy struggled to keep her voice from rising. 'You can't say that. You mustn't say that. I'm Tommy's wife and I love him, so please, please, just go away and leave us alone,' Amy appealed.

Thankfully Jeremy rose to his feet. He gently touched the top of Robert's head, then hers. 'I wish I could, but I can't stay away from you. I'll make that tea now,' he said, at last moving away.

Amy was left trembling as she continued to feed Robert. Instead of leaving them alone, Jeremy was becoming almost predatory. She feared that one day he would snap and tell Tommy the truth.

Jeremy made a pot of tea, his mind twisting and turning. When he saw the intimate scene of Amy feeding the baby, he wanted so much to take on the true role of Robert's father. It could never be, and knowing that, his guts churned.

Dark thoughts filled Jeremy's mind, memories of the time when Tom had been so ill that he'd nearly died. Could it happen again? Would this bout of bronchitis turn to pneumonia, and if it did, maybe Tom wouldn't survive this time. Amy would be free then, and surely she would turn to him? With a groan, Jeremy ran both hands over his face. What sort of man was he? He was wishing his brother dead, yet the thought of going on like this, of having to sit on the periphery of his son's life and eventually hear Robert calling his brother daddy, was more than he could take.

With the tea made, Jeremy poured two cups, giving one to Amy and seeing her tight, tense expression as she continued to feed Robert. She murmured her thanks, but didn't meet his eyes before he went upstairs. Tom was dozing, his face wan, and for a moment Jeremy just stood, looking down on him, wishing that Tom's eyes would never open again.

Black thoughts filled Jeremy's mind again; jealousy, resentment and hate. He put the cup of tea on the bedside cabinet and then his hands, as though acting under their own volition, reached out to pull one of the pillows from under Tom's head. As his brother's eyes opened, filled with confusion, Jeremy pushed the pillow over his face, pressing down and smothering Tom's cries while hissing, 'Robert's mine! My son! Not yours!'

What he hadn't expected was that Tom would have the strength to fight, but he did, clawing at the pillow as his legs flailed. It didn't stop Jeremy. He felt distant, removed from the act as he continued to push down, impervious to the muted bellows he could hear, and though Tom's arm was wildly flapping, knocking the cup and saucer onto the floor, he was barely aware of it.

'What are you doing! No! No! Stop it! Stop it!'

Jeremy's head snapped round and in seconds Amy was on him, pulling, scratching, yelling, tearing at his hands. It was only then that he came to his senses, and as he flung himself away Amy dragged the pillow from Tom's face.

Amy cried out, while Jeremy, unable to look at what he had done, fled. He almost fell down the stairs, but moments later yanked the street door open, nearly colliding with Amy's mother before he dived into his car.

Jeremy's head was pounding, felt like it was going to explode as he drove off, accelerating dangerously. He had killed his own brother! He'd hang for murder!

Foot still down, Jeremy drove straight out onto the main road and into the path of an oncoming lorry. The crash of impact, the sickening crunch of metal on metal, searing, agonising pain and his own screams, were the last sounds that Jeremy heard.

Chapter Forty-Six

For a few moments, Tommy had felt as though his life was slipping away, but then had come the blessed relief of air. He had drawn in a lungful, then another, his chest heaving while Amy clung to him, crying with relief. His head was all over the place, yet the words Jeremy had said while pushing the pillow down on his face kept going around in his mind like a loop. He'd said that Bobby was his; that he was his father – but it couldn't be true, it just couldn't.

There was the sound of footsteps on the stairs, and then Phyllis appeared, holding Bobby in her arms, her expression fearful until she saw him. 'Oh, Tommy, thank goodness. When I saw Jeremy driving off like a maniac, for a moment I thought . . . well . . . that something had happened to you.' She paused then, taking in the scene before saying, 'I found Bobby in his pram, uncovered, mewling, and you're crying too, Amy. What's going on?'

'Oh, Mum, I had to put him down quickly,' Amy sobbed. 'I heard something going on, dashed up here and . . . and saw Jeremy trying to smother Tommy with a pillow.'

'What! But why?'

'I . . . I don't know,' Amy replied.

Still reeling with shock, Tommy croaked, 'Can . . . can I have a drink of water?'

Amy poured it, her hands shaking as she held it out to him, and as he drank some she said, 'I think I should ring the doctor.'

'No . . . no, there's no need. I'm all right now.'

'I still don't get it,' Phyllis said. 'Why did Jeremy try to smother you, Tommy? Was it some sort of game, the pair of you larking around or something?'

'Some . . . something like that,' Tommy replied, unable to believe that Jeremy had meant him any real harm, yet the things his brother had said still tumbled round in his mind. Bobby began to wail, and with his head thumping, Tommy wanted time to think, to make sense of it all. He wanted to be alone.

'I think Bobby needs changing,' Phyllis said. 'I'll take him downstairs and sort him out.'

It was a relief when she left, and wanting rid of Amy too, Tommy sought an excuse. 'Amy, I could do with a cup of tea.'

'Yes, all right,' she said, bending down to pick up the shards of broken china on the floor before leaving.

Tommy sank back, and though he didn't want to believe what Jeremy had said, he began to work out the dates. He'd come home from convalescence in May and Bobby had been born in January, early because Amy had fallen down the stairs.

There was a twinge of doubt then, but Tommy fought to push it away. Amy would never betray him, never; and anyway, he would never forget how he'd felt when Bobby was first placed in his arms, the overwhelming love and joy as he'd gazed in wonder at his son. Surely it wouldn't have been possible to feel like that if Bobby wasn't his?

Yet still there was that niggling doubt. Why did Jeremy think that he was Bobby's father? Why would he think that if there had been nothing between him and Amy? It just didn't make sense.

Amy went downstairs, still shaking with shock. Tommy had denied it, but she was sure that Jeremy had intended to kill him. She would never forget the horror of thinking that she'd been too late when she'd dragged the pillow from his face. She had cried out in fear, but only seconds later Tommy had heaved in a huge lungful of air, life returning to his body as she had clung on to him, sobbing her relief.

'It still seems like a funny business to me,' her mother said as she deftly changed Bobby's nappy. 'And how did that cup and saucer get smashed?'

'I . . . I don't know, Mum,' she said, 'but for now Tommy wants a cup of tea. Do you want one?'

'Yes, all right,' Phyllis agreed.

As Amy put the kettle onto the gas ring, her stomach was churning. She had seen the madness in Jeremy's eyes, and what if he tried it again? What if in his obsession to possess her and Bobby he made another attempt on Tommy's life?

With the tea made, she gave a cup to her mother and then carried one up to Tommy. His eyes were closed and as she placed the drink on his bedside cabinet, her eyes alighted on his prescription as she said softly, 'Tommy, here's your tea.'

He was asleep and didn't respond so Amy picked up the prescription and crept out again, unaware that as soon as she left the room, Tommy's eyes snapped open.

For the next half hour, Amy just watched, her mind still tangled with thoughts as her mother bathed then dressed

371

Bobby. She'd insisted on taking the day off, and Amy was too emotionally drained to argue, just relieved to let her mother take over for a while.

'There, now who looks like a proper Bobby dazzler,' Phyllis said as she held Bobby out for inspection before putting him in his pram. 'It's gone nine fifteen and the chemist will be open now. I'll take Bobby with me, as a bit of fresh air will do him good.'

The telephone rang and Amy rose to answer it, hardly recognising Celia's voice. She sounded hysterical, babbling, her words disjointed, but upon hearing them, Amy's knees almost collapsed from under her.

Somehow she managed to respond, and when someone else came on the line to say that Celia needed someone with her, Amy knew that with Tommy too ill to go, it would have to be her. 'I'll be there as soon as I can,' she said, and then replaced the receiver.

'Amy, what's going on?' her mother asked anxiously.

Somehow Amy managed to say the words; saw her mother's face drain of colour, and then with her feet dragging she went upstairs, knowing that before making arrangements to leave, she now had to tell Tommy that his brother was dead.

Celia had at last stopped crying, but there was a knot of pain in her stomach, as though a part of her had been ripped out. She didn't look up at the sound of footsteps, but then heard Amy's voice as her daughter-in-law said softly, 'Come on, let's get you home.'

Like a child Celia held Amy's hand and allowed herself to be led outside to a waiting taxi, her eyes barely taking in her surroundings as they drove off. There was no sense of time passing, or distance, and Celia only became aware that she was still clutching Amy's hand as they drew up in

Lark Rise. Had Amy spoken to her in the taxi? Celia didn't know, and then the next thing she knew she was in Amy's front room.

'Celia, I'm so sorry.'

It was Amy's mother talking to her, but Celia found that she couldn't respond. She walked past her and up the stairs, but then seeing Thomas the tears came again, flowing unchecked down her cheeks as she sat on the side of the bed. She leaned into Thomas and his arms wrapped around her.

'Mum, how did it happen?' Thomas asked when she was at last slightly calmer. 'I only know that there was a crash.'

Celia saw that his cheeks were wet too and said, 'I know little more than that; only . . . only what the police told me, that . . . that it seems Jeremy drove into the path of a lorry.'

They held each other again then, and Celia could feel Thomas shaking with emotion. He was all she had left now, her only son, and she clung to him as though she was drowning.

Chapter Forty-Seven

Phyllis had never thought much of Celia, but her heart went out to her now. Ten days had passed since Jeremy's tragic death, and there had been a small article about the fatal accident in the local paper.

Celia was inconsolable. She spent a lot of time with Amy and Tommy now, and clung to her surviving son as though he were a life raft. Tommy had recovered from his chest infection and owing to pressures at work he'd had no choice but to return, though like Celia, his grief at the loss of his brother was weighing him down.

'It's only me,' Mabel called as she came in through the back door, bringing Sandra, the little girl she was fostering, with her.

'Hello,' Phyllis greeted, smiling at the child. She was a pretty little thing with blonde hair and blue eyes, sadly handicapped by a heavy built-up shoe that caused her to walk clumsily. Mabel had only been fostering her since Monday, and after being institutionalised for so long it was going to take time for Sandra to settle. The signs were good though, and Phyllis felt sure that in time Mabel and Jack would apply to adopt her.

'I won't stop,' Mabel said. 'I know you're off to work soon, but I just popped round to see if there's any news about the funeral. I'd like to send some flowers from me and Jack.'

'There's been a bit of a delay because of the police investigation, but as no medical reason was found they've put the crash down to reckless driving. At least the lorry driver wasn't badly hurt, and now Jeremy's funeral is being arranged for Monday, a week from today,' Phyllis told her, glad when shortly afterwards Mabel left.

Since the accident and Jeremy's death the incident when he had put a pillow over Tommy's face had never been mentioned again, seemingly forgotten, but Phyllis still found it strange. Not only that, she was worried about Amy and wanted to pop round to see her before she left for work. Of course Amy was upset about Jeremy's death too, but there was more to it than that – more to the anguish she had seen in the depths of her daughter's eyes.

Later that morning, Celia saw Amy as she walked past her window. She was pushing the pram, her head bent against a chill wind, and Celia wished that instead of just passing by, Amy had called in. Maybe she'd stop by on the way back. Celia hoped so.

With tears in her eyes, Celia turned away from the window, knowing that despite the way she had treated her, Amy in return had shown her nothing but kindness and sympathy since Jeremy died. She had thought that Amy wasn't good enough for Thomas; that she was common, but all the things that Celia had once coveted, status, money, and material things, meant nothing to her now.

He was there again, filling her thoughts as he did every minute of the day. Jeremy . . . oh . . . Jeremy. If it wasn't for spending time with Amy and Robert during the day, and most evenings with Thomas too, Celia felt that she wouldn't be able to carry on. They were all she had left now, and she clung to them.

The doorbell rang and Celia, uncaring of her appearance, went to answer it. It was Libby Willard, her next door neighbour, mouthing sympathies, yet with avid eyes. 'Celia, my dear, I would have called round before this, but I didn't like to intrude. How are you?'

'How do you think?' Celia replied bluntly. She had lived next door to this woman for years, had even considered her a friend, but when George had left, Libby had shown her true colours. She had made Celia feel like a social outcast, and nowadays they only spoke when they saw each other in passing, Libby's dinner party invitations and coffee mornings a thing of the past.

'It was such a dreadful accident and you must be totally devastated,' Libby said.

Celia just nodded, unwilling to open up to this woman who had waited ten days to call round with hollow condolences.

Libby hovered on the doorstep, but then seeing that she wasn't going to be invited in, attempted a dignified departure. 'Well, as I said, I don't want to intrude, but if there's anything I can do . . .'

'Thank you, but there's nothing,' Celia said bluntly and with a brief goodbye she closed the door. There was nothing Libby could do – nothing anyone could do to ease her pain.

When her mother had called round before she went to work, Amy had forced a smile that she hoped masked her true feelings. In reality she was almost going out of her mind, desperate to confide in someone, and as Carol already knew the truth about what Jeremy had done it was her friend that she turned to.

She had dressed Bobby warmly and pushed the pram to the café on Lavender Hill, glad to see that Carol was already there. They ordered a coffee each and then Amy forced another smile as she said, 'Thanks for coming.'

'Don't be daft. It's good to see you, but how are you coping?'

The sympathy was Amy's undoing and blinking back tears she said, 'It's been awful since Jeremy died. Celia's in a terrible state and Tommy only speaks to me when he has to. At night, in bed, he . . . he just turns his back to me.'

Carol frowned in thought. 'Maybe it's his way of dealing with his grief. Perhaps he's sort of closed in on himself.'

'I wish it was just that, but I'm worried sick,' Amy said, going on to tell Carol about Jeremy trying to smother Tommy.

'Amy, surely he wasn't trying to kill him?'

'Tommy said he wasn't, but I don't believe it, and what if Jeremy told him why he was doing it? What if he told him about Bobby?'

'If that happened, surely Tommy would have told you, confronted you?'

'Maybe he was going to, but Jeremy died that same morning and . . . and since then, as I said, Tommy's hardly spoken to me.'

'I still think it's his grief, Tommy's way of dealing with it.'

'I hope you're right,' Amy said, finding that sharing her bottled-up fears with Carol had helped a little. Bobby began to grizzle so she lifted him out of the pram, saying as she did so, 'All we've talked about is me. How's your mum, your brothers and of course Eddy?'

'They're all fine, and I've got a bit of news, though I'm not sure this is the best time to tell you.'

'It'll be nice to talk about something else, so go on, spit it out,' Amy encouraged.

'Eddy wants us to get married later this year.'

'Really? When?'

'In September, though we haven't fixed a firm date yet. It won't be a big do, just the registry office and a small party afterwards, rather like your wedding.'

Carol went on happily talking about what dress she might wear, what hat, while Amy found that her thoughts kept straying to her own problems. Was it grief that had made Tommy close in on himself as Carol suggested – or was it that Jeremy had told him the truth about Bobby? It was the uncertainty that Amy was finding unbearable, her nerves almost at breaking point, but somehow she had to carry on.

Tommy was doing his best to catch up on the paperwork, but thanks to Len the most immediate things had been dealt with. He had a lot to thank his foreman for, not least that for the time being Len had taken over sorting out the wages and paying the men. His mother was in no fit state to handle the accounts, and he doubted that she would be for some time, yet somehow Tommy knew that for the sake of his employees and their jobs, he had to carry on.

As he looked at the invoice in front of him the figures blurred as unbidden, his tortured thoughts returned to Jeremy. The last time he had seen his brother haunted Tommy's mind; the things Jeremy had said as he had forcibly pressed a pillow onto his face. At first he'd refused to believe that Jeremy had tried to kill him, but the more he relived the memory of that morning, the more the doubts had set in. It didn't make sense that Jeremy would claim to be Bobby's father if it wasn't true.

He could barely look at Amy now, and at least at the

unit he was out of the house. Tommy knew that he couldn't go on like this; that he would have to have it out with Amy soon, but the thought of being told that Bobby wasn't his son, tore him apart. He didn't want to face it yet – couldn't face it yet, and when the telephone rang Tommy snatched it up, glad to escape his tortured thoughts as his mind snapped back to work and a customer asking for a quote.

Chapter Forty-Eight

As the days passed the stress continued to take its toll on Amy, and her milk dried up. She had to put Bobby on a milk formula, but at first he rejected the teat on the bottle. It was Celia who managed to coax him, and as they smiled at each other in relief, for the first time Amy felt an affinity with her mother-in-law.

On Monday, the day of the funeral, the sky was low, with a dark grey blanket of cloud hanging over Lark Rise. Tommy had shut the unit for the day and when the hearse slowly drove off, only two cars followed it. Celia was sitting between Thomas and Amy in the first one, a black veil masking her anguished features. The second car held Amy's parents, along with Samuel and Rose, just seven of them to attend the service – but when they got to the chapel Amy saw Len Upwood and his wife standing outside, along with other men who worked for Thomas and who bowed their heads in respect when the coffin was lifted from the hearse.

Tommy took his mother's arm as they walked behind the coffin bearers into the chapel, where sombre music played. When they were all seated, the service began, but Amy hardly took in a word of what was said. She was cold, the pew hard, and when they were asked to stand Tommy was as rigid as a statue beside her. She felt the gulf between them, but felt powerless to bridge it.

The last hymn was sung, but they still had to go to the graveside for the interment. There were coughs, the shuffle of feet as they made their way out of the chapel, but close to the back two people were just leaving their pew. It was the couple she had seen in a car at the registry office, and this time there was no mistaking them.

Celia must have noticed them too for there was a gasp, yet they were outside before there was a confrontation. Amy was expecting fireworks, but instead Celia held her head high and in a dignified manner, nodded to her husband and Lena Winters before regally walking past them.

'I didn't know what to expect,' George said as he turned to Tommy. 'At least your mother didn't do her nut.'

'Dad, how could you do this to her, and today of all days?'

'Now look, I saw a piece about Jeremy's accident in the local paper and it shocked me to the core. He's my son too and I have every right to come to his funeral.'

'You didn't have to bring *her* with you,' Tommy snapped, before hurrying after his mother.

George went after him, but then he stopped and just stood, looking at his son's retreating back.

'I told George I shouldn't have come,' Lena Winters said to Amy.

She looked at her former manageress and said coldly, 'I never guessed. I should have, especially on those occasions when we supposedly bumped into each other. You always encouraged me to talk about Tommy.'

'I'm sorry for the deception, but it kept George in touch with his son's life for a while.'

'I can't work this out. How did you meet each other?'

'It was just by chance. I had a broken window, called a local firm and George came to repair it. We talked, got on well, and it just sort of went from there.'

George came back and said, 'Everyone is heading for the interment.'

'You go, George. I'll wait in the car until you're ready to leave,' Lena said.

Amy walked away from them to join the others in the sad procession through the cemetery. Jeremy was now going to be put into the ground, his final resting place, but there was no rest for Amy's tortured thoughts. This was the man who had raped her, the true father of her son, and though dead now, he still threatened to tear her life apart.

Tommy had his arm around his mother and could feel her trembling. He would never know how she managed to hold it together, to show such dignity and composure when it was now obvious that she was deeply upset. If his father had come alone, it might just have been all right, but to bring that woman with him must have been like a slap in the face.

Though he was furious with his father, it did nothing to stop the biting wind from cutting him to the core as they stood by the freshly dug grave. He was aware that Amy had come to stand by his side, but didn't acknowledge her presence. His father was at least standing alone now, a little apart from everyone else, his eyes lowered as the vicar intoned while the coffin was being lowered.

There was a sob and as he felt his mother sag, Tommy did his best to support her, until at last, after she threw a single white rose onto the coffin, he was able to lead her away. They were heading for the car when they were approached by Len Upwood, his wife and the other men.

'We're off now,' Len said, 'but we'd just like to offer your mother our condolences.'

'Thank you,' she said with a tremor in her voice, 'and thank you all for coming.'

Tommy knew she was making a supreme effort, and was relieved when with a few more murmured words of condolence, they drifted away. It wasn't over yet though and as they reached the car, his father walked up to them, saying, 'Celia, can we talk?'

'I've got nothing to say to you, except that I want a divorce,' she said and climbed into the car, adding before she closed the door, 'I will expect to hear from your solicitor.'

Tommy didn't want to talk to his father either, as seeing him only added to the pent-up emotions he was trying to hold in check. Amy walked up to them with her parents, while Rose and Samuel stood a short distance apart. 'Come on, Amy, we're leaving,' Tommy said curtly.

'We'll see you back at the house,' Phyllis called as Amy got into the car.

Tommy climbed in too, ignoring his father, his gaze set rigidly ahead as the car drove off.

Stan walked up to George Frost and said, 'It's a sad day, but after all this time I didn't expect to see you here.'

'Jeremy was my son and I had to come. Until I saw that bit about the accident in the local paper, I didn't even know he was back in the country.'

'There's a lot you don't know. For instance, you've got a grandson.'

'A grandson! I had no idea.'

'I don't get it, George. When a man walks out on his wife it isn't a criminal offence, so why have you been laying low?'

'You have no idea what Celia is like. If she had been able to find me, she'd have made my life a misery, but I kept an eye on Tommy for as long as I could. I knew he was making a success of the business and once he married Amy I felt he was fine, settled.'

'When you left, it was Tommy who had to pick up the pieces and take care of his mother financially. It was a lot to put on his young shoulders.'

'Maybe, but he coped,' George said dismissively. 'Celia just asked me for a divorce so it seems she's moved on. It means I can come out of the woodwork now and it'll be great to see my grandson.'

'Come on, Stan, it's time we were leaving,' Phyllis called.

'I'm coming,' he said, but before walking away from the man he now saw as a selfish pig, Stan left a parting shot. 'George, from what I saw and heard, Tommy wasn't pleased to see you. If you turn up at his door, I doubt you'd get a warm welcome and if he slams it in your face, I wouldn't blame him.'

Mabel had stepped in and offered to look after Bobby while they attended the funeral, but he had been fretful that morning and Amy was anxious to collect him. She needn't have worried. He was sound asleep on Mabel's sofa, a blanket over him, while little Sandra was quietly playing with a doll.

'He's been no trouble,' Mabel said, smiling fondly down on him. 'He went to sleep soon after I gave him his bottle.'

'Can we keep him, Auntie Mabel?' Sandra asked as she awkwardly scrambled to her feet. 'I want to play with Bobby when he wakes up.'

'No, I'm afraid we can't, darling. His mummy has come to take him home.'

'Thanks for looking after him, Mabel,' Amy said as she gently lifted Bobby into her arms.

'Any time, love.'

'I'd best get back. Mum made some sandwiches and a few other bits and pieces which she's put out on my dining table, though I doubt Samuel and Rose will stay for long. I think they can see that Celia is only just holding it together.'

'I haven't had much time for Celia in the past, but I know what it's like to lose a child and my heart goes out to her now.'

Amy couldn't imagine how she'd cope if anything happened to Bobby and found her arms tightening around him. She thanked Mabel again for looking after him and then went home, feeling the familiar tension as soon as she walked in the door. Somehow she got through the next couple of hours, until at last when Rose and Samuel left, and Tommy took his mother home, she was left with her parents.

'Amy, is everything all right between you and Tommy?'

'Yes, of course,' Amy said, hiding the truth.

'Are you sure? From what I've seen Tommy hardly speaks to you.'

Amy clutched for Carol's words and said, 'He's grieving, Mum. Tommy's way of dealing with it is by closing in on himself and shutting off his emotions.'

'Men react differently to women so I can understand that,' Stan said. 'I don't suppose it helped when George Frost came out of the woodwork today.'

'Yes, it must have been a shock for Celia, let alone Tommy,' Phyllis agreed. 'Well, as long as you're all right we'll be off, Amy.'

'I'm fine, Mum,' she said, managing a small smile, which left her face as soon as her parents left.

*   *   *

Tommy was sitting opposite his mother, in no hurry to go home. His emotions were locked inside, yet they were threatening to erupt. Every time he looked at Amy he had to clench his jaws to stop words of vitriol spewing from his mouth.

'I can't believe your father turned up today, and to bring that woman . . .' Celia said as tears flooded her eyes.

'Mum, other women might have lost it, screamed at him like a fishwife, but you were incredible, dignified and . . . and I was so proud of you.'

The tears spilled now, and she said, 'I'm an awful woman and I don't deserve your pride.'

'Don't be silly, of course you aren't.'

'I don't know how I'd have coped without you and Amy. She's been wonderful, but I thought she wasn't good enough for you and did everything I could to undermine your relationship. If it had worked I wouldn't have my lovely grandson and Robert is such a comfort to me. When I hold him I can see Jeremy in his features, and it's as though a part of him remains.'

That was too much for Tommy and standing abruptly he said, 'I need a drink. Do you want one?'

'Yes, a sherry please.'

Tommy poured it and a large whisky for himself. It was followed by another, but neither deadened his feelings. When Tommy reluctantly went home, he barely said a word to Amy as he sat morosely by the fire, staring into the flames as his mind smouldered like the burning coals. The evening passed, and though Amy spoke to him, his replies were monosyllabic, until at ten o'clock he abruptly said he was going to bed.

Amy followed fifteen minutes later, settling Bobby in his cot before she climbed in beside him. In that moment

Tommy broke and he pulled Amy roughly into his arms, wanting to hurt her, to punish her. There was no love in the act, just anger as he forcefully entered her, ignoring her cries of distress.

'Shut up! It's no more than you deserve and if you get pregnant at least I'll know it's mine this time,' Tommy spat as he carried on using her body, pounding into her until at last he was spent.

Amy lay sobbing, but hearing Bobby crying she got out of bed to pick him up, clutching him closely as unbidden words blurted out of her mouth. 'You're as bad as your brother. He . . . he raped me too.'

'What! What did you say?'

'That Jeremy raped me.'

Tommy said nothing at first, but when he did his tone was scathing. 'If that's the truth, why wait till now to tell me? No, don't answer that, I can guess. Jeremy's dead and buried so he can't dispute it.'

Anger replaced tears and abruptly sitting on the side of the bed she spilled it all out. 'Jeremy threatened me, said that if I cried rape he'd tell you that I led him on. I shouldn't have listened – should have told you, but I was so frightened that you'd believe him and I'd lose you. Then . . . then when I found out I was pregnant, I nearly went out of my mind. I didn't want a man like Jeremy to be the father of my baby,' Amy gabbled on, unable to stop now that she had started. 'He suspected he was, but I denied it. I saw him as a monster, hated him, feared him, and . . . and when you held Bobby for the first time and I saw how much you loved him I just couldn't do it, couldn't tell you. I . . . I *wanted* you to be his father.'

'Oh God . . . oh God . . .' Tommy groaned.

Amy heard the anguish in his voice, but she had to get it all out. 'I . . . I think Jeremy had something wrong with his mind. He seemed to forget that he raped me and I think he became obsessed. He wanted me, wanted Bobby, so much so that no matter how much you deny it, I think he tried to kill you.'

'No more . . . no more,' Tommy said hoarsely.

'Tommy, please, you've got to listen. Jeremy raped me, and if I wasn't telling you the truth, if I had wanted him, there was nothing to stop me from leaving you. I could have gone off with him just as your father went off with Lena Winters,' she said, spent now, her body sore and her mind exhausted.

There was only silence now, a silence that seemed to stretch and stretch, until at last Tommy spoke. 'I've been an idiot, my mind all over the place, but I should have worked that out for myself.'

Amy waited for more, but Tommy was silent again. Bobby was asleep in her arms now so she gently put him back in his cot. Tommy threw back the blankets and came to stand beside her, looking down at him as he said softly, 'He still feels like mine. The bond is there and my feelings haven't changed. I love him, Amy, and I love you too.'

'Oh, Tommy,' she said, turning into his arms.

It would take time for the wounds to heal, for both of them, but their love was strong and somehow Amy knew it was going to be all right.